The Shadow Scrolls

Book I

The Vale of Decision

By PD Lorenz

Cover design by Joseph Eldredge

Set in Garamond font

Printed in the United States of America

ISBN **979-8-9882132-6-0**

Acknowledgements

This project has bene a very long time in the making and there are almost too many people to thank, for the journey has brought me across a multitude of pathways. However, some just have to be acknowledged.

First, I'd like to thank God for, well, everything! Id also like to thank my beautiful wife who has always been my number one supporter, sacrificing many hours of labor and encouragement, and for creating the stunning book cover. Thank you to my awesome boys, Joshua, Joseph, and Samuel for their attentive listening skills and palpable excitement. Thank you guys for all the hard work you put into this project.

Thank you to my mom, Janet, who read the manuscript during one of the most difficult times of her life and still found the time to encourage me. Your strength is truly amazing. Thank you to the rest of my family for just allowing to be a part of your lives. Thank you especially to my niece, Kenzie Kate Floyd and Kenzie Kate Floyd photography for the incredible cover pictures. Your wonderful gift is just that to the rest of us, a gift.

A Big thank you to Bob and Johnna Hale for your many prayers and much support throughout the years. Thank you to Nancy Yacher for your incredible work in reading through and editing the raw material. This book wouldn't be what it is, and what we hope it to be, without your giftedness.

Thank you to Robert Eldredge Sr. and Choice Publications who enthusiastically embraced this book.

Thank you to our wonderful friend Keith Curtis and his amazing talents, Craig Bilderback and his family, the Parcha family, Brad and Andrea Parsley and their family, and Brad and Michelle Fallentine and their family for your wonderful help in presenting this work to the world.

Thank you to my brothers and sisters in the fire service; especially stations 31, 30, 11, 8 and 2. Stay safe!

Lastly, but certainly not least, I would like to thank the five father figures that have mentored and guided me thus far in this journey called life. Each of you has been a monumental figure at key crossroads for me.

Therefore, this book has been dedicated to all of you…

To my Father…

Shadows are created when light strikes a substance and casts a darkness beyond. At times, that gloom can reach unfathomable depths, but what if that darkness were not so deep? What if those living in the shadows were not living in darkness at all, but merely, in a lesser light?

CONTENTS

Prologue · viii

Chapter 1 · **A Safe Haven**

The Spring · 33

The River · 46

The Runoff · 54

Chapter 2 · **Pried from the Cobbled Stones**

Forgery · 71

The Arrangement · 82

The Last Meal · 96

Chapter 3 · **An Enemy Within**

The Search Party · 108

The War Party · 118

Chapter 4 · **Taken In**

Wisekoff · 142

The City of Gish · 155

A Warm and Dry Place · 165

Chapter 5 · **Buying In**

The Bridge Ordeal · 181

Throne Under · 193

The Road that Led Him · 209

To the Train · 218

Chapter 6   Meanwhile

A Safe Haven No More   233

The Princess and the Prophet   246

The Peaceless   257

Chapter 7   **The Rise to Power**

The Vale of Decision   267

Rising in Rank and Power   275

The Drums of War   292

Chapter 8   **The Darkest of Cells**

The Threefold Prison   310

A Revelation from the Deep   321

A Piercing Light   329

The Shadow of Light   331

Chapter 9   **A Reuniting**

The Lever and the Door   343

Adjoined Journeys   350

The Reunion   357

The Reconciling   361

Chapter 10   **The End of the Beginning**

The Judgement   378

The Turning of the Point   394

Shades in the Shadows   399

The Sub-Setting   407

The Sent Ones   414

Prolog

Shadow Scroll I

Even from the beginning the blood of mankind has cried out from the ground, but never has it wept louder than one unequaled and compelling day. It was a day like no other, neither before nor since... a day with almost no date; a time outside of time. It was as if the moment itself were held in a sort of suspension, so as to be near to everyone. It was at that crossroads of time that there lived a certain king… a king who did an unfathomable act; an act that would cast a shadow upon all.

The sun broke through the darkness that crisp winter morn with a piercing intensity, its rays sweeping over the Realms of Irenay like the euphoric feeling of an approaching new season. Irenay, a land whose birthright was peace, for so it was named, was about to go through another birthing. It was a birth surrounded by struggle and warfare. And it was all bathed in great streams of blood.

The realm's great white castle, Lock Kalaw, was majestically tucked into a pocket atop the highest peak of the Awlak Mountain Range. Still, it was an elevation that was dwarfed by the enormity and grandeur of the Range of the Unknown, aptly named for no earthly being had ever ascended to its heights. In fact, the lofty peaks no eye had ever even seen, for they pierced the very atmosphere itself and forever lay above the mists and fire of that heavenly shield.

The day that we are speaking of also marked the time when the grand waterfalls of Kalaw broke open to create a torrential outpouring in comparison to the relative trickle of their former majesty. Those said waters were the same ones which flowed throughout the foundations of the castle itself, fed from the lofts beyond. It was said that the waters ran to and fro amongst the gardens and courtyards of the lock like nature's children playing hide and seek amongst the rocks and pillars. However, on that great and terrible day, they surpassed their previous grandeur as the Range of the Unknown poured out even greater drafts from its refreshing springs creating quite a conundrum.

For although the waters increased abundantly upon the land, granting greater life lending liquid, the realm itself was rather decreasing into a fall, that is, a descent to the greatest of depths, as we shall presently see.

The atmosphere of the castle seemed to draw and lose its breath all at once as the giant oak and iron doors of the Southern Gate swung open with no small effort from the immense gatekeepers, for they had swung them open to the dawning of a new day. The entire keep reacted to the breaching of those doors, for the ancient doors of that particular set had never been opened before, reserved for such a day from the building of the foundations of the castle.

Bakers and butlers, saddlers, sewers and smiths all watched with anticipation their breath emanating from their mouths like hundreds of small chimneys growing cold. Even the veteran soldiers-at-arms watched with an air of uncertainty. Never before had the king departed from the Southern Gate; never before had it been breached from without nor within. It had always been off limits to anyone. A perimeter of forty lengths was cordoned around the entrance on the inside, and that for ages. One could hardly see the doors beyond the years of overgrown grapevines which had completely sheltered and shaded them by their growths, growths which were only allowed to be tended to once a year. They were sacred plants and sacred doors sacred and previously locked doors.

Emerging from the darkness of the Southern Gate and the alcove of his own decision, the king strode aside his great steed, Diokalees, a war horse so magnificent that the other coursers of the castle felt depressed whenever he departed. He was the stud to all of the other horses of the royal household, horses that were bred and raised to measure up to the standard of him. Every muscle beneath his silvery coat, every twitch of his silky white tail, every majestic turn of his pillar-like head was marked by power and strength. The blackness that arose from his hooves to his lower legs made it seem as though he were riding on the very air.

And yet, the humility in his loyalty and obedience to his master shone through with each flawless and seemingly effortless movement. The king need only hint in the direction with a slight twitch of the wrist and it would be accomplished with lightening quick reflexes. However, on that day, even the great steed Diokalees shuffled a hoof as the anticipation of the ride grew more thickly.

The king himself was dressed in his winter white furs that covered his hardened leather and forged gold battle array. Upon his head sat the Crown of the People, a crown with a multiplicity of precious stones inside and out. Inside, the stones were polished smooth like river stones to be wearable and fit only for the king himself. Outside, they were cut and angled in so precisely a manner that the colors of the entire spectrum sparkled as the rays of the morning sun flashed from beyond the gently passing clouds. Each step was a measured one. Measured not to create a performance of some sort, it was a measurement from within. And a question lingered in his mind:

Would it be worth it?

The moments hung in the air like the end of a strummed note in midst of an orchestration. It created a silence save for the morning breeze that slipped through the trees. Servants of all sorts observed from beyond the windows and walls of the keep. So did the soldiers-at-arms who quietly followed the king, as did two other servants delicately anticipating any kingly command.

Halting Diokalees, the king ran his powerful vein swollen hand down the extent of the war horse as if to measure the length of his capability, for he knew that the ride would test his steed like no other. Upon reaching the golden horn of the saddle he in one swift movement swung himself aloft the horse and positioned himself upon its back. He was not a large man, so the steed hardly moved beneath his weight.

In fact, when the king walked amongst the population of the keep, he hardly stood out save for the fact that he wore the robes of royalty. At times, he would not wear them at all, and no one would even notice his passing. His eyes were piercingly sharp his face chiseled to a perfect balance between sparse and plump. His arms and legs were powerful enough to stand his ground, if need be, but that of course had never happened for most were awestruck by his shear commanding presence once they looked into his eyes.

What they saw in his eyes was a quiet and gentle confidence that he wore like an invisible cloak and the sturdiness made one think that he were reading the very thoughts of his audience. Perhaps he was. But the day that we have been speaking of had born something altogether different in the king.

It was something foreign, and it captivated the whole castle. Some of the onlookers wept, others shook their heads as if realizing for the first time that what had been written down in ancient scrolls had finally materialized. Still others turned away from windows and doors to corral their emotions for they knew that a change permanent and everlasting had finally come to their world. At long last, the day had arrived and the castle would never be the same.

It would be empty as their king departed, and they would have to leave to be scattered about the realm. They themselves would be empty as well they, like the castle that they loved, would be empty, and it would be void.

A long lone trumpet blast shattered the dark mood and heralded the fact that the time was not a time for mourning, but rather a time for rejoicing. Though change would be difficult, the ride had been prophesied from ages past and the occupants of the castle were well aware of its purpose though they did not fully know the depth of it. They did know, however, that it would be a turning point upon which not only the Realms of Irenay, but all realms would be hinged. And they knew that the hinge and the door attached to them, no matter how rusty and old it would grow, would cast a shadow that future generations would have to pass through and ponder.

Seated atop Diokalees the king fixed his eyes upon the horizon. He gazed past the peaks and valleys that lay between him and his destiny and calculated the time it would take to get there.

Six days should do it, he thought to himself. I'll rest as little as possible and stop even less – only for water – not for food. Food would only cloud my thoughts.

Without interrupting his ponderings, knowing that his faithful servants were by his side, he quietly removed his furs and handed them down to one of them. With outstretched arms the servant received the robes as a tear escaped his right eye. The king gently rested his hand upon the curvature of his head in a reassuring "goodbye" gesture.

Reaching to his head with steady hands he removed the Crown of the People and handed it to the other servant. To that one, he only smiled.

Immediately following the removal of the royal outer garments, his two armor bearers, who were massive soldiers-at-arms, presented weapons to their king.

First to be presented was the long-bow, which was pearl white with ornate victory carvings on its shaft. It was made of Willowfeld, a wood found in only one valley of the realm (it was to that valley that the king had set his course to that fateful day). The wood itself was known for its strength as if petrified and its flexibility as if lithe. Its string was silvery, woven from hairs taken from the tail of Diokalees himself. It was strung as tight as muscle sinew.

Next to be presented was the sword double-edged and as sharp as a stinging winter wind. Its hilt was a crimson hue cured from the leather of a fine red heifer of the realm.

Finally the shield was presented, an exquisite formation of light weight green flint-stone called Emralhearth. It was the only tried and true protection that the king would ever carry into any battle. The shield had sustained an innumerable number of strikes, but had never cracked, never failed, and showed no wear.

To the armor bearers, the king nodded a nod that only comes from the comradeship of battles fought. A comradeship blended like an elixir and mixed with the inner chemicals of elation and relief, triumph, and disappointment. The soldiers knew that they were forbidden to ride with him that day and all they could do was return his nod.

The ride began with a prompting by the voice of the king coupled with a gentle nudge of his steed as he stowed away his armament:

"It is time my friend. Now we move forward," commanded the king to his horse.

Diokalees started with a gentle gait that carried them just past the crest of the mount. Below and beyond lay the Realms of Irenay, and to the south of that, the thickly wooded forests beyond which lay his destiny. Though servants and attendants looked on, the king never once looked back. Not even a glance.

The trot quickly turned into a gallop, and the gallop increased with every stride. First one passed, then two, followed by three furloughs. Each distance passed with rapidity until the swiftness of the war-horse and rider matched that of the clouds above them. The race had begun at last; the horse and the rider became as one, almost blurred together.

The two swept down from the heights of the castle mount and into the hollow below. The king, realizing for the first time that the day had produced a stunning morn, was heartened with a leap of joy from within. Sucking in the fresh morning air he filled his lungs with its newness and encouraged Diokalees with a hearty yelp which the steed responded to with a leap.

Following a road beaten down by the hooves of countless warhorses and wagons they raced through shires over dales throughout forests and across streams. For three days and nights they rode with only the slightest of stops at convenient waters. The small hamlets that they did pass were usually off the beaten path and stood amongst some trees or rivers in the distance. The sounds of pounding hooves were not uncommon, and up and to that point, not a soul had noticed the passing of the pair.

But on the third day contact was made, and it was not by accident.

The rider rested his mount near a lake fed by a canyon creek. He felt that he himself could have continued, but then again, he wasn't the one doing all of the work. Dismounting, he shouldered his bow and sword, for so he wore them upon his back, and he grabbed the reins. He haltered the horse to the edge of the lake where the stream fed the waters. The steed drank in the clear water with ferocity. Before drinking himself, the rider used the cool liquid of the lake to wipe free the sweaty foam that had formed around the edges of the saddle and side straps that led to the stirrups. When the horse had been fully attended to, the king released Diokalees to graze amongst the trees which he was more than happy to do.

At long last the soldier-king drank from the creek himself. By instinct, he refrained from slamming his face into the water though his parched throat begged him too. He patiently scooped the liquid with his hand, always keeping a watch on his surroundings.

His instinct served him well, for presently there happened along two men, who made their way to the edge of the lake from the cover of a bramble of trees on the opposite shore. He could clearly hear their voices as they expressed their frustrations, which reverberated off of the clear mirror-like body of water. They were not soldiers, that much was clear, for their grumbling spoke of the frustrations of a foiled hunt and how close they had been to catching their nemesis of twenty winters past. From the distance, their clothes spoke of the commonality of their livelihoods. One, the shorter of the two, waddled with a limp.

Hunters, thought the king to himself. By and by, they made their way closer to the king's camp and didn't even notice him until, if the king had had ill intent, they were within range of head lopping.

"You're flustered over the hunt, hey?" stated the king.

"Hey, hoy!" shouted one of the men as he practically jumped out of his skin and into the lake.

He was an extremely thin chap whose legs appeared as if they could barely hold up his frame as they poked out from the bottom of his deer hide robe. If it were not for the wideness of his hatchelled feet, he probably would have tipped over in the lightest of breezes, but he had a good and innocent face all the same. The other was stout and spoke with the growl of a bear through a thickened black beard.

"What would be bringing you to our neck of the woods?" asked the stout one.

"I'm on a journey my friend, only passing through." stated the king with an air of humility. "Would that be fine by you?"

"Depends," grumbled the bearded fellow.

"Yah', that d-d-d-depends. It d-d-depends on, well, it just d-depends." The thinly man seemed to be at a loss for words, and maybe even a loss for thoughts.

"It depends on your intents and motifs," said the stout one with a deepening of his voice as if to thrust his courage ahead of his fear, for each of the men had finally noticed the war horse and the hilted sword and slung bow upon the stern frame of the stranger.

"As I have stated, I'm only passing through your dale." He could tell that the men did not recognize him, and he wasn't the type to thrust his authority upon anyone. "It is your dale, is it not?" questioned the king.

"It is but one valley in the Realms of Irenay. It is not our valley, nor our lands, but the king's alone. He has been gracious enough to allow us fief upon it," stated the bearded one.

"Well said, and cleverly crafted. I can see that you are learned," said the king. "By what names are the two of you called?" he inquired.

The king could see that the thin man wanted to speak, for his face twisted and convulsed as he struggled to spit out the words upon his tongue so the bearded one continued as the pause hung on the edge of embarrassment:

"This is Oliver Hunt of the House of Hunt, and I am his kin, Salmon… also of the House of Hunt. We come not only from the finest hunters in the realm, but equally, the surest trackers   as well."

"I've heard of your house, and I hear that it is a respectable one. What were the frustrations that the two of you discussed?"

This time, the stout man called Salmon grew even more grumbled, "My cousin here foiled the trap that I had set, and it snapped upon my foot. A bit of blood, but I'll make it," groaned Salmon.

"D-don't… you mean a f-fountain of blood, cousin?" shrugged Oliver.

"Aye. Spilled blood is the test of a man is it not?" asked the king.

At that, he snapped his finger and Diokalees responded with a start. Both Salmon and Oliver backed away when they saw the approaching horse and it separated them from the sight of the soldier-king. By being in the shadow of the immense horse, they didn't see how effortlessly the rider had saddled his courser, and they were startled when he suddenly spoke down to them with a voice of authority they had not previously heard, his hands resting upon the golden horn of the saddle.

"If you are willing," the king said from his height, "Go back the way that you came, and you will see that the bramble thicket beyond has served as a trap for the prey that you seek. God speed you men." With that he nudged his faithful steed and together they sped away amidst flying mud that segued to dust.

The men stood in silence, contemplating the company they had just kept.

In time, Oliver addressed Salmon. "S-s-s-s-s-s... spill your thoughts, cousin, because I have none."

"I was thinking that I could not possibly walk back to that thicket upon the foot that you have butchered even if I wanted to," Salmon stated with an unforgiving gripe.

"Let's-s su-see how bad it is now."

Together they sat on a nearby boulder to have a look at the wound. To their utter astonishment they found no laceration, only dried blood beneath one robed leg. Salmon was amazed and tried to brush away what, until that moment, had been more or less pouring from the wound.

"Water. Quick! Get me some water!" shouted Salmon.

"Right," replied Oliver as he filled a satchel that had been at his side.

"Pour it here," barked Salmon. "Nothing! There's nothing! No wound, no cut, no nothing! I don't understand, am I mind-broken? Did I not receive a gash from your bumbling?" asked Salmon still mocking his cousin.

Salmon stood to his feet and walked on his legs to test their strength, nay, even jumped upon them. "Nothing! Nothing is wrong!"

For a moment the two just excitedly looked at each other, and then together – as only the best and closest of friends could do – they simultaneously leaped in the direction of the bramble of trees. They ran toward their goal one passing the other until at last they reached the tangled wood.

What they discovered there has been written of and studied for generations, and what they did afterwards has been told around a countless number of hearths since. There amongst the twisted brambles was caught a buck of magnificent proportions. The points of its horns were six apiece and its shoulders nine hand lengths. Too tired to fight any longer it lay on its side knowing that it had lived its last moment, that it was time to give in to the sacrifice.

"What has just happened?" wondered Salmon with his hand to his head in a state of awe. "Who was it that spoke to us, cousin?" He nearly found himself at a loss for words himself.

Oliver created for his first time in his life a most cleverly crafted clearly articulated answer:

"This deer shall feed our village throughout the coming winter, cousin. Once we deliver the goods to the store house, we shall track. Are we not the finest trackers in the realm? Together we shall track this stranger who can be nothing less than a king. Perhaps even our king."

†

It was an ancient valley carved by the receding of a thousand floods and it lay high atop a vista on the far reaches of the realm like a massive basin perched atop a mantle. The king's castle and this ancient valley's heights nearly stood as equals, separated by a relatively small measurement. Over time, it had become known as the valley of all valleys, for it was the finest of vales in the Realms, so naturally manicured invisible creatures might have tended to it, gardenlike.

The trees were Willowfeld, of which we have already briefly been spoken, except for the fact that the branches of those particular trees were coveted and used for the fashioning of premium weapons – nay the most premium of weapons. The Willowfeld were not tall trees as some would assume them to be considering their age. They were rather short and gangly. From their stems proceeded fragrant blossoms of lightening white pedals which, once they had escaped the confines of their buds, would quietly germinate in the ground only to re-bud once again into fresh pearl-white flowers that made the landscape glow like snow.

The rocks of the vale were highly uncommon as well. They were called Sturmstone, and were outcroppings of exposed natural marble columns that protruded through the soil at different angles and undulations. With various sizes ranging from the massive to the small, they were solid, immovable, and appeared to be meticulously placed amongst the dell like a great garden of the gods. All of those ornaments of the valley, if one could call them ornaments, were merely arrayed as such to serve as the bridal train to the vale's one true prize, the waterfalls of Paraketh.

Paraketh was known far and wide as the most beautiful and valuable waters in the entire world. They were the only falls that were not fed from the heights of the Range of the Unknown. Some even called them, "The Bride of the

Unknown," as if the two were entwined, but never touching, separated by a great gulf of peaks and valleys that blanketed thick forests. Unlike all other cascades, its waters were milky white with a tinge of gold and were fed from fathomless springs that bubbled from some unknown well beneath the valley floor. Once those waters had made their way to the top of the natural fount, they would gently cascade over the grandest of all of the conglomerations of Sturmstone that sat atop the south side of the valley. All who gazed upon the tumbling stream were immediately captivated by its beauty. However, its value was even greater than the splendor of its appearance.

Known as, "The Healing Streams of Paraketh," all wounds would be made whole at the mere sprinkle of the milky gold liquid. In times past, animals of all sorts would gather into the valley to bask in its peaceful atmosphere where no predators dared to tread for there was no greater frustration to a carnivore than a prey that could survive every attack, healed by the very mists that were blown about. Some said that even the Guardiers, unseen creatures of the realm, would spend their winters in the place.

Over time, the sons of men began to visit, which subsequently spread the word far and wide. And, such is the nature of men, wars were fought, fought to the bitter end of all that was good and pleasant in that heavenly valley.

So, it was a sardonic sight that presented itself to the king on the morrow that he arrived, though he could remember a time when it was not so. The sight that presented itself on the fate filled six-day ride was not one of magnificence or grandeur, but rather one of desolation.

A desolation that was caused by the countless number of battles fought on what had become the most perfect of battlefields. Where once stood the magically beautiful Willowfeld trees, there stood twisted and dead wind-swept trunks, half pulled up by their roots. Where, at one time, flaming white flowers blanketed the earth like snow drifts, there lay bone-dry powdery dust out of which protruded cracked and crumbling Sturmstone pillars that had long ago served their purpose. They were merely broken old soldiers-at-arms that had sustained a countless number of nicks formed by a countless number of arrow piercing and edgy lashes. And, alas, where once poured the life lending liquid of the Falls of Paraketh, dripped molded and rotted maggot covered moss which emanated a stench of death.

As if the decay were not enough to be overwhelming, what lay beyond the moldy veil was a sight much more ominous. What was then revealed, was the sight of a deep and dank cave of unknown proportions and unknown horrors, for out of it seeped sulfuric mists of yellow and gray. One would have thought that the falls had merely been overtaken by some deep volcanic eruption, if it were not for the far cries of some unknown and tortured creature, or creatures that occasionally escaped from the black jaws of the grotto.

It was that cavern, that throat of the deep, that our rider fixed his gaze upon from across the deathly expanse.

Fear pimpled the fore arms of the king. Thoughts of turning back echoed through the caverns of his mind. The contemplations of his heart trembled within his chest and its pounding galloped in and out of normal cadence. Only the will of his determination to reach his objective, an objective that the whole population of the realm teetered upon, caused him to lean in the direction of the gaping mouth that lay on the opposite side of the vale.

His contemplation was such that he removed himself from the back of Diokalees and crouched down upon the dust of the valley. There he thought only the thoughts that a soldier-king would think, thoughts that arose from the depths of his deep, deep heart. For hours on end, even unto the waning of the day, he never took his eyes off of his goal.

Was it strategies that he contemplated? Was it tactics that flowed in and out of the mind of the captain…? Or was it some hidden and mysterious prize that lay far beyond the blackness of the cave? Perhaps, he was just simply waiting for the perfect timing? Whatever be the reason, it was just long enough for two stragglers to appear high upon a crest of one the walls that helped to create the bowl for the valley to be housed within.

Oliver and Salmon had been tracking the king for three days. They barely had time to drop the deer that the king had mysteriously provided to them at the manor hut in their hamlet before they saddled the only two horses the shire owned. With the speed of the king ahead of them, and not knowing his destination, they trudged forward only stopping to examine the direction of the war-horses' hoof prints as they left the earth to fly across some stream, or at times, some river.

With a steely determination to meet again the stranger that had so affected their lives, they finally found him far below the perch that they had climbed to. Winded and exhausted, they had just enough time to catch their breath when they saw the stranger rise from his crouched position and saddle his horse. What they witnessed after that would only make their stories even more remarkable, remarkable, and difficult to believe.

Diokalees neither shuffled nor swayed as he could clearly distinguish the expanse of the battlefield, for he was a war horse and was bred and raised for such confrontations. He, like the king that sat upon him, was determinate. Together horse and rider paused only long enough for the sovereign to drop his weapons to the ground beside him, a movement that made the two onlookers high above gasp.

"What soldier enters a battle minus his weapons?" whispered one to the other.

First, the bow with its tried-and-true handle carved from the very trees that now lay in heaps about the valley. Then the double-edged sword which, as it dropped, pierced the ground and held fast. Next, the shield was flung away. It was the only weapon that the king took a second glance at after discarding, for it was his only means of defensive protection.

Finally, with the finality of a choice made solid, he removed his battle array. Breastplate, armguards, and flank-girds all fell to the side like a rain of unneeded wear. Where before the king had stripped himself of his royal garbs, including the Crown of the People, he then removed his soldiery and became like most of the inhabitants of the realm he ruled: simple, peasant-like.

At last, the rider and his horse entered the valley, and the inner chemicals that surged through their bodies caused their pupils to fixate upon the goal, the deep dark maw of the cave.

They started slowly, as they had done when they began their journey six days prior on a crisp winter morn. The ground beneath released its black ash-like dust with every step of the horse. A northerly breeze picked up as they began, and its hint of warmth touched upon the king. For a moment, it encouraged his soul as it lightly blew upon the back of his neck as if to remind him that the bitter cold of winter would, at some point, release its grip.

At the same moment though, a southerly heat and anger-filled wind beat back the pleasant breeze and its piercing stingers penetrated the corners of the rider's eyes as if to mock his approach. It was the winds of war and the battle had begun, but the airy fight served only to solidify the severity of that purposeful moment, a moment that hung on a branch that hovered near the edge of eternity.

Together, more one than ever, the horse and rider increased in march and step as they proceeded into the vale and to the gape of darkness. At first, there was no resistance, but that quickly changed, and the once soldier-king turned peasant-rider could see that bows were being lifted from near invisible hiding places amongst the tree trunks with their tangle of roots.

With that recognition, he urged Diokalees forward and gripped the reins even tighter. The bows that had been previously raised then produced reflections of sunlight as the polished arrowheads were lifted in the direction of the swiftly moving target.

The king could hear the strum of numerous war instruments as their shafts left their strings, and he waited for the inevitable stingers… but the fires of laceration never came. It relieved the king, for he was in full anticipation of the pain, knowing that the soldiers were well trained and well-seasoned warriors. Then the second wave flew.

Three of the strikes sunk into his back, and two into his thighs, one in each leg. With a wince, the king dropped his head and focused upon his hands. He could see the white of his knuckles beneath his skin being covered with the red of his blood as his grip began to loosen. That's when another wave hit.

More of the projectiles lodged into his back. That time, from his neck to his right flank, another in his leg and one in his arm. With that second strike, the sovereign slumped upon the back of the war horse, but still held on tightening his wounded thighs around the contour of the steed's mighty back. The horse could feel the squeeze and perceived the need to increase his speed, not so much as a prompting from his dear friend, but rather as a cry for help.

A moment passed before the king regained the strength which was quickly draining from his body to raise his eyes toward the cavern in the distance. He judged himself to be not quite halfway across the battlefield and could see more of the stealthy warriors rustling amongst their nests ahead and on his right and left flanks.

More arrows flew, and again the king was surprised when they missed his body all together. That's when the horse beneath him was struck several times and the rider realized that the enemy was not aiming for him at all. They were truly in this trial together and it disheartened the rider to think that his trusty friend was suffering as well. However, the previous onslaught only served to strengthen the horses' cadence and it was yet one more occasion for the king to be proud of his steed.

At the three-quarter point, that is, at about twenty six lengths, the third wave of arrows found their marks. They were the ones that produced the most damage for they had been let loose at the closest range. The grand outcropping of Sturmstone that once served as the fount of Paraketh, and then helmed the depths of darkness, also served as the position on the field of battle where the enemy had created their redoubt.

Determined not to allow the horse and rider to reach their goal, the arrows that flew from the bowmen nestled into the base of the cliff were duel headed and flew in a circular trajectory thereby striking with greater damage and ferocity. It was those missiles of destruction that caused the once mighty Diokalees to finally stagger, and the once majestic king to finally let go of the reins for the pain was too much to bear and the devastation too complete.

At that point, their path was not a straight one as it had been. For the first time, they were removed from their heading as Diokalees stumbled to the right, and the king slumped to the left. If it were not for the arrows that were lodged in the side of the courser, the rider would have fallen all together, but he managed to hang on to two of them   which were fastened side by side on the fourth quarter of the left shoulder.

Seeing their last strike moment approaching, enemy combatants began to emerge from their hideouts with unsheathed swords in their hands. Like a tumbling projectile approaching them, each one craved for the fame of delivering that fatal swing, a swing that would never connect.

As the man and horse staggered closer and closer to the mouth of gloom, there arose one more arrow upon one more bow, and it was from high atop the Sturmstone tower.

Appearing upon the mount was a warrior-prince of unrivaled splendor, second only to the king himself. Prince Magreth stood as a powerfully built and well carved leader of hordes. A thousand battles would only begin to describe the fullness of his list of achievements. He had become the ill-gotten owner of many manor houses, lands, and even a city all obtained by deceitful gain. His dress was that of hardened battle array stained pearl-white from dye that had been obtained from the felled petals of the Willowfeld trees ages past. His helm was also carved from Willowfeld, but coated in silver and gold that, at that moment, glowed in the sinking sun. He held a bow of magnificent enormity and, it seemed, could only be raised and aimed by the strong arms that were fitted to his immense and towering body. In a strange way, his voice resembled a herald's trumpet and a player's lyre all wrapped together, or some other sort of wind and stringed instrument that had been formed and fashioned to announce war. And a war cry he did raise.

"My kingdom shall rise and never fall," he harmonized from above.

It echoed down through the cracks and crevices that were inherent in the shear angles of the Sturmstone perch. The melodious voice had a hint of victory song hidden in its chords that caused the sauntering soldiers far below to stop in their tracks. It even produced a start in the heart of the suffering king and caused him to pull back his bloody head and tilt his whole body backward so that he could look upon his conquering foe.

Prince Magreth may also have discovered that two sets of additional ears on the opposite side of the valley had heard his decry if they had not been scrambling down the back side of the basin. However, even being around the corner from the entrance to the vale, Oliver and Salmon shuddered at the sound of his echoing decree. It beckoned them to speed their descent, and they managed to peer around the entrance into the dale that lay before them.

That was when they witnessed the last strike, but it was not completed by any mere foot soldier. No, it was Magreth himself who delivered the blow.

His arrow was not double pronged or even single pronged. Neither did it have any flight feathers. Nay, it was a single shaft so elongated and perfectly balanced that it was more like a spear than a simple fetcher's arrow. It had a thickened mid-shaft with beveled ends and when it was let loosed, it neither quivered nor quaked. So straight and true did that arrow fly, that when it struck the heart of the king, it passed right through his body and halfway into the hind quarter of the war horse upon which he sat.

He had timed the shot perfectly, and both the horse and the rider fell, rolled, and finally slid to a stop just short of the mouth of the gaping cavern, a tangled mess of blood, sweat, and mud.

There they lay, steam emanating from the bodies in the sudden appearing evening chill with great beads of blood leaking into the dust of the valley that swallowed it like a dry and parched throat. A swell of victory cry grew within the diaphragms of the enemy soldiers, and they surged forward toward the felled king, knowing that their plans would continue uncontested. However, before their victory cheer could be released, the most unnatural of occurrences happened, and it caused even them to pull back from their advances.

It began as a peculiar wind and it swirled into tiny tornadoes about the valley. From deep within the cavern, a bellowing vapor arose from the deep. And then, as fear swallowed the atmosphere, two sets of mysterious tracks emerged from the gloom of the grotto.

One would have only known that there was some sort of creatures emerging, because the tracks could only be seen by the dust that they produced. As far as the creatures themselves, they were invisible to the human eye. Oliver and Salmon could see that something darkly mysterious was happening from a distance, and it deepened the darkness of the mystery, nay, the blackness of the nightmare they had   been witnesses to.

All eyes followed as the tracks made their way to the bodies of the king and his horse. When they stopped, what was then observed could only be described as nothing short of menacing.

In a moment of time, the invisible specters thrashed and tore at the blood-stained clothes of the motionless body of the king that shuddered in response to their attack. Like a victory dance, they tore and thrashed about unaware to the human eyes save for the clothing, flesh, and blood that was flying everywhere. The thrashing continued uninhibited like a festivity of rage until all of a sudden it stopped, and for a moment all that saw were filled with a dreadful awe.

Then, ever so slowly, the torn and broken body of the king was dragged into the heart of the abyss. Like a macabre procession, he sank into the depths of darkness pulled by seemingly invisible claws on seemingly hideous and unseen arms.

A moment later and a long way from there, in the farthest distance north of the vale, the Range of the Unknown released a great flood of waters. It was as if the mountains themselves were convulsively weeping. The waters tore through the white castle of Kalaw and half demolished the structure, and its crumbling shook the sides of the mountain from the summit to the base.

After that, all fell quiet upon the vale, and the soldiers slunk away one by one after Prince Magreth had removed himself from his lofty perch. The hot wind eventually died down and the ashy dust settled upon the ground once again.

Then silence prevailed.

The next day, when all seemed to be clear, Salmon and Oliver made their way to the war-torn body of the great horse Diokalees, and dug a trough next to the place where he had fallen. While they dug, neither spoke to each other, and only thought of how they could possibly tell the tale of what they had seen.

They wondered if any would believe the story of a warrior, possibly even a king, who had decided, and stripped himself of his soldiery, surrendered to the lances of a thousand volleyed arrows, and was dragged beyond a macabre gate into a well of darkness. And, as they pondered the meaning of it all, they hauled the body of his horse into the shallows beneath the floor of the valley, a valley that would forever be known as, The Vale of Decision.

Over the years Oliver, the once stammering hunter, became an orator and carried the story to the far reaches of the realm and beyond. As for Salmon, his once angry and bitter cousin, he quietly and peacefully communicated the account through the written word, for the bitterness of life had long lost its purpose.

And the story which he wrote, he writ upon a scroll, nay, upon a number of scrolls, for that which you have just read was only the first of the Shadow Scrolls that I was compelled to write.

For that was not the end of the tale… that was merely the end of the beginning.

Chapter 1

A Safe Haven

"Heroes are not born, they are forged... And most often, it is by fire."

- Ancient Irenay Scribe –

†

The Spring

"So, some strange far-off king was killed and dragged into a pit!" he fired. "The story is centuries old, Da'. What has it got to do with me?" challenged Jonathan as he defiantly stared into the blank, soot surrounded eyes of his father seated in front of a hearth-fire pumping away at its billow. The creaky wooden contraption sounded like a ship being rocked by the sea, and somehow, it strengthened the boy.

Jonathan of Scharp was a young man of fifteen when he first began to feel his oats. Raised the son of a weapon master, his father John of Scharp, had created quite a name for himself by having fashioned a multitude of fine weapons of warfare made famous by the fact that (so it was said) not one had ever failed in battle. It was an unverifiable rumor of course, but nonetheless, it had served its purpose though the weapon master had never condoned such a statement.

Be that as it may, the fame cast a shadow whose shade the son was destined to grow up within, and therein lay the problem. For its boundaries, as Jonathan would often think, threaten to choke the life right out of me.

From an outsider's point of view, it seemed only natural that the son would follow in the footsteps of the father and to carry on the work of the family. Even their appearance spoke of their commonality. Each had green penetrating eyes save for some subtle differences which shall be revealed shortly, and each had flowing black hair that poured from their heads like waves flowing in from the sea.

These and more, they had inherited from their grandfather, a hunter of the Scharp line. However, John of Scharp was the first to depart from that infamous family procession to forge ahead anew by no choice of his own, the reasons of which lay locked away in the deep caverns of the weapon master's heart. Nevertheless, it was a break in a long line of hunters, that is, pseudo-warriors that had served the kingdom for a multitude of generations.

Both John and Jonathan supported a stout frame with powerful arms and legs made stronger still by the fashioning of fine instruments of war, a work they had spent countless hours perfecting. Jonathan himself had been an apprentice to his Da' long before his memory would allow him to remember. And alas, both were stubbornly devoted to whatever task their heart had fixed itself upon. Unfortunately for the weapon master, the son's heart had begun to fasten to another life altogether different from the one that had been laboriously carved out for him like a bow from a Willowfeld branch. Unlike the obedient materials of craftsmanship, the human heart and its will was most unpredictable, as the master forger was about to discover.

For young Jonathan, his heart was set toward a life of soldiery and adventure which he dreamed would take him far from the village he had grown up within. Though Safehaven was a respectable township and had recently outgrown its status as a village, due in large part to the hard work of John himself, its size was not the problem at all.

It was, rather, an inner turmoil that had been forced to the surface. It was as if a deep, unfathomable, and long forgotten well of water had been waiting to spring to life, and when it was finally uncorked, it created a wave that the young Jonathan would have to ride nay, was thrilled to ride. It was that urge, or rather surge, that pushed the younger to challenge the elder.

"Do you even know what the soldiers fight for?" asked Jonathan snidely. "Where they go? What, or who your precious weapons are used on? Do you even know that, Da'?" It was a line of sarcastic questioning with a purpose. It was a means to an end like a series of levers that were being pulled one after another in the hope that it would produce some expected result.

As for John, the weapon master of Safehaven, he was oblivious to the fact that he was about to be blindsided by such a line of inquisition. For the moment, he was hardly listening, and was only thinking about how he had groomed his son well and that his final task of forging the boy would lay in his belief system, a system that John had come to depend upon and even live for.

Therefore, even as the son spoke to the father in defiance, a smile escaped his mouth while he secretly thought of how proud he was of the boy. Time has passed so quickly, he thought to himself. I have carved out a life for him here. He will carry on this work, make a name for himself, and start a family of his own… Yes, a family of his own.

"Are you even listening to me, Da? Do you even care about what I'm saying?" Jonathan, as was usual, found it always difficult to communicate with his father. For as long as he could remember, he was never quite sure what his father was thinking behind his quiet, gentle, and at times mysterious demeanor. And then, there were the times when it became quite clear. In fact, at that moment, Jonathan was trying produce one of those times.

"I don't want to do this work. I want a life of soldiery." He flatly stated.

Jonathan watched the hands of his father closely for he knew that if they began to shake and tremble, that would be the sign that the earthquake was about to strike. Even with fear in his heart, his adolescent chemistry would urge him beyond any caution signal that would arise.

It was a long-planned speech, months of preparation had been leading up to it, and he hoped that it would become the pry-pole that would create an argument designed solely to lever him free from life's niche that he felt he was destined to be stuck into like one more indistinguishable brick in the gray prison of life. It was not that Jonathan didn't love his father, no; it was something much larger than that. Though he could not put his finger upon it, the specter ate at him for a long time and was pushing him toward a life of defiance if not rebellion. The shadow could not be explained nor understood, and it couldn't wait any longer.

John, seated at the fiery billows of the hearth, continued to pump with his leg, causing the fire to glow hotter and hotter. A sword, which lay atop the coals, grew brighter.

All the while, without even knowing it, John's hand began to shake as he formed a fist. This, Jonathan took note of and quickly yet silently made his way across the hardened clay floor of the weapon master's hovel. Like a thief in the night,

Jonathan lifted a small stool and silently placed it between him and his Da'. With his back to his only means of egress, and facing his foe, he purposely raised the stakes in the male-to-male challenge.

"One day, one of your weapons will fail in battle and the people who admire you will turn on you and they will turn on our family. Where will that place me in this society that you so love? Where will my life be at that point?" Jonathan watched his father carefully, knowing that his powerful hands could snap him like a twig, and yet there was still no response save for the clenching of the fist.

It was time to cinch the knot tighter. "I have learned to use some of the weapons we have fashioned together. Against your orders Da', I have practiced this art of war." Jonathan threw out the statement like a fishing line in hopes that it would produce some sort of bite.

"Art of war?" John bellowed as he stood to his feet. At last, Jonathan had touched upon a subject he knew would arouse his father, the famous weapon master known to outsiders, at least, for his intricate weapon-forming patience.

Perhaps it was his father's voice or the way his eyes seemed to light up even though dim. Nevertheless, in that moment of challenge, Jonathan's memory leaped to the surface and threatened to defeat the assault even as the gauntlet had just been thrown down. The produce of memories nearly caused him to abandon his challenge for it was a memory of a far off time when he and his Da' had first connected as a father and son...

It was upon a great rock that they had climbed together. The two sat upon the height overlooking small lakes and the river that fed them as it meandered from one shire to another. A canyon over, and a bit above their height sat the crumbled remains of the majestic castle Kalaw tucked into its pocket beneath the heights shrouded it in mist; mists that gently descended from the lofts beyond, a residue created by the outpouring of torrential runoff. It was the first time that Jonathan had seen the world beyond the surroundings of his home, the then village of Safehaven. Together, they faced the world beyond. To the younger it was a revelation of grandeur for what he saw; he described it to his blind father:

"I see grand forests with a million trees, Da'. As far as I can see, there are trees. They're like, like great armies filling the mountains and valleys." he explained, his excitement palpable. "And the river is like a train of war wagons all tied together and carrying the weapons and supplies." His wonderment was tangible, and John felt the satisfaction of being a father.

"And we are the ones that supply those soldiers with their weapons, son." It was the statement of a man who knew that he and his work had would make a difference in the world. However, his son's following statement would connect and disconnect the two of them all at the same time.

"Where do the soldiers go to fight, Da'?" the younger asked innocently.

After a long pause, his father answered:

"Past the trees and beyond the forest, Jonathan. They go to a place where darkness reigns supreme. A place we don't need to think about. As long as we supply the soldiers with their weapons, they can hold off that dark tide, and it won't come near us at all. Not near you, your mother, or your baby brother." Though blind, John seemed to be looking at objects in the distance.

"Were you born blind, Da'?" the son asked.

With that, a longer paused prevailed.

"We need to return to your mother, son. She's expecting us for victuals. If we're not there, she'll be cooking our hides for sure. Come, lead us home, boy." John rose and urged his son to abandon the conversation, but Jonathan remained a moment longer gazing past the horizon and beyond.

Thus, a seed had been sown. A seed that would produce a tree, whose branches would, for a long time, form a distinct intersection.

"Thank you for taking me here... I love you, Da'."

Jonathan's maturity never ceased to amaze the weapon master.

So that was the intersection, the deep connection, and at the same time, the deep dividing fissure that would become a chasm in their relationship; a chasm that would take only the greatest of blind leaps to re-cross.

"I never wanted to be like you!" shouted Jonathan to his fuming father. "I never once wanted to carry on your work!" It was an adolescent icicle that pierced John's heart and for a moment Jonathan regretted the whole idea of the attack, regretted the whole idea of freeing himself from the confines of the status quo, but alas it was fleeting.

Jonathan made his way across the clay floor of the shop, and John could hear a weapon being removed from the wall. It sounded like a war hatch, the throwing axe that he completed just one day prior.

How angry is this boy, thought John to himself. What, or who, has pushed him to this point?

Jonathan had taken the war hatch from the wall and if John could have been looking, he would have seen the emotional turmoil that rippled across the face of his son. It was not a look of murderous rage, but rather the look of a young man desperate for a life of his own.

"I wish that you could see me, Da'... but you can't. Here I stand, thirty steps from the Willowfeld tree that you were awarded. Our horse is tethered to the tree and to her leather lash I set my eyes, but before I throw this axe at it, I close my eyes... Now, I'm just like you... I cannot see Swift's tether, or the tree." His voice quivered as it trailed off and a pause hung in the air as the boy's adolescent and impulsive chemicals assaulted his emotional control. Only the crackling of the hearth fire made itself known.

John, with his keen senses, could hear his son positioning himself to throw. "That throw will be the beginning of the end of our relationship, son. I beg you not to do it," John cautioned.

With closed eyes and a wince, Jonathan let the instrument of war fly toward the tree that sat just outside of the weapon shop. Little did the boy know, but at the same moment a warrior of unprecedented size stepped into the doorway of the weapon master's shop!

If it were not for his keen fighting abilities, Nathan, the captain of the king's army, keeper of the castle, and leader of the Council would have had his forehead split asunder. The axe traveled end over end, within inches of his face, and beyond the door to the tree where it cut in two the leather strap that held the family horse. With a whiny, the mare took off in a gallop.

Jonathan watched the pregnant horse scamper down the hill toward the forest in the distance. At the same moment, John had reached his boiling point.

No longer could he tether his famous patience, and sprung in the direction of his son bent on teaching him the lesson of his life. Jonathan turned just in time to witness his blind father trip over the small obstacle of a stool which he had placed earlier and slam onto the floor with a whimper. To Jonathan, it was a bittersweet moment, for he knew that the thrashing he would have received would have been bone crushing, and yet, for the first time in his life he had seen the utter weakness of his Da'.

It was the culmination of the fuming frustrations of unanswered questions and what seemed to him to be a boxed-in life. At the same time, he knew it was the final axe blow to the creaky wooden bridge that barely held their relationship together.

With a face covered in dirt and blood, John struggled to his feet and bellowed toward his son. "Jonathan, go get that horse, now! Only God knows where she'll run too, but if it's to the farthest reaches of the realm and you are gone for months on end, then that will be just fine with me!"

Jonathan slunk out of the shop with a defiant and quiet anger coupled with pain, not even glancing at the warrior he had nearly killed. One step led to another that quickly turned into a sprint. As he ran, tears welled up and tracked horizontally across his cheeks.

The crackle and pop of the forging fire was still all that echoed off the walls of John's shop. In his dimness, he did not perceive the entrance of Nathan into the hovel, a rarity, for his keen ears had been finely tuned over the years. The weapon master struggled to his feet and the blood that trickled from his nose threatened to cause an uncontrollable sneeze to tickle its way to the surface. John held it back for as long as he could before it finally gushed out all over the floor.

"Bless you, my friend." announced the Captain of the Guard.

John faced the direction of the voice. The bloody sneeze made his face look as though it had been smashed in with a stick. "Nathan, is that you?"

"Aye."

Nathan was an enormous man trained in the art of war from a boy. A man groomed by meticulous repetition and forged by the fiery trials of constant sorties. At that moment, he was not arrayed in his battle fatigues, but rather in his royal business attire. An immensely thick cloak, as thick as a normal man's forearm, draped his blackened frame and only added to the enormity of his size. From beneath its folds, his arms reached down to his wounded comrade.

"I haven't seen you look this bad since the Campaign of Eight," Nathan declared.

"Ah, Nathan! You have always had impeccable timing. Again, your arm reaches to me." John could feel the strong squeeze of the captain's hand around his bicep and took note that it encircled the entirety of his forger's arm.

It reminded him that his friend was no mere man, but rather a descendant of the realm's great warrior families. Struggling to his feet, he wiped the free-flowing blood with his ever-present slog towel which hung at his side from his leather apron. Through a pinched nose, he continued his conversation:

"How much of that exchange did you see?"

"Enough to know that you've got a fighter on your hands." stated Nathan with his deep and hardened voice.

"Aye, a rebellious boy that needs the billows of discipline, not the fires of war," John said flatly.

Nathan made his way to the fire where the sword John had been forging still lay in it, its white-hot metal beginning to spark. "This sword that you have been forging... What would happen if you were to leave it sitting here in the billows?" questioned the captain. "Would it not fight for life, spark, crackle, and hold on to its form just before it smelted into something else, altogether different?"

"I know what you're saying, Nathan." interjected the weapon master still blotting his stained face. "But my son is not hardened metal. He's just a boy that's grown up in this village. And Safehaven is just that for him. It's a place where he can have the goodness of life. Have we not worked toward this safety? Have we not bled for such a place? Now that it has grown into a township, it has become the perfect place for him to begin a life of his own, forging his own name in the world. In this safe world."

Nathan watched as John settled himself onto the stool that he had fallen over, brushing his clothes off.

"He built this stool on his own. It was his first craftsmanship. The fire was too dangerous for him, so I told him he could start by working with wood. He so much wanted to be like me back then. Now, things are so different."

"When your campaign days were over, and you were finally healed of your wounds... When I brought you here... you knew that sense of confinement as well. John, it was like a prison sentence for you. You told me that, remember? Why do you expect your son, your first-born not to feel the same way?" asked Nathan.

"My wounds were barely survivable, Nathan," John replied, his voice gaining in strength.

"But you did survive," Nathan quickly interjected. "We all did."

"Only by the merciful grace of God did I survive my infirmities. I don't want him to go through that ever. He wants soldiery. And soldiery is certain destruction. Nathan, we go back a long way, but I have to disagree with you, respectfully. My son cannot have that life. I will not allow it," John stated with finality.

"And I will not push you, my friend. I cannot." Nathan replied after a long pause. "I will only say this more. You are a forger of weapons, a weapon's master. A weapon is not fashioned to merely hang on the wall or ornament a living quarter is it?"

The silence grew thick as John stood to his feet and made his way to the still baking sword struggling for the life of its form. Nathan thought that he may have pushed the issue to the edge but trusted that their years of fighting side by side in death-defying situations would hold them fast.

"John, I did come on business however," The silence still palpable. "I've come to ask if the latest order of weapons could move ahead of schedule by three days. I know it is a lot to ask, but I've brought workers to assist you. They're waiting outside if you need them."

Still John's silence continued.

"This is the kingdom's and the council's command, John, and our need is urgent. We have never seen this kind of enemy movement since, well, since the Campaign of Eight.

Our spies are not returning from their missions anymore. Only a handful has made it there and back again and they've reported an increase in activity." Nathan's voice was taking on an air of authority that was his just due, and John slowly perceived that his small world issues were becoming of minor concern.

Removing the sword from the fire, John struck it a couple of times with his forgers hammer and placed it into the water basin that sat next to the hearth. Instantly, a massive amount of steam and hissing exploded, filling the room with its humid odor. John's forehead beaded and dripped with sweat that mixed with the already drying blood on his face. Together, the crimson hued streaks ran around the forming smile on his face. Nathan responded in like manner, satisfied that their friendship had held intact.

"I can have the order done and I won't need the workers, though I thank you for the gesture. My son and I will accomplish this task together, or only I will," stated John with a warmed heart.

"I can always count on you my friend. I always have." With that, Nathan slapped John on the back and exited the hovel of the weapon master's shop. John held the sword over the basin momentarily before plunging it into the swirling water once again. At times, he imagined that he could see his reflection, but alas, it was only the distant memory of a face much younger, younger and more naïve, more like his firstborn son.

†

The River

Jonathan approached the swirling liquid of the river cautiously. He tried not to startle the already jittery horse as she drank from its crystal-clear waters at an eddy near a crop of trees. The horse was the family's backbone of sorts, due to her tireless and burdensome work that she had always performed with blind obedience and yet, Swift, as she was called, was pregnant almost to her full term.

Her gray coat was beginning to take on its winter thickness. Only by the closeness of their camaraderie was Jonathan allowed to grab her broken reign and calm her demeanor. If it were anyone else, she would have turned and taken off in another direction.

Life, as of late, had not been easy on Jonathan, for everything that Swift had been utilized for, he had to shoulder himself. At times, his younger brother Samuel would help, but he was only seven years old and that was enough to make most tasks more frustrating than fruitful.

The river, Safehaven's natural southern border, separated Jonathan's homeland from the vast wilderness that lay beyond his understanding and had become the demarcation line between the life that he had and the life that he had longed for. He had visited the shore many times throughout his lifetime for the family had spent many hours eating by its shores, playing in its waters, and of course, drinking from its life-giving sustenance.

It was an endless source of refreshment and a place of peace in the midst of an often-difficult existence. Endearing were the memories when his father would explain, and re-explain, to the family what their role in the kingdom was and how they, "as an important brush stroke in the painting of progress," fit into the larger fresco of life.

That's how the young Jonathan learned that Safehaven was just one of seven establishments throughout the realm, and how theirs was the most fortunate to have been assigned as the productions capital when the lots were cast. And, that their contributions to the supply line played one of the most, if not the most, important role in the kingdom. It was also at those riverside chats that John of Scharp would speak of a dynasty of weapon forgers such as the world had never seen, perhaps even producing a plethora of guilds. They were dreams and concepts beyond the youngling's years, but the family enjoyed seeing the enthusiasms by which the "Da'" had made his grand speeches and colorful tales, for where he lacked in sight, he made up in imaginations and stories.

And what stories he could tell.

As of late, the task of fetching water was passed from Jonathan to his younger brother although the elder would often defer, or rather refer, the task back to himself. This served the purpose of slipping away for moments of respite amidst his tiresome task-filled days. It was thus that Jonathan grew to cherish the times he spent by the shoreline. So much so, that he would often make up excuses or even create circumstances to get away to the water's edge. Once there, he had grown fond of a childhood game that was once revealed to him by his father but had quickly become more of an obsession. Nay, more of a mission.

The simple task of skipping stones had, in Jonathan's heart, become much more than a mere children's game. As he grew in strength, he realized that his arm would afford him the opportunity to skip the stones further and further into the passing current and thus, closer to the opposite shoreline.

It was an undiscovered land that had come to represent the life he had longed for. Was it the monotonous task of day-to-day life that urged his heart to wonder, or was it the mere fact that there had to be more to the life than that which was apparently laid out before him like a walkway made of immovable steppingstones? Whatever be the reason, young Jonathan's heart was determined to change his world, and the unfortunate stones that lay upon the shoreline would have to bear the brunt of his adolescent chemical which created the frustrations and determinations for his symbolic escape.

A stone tossed and skipped across the water was no small task. The river itself was vast, approximately forty lengths as the shadows moved, besides the fact that the current raced by at a furious pace and more so in the spring months. Fortunately for Jonathan, the runoff had run their courses being fall and the river had finally slowed to a mere surge rather than its normal torrential state. A stone that had the potential to reach the other shore would land well down river from where he stood, but he had found a remedy for that.

Jonathan had perfected the trajectory of his throw so that he could face upriver, throw against the current, and by the time it would reach (or nearly reach) the far side, it would be directly across from him. Thus, there seemed to be no better time to accomplish his "mission" than the present, for did not his father state that he could have been removed for months at a time and it would not have mattered?

Jonathan easily tethered Swift, for she had become quite the opposite of her namesake due to the fact that a new foal was growing within her womb. He had always had a respect for the family horse and their relationship was a special one. She was a gift to the family at the birth of Samuel six years prior and it was assigned to Jonathan to care for her.

For instance, he was tasked with the "mucking" of the stall, the grooming of her coat, the caring of her boarding on cold winter nights, and her retrieving when she had escaped in the swift blink of an eye; hence the namesake.

It was during those many horse retrievals which taught Jonathan to know where to begin his search for her. And she would always run to the same place: the river's edge. Consequently, when he had cut her reigns asunder, he instinctively knew where she had once again escaped too. The location that he was all too eager to go there himself for the river had become their common secret place, hidden away from life's hurts.

Returning to the river's edge, he meandered among the stones trying to find the proper ones used in the art of skipping. He had learned long ago that the shape and size of the stone determined his chance of succeeding in his task.

While he searched, thoughts of his father and their fight coursed through his mind like hidden specters flashing mocking smiles at his already restless mind. All at once, they caused not only remorseful memories, but also fleeting surges of rage. It was a conundrum of emotions that could not be contained nor understood. At times, he even thought that perhaps they were thoughts from another world, all together like voices from the shadows that seemed to want to envelope him in a swirling mist. The only way that he could assuage the problem was to throw, throw, and throw.

The stones themselves had to be smooth. Stones the river had tumbled and polished. They also had to be flattened, but not too flat. Too flat, and they would take flight on unseen wings and curve off in wrong directions. Too round, and they would sink before even finding the light of day. At last, he found seven smooth stones and made his way to his favorite place from which to pitch them. Near the shoreline, he had long ago found an outcropping that lay about five hand breadths above the surface of the water. Behind him, some felled trees created a closed in wall.

It was the perfect spot from which to hurl his stones and it was also hidden from sight in case any passers-by would happen along. With rage and remorse still brimming within him, he cast a look across the wide expanse of swirling water and fixed his gaze upon the opposite shore determined to complete the task his heart had been fixed upon for years.

The boy took the first of seven stones and threw his hardest. The first fell to the side and quickly sank into the depths swallowed up by the mysteries of the deep as if to mock his meager effort, yet for Jonathan it was the usual warm up (and cast aside) attempt. The second and third tosses produced better results, but they too were at odds with the contour of the water's surface and glanced off in equally odd directions. The fourth skip however, finally produced results. It excited Jonathan to no end for it had become the longest distance he had ever thrown a rock. His heart leaped as the stone raced its way to the far side. Farther and farther it went bouncing with purpose. He even began to cheer it on.

"Go, go, go!" he shouted at the emotionless stone.

He would have released a triumphant bellow if it had bridged the distance, but alas it fell just shy of the far shore. With new hope in his heart, the young man took another, his fifth stone, and slung it as hard as he could. It was more out of frustration than finesse, for although it did leave with force, it caught a small wave and shot into the air and nearly back in the same direction it had been fired from. Gathering himself, the boy settled into the task at hand with his whole heart, the anger and frustration of the day yielding to his new goal, or rather, the old goal that had found new purpose.

The sixth stone was another foul, but it showed more promise than the last. Finally, with the last stone in hand, Jonathan made his thoughts audible:

"This has got to be the one… Come on, just once…, just once make it to the other side," he pleaded with the clouds above as if they were listening at all. It was the first time, however, that he noticed their racing past as if they were foxes being chased by an angry storm of dogs.

Without a second thought, he let it fly.

It was a picture of beauty as it left his hand and he knew it. He felt it in his gut. Its trajectory mirrored the fourth throw, but appeared as if it had invisible angel's wings that majestically flapped with each kiss off the water. For a moment in time, it was as if the current of the river had all together stopped. Farther and farther it traveled skipping like a rock with a mission and as it began to approach the far shore it even seemed to pick up speed as if someone had magically roped it in and was pulling it hand over hand and closer to its mark.

Within a breadth of a man's arm though, the stone abandoned its strength, and it fell short of the goal by mere wisps.

It was the defeat Jonathan had grown accustomed too as if creation itself had conspired against him and doomed him to failure. The task of rock skipping and stone throwing had become the defining moment in his adolescent life. With all of his heart he wanted just one of his stones to reach the far side, the new world, the adventure of a lifetime. Somehow, he felt that just one stone's liberation from his side of the world to the other would somehow liberate his own soul as well. Alas, it would not be, not for the moment at least.

His face fell and it seemed that his brooding had carried not only his facial features, but also his shoulders towards the dust of the ground below his feet.

Defeated, he turned on his heels and sauntered back in the direction of Swift, back in the direction toward the life he had ever known, and would ever know. Oh, he could have thrown more stones, but he only ever afforded himself seven tries. That was an unwritten rule he would never break. It was only ever seven stones.

On the edge of the outcropping, Jonathan continued to amble back into his past life, his eyes seeing the ground before him but his focus elsewhere. Elsewhere, that is, until he spotted a sight that yanked his seeing into a rapid focus. There, before him, lay a stone half hidden by the shoreline sand. Though partially buried, it seemed to enlighten the surrounding silt, and indeed it did.

Kneeling down, Jonathan reached for what would be the most perfect of stones. Freeing it from its confines, he brushed clear the clinging earth. The stone filled his hand almost to its full breadth. It contained a near perfect balanced weight, a bit on the heavy side, yet easy to handle. Jonathan's heart leapt at the discovery. Though it was mostly covered in mud, he hoped beyond hope that what he was holding was really what he thought it was. Racing to the shoreline, he plunged the object into the water and cleared away the grime.

From the water emerged the most beautiful sight he had ever seen. In his hand lay a single piece of Emeralhearth, a majestic green rock so perfectly formed and polished that it was nearly transparent. Looking into its depths was like looking into the heart of nature itself, for a distant light burned deep within. It was like the light that streams through the branches of trees in the waning hours of a glorious day.

He had heard of the stone, but never believed it to be real in any way, shape, or form. To him, it was only a legendary substance fashioned into a legendary shield for a legendary king. If true, its worth would certainly be legendary for it would be much more valuable than fine gold.

Jonathan's mind raced at its discovery. He thought that perhaps he had found a future in it, a way to buy his way out of his ordinary life. As he pondered its potential, he soon found another discovery and it nearly stopped his rapidly beating heart. Rolling the gem across his fingers, still amazed at its exquisite beauty, he dropped it into the then murky water. The moment lingered on the edge of self-destruction for it had disappeared beneath the surface, yet to his utter amazement, the item that had sunk suddenly bobbed to the surface once again.

"A stone that floats upon the surface of the water? Do my eyes deceive me?" mused Jonathan out loud.

The young man picked up the stone again, and again dropped it into the water where it again descended into the depths, but soon rose again to the surface. Then a thought occurred to him.

I am more than sure that this stone of stones could span the distance of the river. Just one throw, perhaps even just one skip with an eighth try could more than bridge the gap of my frustration. But I am equally sure that it could buy my freedom as well. Perhaps elevate me to a position of power in the realm. Maybe even to the hand of my princess?

For there was yet another obsession tucked secretly away into the son of the weapon master's heart.

Thus, in an instant, the boy grew to be a young man; a young man with real opportunities, with real temptations, and with real choices. Do not all suddenly discovered treasures have a tendency to produce such quandaries… such inner battles?

✝

The Runoff

Samuel was seven and almost seventeen at the same time, the second son of Kathryn and John of Scharp, a young lad ahead of his actual days. The night before his birth, his mother had a dream whereby he was found to be lying upon a forested bed in a nest of feathers and guarded by majestic birds of prey. They were birds of multiple hued feathers with talons as long as thorn pegs.

In actuality, he was born with two umbilical cords, and his mother often stated that half of him was for her and the other half belonged to the heavens. His eyes, even at birth, seemed to be seeing somewhere else and unlike his Da' and his brother's green eyes, Samuel's eyes were as clear as a bright blue sky.

Though somewhat absent from this world, he was a good and obedient boy and at the moment was making his way to the river's edge, looking very much like a monk for his hair was cut so short around and above the ears that his scalp could be clearly seen. Around his shoulders he wore a thick brown cloak made of bear skin that his mother insisted he wear for the long and forlorn winter months were rapidly approaching. In his hand were two thatched buckets lined with pitch used for carting water to and from the family's small stone cottage. While he walked, he hummed a tune (for he always hummed a tune) and somewhat post-toddled his way toward the river's edge.

Once there, he found his brother, seated by a clump of trees daydreaming about some far off place and perhaps even some far off time as well. Samuel was always ready for a game, and when he spotted Jonathan near the clump of trees where he had often found him flinging stones into the current, he decided to sneak up on him.

He had looked up to his brother in not only a literal way, but also a figurative one as well. It's only natural, I suppose, for a younger brother to admire the elder. Perhaps it was due to the fact that the elder had braved the rapids of new and naïve parenting or perhaps it was the fact that the elder was just simply the larger of the two. What had never crossed his mind, and what Samuel could not possibly fathom, was the fact that there were actually times when Jonathan would admire the younger with equal vigor. And that, perhaps, was due in large part to the way in which the parents treated the younger for at times they treated him as if the younger had been the actual firstborn. Nevertheless, the two brothers ended up with a mutual respect and admiration that allowed them to interact on the friendliest of terms.

Therefore, when Samuel snuck up on his brother with a large stick in his hand, he was confident that a game would soon be afoot.

Samuel hurled the stick up and over the clump of trees with all of his strength not knowing at what angle it may come down. To his utter amazement, the stick came down right between Jonathan's legs and stuck fast into the mud that lay in pools before him. Jonathan didn't even flinch, so lost was he in contemplation, about what Samuel could only guess. Searching for another projectile, the younger continued to steal his around the clump of trees.

Surely, the breaking of branches will snap him out of his thoughts, thought Samuel to himself. However, his rustlings produced no response from the elder, so it was only right to toss another in his general direction. Thus, up and over the hedge went another stick of considerable size which, at that time, would have ended up almost directly upon the head of Jonathan if it were not for his quick reflexes.

Jonathan, consummate would-be warrior, instinctively kept one ear and one eye upon his surroundings at all times. He had known that his mischievous brother had approached earlier and had also known the precise moment that he was present and thereby had hidden the green gem in the folds of his cloak. He also knew that with the toss of the first stick in his direction, a second would be a calculable fact which was proved correct. (For what seven-year-old could possibly show any respect let alone restraint whatsoever?)

As the second projectile was on its heading to strike Jonathan on the top of his lid, he snapped his eyes in the direction of the danger and instantly made a sweeping arc with an outstretched hand thereby catching the stick in mid-fight. As he whirled around, he thought the better of returning the missile from whence it had come due to the fact that serious bodily harm could have been afflicted upon the young misfit. Electing rather to sprint in the direction of Samuel, he could hear the giggling yelp of the younger as he took off in another direction all together.

Thus, the chase and game were on.

Samuel ran like a leaping roe in and out of the shoreline dodging low branches on the way and yelping the whole time. It was just what Jonathan had needed at that moment to shake him out of his very adult-like contemplations and he was more than happy to play along. It was one of the things that caused the elder to admire the younger. Somehow and someway Samuel had a way of bringing peace, if not healing, to whatever situation he happened upon.

That was his gift, and it was always a welcome one in the Scharp household.

Jonathan slowed to a trot, and with stick in hand, prodded Samuel on his backside which produced only more hilarious yelps from the youngling.

"No, you can't poke at me! That's not fair!" yelped Samuel.

"But you can throw gigantic logs at me, eh brother?" taunted Jonathan.

"But I never hit you!" continued Samuel as they both raced along the shoreline, splashing in the water the whole way.

Samuel was oblivious to the fact that Jonathan and the Da' had a falling out as of late, that made Jonathan's willingness to play along undiminished. Finally, beginning to tire, the elder gently tossed the stick in front of Samuel's legs where it just caught the pitter patter of Samuel's feet at the right angle to cause him to trip and fall into the water. Falling face first into the current, Samuel outstretched his arms and momentarily bobbed… then suddenly became a still and seemingly lifeless object floating deeper and deeper into the river's sway.

All at once, Jonathan felt the emergent feelings of guilt and panic.

"Samuel…? Samuel…!?" he shouted at the still lifeless form.

It was one of those moments that freezes one in time. A moment that feels like an eternity when in actuality, it's only seconds long.

Without a further thought, Jonathan leaped with lightning-fast reflexes into the swirling current and placed a hand on the floating bearskin cloak of his brother and flipped him over. Once there, he was met with a rather sheepish grin emanating from the face of the younger.

"What, you were jesting?" questioned Jonathan.

Samuel snickered the only kind of snicker that would fend off a slap in the face.

"You're fortunate enough to have the face that you have, or I would drown you in the surf, you skunk!" retorted the elder brother as if he were a parent himself.

Together, the two made their way to the river's edge and onto the shoreline once again. There, they sat in the mud and just laughed together, Jonathan's heaviness melting away like a spring runoff. The mud that they had collected upon themselves would have had their parents verbally raising the rafters of the family's home. In fact, at the moment, the two of them even pictured the thatched roof coming apart at the seams and the anger of the Da' beginning to light the straw on fire. They read each other's thoughts and at the same time turned to the other and verbalized their inner converse:

"WHOOSH!" they said aloud and laughed like raucous old hunters after a long night of tracking.

In time, their hilarity died down and they just sat together in silence until the younger broke it with a line of sincere and heartfelt questioning.

"Brother, what were you thinking about at the river's edge when I found you?" inquired Samuel.

For a moment Jonathan, in his adolescent manner, thought it strange to think about engaging in a would-be conversation with a seven-year-old as if the seven-year-old were seventeen and his peer. But long ago the fifteen-year-old Jonathan had learned that his baby brother was especially gifted in the art of listening beyond his years, and he abandoned his line of thinking to answer the sincerity of the would-be teen.

"I was thinking of a time before you were born. A time when I first saw…," his words fell short of near revelation.

"When you first saw her?" Samuel questioned after a long pause.

"You don't know what I was going to say," defended Jonathan.

"I do know… but I haven't said anything to anyone."

"How?" Jonathan questioned.

"Brother, we sleep in the same room. I hear your dreams. Between snorts and snores, you talk, talk, and talk," giggled the younger.

With that, Jonathan scooped a clump of mud and placed it upon his brother's head like a mucky hat that dripped down the sides of his monkish head. Samuel just shook it off with a shake like a water shedding pup.

"Tell me the story though, please. I want to hear it." Samuel inquired.

"Well, just before you were born, when Ma' was pregnant with you, we were at the last Festival of Blossoms."

"Oh, like the one that's about to happen again?" interrupted the youngling.

"Story, Samuel. I'm telling the story," frowned Jonathan, with his hands raised in the air.

"Right, sorry," repented Samuel.

"It was a great day. We arrived at the hollow with grand excitement. I'll never forget how the hollow looked that day. A wind had been blowing and the cherry blossoms were shedding their petals to look like snow falling from the sky. The blossoms were not falling straight down, but rather swirling in circles as if they were dancing to some sort of music that only they could hear. The ardent play had already begun, and it was the first year of the new pavilion. The three-plat-formed stage was a great sight to see back then. Everyone was excited about the whole thing. It also marked the beginning of Safehaven becoming a township." Jonathan watched his brother with discernment and discovered that he was certainly intent upon listening, and it afforded the elder encouragement to continue his discourse.

"Back then was different from now. The Blossom Festival used to be so fun. Now, it's only serious talk with no games."

"There used to be games? What games?" inquired Samuel.

"We used to play fun games as kids… That was where I first met her, and him."

"Who's him? You never mentioned 'him' in your dreams," Samuel interrupted.

"Yes, there's him," Jonathan stated as his furrowed-brow thoughts carried him away to a distant time.

The game was called, 'catch the squealer,' and all the kids of the village-turned-township looked forward to participating every year at the annual festival. The parents looked forward to it as well because it gave them a chance to have fellowship with friends without the constant interruptions of cloth jerking little hands and their constant neediness. Once gathered in the gigantic stall behind the butcher's shop, the kids would anticipate the appearance of His Sir-ness as Bart of the Forest was called.

Sir-ness was the affectionate name that he had earned because of his great generosity towards those in need. There was nothing more satisfying to the butcher than the chance to help out fellow villagers in times of need and he spent most of his time stealthily spying out those who were lacking, so he knew their need even when no one else could have known. His favorite time of year was the annual festival, no matter in which of the seven towns it was being held, for he was the supplier of the massive amount of mutton and victuals that generously fed the masses. His appearance at the back door of his butcher's shop brought yelps from the children as the anticipation of the chase was about to commence.

Bart of the Forest was a portly man, but as strong as an ox and his second favorite past time was to hunt wild boars in the wood. Armed with only a deer horn dagger, he would often coat his bald head with inky mud before setting out on foot into the vast wilderness where he would be gone for days at a time. Although a vigorous hunter, he was also known as a kind and gentle man when he was in town and always cordial to his customers.

When he appeared in the doorway, in his hands were one of those wild boars, but only a young one whose tusks had just begun to appear and therefore were dull and harmless. Lathered in lard, the young hog was set loose by his Sir-ness and the kids scrambled to catch it as it darted away with a small explosion of squeals.

Jonathan was the first to touch the wild beast. At only eight years old, his fleet feet carried him faster than the other kids of the town. With a great and remarkable slide in the mud, he was able to grab the hind quarters of the small prey. Once attached, he was able to hold him for a whole ten seconds before the little creature slipped away, bucking and snorting. Instantly, a gaggle of kids clamored after it, all of them falling well short of its wiggly scamper.

His "Sir-ness" laughed a hearty laugh that made his whole body shake, and as Jonathan watched, he winked at the boy in a "good attempt" sort of way. Jonathan slathered his way to his feet and nodded in the direction of Bart before turning once again toward the little pig.

The wild boar itself was a determined little fellow and at the moment was making an attempt to leap over the stone wall that created the barrier to hold the animal within the field of play. Unfortunately for the boar, the barrier was an immoveable one and with a great thud, the animal failed to clear the wall and fell stunned and back into the arena. What followed was an absolute pig pile!

Children's arms and legs leaped from all directions upon the poor creature, and it was instantly buried beneath the small mountain of flesh, but that was what made the game so fun. At the same time that the avalanche of bodies settled upon the ground, a wave of muddy water sprang up into the air and inevitably upon each and every child present. Jonathan was saddened and elated all at the same time, for although he had missed the pig pile, he spotted the small fiend of a pig wiggle free from the fleshy mountain and scamper across the yard again, affording him a second chance at the prize.

What was the prize? The pig, once caught, would be awarded to the child's family and in turn the family would be free to do with it whatever they saw fit or perhaps had need of at the moment, for if sold it could fetch a handsome sum indeed. It was also a chance for the winning child to be as if they themselves were a great hunter and perhaps, for the first time in their young lives, bring home the game for the family's needs. At the end of it all however, it was simply yet another token of generosity by the gentle butcher.

Jonathan saw his chance to make his Da' proud and sprang into action. However, as he approached the cornered piglet, he was halted in his tracks by a flash of whirling blond hair that leapt in front of him. With the swiftness of a lightning strike, the small boar and boy were caught dead in their tracks.

Although muddied to no end, she was the most beautiful creature Jonathan had ever seen.

Her matted hair released ringlets that fell down over her eyes like a royal veil. Through those ringlets, clear eyes shone underneath eyebrows that were like waxing crescent moons on a harvest eve. Her nose elegantly descended from there like a gentle fall line from a majestic mount only to touch lips that were full and rich in a reddened hue.

Having corralled the piglet, she laughed and turned her head toward Jonathan, causing his world to slow down for that one moment. All peripheral sights clouded on his left and right, and all at once his focus was upon the creature that would prove to haunt many of his dreams, though it would become a welcomed haunting indeed.

Unfortunately, the dreamscape was quickly smashed like a boulder falling through an icy river by a boy bearing the name James the Younger, son of James the Good, Nasgroth of Trelane, one of the other townships of the realm.

Jonathan could hardly believe his eyes as he witnessed the ten-year-old James approach the eight year old girl, slap her in the face, and peel her off of the piglet only to throw her aside like an empty burlap sack where she fell with a whimper. Jonathan had never felt such a surge of chemicals in his veins. His heart leaped like the little piglet had as it left the arms of Bart the butcher and before he could even think, he had smashed the boys' nose and had him pinned against the stone wall with one hand on his throat and the other with a fist full of nappy brown hair. Poised and ready to slam the back of James' head against a stone, he stared down into the blood spattered and defiant eyes of his would-be nemesis.

Suddenly, he found himself dangling above the boy as he was being held one-armed by the vice like grip of his Sir-ness, Bart of the Forest.

"That will do, boy." Bart turned Jonathan toward himself like a door swinging on a hinge and looked approvingly into his deep green eyes. "You can beat your enemy down, but never, never kill him. That's not your decision to make," Bart stated with what seemed to be an echo in the hot anger filled ears of young Jonathan.

Then, as quickly as it began it was over, and Jonathan found himself on the muddy ground once again. He could feel the steely eyes of James the Younger burrowing a hole into his chest, but he brushed it aside and made his way over to the girl.

Offering his hand down to her, he cherished the moment she placed her hand in his and heard her speak for the first time.

"Thank you, my prince," she whispered.

"And that was the first time that I saw her," stated Jonathan to his attentive little brother.

"Have you spoken to her since then?" questioned Samuel.

"Not once, not even in my dreams."

"That's not right. I'll tell Ma', she'll make it right."

"No, you won't," Jonathan stated flatly.

"Yes… I will," jested the younger.

"No, you won't," responded the elder with a touch of anger.

"Oh, yes," said Samuel as he rose from the shoreline and threatened to run in the direction of home.

Jonathan rose in unison with the little skunk and grabbed him by the arm as the younger tried to pull away. Samuel giggled in his own silly way and tried to pull away again, but Jonathan picked him up and tossed him into the river's awaiting water. He then jumped in after the little one and together commenced a war of water that lasted nearly a quarter of an hour before they were then interrupted by an ironic twist of fate.

From the forest that lay upriver there emerged a war party led by soldiers of the kingdom riding upon the magnificent coursers of the royal stables. At the moment, they had just completed a scouting trip of the southern border lands, and when they stopped at the banks, Jonathan was more embarrassed than Samuel when they were caught frolicking in the water.

They instantly stopped, water dripping from them like the end of a morning rain. Among the party was an older James the Younger in training as a would-be soldier with mentors of the royal soldiery. Also among the would-be warriors was she, the girl Jonathan had rescued seven years earlier. He had seen her many times since their very first encounter, but still had never spoken to her. He didn't even know her name. Jonathan stood dumbfounded.

The war party hardly took notice of the two peasant looking boys, but one amongst them did and she smiled at Jonathan as he stared in awe. It was his 'princess'. She was dressed in battle fatigues and sat atop a mocha-colored horse that was also arrayed in the dress of war. Together they matched, with her darkened leather garbs and a saddle of the same shade. The way that she was seated in the saddle made it look like they were nearly one. An array of small daggers was lined end-to-end up the left forearm of the girl, but it was clear that her main fighting weapon was a crossbow that was slung over her head and hung upon her back.

It had the distinct characteristics of his father's craftsmanship and in an instant, he wondered if he himself had a hand in its formation. To Jonathan, she seemed to fit the position like a veteran of the realm although it was clear that she was merely in training due to the way that the true veterans had been barking orders to the trainees.

Upon hearing the gruff growls of the battle-hardened mentors, both James the Younger, the 'princess', and two other newling's scampered from their horses and to a small wagon being pulled behind a servant-at-arms. Once there, they produced watering troughs and cups and commenced to fill them at the river's edge. It was a sight that produced in the heart of Jonathan a sense of humility and jealousy all at the same time, for there was his nemesis at the side of his princess and they were both in training for the greatest desire of his own heart, to be a soldier of the realm.

The feelings flooded his soul once again just at the moment he had completely forgotten the tiff earlier in the day.

"Why don't you go and talk to her?" interrupted the young Samuel.

"What?" Jonathan questioned as he nearly shook his head to clear his daydreaming state.

"Go and talk to her." repeated Samuel.

"I couldn't."

"Yes you could… You know that you want too, right? Or are you tongue tied brother?" There was an air of challenge in the young ones' tone, and Jonathan sensed warm blood filling his still water doused face.

"Never mind," shied Jonathan at the dare.

"Then I will for you," Samuel stated as he started to make his way in the direction of the war party.

"No, no, I'll do it," was the older brother's answer.

Jonathan approached the party tentatively, waiting for the right moment when the girl would be alone and not busy attending to the others. The moment presented itself after she had finished her duties and when she had at last begun to attend to her own courser. For a moment, she was alone by the water and Jonathan snuck below the sight of the rest of the soldiers including Jaes the Younger.

"Hello," he spoke with a conscious effort to keep his voice from shaking.

"Hello," she replied with a voice that sounded like some kind of music to Jonathan.

Her beauty was still just as intimidating as it had always been, and Jonathan could feel the great gulf between them threaten to grow into a wider chasm. He fought it off with the only words that came to his mind at the time.

"Do you remember me?" he questioned.

The pause hung in the air like a note in mid-orchestration. Her face had a kind expression, but the words hadn't come just yet. It was impossible for Jonathan to discern what her anticipated answer would be, and his inner conversation clouded his emotions. 'Has she ever thought of me the way I have thought of her?' he mused.

"Ho' there," boomed a voice that broke through the moment like a stone that breaks the ice of a thawing creek.

It was James the Younger, mounted upon his steed and dressed in his own battle array. He managed to move his horse between the girl and the drenched Jonathan. From his height, he addressed the still dripping weapon-master's apprentice.

"It's not proper to approach a soldier without an invitation too, piglet chaser," bellowed James.

His condescending manner of speech reminded Jonathan that the privileges of the wealthy included an education in the tongue of the upper class.

"Who is looking down upon whom now, apprentice?" said James.

"Still polishing the saddle of your master's horse, hey youngling?" retorted Jonathan.

"Yes, well, by the time I join the war effort and am actually using the weapon's that you grovel to create, you will still be fetching water for your Ma' from this river here."

It was a stinging accusation, and before Jonathan could react, the veteran mentors demanded that they continue on their journey.

James deliberately kept his horse between Jonathan and the girl until she had mounted hers and the party was off once again. As they disappeared into the forest, the girl shot a glance behind her and in the direction of Jonathan. It was a moment he would remember for years to come.

Samuel slowly scuttled next to his brother with a tethered Swift in hand and allowed the horse to nudge his older brother on the shoulder.

"I'm sorry, John," said Samuel.

"John, not Jonathan?" questioned the elder.

"Aye, for you are John of Scharp; much older than James the Younger. Older and 'gooder', brother," declared the seven-year-old.

"Thanks," Jonathan said as he slung his arm around the neck of his sibling and friend.

Together, they filled the thatched buckets with water near a small rapid created by some boulders in the river. Then they each grabbed a rein to handle Swift and slowly made their way back in the direction of their home just as the first drops of rain began to fall from the newly arrived storm. As they started to enter the forested canyon pass that they had traveled for years, Jonathan felt for the precious stone that still lay hidden within the folds of his cloak and contemplated its weight in silence.

Behind them, and unbeknownst to anyone that had been previously near the water's edge that day, there emerged from the shallows of mud and mire a figure nearly invisible.

So stealthy and camouflaged was the enemy scout that the whole of the war party had watered their horses a mere hand breath above its hiding place. And like a shadowy serpent it had passed silently and within a whisper of the frolicking Samuel and his older brother, Jonathan of Scharp.

Chapter 2

Pried from the Cobblestones

†

Forgery

It was a long walk home for both Jonathan and Samuel. Neither of them spoke many words except for the few times that they expressed their mutual desire for Swift to pass her foaling so that she could get back to work and their loads would be considerably lessened. As they emerged from the forested pathway and into the land that their Da' had acquired, their countenances changed considerably with one lightening and the other dampening.

Samuel, with his buckets of water in hand, scurried in the direction of the cottage, a laminar smoke emanating from the chimney. Jonathan, on the other hand, sauntered with Swift in hand toward the weapon shop which the stable was attached too. The smoke that emanated from the hearth was noticeably thicker and darker than that of the cottage.

The land that the homestead sat upon was bequeathed to John after his faithful service to the kingdom during the Campaign of Eight and in the wake of his healing; a healing which we have already briefly spoken of but in time shall be revealed more fully.

Though he had never laid physical eyes upon the plot of ground, which was approximately forty full acres, he had searched it far and wide utilizing the eyes of his wife Kathryn as they would often walk hand-in-hand throughout the land. She had been pregnant with Jonathan during the infamous campaign and often feared she would be left alone to fend for herself, and nearly was. After her husband's return and recovery, and upon receiving the news of their inheritance, she was more than happy to help him with the homestead in any way possible and together, they vowed to build a home to settle in for the rest of their lives.

It was inevitable that they built, or rather, supervised the building of the compound toward the rear of the property because it was the area closest to the river and the infinitely valuable water source would be vital not only in the construction process, but also in the future of any forging. Hence, both the property and the business were included in the reward for faithful service to the kingdom.

The pathway to the river, of which has already been revealed, but will play a further prominent role in the unfolding of this story, ran from the Scharp property and down a long ravine that passed between two stark canyons that became so narrowed toward the end that it appeared to become boxed in. In ages past, a branch of the river had run through it thus creating the gorge and thereby forming a forest of felled trees whose wood had been smoothed by the passing of ancient waters. Though long buried, the hardened substance could be acquired if one were to dig beneath the topsoil about the height of a work horse. It was in those diggings that John of Scharp had found the unique wood to support his livelihood, but as of yet, was still in need of a crafting pair of hands.

The idea of becoming a master carver and forger of weapons had never even crossed his mind before, for he had been raised as the son of a hunter. Other than creating the bows and dagger handles used in the hunting of wild game, no one of the Scharp line had ever taken up the craft of weapon forging. After his eyesight was taken from him, John had lost all hope of ever being useful to anyone; that was, until the Council of the Castle, led by his good friend Nathan, bestowed upon him the task of a weapon master for the kingdom, a true step of faith by the Council that was for sure. (In fact, the act was one of the many occasions for John to admire their leadership abilities for they had a tendency to see the people of the Realm for who they could be, and not for who they appeared to be.) Needless to say, John was compelled to become self-taught, for in those days folks were expected to be hearty and self-reliant. Therefore, he had no other choice but to figure out the craft all on his own.

Hours that turned into days and consequently into weeks were spent in frustration as he tried to figure the art out. There were many times, as Kathryn would attest to, that the forger would spend in complete and utter silence having completely forsaken the task in shear exhaustion. One particular spell lasted close to nine weeks and Kathryn thought that she had lost her love forever, for unlike his physical injuries, these were psychologically incapacitating.

During those nine weeks of darkness, Kathryn would attend to her husband almost every hour at the top of the hour. She was the kind of woman who would keep herself up because she so dearly loved her husband and possessed a devoted heart. Though naturally beautiful, she was always attentive to her appearance even though she felt that her husband's eyes would never see the light of day again.

She became more and more worried for him as he seemed to descend deeper and deeper into the chasm of his own soul. The only thing she knew to do was to pray. Therefore, prayer became an hour-by-hour ritual just before she would check in on him.

Whether it was the constant prayers or pure coincidence, although it should be clear where Kathryn's opinion lay, the darkness was shattered one spring morn when she heard the sound of craftsmanship emanating from the weapon shop which lay across the flowered and spice filled gardens adjacent to the cottage; a garden that she had attended to with the utmost of care.

Sweeping past the spices and next to the vegetable rows, her eyes rested upon a number of hummingbirds that seemed to pay no attention to her passing. She counted at least seven of the creatures all hovering in unison about the flowers, their wings creating their own type of musical score.

When she arrived at the entrance to the shop, she was shocked when she opened the door. There, before her eyes, sat her husband upon a stool with a staff of magnificent and ornate beauty such as she had never laid eyes upon before. It was lying across his legs and with his hands he was carving another in the exact dimensions and design of the first, although in a lesser wood.

The first was a white type of substance that appeared to be wood, but looked like some sort of stone as well. Its top, or what seemed to be the top, was thick and could have been used for a club. Below the head was a gilded handle that appeared to be the handle of a broadsword. From there, the shaft gracefully descended with a slight bowing effect toward a beveled end that was thinned to a point. At the point, an ornate head of gold continued to a sharpened place that appeared to be that of an arrowhead. Throughout its length and breadth, the carved wings of birds of prey were effortlessly wrapped around the circumference and lined with a silvery-blue substance. All in all, surmised Kathryn, it appeared to be four or five weapons all melded into one.

The one that John was carving was well on its way to becoming a near exact replica, minus the gold and silvery-blue substance of course.

John's countenance was full of light and life and his eyes seemed to be seeing something that Kathryn could not. For a moment, she thought that somehow his eyes had been healed, but the thought escaped her when he dropped his carving tool and had trouble finding it again as he searched for it with fumbling hands.

"John?" she quietly inquired.

He seemed to not hear, or not even care until she asked again, "John?" she nearly whispered.

"Kate? Oh, my dear sweet wife. You'll not believe what has happened," he declared as he turned his head in her direction.

"What is it?" she asked in an almost incredulous way, awed by what she was witnessing.

"The darkness has faded and I'm seeing with new eyes."

"I'm not sure what you're saying… Are you telling me that you can see now?"

"Not exactly… but where there was only blackness and deep darkness, I can see what looks like mist. It's hard to explain… It's, it's almost like water swirling around my eyes. It's incredible!" he finished with a joyful hush.

Still in awe of what she was witnessing, she felt the need to question further if she were to grasp an ounce of what was actually happening.

"Where did you get that… that weapon?" she inquired, not quite sure what to call it.

"He called it a Willowfeld Shunt."

"Who called it that?" she inquired.

"He didn't say his name… I was seated right here, where I've been for weeks, and all of a sudden I heard a knock on the door and it opened without my reply. I thought perhaps that the wind had somehow blown a branch into it, but when it opened, it was as if the darkness was swiftly chased away. The next thing I know, this 'shunt' is being placed across my legs as you see it now. And then he said, 'This is a gift from the one true king, and it comes from the courts of the one true castle.' I didn't even know there could be another king, let alone castle," stated John with a hint of disbelief in his voice.

"Was that all he said?" asked Kathryn.

"No, one thing more. He said, 'Follow,' and quickly left. Somehow, I knew he didn't mean to physically follow him. That's when I started carving. I can't explain it to you Kate, but I now know how to create. It is as if I can see a thousand weapons with my hands. I don't know how… I just know how," John finally stated and continued to mimic the staff that lay in his lap by feeling it and then carving, feeling again and then carving some more.

Kathryn was in awe, altogether filled with joy, and merely watched her husband as a new focus and purpose began to register upon his face and about his countenance.

"Thank you my dear, Kate," he finally said. "Thank you for taking care of me. I knew you were there each and every hour that you checked in on me, and I thank you. I'm sorry for disappearing on you." The love with which he made his last statement convinced Kathryn that her prayers had been answered in a way that she could not possibly explain and didn't even care too.

This had all taken place just before the birth of Jonathan, and as experiences such as those have a tendency to become dull in the light of new generations, the importance and meaning had been lost in the translation of the stories to his boys as John would try to pass them along for the purpose of helping them to form a belief system.

Such is the nature of the human heart. One's life experience can be talked about and told, but somehow the viscosity of its meaning becomes thinned in the mere hearing of it. Perhaps all stories are of such a nature. That is, stories that are told in the light of one's own perspective according to the way one has perceived it, becoming dulled to a point so as to merely become a signpost on the road of life, to be used to point another in a direction and according the outcome, either toward the good, or toward the bad thereby giving the listener a clue to which direction he or she should flee toward. This, of course, is supposing that the listener has heard the hearing at all.

What John had meant to convey to his sons through the telling of the stories was meant to spur them in a similar direction of his own, one based upon his own understanding of the ancient belief system that had been laid out in The Shadow Scrolls whereby the King had given himself over to the powers of darkness and the inky blackness of the realm's shadows.

However, what had happened in reality and what he had at long last discovered was the fact was that his boys had their very own human hearts. In other words, though flesh of his flesh, his boys had their own minds, their own wills, and their own emotions, i.e. their own souls, those very human entities which are uniquely individual and not controllable or lead-able by any outside force unless, of course, that individual yields to the leading.

Now, pulling back from the past and focusing upon the present once again, allow us to catch up with the eldest son of the weapon master of Safehaven who found himself bypassing any 'sign posts' and was being led by something else altogether; something that he could not quite put his finger upon even though it was gnawing at him with an unyielding nibble.

Jonathan, his clothes still dripping with the river's mists, arrived at the door of the shop in silence after putting Swift back in her stall and could see that his Da' had been working without a break since the early morning, or at least since the time that they had head-butted. John's mid-day victuals sat untouched upon a small table and Jonathan knew by experience that the latest order must have been pushed to an earlier date. He knew this because his father would only work non-stop in such demanding circumstances and would otherwise never dream of missing mid-day meals, being heavily indebted to time with Kathryn so as to make up old losses. Although the little shop was a cacophony of noise, John almost always knew when someone entered his hovel unannounced.

"Jonathan… How's the horse?" he inquired.

Jonathan made his way through the shop and began to quickly assemble the tools and materials to begin a new weapon. The one he chose would eventually become a hand crafted, carefully fashioned cross-bow similar to the one he had seen hanging upon the back of the 'princess'.

Seated at his work space in the rear and darkest part of the shop, he refused to answer the inquiry of his father when he asked a second time and merely started his project in silence. With wood slab in hand, he closed his eyes, and like his father, blindly yet instinctively began whittling away as shavings from the material curled up and fell into balls in the corner of the shop. His was a craft that had been passed down to him and out of love and admiration for his father, at least when he was younger, he had learned to whittle blindly.

"When your mother and I were married, it was like an arrangement made in heaven. I felt like I was engaged to an angel. She was so beautiful, but she was not the person I had originally pictured in my mind you know. I was picturing someone altogether different," John began, knowing that his son could hear him even though not necessarily wanting to. "In this realm's society, you have to learn to take what comes your way with gratitude knowing that things happen for a reason. Jonathan, you can't swim against the tide your entire life! You'll eventually wear out. Can't you just have some faith in the way things are run here? Some trust in me as your father?"

Jonathan was working at a fever pitch on his construction. Faster and faster he whittled taking his frustrations out on the innocent piece of wood. Though his Da' continued to bolster him with words about his own beliefs and philosophies, the boy knew that it would be fruitless to commence arguing as he had done before, and it further solidified in his mind his utter need to escape the confines of his surroundings. That was when he remembered the precious Emralhearth stone stowed away on his person. It brought him comfort to know that the precious light that flickered deep within the heart of the rock would also produce a ray of hope into his hopeless situation. It also gave him occasion to redirect his father's line of thinking.

"Da', he interrupted, "Have you ever seen an Emralhearth stone?" he asked with a needle prick of sarcasm although he did not overtly mean too.

"No… why do you ask?" inquired John.

"Then how do you know that they exist?" prodded Jonathan.

"It's as I have been telling you, son. Some things you just have to receive on belief alone. I know that it exists because of the stories I have heard. It's that simple. In the reading of the Shadow Scrolls, Emeralhearth is mentioned many times, so I know it to be true," surmised John as he diligently continued his work.

Jonathan found himself in a quandary, not knowing whether he should continue his discourse and run the risk of his secret being discovered. Just as he was about to spring the question about whether someone had discovered a piece of the legendary mineral, if it were that mineral, a rap on the door occurred followed by the entrance of Jonathan's mother Kathryn, his Ma'.

"Is your plan to work through the night you two?" she jested, oblivious to the complexity of the day's events.

She thought that she could sense a frigid air in the room despite the ever-present heat of the hearth fire, but she figured it for a different reason, a reason that was just about to hit the ears of the young lad like a thunder crack from above.

"We have to be at the Festival of Blossoms one hour following dawn's break. Have you told him, John?" She asked while keeping her eyes on her son with a wry smile on her face.

"No Kate, we haven't got to discussing it yet." John replied with a hint of irritation and continued his work.

"Being tomorrow is the day of the announcement; I think he should have known by now. Don't you?" she continued, a slight excited sway in her stance.

"Aye, you're right woman." John started, following a deep-breath sigh, "Jonathan, we have a surprise for you, although I don't know whether it will be a welcomed one, but nevertheless… The good Nasgroth of Safehaven will be asking us to join him on the stage tomorrow for an announcement to the township."

With that John hesitated while he carefully thought things through, and then continued, "I don't know if this is the right time Kate. I think we should wait," John said flatly.

"John, I think it should be now." she retorted.

"What Da', what is it…? Ma'?" Jonathan searched with wonderment.

"No, now is not the time. It's not the right time." John finalized. "We'll set out at dawn's early light. Jonathan, I'll need you and Samuel to have your daily tasks completed before daybreak."

With that, John arose and made his way to the door of the shop, but before he passed through the exit to be alone with his thoughts, he concluded his conversation, "You'll be dressed smartly with some new clothes that we bought for you. Make your hair presentable and try to remember the things I've been talking to you about."

Kathryn just shrugged her shoulders at Jonathan who suddenly felt an urgent need to recheck his pocket for the Emeralhearth stone… it was still there.

†

The Arrangement

The storm that had been gathering became more intensified throughout the night. It was one of those storms that breaks the back of the previous season, and at the same time, ushers in a brand new one. When Jonathan arose from his straw filled sack that morning, the first thing that he did was to cross the tiny room where he and Samuel slept, and it took him all of three steps to do so.

At the window, he paused before opening it in the hope that the storm had somehow made it impossible for the Blossom Festival to occur. Alas it had not, for although the darkened clouds were still marching by, there was blue sky in between them that afforded sunlight to streak through in various areas around the realm. Jonathan could see the remains of the majestic castle high upon the mountain in the distance tucked into its pocket beneath the heights of the Range of the Unknown, and as usual, he pondered what it would have been like to wake up as a soldier from that height ready for duty.

Samuel woke right after Jonathan and, as was unfortunate for the elder, reminded him of their duties. That's when the thought struck the both of them: They were supposed to have their daily tasks already completed!

Both sprung into a frantic scramble for their clothing, Jonathan stumbling over his younger sibling.

They had barely gotten into their undergarments when 'the Ma' came knocking on the door.

"Never mind the rush, boys. Your Da' has done all of your chores for the day. He said that he couldn't sleep last night anyway. Here are your clothes," she whisked in and out of the room as she handed the boys the new garments.

For Samuel, he had been given what seemed to be a long lower half of a robe dyed green, which he fastened with a whitish rope that had been woven into the top edges of it. Above that, he pulled over his head a shortened top half of the robe nearly the same color as the rope. Never before had he worn two halves of a robe, and never even conceived of having a different colored top and bottom half. It was only ever one full garment and one full color... a dirty brown. In addition, everything seemed to be one size too large, but it did not phase the young boy for he couldn't have known that the Ma' had purposely ordered them too large for his inevitably growing frame. He figured that they were just meant to keep him warm which seemed to be the favorite past time of his mother anyway, that is, to dress him warmly. It could have been the middle of summer and there could have had beads of sweat on his forehead and she would have still been worried whether he was dressed warmly enough.

As for Jonathan, he began to dress in clothes for which he couldn't figure out the front or the back. For as long as he could remember, he always wore a woven cloak sewn together at the top and sides where holes for his arms were placed. It could have been worn forward or backward for either way the clothing was the same. The new top half, or what he guessed to be the top half, had actual arm coverings that stretched the full length of his span. Like Samuel's, it had a whitish rope that was woven into it at about the level of his navel. The bottoms were similar to Samuel's which was something new altogether for him as well. To his shock, each leg had its own sleeve to slip into. Again, it was dyed green but almost dark enough to be called black. It too had a whitish rope that was sewn into the top of it.

Both Samuel and Jonathan left their old clothes bundled together, kicked them under their cots, and rushed out the door feeling that everything was changing so quickly in their world, and truly it was. They were dressed 'smartly' as their father had stated, and although the new garbs were uncomfortable, they felt like different people.

"Still no games like, 'catch the squealer,' today aye' brother?" asked Samuel in a low tone to Jonathan.

"Not with this type of clothing," he replied.

Once in the courtyard of the compound, the Da' emerged from the stall with Swift towing a small wagon. In the wagon were the nearly three-quarter-completed order of weapons. Jonathan always felt an ounce of pride when the wagon was loaded with the cache of weaponry. Despite his bitterness as of late, he still took pride in the fact that he and his Da' produced weapons that would be used by the royal guard. It had been a while since Swift had towed the wagon and it created questioning furrows upon the brows of both Kathryn and the boys.

"Are you sure she should be towing the cart in her condition? She's due to foal any day," stated Kathryn with concern.

"I have no choice. I can't have the boys tow it with their new clothes on," John stated as he stopped to ask his wife to give them a look over, "Are they smartly dressed gentlemen?" he asked.

"Very smartly..."

"All right then. We'll be going." John stated.

With that, the family headed out to the road that passed the length of the Scharp property. It had always pleased John to travel the length of his land for it would take close to twenty whole minutes before they would reach the end of it and where the town limits began. That day the trip had taken considerably more time because the family horse was in her weighted condition. It was therefore, almost forty minutes before reaching Safehaven. As they began to get closer, they could hear the rumblings of the townspeople as they too made their way to the central square.

Where at one time a loose conglomeration of hovels existed, the town had begun to take shape over the years with small stone buildings springing up along the central roadway. John could remember a time when he and Kathryn had first arrived and there was merely a narrow pathway that bisected the village. John's weapon 'factory' was certainly not one of the first businesses to be established in the area.

A stone quarry had been in existence for as long as anyone could remember, and many a villager would take pride in the fact that the castle that overshadowed the realm contained rocks from the very same quarry which was located in the opposite direction from John's land and closer to the mountains. After that, farmlands were placed with a variety of pasture animals and their multiple uses. The first significant structure to be built in the village was the hunter's lodge, a guild for the weary warriors who would spend weeks at a time south of the river's border searching for prey amongst the thickest forests of the realm. It was a hunting ground ages old. The lodge itself had been built and re-built time and time again. John's father had actually been a member of the guild before losing his life to The Great Hunt long before John himself could remember. No hunter actually lived in Safehaven, but merely had a lodge present. The hunters of the realm actually lived in Trelane, the closest township to the castle remains and which sat atop the plateau that lay beneath the castle itself. The hunters would occasionally be called upon to serve the war effort as spies, trackers, and at times, pseudo-soldiers when the numbers of actual soldiers were thinned.

As the Scharp family entered the central square, they were shocked to realize that the old three-tiered platform and pavilion was once again in use. As Kathryn described it to John, and as the boys could observe, upon it were actors dressed in different costumes of soldiery and they were warming up with different acrobatic feats. For instance, there was one small band of players, about four or five, for it was hard to tell who were working with which weapons or who were throwing dulled axes at each other and pretending to be struck, at which time, one would fall to the boards where not only one trap door would open to the floor below, but also when the actor would fall through, another door would open on the bottom floor leading to some kind of sub-floor. The graceful manner in which the players would fall made it look as if they were descending in slow motion, but unbeknownst to the gathering crowd, they were suspended by thin ropes. The sight mesmerized the entire citizenry who were beginning to fill the square and create quite a large gathering.

To the right of the pavilion, a conglomeration of Council of the Castle representatives was gathered, and it sparked the interest of Jonathan who was more interested in them than the players upon the stage. With the wagon loaded down with weaponry, Kathryn led John and the horse in their direction for the reason of transacting his business. It would be a welcomed partial payment, for he still had a full quarter of an order to go but was hoping to receive a partial payment anyway. The convenience of being in town, coupled with the fact that they had brought their wagon gave them the occasion to anticipate the stockpiling of food, materials, and goods, not to mention payment for the new clothes.

All in all, it was an exciting time for the township of Safehaven and for the family of Scharp because of the arrival of the Blossom Festival. Seven years had passed, and the event afforded an occasion for great excitement and even greater opportunities for all of the townships for they would annually gather from far and wide.

The Scharps settled in near the stage and John, after direction from Kathryn, left them to transact his business with the Council representatives. Jonathan could see him talking with his hands and trying to convince them to receive his partial order. After some persuasive words, he watched one of them make his way toward the wagon. Jonathan took note that he was an enormous man with long red hair upon his head and his arms. As he came nearer to the family, a distinct scar came into focus, for it ran the entirety of his forehead just above his eyes and around to his right ear where a part of that was missing.

"Good morn," the enormous soldier stated as he neared the family, to which Kathryn responded in like manner but with an added curtsy.

Jonathan watched in awe as the man with arms as large as trees picked up a number of the objects to test their balance and weight. He could only attempt to fathom what had caused such an enormous head wound and consequently enormous scar. With swinging motions and aiming eyes he calculated the weapon's cost and seemed to be pleased when he turned to Jonathan's father and saluted him with his words.

"As always, the finest in the realm. Nathan will be pleased yet again. When can we come to acquire the rest of the order?" he asked.

"My son and I will have them completed in two days as has been requested," he replied.

The soldier looked at Jonathan with an approving nod, "Quite a young man to have accomplished such fine and intricate work. Well done, boy," he said as he ruffled his hair. "Very well, we will be by in two fortnights," he said as he opened John's hand and placed into it the gold squares of the kingdom. "Enjoy the day's festivities," he said as he left the company of crafters.

It was not long before the festivities began, and they began with a bang.

All eyes were fixed upon the stage, or rather stages, as the actors portrayed a reenactment of the legendary ride of the King. Complete with battle scenes, the first of the Shadow Scrolls unfolded in live action before an awed crowd of Safehaven and surrounding townspeople. Nothing moved the crowd more than when small explosions of smoke occurred during the battles for the acting troupe had figured out a way to cause the tiny bombs which they coupled with concealed fire blowers positioned in strategic locations. Even at the distance to where Jonathan and his family were settled, they could feel the warmth of the small explosions followed by the blown fire. Kathryn described every moment in the ardent play to her husband whose face was alight with joy for never had the story come to life in such a way and it delighted him to no end.

The crowd had swelled well beyond the actual population of the town because it was not uncommon for neighboring towns to travel to the festivities, and not one among the travelers was disappointed with their decision to make the trek including the family of James the Good.

The Good family was from the almost city-size town of Trelane, and they had traveled the farthest of all. Upon their arrival, there was no small commotion when room was made for them near the front of the crowd and within arm's length of the stages. Jonathan could see the wagons that they had arrived with, and they almost mirrored the likeness of the Council of the Castle's very own royal coaches. Also amongst the Good family was James the Younger, the youngest son of the James the Good. He was seated amongst his brothers and sisters, and yet stood out among them having achieved the status of royal soldier though still only in training. Needless to say, it irked Jonathan to the core and he tried to avert his eyes as often as James the Younger glanced in his direction.

James the Good was known throughout the realm to be one of the most successful and wealthiest men in the kingdom, outside of those who served in the Council itself of course. His was quite an accomplishment, and some said it was an even greater position than that of being a Council member because he was self-made rather than being elevated by royal appointment. He was therefore free to run the town in the way that he wished albeit within the lucid confines of royal decree.

Perhaps some sentences on this should be inserted into our story, although the realm's politics could fill another yarn altogether. However, for the sake of the interested, we will divert momentarily away from the tale of the young man Jonathan to attend to the business of higher thinking than his, although his mind will eventually move to higher places as well, but that will be more out of necessity than desire, as we shall see.

It has been stated, although whether some believe it to be true or not is entirely up to each individual of the realm, that the king had appointed the Council of the Castle members before his infamous ride to the Vale of Blood many, many years prior. Far too long for any present eyes to witness, or even an eyewitness of an eyewitness to be present to verify. The legend states, (whether you think it to be a legend or not, you decide) that letters of conscript were hidden within the clothing of various simple servants of the castle the fortnight before the said ride.

It has been stated that it was the servants of the king whom received the letters, for the king himself had no family of his own flesh and blood, (or rather of the flesh only) let alone son or daughter to bequeath his kingdom upon. Nay, they were servants; servant like bakers, tanners, fletchers, blacksmiths, cobblers, and handmaidens, for there were women who received the decree as well, simple folk like you and I. As the story goes, each of seven individuals received the letters but did not discover the parchments until well after the time they had vacated, or rather abandoned, the king-less castle keep.

Some of the seven said-servants had families and some did not. At least two of them, as some stories have been said, were actually orphans of the realm and had been taken in by the king himself, having found them within Irenay's own forests and abandoned near tree stumps.

Once there, they made out a livelihood amongst the keep. One of the orphans was said to have been personally raised by the king's mysterious secret soldiers called, 'The Guardiers,' which is yet another direction that our story could take, but would be too far off the track to take at this time. Perhaps, those said 'Guardiers' may be revealed in due time if we walk softly throughout our own telling for they are mysterious creatures indeed.

As for the servants, each one, whether with family or without, was scattered throughout the realm to create settlements within sight of the crumbled castle, for as the first Shadow Scroll has stated, the castle had been destroyed shortly after the death of the king by a great flood.

For many, many years the ruined castle sat abandoned in its mountain-top pocket overlooking the seven settlements as they slowly grew according to the natural unfolding of the families. Years passed as the original servants maintained control of the sapling colonies until the time when they were forced to join as one to fend off a mysterious invader within the land.

Together, the original seven passed on the control of the settlements to become self-taught warriors and to band together to train in the art of war. It was more out of necessity than desire, for it was clear to all that the invading army had set their sights on the re-building of the castle itself and thus, control of the entirety of the realm; the Realms of Irenay, and in fact all realms.

It was within the walls of the old-abandoned stronghold that the seven trained together and eventually became the Council of the Castle and lit individual candles to tie themselves together. Some legends even state that the candlesticks, which they originally lit, still burn somewhere hidden and deep within the heart of the castle ruins, each protected by its own ancient Guardier. Although they learned their craft, the seven never re-built the castle. Some have said that it was out of respect for the king but others, with perhaps a more grounded view, have said that it was for the purpose of raising seven armies that they felt were needed to combat the coming onslaught of the enemy.

However, the offensive attack of the enemy never materialized and that was due perhaps to the enemies' conviction that victory was an impossibility, or at least it was for the time being. Or perhaps, as some have said, the enemy has lingered for eons of time to patiently wait for a more perfect and more opportune time. And, I dare say, that if the latter were ever proved to be right, the enemy would be a cunning foe indeed, for his patience would be almost immeasurable.

The ancient family line of James the Good had been the fortunate inheritors of the most successful, and consequently, the leading settlement of the Realms of Irenay. And, in yet another eddy in the familial histories of Irenay, James the Good was elevated to a leadership position by a no small act of political cunning after being cut off from the original inheritance, and thus, being self-made or rather pseudo-self-made.

As has been mentioned earlier, Trelane was home to the hunters of the realm and all of the seven townships including Safehaven were sustained by the meats that were distributed throughout the lands – at a price of course. That price is what set James the Good apart from any other Nasgroths of the towns past or present, for that is what the rulers became to be known as, Nasgroths, a word meaning paternalistic leader, even though some were women…

So, Jonathan of Scharp from the township of Safehaven, the productions' capital, watched the said Nasgroth of Trelane, the hunting capital, as he rose from his seat and ascended the stage at the bidding of the Nasgroth of Safehaven, Framington, who was cousin to James the Good.

He could feel his knees becoming weak and his stomach beginning to turn as the momentous announcement was nearer than he cared to think upon. With everything within him the son of the weapon master wanted to run away, and yet, there was an ounce of curiosity that begged him to differ. Could it have been a new assignment to the soldiery? He had heard of such drafts in times of need, but there hadn't seemed to be a need as of late. Jonathan thought that somehow, just maybe, his Da' had finally come around and that somehow, just maybe, he had made his argument break through the ancient icy ways of his Da's belief system. After all, his argument had taken months in preparation.

Thus, Jonathan waited with bated breath, and as he did, he shot a glance toward the darkening skies above where it threatened to crack open its water swelled clouds once again.

"Citizens of Safehaven," started James the Good, "I have been invited here today by my good cousin and your Nasgroth to speak on his behalf, seeing he has been struck with a certain throat ailment. By the way, I've brought my own apothecary to assist you cousin," he said aside with a little more than a lowered voice.

"Allow me to ask, has he served you well in this newly formed township as it has moved on from being a mere village to something more?" The question was a well-received one with a well-rounded applause, and it became instantly clear to Jonathan just why James the Good had become so successful.

"The Council has also asked me to present a few official statements on their behalf," James continued as he nodded in the direction of the royal coaches and the soldiers-at-arms that had done business with John. "It has been discovered, as of late, that the enemy has been sending more and more spies, whom are called Snipes, to our homeland. From the ones we have sent in response, very few have returned to report their findings. The counter-spy reports have been vague to say the least. Sad to say, we have found that a greater number of missing people have been reported this year than the last by half a dozen, for which we pray and will continue to search for…"

The mood of the crowd was instantly hushed and sedated as if the morning festivities had merely been the anesthesia to numb the reality of what was really happening in their midst. Underneath the surface, Jonathan's heart leapt with a silent joy for perhaps the draft was truly possible, but he concealed it as James continued his discourse:

"In the light of these latest developments, it has been decreed that each community, including my own, must immediately begin to build defensive walls to surround each town's limit." The shock rippled throughout the crowd and James the Good felt the need to steer the direction of it to a lighter waypoint, "The good news for you, citizens of Safehaven, is that most of the stone that will be used in this grand endeavor will come from right here. The other towns will be sending trains of wagons and I, and your good Nasgroth, have come up with a levy for each individual who volunteers to work the quarry." A tentative applause arose and James altogether felt satisfied that he had piloted correctly, "Greater work with greater payments!" he pronounced as the applause increased.

The ways of the small town of Safehaven were thus set on a new course.

"Now, on to even more localized good news," continued the Nasgroth who was obviously basking in the light of his position. Jonathan's heart once again took a leap of anticipation as James continued, "Will the fine weapon master, John of Scharp, please come up here with his lovely family?" James requested.

Jonathan felt the first few drops of rain hit him in the head and on the side of his face as he caught his stumbling Da' who was ascending the stairs right in front of him. His quick reflexes had saved his father from a very embarrassing moment indeed. Once upon the stage, blood flooded Jonathan's face with embarrassment as the enormity of the crowd slapped his perception with a great strike. At no other time did he want so desperately to escape to the river where he had spent hours in solitude. Even the mere thought brought an ounce of comfort to his soul.

"I have been getting to know my now good friend, John of Scharp as of late," James continued. "Did anyone know that he had taught himself how to craft the finest weapons in the realm?" Yet one more applause followed, causing James to have to escalate his voice. "Others have tried to mimic his work, but have failed miserably in trying, elevating only him to become the greatest weapon master in the realm. We have even discussed the possibility of a guild being formed right here in Safehaven, which would create yet more opportunities for greater work." At that, the crowd began to chant:

"Greater work, greater work," they sounded, and James knew that his newfound relationship to the blind weapon master was truly a masterful political stroke.

"Therefore," he tried to interrupt, "Therefore… we have come to a mutual decision."

And there it was the announcement. Jonathan could feel an ache begin to form in the base of his feet and it increased all the more as James made his way over to the young lad as he placed a hand upon his shoulder,

"His son Jonathan is to be married to my daughter, Serenity, at the very next Blossom Festival, to be held", A roar broke out in the crowd, "To be held in Trelane one year from today, and he will be starting his own weapon shop right from there!" proclaimed the Good leader of Trelane and in a sense, Jonathan's new non-understanding father.

Again, whether coincidence, fate, whatever or whomever ruled the air above the Realms of Irenay, the rain was let out of its pent-up cage and poured forth what seemed to be a solid waterfall whose precipitation wouldn't yield for days on end. The announcement had struck Jonathan with such force that his mind swirled in another one of those dizzying moments in time that causes all things around to slow down.

His eyes raced from the Nasgroth, to his Da' to the not so beautiful 'Good' girl and her brother to his mother to Samuel who was looking like he had just been shot through with an arrow.

The spinning effect finally stopped as he rested his eyes next to the red-haired Council warrior with the massive facial scar who was, at the moment, standing next to his war-horse and watching the crowd which was rising to a crescendo. His only instinctive thought was to spring in that direction to spring for that horse and his only possible means of escape.

And sprang he did.

✝

The Last Meal

Kathryn was shocked as she watched her firstborn son sprint across the stage away from the family and in the direction of the massive war horse and for an instant her mind asked her to tuck away the image within her heart. She had been aware of her son's desire to become a soldier, but never really judged it to be a possibility, having been a product of her society since her birth and knowing that it was a rarity for a citizen to break free from the mold that they had been born into.

However, at that moment, she realized the utter determination of Jonathan to pry himself away from his surroundings and knew that his path would be a rough one. Perhaps even to that of an outlaw.

'Please be with him, God,' she silently prayed.

Jonathan flung himself from the stage and in the direction of the red-haired man's stallion with the ease of a flying squirrel. All eyes were upon him as he leaped the leap of his life. It was the distance of about five lengths and he landed upon the rump of the courser which jumped in response. Jonathan clasped his hands on the rear edges of the saddle and held on with all of his strength. The war horse rose upon its hind legs and let out a war cry like no other.

So straight up stood the horse, that the boy could touch the ground with his feet and it gave him the opportunity to kick himself higher up upon the back of the stallion. In an instant, he grasped the mane and pulled himself closer to the saddle as the animal took off with a jump, kicking mud behind him.

The red-haired soldier of the council was very nearly kicked in the face as he spun around too late to do anything to stop the duo. Turning toward his comrades, he motioned with his hand to mount up and five of them responded as the ready warriors that they were. The eyes of the crowd followed the action with intensity for they had already been witnessing the drama of the ardent play and the thought occurred to some that it was merely an extension of the day's dramatics. Kathryn yelled out for her boy, but he had already disappeared beyond the mud of the fleeing horse and following soldiers. John demanded her what had transpired, and all his wife could say was that Jonathan was gone.

The red-haired man was then upon a horse, not his own, and addressed Kathryn, "I'll bring your boy back from wherever he runs too, I promise," and took off with a start.

The war horse carried Jonathan farther and farther away from the township of Safehaven, and that was exactly what he had wanted. He had dreamed of what it would be like to ride a horse bred for battle, but had never anticipated it to be the thrill of a lifetime. What shocked him the most was the shear power by which the horse charged forward without breaking stride. Together, they rode through a forested path and into a dale that lay beyond.

The continuing rain began to sting the eyes of the young man as he and the horse broke free from the protection of the trees, but it mattered little to Jonathan. The dale itself was made up of tall reeds that a meandering stream had created, and in certain sections, produced a marshy ground. The horse that carried Jonathan cared very little of the soft undergrowth and even seemed to pick up speed as they crossed the area on their way to a mountain's steep pass.

At about the halfway point, Jonathan heard the yelps of his chasers as they too entered into the dale. By that time, the man with the red hair had overtaken his comrades and was leading the charge after the boy. His flowing red hair mirrored the flowing mane of the horse upon which he sat, and Jonathan felt the urgent need to better position himself upon the back of the horse.

His legs barely wrapped around the contour of the stallion's back and his feet didn't even come close to the stirrups. Nevertheless, he urged the courser with a slap on the neck as the two began to enter into the steep pass of the mountain trail. The trail itself ran up the side of the mountain and out of necessity followed switch back after switch back as it ascended the side of the steppe. Jonathan could feel the horse beginning to slow due to the shear angle of the pass and as one switch-back turned into another, he caught glimpses of his frustrated followers as they urged their own horses up the side as well.

Judging by the look on their faces, it seemed as though they felt that they were losing ground.

Higher and higher they rose until at long last, the horse upon which the boy sat suddenly abandoned its charge near an outcropping of boulders. Try as he might, Jonathan could not get the horse to move another inch and he could see the hunting party gaining ground on him from his lofty perch.

With no choice but to abandon his courser, he stood up upon the back of the war horse and for the first time noticed the enormity of the beast. He felt like a mouse in comparison to its sheer size. He had no choice but to leap from the back of the horse and onto the outcropping of rocks.

Once upon the boulders, he spied an opening in the top and jumped down into it, not caring where it would carry him to, as long as it would hide him from the rapidly approaching hunting party. Through the darkness he fell…

Bouncing from one side of the rocky chute to the other Jonathan could feel the scraping of his back and his stomach as he passed jagged edges on his way to the bottom. Finally, with a thud, he landed in a patch of dirt on the bottom of the chimney and commenced to swipe away the spider webs that had clung to his body and hair.

By the time he had cleared the cobwebs from his head, he could hear the hunting party gathering above him upon the top of the outcropping of rocks:

"He may have jumped off the side," ruffled one of the soldiers. "Desperate little rat, aye?"

Jonathan thought for certain that the soldiers would have abandoned their search, for they had obtained the horse that they were after. Alas, he was shocked as he heard one of them beginning to descend into the chute, cursing as he did. The realization jolted Jonathan out of his momentary comfort and caused him to begin to search for a way out of his cave-like surroundings.

Turning over rocks, he desperately searched as the soldier above neared his position. Finally, pushing on one of stones, he triggered a small avalanche of sorts and the light of day streamed through a small opening where Jonathan figured he may be able to squeeze through. Having inverted himself, he poked his head through the hole and commenced to shimmy his shoulders through as well. He nearly dislocated his right one trying to escape the confines of the cave, but after he managed to free himself, the rest of his body simply poured from the rocks.

Having freed himself from the boulders, he ended up in the waiting hands of the red-haired man, with the scar that ran the distance of his face and half way through his ear.

"The game is over boy," he stated as his powerful hands wrapped around his arms and nearly dislocated them again, "Good work men, we've captured ourselves the rat," he yelled to the others.

The soldiers tied Jonathan hand and foot and draped him face down over the rump of the red-haired man's war horse, the very one he had tried to escape upon. From that vantage point, Jonathan watched the dirt path below him shake back and forth as his vision was subject to the swaying motion of the horse's hind quarters. Switch back after switch back tossed him to and fro as the hunting party made their way back down the mountain pass. Finally, they made their way back into the marshy dale and followed the road which led back in the direction of Safehaven. Jonathan's demeanor sunk further than it had ever been as he watched the entrance to the mountain pass grow further and further away.

Not long after however, and almost before he saw the rustling of some bushes in the distance behind them, he heard the sound of a flying arrow as it zipped past him and within a hand breadth of his head.

An instant later, he heard the shear pain-filled cry of one of the soldiers and he surmised that the arrow had struck its mark. Jonathan just caught the glimpse of another arrow as it flew from the bramble of shrubs shot from a soldier that seemed to blend perfectly into its surroundings. After hearing the passing of the second arrow, another fatal cry was released from a wounded soldier.

For Jonathan, his world spun around in a great circle as the red-haired man swiftly turned his horse in the direction of the foe. In the process however, Jonathan was flung from the back of the beast and thrown to the ground. The pain shot through the entirety of his body, but as he rolled in the mud, he discovered that the throw had also managed to loosen the ropes that held his legs.

By his sheer terror he was able to find the strength to rise to his feet and run in any direction that he could. It so happened that the direction was toward the mountain that he had been climbing earlier, but he was well away from the pass's entrance where the ambush had begun. He could hear the skirmish of the attack continue behind him, but he dared not turn and only focused on his escape.

Through the reeds and marshy ground he continued, the battle fading fainter and fainter behind him. When he at last reached the base of the mountain, he stubbornly ascended straight up the side of it. When he felt that his heart could not take any more of its abnormal cadence, he finally allowed his body to rest, but his mind had refused too. The moments were not wasted, and he found a sharpened rock to which he could cut the cords that still held his hands. Once free, he refused to listen to his lungs that were screaming for relief, and he continued his climb up the shear side of the mountain.

Higher and higher he climbed, only stopping for a moment to give his heart just enough time to recover before pushing it to its max again. With every step, he sensed more and more freedom, and it urged him upward like a calling from the heights beyond. At long last, he had reached his goal, the top of the mountain.

The rain that had been pouring from the sky had relented, stopping its torrential flow, and for the moment at least, Jonathan was able to catch his breath as he looked about. To the south, he could see the vast, thick forest with the river leading into the heart of it. To the north, he could almost see the seven settlements of the realm which dotted the landscape far, far below. Across from him, and considerably higher than he was, he could barely make out the contours of Lock Kalaw, the ruined castle of the realm as the low-lying clouds enshrouded it in mystery. Then the thought struck him that his was the same spot that he had climbed too with his Da' years earlier. The rain began again as if to mock him, and caused Jonathan to search for any shelter that he could find.

The tree that he scurried beneath afforded him some protection from the elements but not a lot. For the first time since his escape Jonathan felt cold, the adrenaline within his system having subsided a bit. Also for the first time, he noticed that the new clothes that he had been given were looking like mere rags hanging from his bruised body. Although somewhat shredded in places, they were keeping him somewhat warm. The meager warmth in turn caused him to think of his mother and that led to his thought about what she had must have been going through. His escape had not been thought out like the argument he had started with his Da' the day prior, and he hadn't planned on being in the position that he was currently in. In fact, his life had been changing so quickly as of late, that he hadn't thought of anything as far as his survival was concerned.

Survival, he mused to himself. What of the soldiers in the dale? Had any of them survived the attack? And what of the enemy that waited, hidden amongst the realm like camouflaged serpents? In a sense, he was thankful for them for by their actions he was released from his captors. What about the man with the red hair and scar? Had he survived?

In his ponderings, Jonathan grew colder and searched for a warm place to put his hands. He found the warmth he desired in the comfort of his new pockets. That was when he finally remembered that he had discarded his only possible means of financial security, the Emeralhearth stone that he had left in his old set of clothing and that he had mindlessly kicked under his bed in his haste to be ready for the festival. Jonathan banged his head against the felled tree trunk just above his head and verbalized his disappointment:

"Stupid, stupid peasant."

He sat for over an hour contemplating his next move.

Thoughts of his family filled his soul. The good times that they had had over the years were a security to him. Also flooding his mind was the reality of what he had seen in the appearance of the strange soldiers hiding amongst the trees. Perhaps, he surmised, becoming a soldier was inevitable due to the fact that there would be no time to build the defensive perimeters around the towns anyway. Perhaps, it would all take place sooner than anyone thought. But what filled his mind most of all were the thoughts of his far-off love who felt further away now than ever before.

He could almost see her face if he were to but close his eyes for a moment. However, the fact that he might fall asleep and freeze to death kept his weary eyes open. The darkness of the night began to creep in over the Realms of Irenay and he knew that staying in the cold overnight could cost him his life, for besides the fact of the thinned atmosphere of that height; the snows could arrive early.

It was a full two and a half hours before he completed the long trek back to his home. The darkness had set in long ago, but all the same, he had at last found the small stone cottage of his childhood. From a distance, he could see the warmth of candlelight emanating from the small windows. Jonathan remembered the time when he had assisted his Da' break through the walls of the homestead in those areas when the advent of glass windows had arrived at Safehaven. It was a foreign concept, but it had let light into their living space and consequently into their lives.

As he approached the door, he hesitated one last time knowing that on his side of the wooden door was his longed for freedom, but on the opposite was his step back into the prison of the past and the warm arms of his mother.

Was it that bad of a past, he questioned to himself. My life has not been so poor. At least my relationships to my brother and mother are still intact, but my father? It may, someday, doubtful, but maybe be… With that he forged forward and swung open the door before him.

The Da' was seated at the head of the table; his Ma' at the foot. On the side of the dilapidated wooden table sat Samuel, his eyes still reddened from a day full of weeping. It was obvious to Jonathan that the victuals which had been prepared had sat there for quite some time. Both Kathryn and Samuel started to jump to their feet with excitement, but before they could, John interrupted them with a bellowing howl.

"Let us pray! Let's pray for what we are about to receive." Jonathan slid his broken and still dripping body into his seat at the table as the weapon master continued, "God, we give thanks for what we are about to receive. We give thanks for-"

Little did the family know that at that precise moment a thick black snake, as thick as a boy's waist, was slithering its way into Swift's stall perhaps to find comfort from the storm or, perhaps, to find its last meal before the soon coming snows of winter. Swift wasted no time as her only thought was for her foal. She instinctively kicked against the wooden wall of the stall and sent it crashing to the ground.

That was the sound that interrupted the prayer of the weapon master.

The family jumped from their seated positions and ran to the door. They opened it just in time for Kathryn and Samuel to catch sight of the fleeing horse as she disappeared into the darkness of the night's storm. John had already been reaching for the Willowfeld Shunt which he kept hidden in a locker buried near the fireplace when Kathryn declared that Swift had disappeared.

"I know," he stated as he made his way past the family and into the courtyard that led to the canyon pass and river beyond. He had crossed the courtyard a thousand times, but what he had not anticipated was the torrential rain that had caused the cobblestoned ground to be washed away, thereby creating deep fissures in the earth. As he was just reaching the gate, one of those fissures made itself known and he stumbled over it, slamming onto the ground with a cracking sound.

"John," Kathryn shouted as she sprinted out into the rain and to the side of her felled husband. His ankle had been broken and Kathryn could see the bone protruding from the side of his leg. Blood poured from the wound and was lost to the surrounding puddle that was threatening to become a lake around the home.

"We have to get that horse," John replied through winced pain. "Our future would be lost without her and her new foal." Before Kathryn could argue her point to him, Jonathan whisked past the two of them making a final gesture as he did.

"I'll get her! I know where she'll be!" and off he disappeared into the darkness of the night.

It would have been impossible for him to hear the cry of his mother's heart as she begged him to come back, and it would have been equally impossible for him to hear the cry of his father's heart as he released a heartfelt statement:

"I'm sorry son, I'm so sorry for everything…"

Swift was right where Jonathan knew she would be, but to his shock and horror the family horse had fallen into the rain swollen river and was in the process of struggling to swim to the far side. She was only halfway across, and the current was beginning to win the battle.

Jonathan was awestruck when he realized that the river had nearly doubled its size due to the ferocity of the storm. He stood on the bank that had been newly carved and which created an outcropping over three times his height. Into the night, he cried out to the horse:

"Swim girl, swim!", fruitlessly shouted for he could tell that she was frantic and losing the fight, "You can make it!" he repeated while all around him the shore was giving away and caving in as if the very earth were shaking the ground like a liquid filled basin.

Rocks, bushes, logs, even whole trees were tumbling into the swiftly passing waters as it continued to carve a swath through the land. Jonathan cried aloud when, for the first time, he saw Swift go under the water. However, his cry was not for the fact that the horse was completely being swallowed by the current, but rather, because he had suddenly found himself falling into the surf as well! The bank he had been standing upon and shouting from had completely collapsed and Jonathan felt the surge of current all around him.

It was the most powerful thing he had ever felt; infinitely more powerful than the gallop of the war horse he had been upon earlier. It took all of his might to just keep his head out the water and he desperately fought to keep his head above the surface. If it were not for a passing tree limb, he would have succumbed altogether. He clung to the branch with all of his strength he could see the edge of the shoreline passing by him with greater and greater speed as he struggled for his life he perceived that he was heading deeper and deeper into the canyon that carved its way through the thick forest of the southern edges of the realm. Somehow in the midst of his struggle he took note that his old life was quickly disappearing behind him as he was being swallowed by the darkness which lay ahead.

Darkness he could not even begin to fathom the depth of.

Chapter 3

An Enemy Within

†

The Search Party

They arose early and opened the door of the cottage to discover a sight that altogether shocked and amazed them. Up and to that point, they had figured that Jonathan and Swift had spent the night in some covered and protected shelter out of the storm's fury. However, the moments that followed the opening of the door were a fright to their entire systems.

Where the courtyard had once stood, and where mere fissures had formed around the cobbled stones the night prior, were then great pits that if one were to mistakenly step into them, one would be swallowed by the earth entirely. The gate and wall which led to the river pathway were no longer present. Even the heavy stones used for the base of them had been carried to some unknown destination. Overarching everything was a fresh blanket of snow, which spoke of a cold night indeed. All of this, Kathryn described to John, prompting him to bark an order to his youngest son.

"Get into town, boy, and tell Nasgroth Framington what has happened. Tell him we need to assemble a search party, and tell Bart of the Forest as well… Go, boy!" he ordered through clinched teeth, for the pain of his fall the previous night was still a very pronounced irk. "Let's head to the river, Kathryn."

"I don't think it would be a good idea… We should wait for the search party to gather here," she stated. "You can't travel in your condition. It took me three hours to finally get the wound to stop bleeding. You're still as pale as a ghost."

"I have to find the boy," he softened. "This is my fault."

"John, it's not. You can't direct his heart. He has become a man, a bit early, but nevertheless…"

John knew that she was right. In times past he would have barked at her too, but everything was rapidly changing; changes that had arrived and were currently pounding on the door of his heart with aggression. He even pondered whether there must have been some sort of indescribable blanket darkness that had descended upon his world, arriving just as life was about to take off in a way that he had only dreamed of. It made him feel small, small and humble.

"Can you help me wrap my leg tighter so I can join the party when they arrive? I promise to go slowly, okay Kate?" he softly spoke, using his nickname for her.

Kathryn could sense that her husband was changing, and it caused her staunch strength to diminish some as well. "Do… do you think he's okay?" she somewhat stammered.

"Dearest Kathryn," he stretched his arms out to her for a hug. "Our boy is a fighter. Wherever he is, I'm sure he's fine. I'm sure of it."

After the reassuring hug, they made their way back into the cottage, where John gathered some excess cloth and began to rip it length-wise so as to create strips that Kathryn could fashion into a splint. Next, he took some of the small logs used for firewood and felt around for the small hatchet used to split the fuel with. Kathryn had made her way into the bedroom to acquire some warmer clothes for the two of them. Knowing that she had done so, John hesitated when he at last found the small axe, for the feel of the weapon had caused the thoughts of his son to flood into his emotions like a whirlpool.

It felt like a rising tide that started in his feet and quickly wound its way up his entire body until at last, was released through his eyes. They were tears of fear and sorrow mixed together like some salty liqueur and he could not fight its sway any longer. He had been secretly feeling that way the entire night, ever since the moment he had heard from his wife that Jonathan appeared at the door looking haggard. He could only imagine what travails the boy had endured without and within. He would have loved to have gone searching for him the previous day after his disappearance from the festival, but he had long learned that his lack of sight would have only complicated things.

He had long ago vowed to never shed a tear over his own condition but would simply accept his own limitations. His thoughts then began to drift back toward the search and his son once again.

Kathryn returned from the other room with warm clothes for them to wear, dropped them near to where John was chopping the log to create the splint, and quickly whisked past him without noticing his tears on her way to the boys' room to retrieve warmer clothes for them, if and when they found Jonathan.

She was very thankful that the clothes that she had purchased for her oldest child had been doubly thick. Though they were a strange new style, she was sure that they would keep him warm. However, she knew that when she found him, he would need a dry set of clothing and would probably appreciate his old clothes once again. As she entered the room, she was not prepared for the emotions that would flood into her own soul for it was in that room that she had spent many a time talking with Jonathan into the waning hours of the night when the boy could not sleep. Together, they had laughed over the silliest of things.

She remembered a time when they had spent a whole two hours playing shadow games on the wall as the moonlight streamed through the newly formed window and cast images beyond their hands. All that, while Samuel slept snoring to his heart's content. His occasional snorts caused both Jonathan and his Ma' to laugh uproariously. She also remembered a time when he had mentioned a girl he had seen but figured that he was too young to be thinking anything very serious. She hadn't thought of that until the moment the announcement was made and saw her son take off like a lightning bolt. That was when the seriousness of the long-ago images touched upon her memory.

All of those thoughts and more filled her facial features, and she too cried gushing tears, so much so that she had to gain control of her shaking body. She finally accomplished that by quickly busying herself, gathering clothes which she found underneath the boys sleeping cots all balled up into bunches.

At first, Kathryn didn't pay much attention to the lump she discovered in the folds of Jonathan's cloak, but the more she thought about it, the more curious she became. She laid the cloak upon the straw filled bedding, and gently peeled away the layers of cloth as she searched for the source of the protuberance within. She first felt the object with her hands and took note that it felt like no mere stone, but when she pulled it from its secret place, she was taken aback by its sheer beauty. With awe that equaled her son's when he first discovered it, she looked deeply into the heart of the stone and could see a flicker of light within, and a sparkle of hope chimed within her heart as well.

She had seen rare stones before, most notably, the blue substance that was embedded in the mysterious shunt that her husband had been given by the passing stranger. However, she had never seen anything like the one she was currently beholding. She had heard of it, perhaps. She thought that it could be Emeralhearth, but that was only a legend, or was it?

As she rolled it from hand to hand, she could only imagine what her son must have experienced when he discovered it for the first time. The consequences of the discovery caused her to contemplate all of the sudden changes that must have been taking place in the young man's world. And for the first time since his birth fifteen years prior, she was seeing through the eyes of her son and felt a pang of guilt that edged out the sparkle of hope.

Could she have somehow grown closer to him? Could she have somehow been the one he could feel comfortable talking too in his most urgent hour? The battle within caused her to kneel and say a silent prayer for him, and when she was through, she felt that somehow she should return the stone to the place that she had found it… hidden within the folds of the clothes which she kicked underneath the sleeping cot.

The door of the cottage flung open in a way that only a seven year would do, that is, without a care as to whether it would splinter the door as it slammed against the stone wall. Wood fell from the door as the crash happened and Samuel came running through.

"Da', I found Bart of the Forest! He's coming behind me, but no others," Samuel panted as he fell into his father's arms. "I'm sorry. The Nasgroth said that there are many others that have gone missing as well… And the town…" Samuel tried to catch his breath but was having a difficult time of it.

"Slow down, boy," John interrupted. "Take some breaths first."

"… The town looks like a mess! It's worse than my room looks when you yell at me to clean it up," Samuel said matter-of-factly.

"It's a truth, John." said Bart of the Forest as he entered through the front door.

At the same time, Kathryn was entering the room as well and was still wiping her eyes. "What does it mean when so many of our people have gone missing?" she asked as she entered the space.

"My lady," Bart nodded as he saw Kathryn. "The leaders of the town believe that the enemy took advantage of the storm last night and attacked with full force, stealing the folks in the night. I came here to see what I could do to help," Bart trailed off realizing the delicacy of the moment.

"Oh, God… Don't tell me that Jonathan was taken, that can't be!" cried Kathryn.

"Now hold on to yourself, Kate," John replied. "We don't know that for sure. We saw him chase after the horse. That means that he went to the river, as he always does. Who's to say that he's not still down there?"

"We have to find out then, Da'," stated the youngest Scharp. "He's probably skipping stones anyway."

The thought brought slight smiles to Jonathan's parents and for a moment sparked hope within their hearts one again.

Thus, after securing John's splint, the small search party of four set off down the long and deep canyon trail that led to the river. John trailed behind Kathryn and used a stick to support his weight. The pain in his leg was palpable, but he was determined to complete the quest. Together, they brought up the rear of the party. Bart of the Forest walked out in front of the others with Samuel close by his side. If there were still any enemy soldiers present, he wanted to be the first to confront them.

The canyon path had become more of a gorge of sorts due to the tremendous amount of water that had been released by the storm. At the moment, the sun seemed to have the upper hand as it fought back the still swiftly passing clouds. Though the snows had arrived, only small traces of it were lingering upon the ground and steam emanated from the leftover patches as the passing sun's rays warmed it.

Massive boulders had been dislodged from their resting spots as well as whole trees, which had been uprooted entirely. The forest canyon itself laid silent save for the remnants of water that had slowed to a mere trickle. If there was one bright spot in their day, it was when Samuel pointed out to his father that there were many ancient logs and branches that had been exposed by the storm and that the long hours spent digging for them would not be needed any longer. John saw it as only a ray of hope, for although a greater number of weapons would be needed for obvious reasons, so would his help have to be temporarily replaced. It was a thought which brought his heart low once again. Not another word was said as the search party continued making its way toward the river.

It had taken them twice as long to reach the water's edge due in large part to the trail's broken pathway, but also due to the painful process that John had to endure. However, no one dared mention that fact. Not a sign of Jonathan or the horse had yet been seen, not even a hint that they had come in that direction. The party was searching on mere instinct alone and both John and Kathryn were very thankful for the presence of Bart in the search.

It was Samuel who discovered not only a hoof print in the mud, but also a footprint as well. He had made his way to the creek because of thirst, but abandoned his quest for drink when he spotted two sets of tracks which sat side by side. Bart figured that Jonathan had been tracking the horse by the fact that not only had there been a human's footprint, but there had also been hand scrapings near the hoof print; a tell-tale sign that Jonathan had been feeling his way in the darkness. They all surmised that it must have been a long night for him, but the tracks most definitely led in the direction of the river.

The small party of four finally reached the water's edge where Kathryn and Samuel's shock equaled, if not doubled, the moment when they had first opened the door of the cottage. The enormity of the storm was greater than anyone had imagined.

The rain swelled canyons had released a massive flood of water and debris into the river basin that had, overnight, become twice the width as it had ever been. Much of the water had subsided, but the river was still racing by at a frantic pace. Occasionally, a shoreline would give away and completely collapse into the passing current seemingly of its own accord. The water itself was dark and muddied and the thought struck the hearts of the entire search party that perhaps their brother, son, and friend had been swept away by the tyranny of the current. All at once, they put the unspoken thoughts out of their minds.

The party stood upon an edge of the shoreline. 'Edge' because there was no more defined slope, but rather gigantic drop-offs due to the whole new canyon that had begun to form. Looking in the southerly direction, Bart could see that much of the thickened forest that he had often hunted within was chewed away by the passing of the river. He was scarcely able to call it a river any longer for it was much wilder than it had ever been.

He even voiced his thought to the others when he ventured aloud to call it something altogether different, "The *'torrent'* would have carried the horse to the south," he started, "That is, assuming that she had been taken by the current. Sorry to say, it would have carried her in that direction," he pointed toward the ominous forest. "I say we head down stream. If Jonathan had been tracking her, which I think he was, he probably would have surmised the same thing."

The party agreed and began to make their way along the cliff line, congruent to the torrent. Shortly after heading in that fateful direction, they were halted by the sound of approaching horses. Their first thought was to hide amongst some felled trees in case it was the enemy returning from one of the realm's towns, but John persuaded them differently.

"It would not be the enemy," stated the weapon master. "If it were, we would be either dead or stolen away. There is a reason we have never seen them. They have the ability to move freely among us without detection and without remorse. Frankly, I'm surprised that they've not completely invaded the land already after last night's sorties. It's beginning again, Kate." John said to Kathryn.

"What's beginning, Da?" pleaded Samuel as he tucked himself closer to the covering of his mother's arms.

"The prods," declared Bart of the Forest.

"Aye, the prods," John followed.

With a sound like thunder, mighty war-horses broke through the shrubbery that separated them from where the search party had stopped to wait for their arrival. The small party of four backed themselves against the canyon wall as a conglomeration of twelve soldiers-at-arms arrived to their location. Not expecting to see anyone else save some enemy soldiers upon the new trail that they had been reluctantly carving, the heavily armed war party of the Council halted in front of the four searchers.

Without a word of direction by their leader, six of the soldiers steered their horses, two by two, and positioned them to face in all directions to keep watch on the surrounding forests and thereby create an armed perimeter around them all. The seriousness of the situation shone upon their faces as each one moved upon their coursers with deliberate discipline and an ever-watchful eye. If it were not for the context of events in the last two days, the search party would have thought that they had been witnessing the royal council soldiers upon their parade grounds. The totality of the weaponry they carried suggested they could have started their own war if they so desired.

Samuel, perhaps for the first time in his life, could understand his brother's lifelong obsession of becoming a soldier. The sight was awe inspiring and at the same time fear striking. Also for the first time in his young existence, he felt proud that the majestic weapons that they were supplied with had come from their very own 'factory'. His shock and awe was obviously evident prompting John to reach for his son's short hair to assure him that he was safe.

Nathan, the captain of the king and council's army, was at the lead of the war party and once he was sure that all was clear, he dismounted his giant war-horse and approached the four searchers to inquire about their business. Samuel shrank deeper underneath the folds of his mother's garment as the dark skinned man approached. To the little one, he appeared like a walking tree, and the clanging sound of his weaponry mixed with the crackle of his leather garments caused Samuel to think better of ever wanting to become a soldier, especially if he would ever have to face such an enormous creature. Even the portly Bart of the Forest seemed lost in the warriors shade.

†

The War Party

"What news my friend?" bellowed the massive soldier as he addressed the weapon master.

"Nathan, we've come to search for my boy. He left last night to fetch our escaped horse during the storm after she was spooked by something," John replied still wincing in pain.

"You're injured?" inquired Nathan.

"Aye…"

"Do you know what spooked the horse?"

"Not a clue."

"We've had reports of serpents being released within the realm. Thick black snakes, some as thick as a man's waist."

"We've killed several already," interrupted one of the soldiers assigned to keep watch on the surrounding parties.

The disruption caused the great captain of the guard to shoot an annoyed glance at the soldier, who was obviously not paying attention to his assigned task. The soldier was mounted upon a black stallion and was arrayed in leathered garb. His browned hair was noticeably short, and his gangly arms made it look like he didn't fit in with the other soldiers. At his side, he wore a sword that was thinner than the normal broadsword size yet sharpened on only one side of the blade as opposed to both and curved in a similar way to a bow.

"Was that the younger Good?" John whispered to Kathryn.

"Aye, it was."

"Has he got the sword his father ordered for him?" he continued in a hushed tone.

"Aye, he has!" retorted Nathan. "And he should be watching our perimeter," he continued, loud enough for all present to hear his rebuke.

All the same, the newling had made a true statement. The Council Army had been called upon all over the realm to deal with the wicked creatures. James himself had killed three already and it had impressed Nathan. For where he had lacked in his size, he had made up in his courage and quickness. Nasgroth Good, the newling's father, had been told of his unique fighting traits by those who were in charge of his training and had personally come to John a year prior to speak with him regarding his son's weaponry.

That was the first occasion for the two to have met, and from that time together working and re-working the designs, the two had begun a friendship.

The mere fact that the boy was currently riding with Nathan was impressive to John as well, for he knew that the captain had always surrounded himself with only the very best of warriors. And he should have known, for there was a time when he was one of them… However, the boy's interjection betrayed his newness and made it quite clear that he was still a trainee with loosened lips.

"Those snakes, any idea who or why they've been sent to us?" asked Bart of the Forest.

"Not only that, has anyone been killed by any of these serpents?" added Kathryn.

"It's a new and ominous tactic of our enemy, my lady," explained Nathan, "And it's obvious that much breeding has gone into their formation. We haven't had any deaths reported, but we have heard of the slippery creatures stealing folks away, even adults have been taken." explained the captain.

"How is that possible?" asked the weapon master.

"Apparently, they've been trained to hold them within the grasp of their third quarter, and by their shear size, they are able to drag the unfortunates away."

"Where-where too…, sir?" piped in Samuel.

"Most likely, the Vale of Decision son," replied Nathan flatly. "It's where we ourselves are headed to now."

Although the young Samuel had barely heard of the dreaded place, he surmised that it must have been an awful one indeed judging by the reaction of everyone else who was present at the moment, for a deathly silence had descended upon them all. The realization struck not only the small search party, but also the war party and it appeared, at least to Bart of the Forest, that it was the first time that the other soldiers had heard confirmation of their mission.

"Is it true that the prods have begun again?" asked the kindly butcher, Bart.

The prods, as they had been called, had been a sign that the enemy was on the prowl again. It had been a tactic of the foe from as long ago as the original formation of the Council of the Castle. In fact, the prods were the reason the Council was formed in the first place.

From ages past, the threat that the realm's castle would one day be attacked and captured had almost fallen not only into legend but fable, save for the fact that the prods had continued off and on for the entire duration. Ironically, that tactic had, in effect, caused the opposite results to occur. Instead of creating a false security in the hearts of the people of the realm, the fact that the enemy occasionally appeared to wreak havoc in the everyday lives of the citizenry kept a remnant of people keenly aware of their presence.

There were even a small number of scrolls, albeit a very small number, which had been issued by certain sages who had proclaimed that if it were not for the prods, the enemy would have succeeded in dulling the ears of the entire realm. Therefore, the dulled-ear-effect, if you will, would have achieved total victory by the fact that the element of surprise would have been so widespread throughout the kingdom, laws would have inevitably been passed proclaiming that a need for a standing army was null and void. Thus it was the prods that kept alive the fact that the enemy truly did exist, and that was that history that prompted Bart to question the captain along such matters.

"Aye, it's true, butcher, but we've never seen this type of escalation of enemy activity," replied Nathan. "And with the appearance of the snakes, the tactics have become even more aggressive than the in-famed Campaign of Eight. It has prompted the Council to declare a new, still unnamed campaign. We are now riding on the first of many scouting trips into the enemy territory beyond the forest to pre-empt any war efforts. In fact, we may call upon your hunting skills in time, butcher," implied Nathan.

"I'm ready right now if need be."

"Thank you, my friend. For now, assist the weapon master in his search. John, I can spare two soldiers to assist you as well. I'm sorry for your troubles Kathryn. I hope you can find the young man. I am more than certain that he has the fight in him to survive whatever lot the realm has cast for him, and I'm equally as sure that he feels your prayers even now!"

Nathan, though a hardened warrior, had possessed a wise and compassionate heart and it was only one of the many reasons why he had become the leader of the council and keeper of the castle in the first place. Incidentally, a fact known to very few, Nathan had hidden within his watchful eye the very Crown of the People, passed down for safekeeping by the hands of the king himself. He was, therefore, more than able to hold the hearts of the realm's people in his comforting and powerful hands, a fact that Kathryn remembered even as he spoke. It had comforted her heart from the moment that her husband had originally revealed it to her.

The captain then issued orders to the soldiers that would be left behind to join the search party. One of them was a long red-haired man who had a scar that ran the distance of his forehead and though the top half of his right ear. He was addressed as Thomas by the captain, and Kathryn recognized him instantly. It was only fitting, for he was the same one that had promised her at the festival that he would bring her son back to her.

Samuel was the one to recognize the other soldier, for she had flowing and darkened hair that somewhat covered her face with ringlets. Upon her left arm, she wore a string of daggers each with red stones upon the hilts, and upon her back was slung a crossbow. She rode upon a mocha-colored horse, and Nathan addressed her as Jacqueline. Also notable to the seven-year-old Samuel was the look of anguish that flashed across the face of the lanky warrior with the narrow sword, James the Younger, as the girl more than enthusiastically turned in obedience to the command of her captain.

"We'll do what we can to help in the search for your son," declared Thomas. "It would be an honor to serve you in whatever way you need us to, weapon master," he said to John.

"We are at your service, sir and my lady. Your son has been admired by many of his peers," continued Jacqueline to the parents of Jonathan.

Unbeknownst to either of them, Jacqueline had fancied their eldest son for some time, a fact that had never been expressed to Jonathan. Her statement sparked the interest of not only Kathryn, but an inquisitive Samuel, who was looking deeply into her eyes as she spoke. She took note of his observations and found it difficult to look into his clear blue eyes in return, knowing that the abundance of her heart may have just betrayed her secret. Also listening was James the Younger, and her words struck him to the core.

"I bid you farewell," declared Nathan as he spurred his war-horse along the cliff line adjacent to the river.

His war party followed suit, and together the ten of them rode in the direction of the vast forest to the south. The rumble of their departure nearly shook the ground from beneath the feet of the search party.

✝

The thick forest, as well as the river, had remained officially unnamed by the Council of the Castle. It was surmised that the naming of them, which was the clear demarcation of the southern boundary, would somehow create in the hearts of the people a familiarity with the forbidden border and thereby create within their hearts a subliminal lack of fear to venture beyond it.

The fear was necessary.

But it was one of the few 'written laws' that had been a mistake of the Council over the years, for it was a futile way to exact control over the population. What they had failed to recognize in its penning so many years prior was the same that the weapon master had failed to recognize in his son; that was, the inherent need for the human heart to have the freedom to make decisions for itself and to have the liberty to make the choices it so desired.

The law merely created an imaginary fence line that the more adventurous would venture to breach simply by the fact that the law itself was in existence. Rather than enforcing the fear of the unknown in such individuals, it produced in them the strength to become outsiders to the law, 'outlaws.' At the same time, the realm would not have survived over the ages without those said outlaws, for it was they that became the realm's greatest hunters, and their captured game from the forest that lay beyond the border was a section of lands that produced the most plentiful and choicest of meats in the entire realm. However, the conundrum as of late had been attempted to be addressed by the Council as it commissioned the productions of the ardent plays which tried to reveal the dangers that lay beyond the realm's borders.

Still, the inherent freedom within the human heart caused most to have to experience the dangers for themselves, a fact that no law could contain. In the end, the law proved to be similar to trying to hold water in one's hand... the water, like the freedom within the human heart, would always find a way to escape the clenching grasp. There were some, however, that had understood and trusted the good spirit by which the law was written, but most had seen it as a mere rule that was meant to be broken. In turn, it broke them, and the price would many times cost them their lives.

James the Younger had always been one of the more adventurous sorts though tempered enough to become a soldier and had never ventured beyond the border outside of the law. However, he was fond of calling the forbidden forest The Dead Forest, for that was what most of his peers had called it growing up. The river had been nicknamed The Tongue of the Dragon, for it sank into the depth of the trees just like its namesake.

At the moment, it was James' first venture into the heart of the so-called dragon, and he was more than thrilled by the adventure of it all. At the same time, he was thankful that he had waited to cross the border on legal terms for at the back of his mind he chewed on the fact that they were heading to the dreaded Valley of Decision. Therefore, when Nathan had ordered the scouts to venture deeper and deeper into the forest, James silently pondered in his young and naïve warriors' heart the very real and very dangerous mission that lay before him, and instinctively he knew that it would change his life forever.

It was the moment that every soldier confronts within his own soul. That was, the realization that one's life was merely a breath away from eternity and was hinged to a higher purpose. At the moment, it was that higher purpose that strengthened his heart to face the day, a purpose made solid by the fact that his very own sister had been taken by one of the aforementioned serpents, which had stolen her into the night. Word had reached him just as the war party was departing from the royal stables that were adjacent to the barracks, a mere stone's throw north of his hometown of Trelane.

The forest itself was made up of an abundance of trees so tightly grown together that there was hardly room enough to maneuver. The thickness created a constant, silent and slowly fought battle between the various types of foliage, for water had become the treasure that they constantly fought over. With such an inherent denseness, there was never enough of the life sustaining substance to go around. Therefore, most of the forest had lost its immunity to the internal killing of invading beetles and simply dried up and died. Some among the war party saw it as a metaphor of what was happening in the entire realm. Hence, the deadness of the dying forest, and it made the journey of the war party that much more difficult.

At times, Nathan's band of warriors would have to send two or three of the troops ahead of the group to slash and cut through the thick brambles. James had been selected as one of those to perform the task.

His sword was a proven companion, and he appreciated not only the lightness of its craftsmanship, but also its strength. He cut and slashed on the right flank of the group. In the middle was one of the elder warriors and mentor of James the Younger. James had come to admire the man tremendously and he occasionally shot glances in his direction as he made his way through the forest, each slash of his broad sword clearing a swath the width of a horse. He had been named Edgemont for good reason, but later 'du Val' was added as we shall see. He was from one of the realm's long line of warriors just as Nathan had been.

On the far-left flank, a hearty woman by the name of Brenda of Hilt was cutting a path with her massive battle axe, the most appropriate of tools for the task at hand. She was Jacqueline's assigned mentor and at the moment seemed to be oblivious to the fact that blood was flowing down her arms due to the many thorn bushes that she was currently clearing. Both the mentors had been proven time and time again in the foray of battle and Nathan was more than confident in their abilities to be the ones to train up the new candidates.

The party continued at a snail's pace as the foliage continued to make the trip a difficult one. As they approached a certain area that seemed to have an ominous look, with good reason, Nathan ordered the progress halted. The trees of that particular area were massive and had an appearance foreboding. In fact, the trunks had been steadily growing larger and larger as the party moved ahead. Some soldiers had noted the steadily growing thickness, but had never really voiced any concern, for there was no militaristic reason to do so, that was, until they had halted their progression.

The area echoed with an ominous sound that filled the air around them and slowly grew in strength. It seemed to be coming from the base of the trees at first. Nathan ordered the three in reconnaissance out front to investigate. Edgemont was the first to look into the openings, and there appeared a den of sorts. James and Brenda soon joined him and together the three reported their findings to their captain.

"It appears to be a subterranean entrance for an animal of some sorts," Brenda shouted, being a good distance from the captain.

"Only it must be of considerable size. Perhaps wolves," reported Edgemont du Val.

Not one among the party was ready for what happened following the discovery of the holes.

All at once, the forest began to rain with dripping poison and the sweet smell of its noxious fumes was nearly overwhelming. Though toxic, the aroma was at the same time completely attractive. If it had come in a kinder context, it surely could have been emanating from a dessert baker's kitchen.

The ten soldiers of the war party turned their faces to the canopy of trees above their positions and were met with a sight that proved menacing indeed. To their shock and horror, hanging from the branches were thousands of the black snakes that they had encountered within the realm, only these were in their infancy. What they had actually stepped into were the very breeding grounds for the monsters. Simultaneously, the little devils released a cacophony of hissing that threatened to pierce every human eardrum like a high-pitched note that shatters a finely-crafted goblet of glass.

Instantly, James the Younger's body refused to move for he had instinctively inhaled the sweet smell into his lungs with gusto. The vapors then overwhelmed his bronchioles and he staggered to his feet as the fumes that were continually being released by the droppings threatened to paralyze him. With that realization, he tried to hold his breath and stagger his way in the direction of the rest of the war party where his horse had been being towed by those who had not been slashing at the trail. For a moment, he suddenly understood how his sister must have been swayed and captured by one of the larger serpents, for she was always partial to fine confectionary delights.

A few of the slithery creatures fell around him like giant leeches falling from the sky. Fortunately, most of the baby ones had held to their positions, not wanting to leave the protection of the nest. The few that did fall to the ground, however, lunged at the three fleeing trailblazers, and James found himself one of the victims of tiny fangs that sunk deeply into the back of his leg.

The creature attached itself to his calf muscle. Instantly, he felt a numbness as the venom began to leak its way into the meaty section of his leg. It felt like bleeding cold blood, only it was moving in the opposite direction of the way it normally would have. He wasn't sure how much of the poison the little creature contained, but he thought that if it were enough to reach his heart it would surely fall asleep as well.

The fumes continued to cloud his thoughts and through hazy eyesight he could see that Nathan had dismounted his steed along with the others and was barking orders to each of them.

Through the fog, he could see that the order to light a fire was being carried out, but that was beyond four of the others who were making their way closer to his struggling form. His head began to swim into a deeper dizziness, and his eyesight felt as though it were beginning to fail him completely. As he felt an arm reach around his waist and lift him to his feet again, he turned to see Edgemont struggling to raise him upon his utterly failing legs. Though echoed, he could see his mentor's mouth moving and could hear him shouting something about 'standing upon his legs again, soldier'.

As one of the rescuers reached the two them, he suddenly felt the sensation of flying as he and Edgemont were being lifted and carried to safety. His last sight was that of the captain who was still making a defensive stand with the remaining war party, then for James, life went dark.

Nathan ordered the others to light their arrows with the flames that they had produced. Those that had been armed with shooting weapons did as they were told and commenced to fire into the tree canopy that housed the thousand foes which were still hanging from the branches. As for the few snakes that did fall to the ground, once they had bitten their prey, they had quickly expired, for the bite of that particular snake proved to be their last defensive mechanism for the purpose of protecting the nest as a whole, thus disproving the notion that there is no honor among thieves.

Flaming projectiles were released into the area of the hanging foe by the members of the war party and the sweet-smelling perfume that shrouded the air instantly ignited before the missiles had even reached their targets. The ball of fire was tremendous, and the wail of agony that followed was even greater. So hot did the fire rage that not only had it completely consumed the nest, but it also completely removed the canopy of trees above them so that the war party could see the intermittent blue skies above their heads. It strengthened the hearts of the soldiers to know that the sun still stood in the sky though they themselves felt as if they were in a dark, dark tunnel.

The evil that they had just faced and vanquished was even new to the great warrior Nathan. Never before had he witnessed this sort of escalation of darkness, and that was saying quite a bit. What he had been feeling about the enemy's movement was altogether solidified with the encounter. He took stock of his war party and was relieved to discover that though three of them had been bitten by the serpents, he had not suffered a loss of life... not yet at least. With a determination to continue with his mission, he gathered his troops, including the young one that was still unconscious, and pushed deeper into the forest, ever aware to keep an eye out above him.

Farther and farther their quest led them away from their homeland and closer to the Vale of Decision. He had been to the valley before, but it had been quite some time, and the question that raced through the mind of the leader of the king's army was to what level had the enemy descended, or rather ascended. What new evil awaited them in the shadows of the valley, and to what heights had the darkness grown?

✝

The search party and the war party were intricately woven together, only they were woven in such a way that the saying, 'coming apart at the seams', fit the two of them perfectly. Ironically, the moment just after the war party had faced the first of what would be many foes, the search party had faced an enemy of their own.

They had been searching the banks of the Dragon's Tongue and were making their way closer to the forest that the war party had disappeared into.

Still no sign of either the horse or the boy had presented itself since the time that Samuel had seen the tracks in the canyon. The banks of the river had continued to crumble around them, and more than one time the tiny avalanches had threatened to swallow the party, prompting the added soldiers – Jacqueline and Thomas – to dismount their horses. Each failure of the bank had dreadfully solidified the presumption that Jonathan had somehow fallen into the current and was carried beyond the southern borderlands. Still, they hoped against hope that he had made his way to the shoreline where some eddy had taken him in to its swirling hands.

The foe that faced the search party, as has been mentioned, confronted them just as Jonathan's mother and Jacqueline were starting to get to know each other. At the prompting of little Samuel, the two had begun to discuss the only encounters that Jacqueline and Jonathan had had, and when Kathryn grew enlightened about the latter meeting, the picture that emerged regarding her son's strange behavior became more and more clear.

Kathryn had learned, for instance, that Jacqueline had been raised in a family who hailed from the fishing township of Marshai. She had never been to the town herself but had heard stories about the famed sunsets that occurred over the waters of Brittle Marsh, which the town had been situated upon. In fact, the entire town had been built upon stilts and strangely stood with each building attached by a conglomeration of narrow wooden bridges.

It was one of the two settlements that had been founded by a woman Nasgroth and it had held to that tradition from its inception. As for the sunsets, it was said that the dipping sun's rays would glance off the material that was abundant upon the waters of the lake. Tiny creatures called Millified Shams produced in their wake crystallized wood that was built up throughout the large tarn and was the end result of their digestion as they took into their systems the silt of the depths. Consequently, the said rays would be refracted by the crystal substance and would cast a reflection that magnified the majesty of the sinking sun.

The two women, for Jacqueline had reached the age of sixteen, had just been talking about the teen's mother and how she was the personal servant of the current Nasgroth when the party fell into disarray.

Thomas had just re-mounted his war horse, and the others in the search party were beginning to question his judgment, seeing that they were upon a precarious precipice that stood about triple their height over the swirling waters of the river. They had climbed to the bank to gain a better perspective upon their surroundings when it suddenly started to crumble beneath their feet, but it was not due to the previous night's storm. The weight of the horses could have been sustained by the earthen shelf, but Thomas suddenly decided to climb upon his steed and in a moment, leaped from the edge and spurred his mount in the opposite direction.

Together, the pair jumped from their current position and caused the bank to crumble. As the rest of the party began to lose their balance, they were shocked when Thomas completely abandoned them in their moment of need as he and the horse galloped away.

Samuel and his father were the first to fall from the height, for the blind weapon master could find nothing to cling to as he groped about for a hand hold. Samuel had instinctively grasped a hold of his Da's leg, and in turn, it caused the two of them to drop like the rocks that were tumbling beneath them. Kathryn and Jacqueline were able to hold to their position for a short while, but in time they too lost their footing as the shelf upon which they were clinging completely disintegrated beneath them. Bart of the Forest had found a place that was not disappearing beneath him, but when he saw the others fall into the depths, he simply jumped in after them and into the swiftly passing waters himself. All together, the remaining search party found themselves treading water in a pool far below.

Fortunately for the five, the river had carved itself into the side of the canyon and created a small cave toward which the waters had simply begun to turn in circles. However, at the same time that the circling waters continued to gently carve a hole in the wall, it had also found a bottom drain to which the water escaped into a subterranean river system. Though they had survived the fall, they alas found themselves struggling to free themselves from the funnel effects of a giant whirlpool.

That was when the strength of the kindly butcher, Bart of the Forest, truly paid off for the remaining party.

Samuel barely had the strength to fight the current and it was a good thing that his parents had allowed him to play in the river a number of years earlier for it afforded him the experience to fight against it. He and John remained clinging to each other as they fought to escape the swallowing currents. Though injured, John was able to supply his youngest son with the edge that he needed to keep his head above the water. Bart reached out to them first, for he had managed to grab onto a root that protruded from the side of the cave's wall. As he did, he reached for the arm of the weapon master and found his wrist. With all of his might, he held on and allowed the natural flow of the whirlpool to cast them toward the only shore that provided a resting point. They managed to barely reach it after the help of the butcher.

Bart could feel that the root system had begun to fail, but his mission had not yet been completed, for Kathryn and Jacqueline were still treading water and fighting the river's sway. At first, the butcher turned his eyes to the elder of the two women thinking that the younger would certainly have more fight in her, but the opposite proved to be true.

"Reach out to me Jacqueline," Bart shouted as the girl passed by just out of his reach.

"I can't fight the current," she yelled.

"You have too! Just reach out! I can't help if you don't!"

As she came around to his position, she reached with all of her might, and it made her feel like she would come apart at the very seams. Stretching out with one arm, Bart was able to just grasp hold of her fingertips. Instantly, he could feel her knuckles crack beneath his grasp as her tendons strained to maintain their integrity. He was able to capture her from the pulling effects of the water and move her in the direction of Samuel and John.

"Reach out to her, Samuel," Bart shouted!

"I've got you, princess!" Samuel shouted in return as he grabbed her hand and directed her to the waiting arms of his Da', who in turn pulled her from the current.

Kathryn had been continuing her struggle against the swirling effects of the funneling water but was quickly losing the battle as she was drawn closer and closer toward the center of the conduit. She was well out of the reach of the butcher as she passed by him the first time following the rescue of the girl. Bart knew that he had no choice but to abandon his hold on the root that he was clinging to, figuring that the next turn around the circle would be the last before she would succumb to the descending current.

"Hang on Kathryn! The next time around I'll come out to you!" proclaimed Bart.

He could see the fear on her face and for an instant it reminded him of the young animals that he had so often caught in his traps on his myriad of hunting trips into the forest. When she came around closer to his location, he let go of his hand hold and swam out to her. He wrapped his arms around her just as she was losing the strength to fight any longer. Together they took one last ride around the circle and when they reached the position to which the rest of the party had landed, he pushed her against the heavy current in that direction. She used her last ounce of strength to reach out to the waiting hands of Jacqueline, John, and Samuel. Bart had lost his own altogether.

The search party could only watch as the kindly butcher, 'his Sir-ness', succumbed to the whirlpool, sank beneath the waves, and into the subterranean river system. He even managed to raise a farewell hand from beneath the waters' surface as he went down.

It was a gesture that the others in the search party would have to describe to the weapon master for his eyesight was more watery than ever and could only make out shadows in his dimness; especially as liquid sadness escaped his eyes in the form of tears. In his silent weeping, he admired how much the butcher had become just that, a shadow in the shade of the fabled king's sacrifice, and wondered whether he were heading to the very same place.

†

Although the opposite edge of the tapestry, the war party, had survived the encounter with the thousand tiny serpents, they too were about to break down in the fray. The decision to forge deeper into the forest and closer to the vale had been made, and that in and of itself produced a whole new set of circumstances. It was a decision full of fate, for unlike the search party, Nathan and his soldiers most definitely discovered traces of Jonathan's journey.

The company of soldiers had made the decision to set up camp for the night on the outer edges of the forest that they had cut a path through. They were not quite the full distance to the Vale of Decision and still had a few minor passes to cross, yet continued to follow the river's course. The forest had already succumbed to, and the river had just begun to succumb to, the shear dryness of the outer reaches. They camped where one realm ended and another started as the landscape shifted from that of a mountainous terrain to that of a vast desert land.

The Vale itself sat beyond the very last canyon pass that the river flowed to and created a bowl that at one time teemed with life as the first of the Shadow Scrolls has described. Like Samuel had done earlier, James the Younger had made his way to the river's shoreline to refresh himself from its life sustaining liquid.

He had woken from his coma just prior to emerging from the forest. When he had come around, he found himself strapped to the backside of his horse and loosely tied with its tethers. Edgemont had to loose him from his bindings and ribbed him about falling asleep on the job. After tumbling to the dust beneath his mount, he found that the ingested poison had left him parched with thirst, a thirst that drove him to seek the river's edge.

When he reached it, he was surprised to see that the once raging rapids had slowed to a mere trickle of foggy water that caused him, despite his raging thirst, to hesitate before slamming his face into the murky mess. Between slurps and slurries, he heard the whimpering of some sort of small animal and surmised that it must have been just as thirsty as he was. After his quenching, he made his way in the direction of the sound which happened to be behind a series of large boulders a little further upstream and back in the direction that they had come, surely the last of the mountain's great grandchildren of stones.

The others hadn't noticed his venture, having been busied with the work of building the camp, but when he called out to them, they all responded to his position. What James discovered caused even the Captain of the Guard take a step back in hushed awe. No other sight had spoken louder to them about the ebb and flow of existence, and ironically it occurred within hours of the Vale of Decision. As the party answered the call of the Younger, they were met with the sight of Swift, and her newly foaled colt. Unfortunately, the mare had expired, and the new colt was near to that end as well.

Nathan figured that the horse must have stayed alive just long enough to last the distance of the river's reach. Though she had failed in her personal fight to preserve her own life, she had managed to create a safe haven for her newborn, to at least afford it a fighting chance at survival.

By instinct, she had foaled at the base of one of the boulders that had an overhang where she could lay. After the birth, she had wrapped her body around the little one with her backside facing in the opposite direction of the giant stone. In essence, she had created a nest for the colt to lie within. If it were not for the soldier, James the Younger and his insatiable need for refreshment, the tiny horse would have most likely succumbed to the elements within a few hours.

The great leader of the army gently scooped the foal into his arms and ordered a burial for the mare.

Carrying the colt to within the confines of the newly constructed camp, he bedded it down amongst the surplus hay that had been brought for the war-horses. After watering and caring for the little horse, Nathan watched as the mighty larger ones began to care for it as though it were their own. The thought occurred to him that the beasts of burden were truly incredible creatures indeed, for although they were fearless in the midst of the mightiest of battles, they were gentle enough to become the servants to the helpless tiny brother. It strengthened the heart of the captain to know that he had spent his entire life serving a kingdom that produced such beauty, and for the moment, allowed his mind to forget the prospect of a war that potentially lay ahead in the shadows of the shear evil that was produced beneath the Vale.

The night that fell upon the war party's camp was darker than any one of the soldiers had previously seen, save for Nathan himself. Each took their turn at not only keeping the campfire lit, but also keeping watch on their surroundings. When James' turn came around at about the fifth hour, he was surprised to be visited by his friend and mentor, Edgemont du Val. In the light of the flames, his form appeared even larger and more menacing than he was in actuality. However, when he approached the newling, James felt comfortable enough to rib the man as he had been ribbed earlier and pointed out that leftover victuals of some dead foul had found a nesting site within his thickened beard. In return Edgemont, having never been an individual to have been one-upped, grabbed him, and commenced to wipe his face upon James's cloak.

"Not funny, Edge," James squealed as he pulled away.

"But so necessary," decried Edgemont.

They both kneeled near the fire and Jonathan could see the wrinkly smile of his mentor fade into a more serious look just before he released new news upon the seventeen-year-old soldier.

"We'll be continuing the scouting trip on our own," he started. "The captain will be returning to the royal stables with the colt, something about paying his respects to an old friend."

"The Captain of the Guard is going to abandon the mission? Where does that leave the rest of us?" questioned James.

"He's already gone…"

"Who's in charge now?"

"I am," Edgemont flatly stated. "He's left me in charge of the team. We'll leave before first light and I'll need you to stay on your toes, hear me? We need to be ready for anything."

"Where do we go from here?"

"The Vale," said the lieutenant. "We have to bring back a scouting report with us. Nathan wants to know of any new changes especially any troop build-ups."

"You've seen it before?" questioned James.

"Aye, it's why du Val was added to my namesake. It was many years ago. Can't say that I'm happy about returning, but I suppose it's only considerate to visit the graves of one's comrades, to visit, the many graves." Edgemont's thoughts trailed off after that and James knew that the conversation had faded as well.

The mentor relieved his newling from his watch and sent the young man to the covering of his own tent for some rest.

Needless to say, James the Younger could not sleep.

The war party assembled before sunrise and arrived at the dreaded valley's rim just as the daylight was beginning to inch its way over the bowl that it was housed within.

The scouts were taken aback as, fathoms below them, the utter blackness of the soil made the sight look as though there were no floor at all. From their great height, it appeared that there was nothing more than a bottomless pit which fell into the depths of the earth. The last thing James heard was a sentence that was released by his mentor's lips which said that things had become much worse than he had ever imagined.

That was right before a sudden and violent hot wind met them head on like an invisible and charging army that struck a blow to their meager numbers. It was a blow that caused all of the soldiers to lose their balance at the same time and fall headlong into the awaiting valley below.

Thus, the entire war party fell into the macabre arms of the dreaded and infamous Vale of Decision.

Chapter 4

Taken In

†

Wisekoff

Jonathan would have awoken to a silvery day. Silvery because that would have been the best way to describe the wind, cold, and snow that would have caused the atmosphere around him to penetrate and permeate his soul with icy feelings. The clouds that swiftly passed above him were refracting the sun's dawning light in such a way that the edges of them appeared to have silver linings, though their hearts were dark and mysterious. The sight above, that revealed the glimmer of hope, would have been the sight to have greeted him if he were not still sleeping within the depths of an exhausted slumber. However, at the moment, he was still within the confines of what would be the first of a recurring dreamscape.

In his netherworld, Jonathan found himself beside a stream. Around him were grasses whose greens were lively, bright, and punctuated with the flaming colors of a myriad of flowers. The trees of that heavenly place were shimmering Willows and Aspens whose trunks were a milky white and whose leaves were flashing golden responses to a warm light breeze that caused them to whisper in hushed tones. He himself was arrayed in the garbs of soldiery and had just sat upon a felled tree next to the babbling brook. After refreshing himself with the passing waters, he turned his head in the upstream direction. Beyond the winding, sun-reflecting waters, he could make out the shadow of a figure emerging from the depths of the surrounding forest, and it froze him in his tracks.

The image was altogether captivating, and the normal foreboding at the sight of the approaching stranger was completely absent. Jonathan watched the female form as she skipped over the rocks within the stream. She was approaching nearer to his position, but not upon a straight course, but leaping from one side of the brook to the other. He thought it strange that she didn't approach in a more straightened line, but it occurred to him that there must have been a reason for her mysterious behavior.

She was dressed in a black cloak with a hood, but when she would leap from side to side it swayed in the wind, revealing the clothes beneath that hugged the contours of her form. However, he could not discern what type of clothing they were due to the flickering of the sun's refractions off the water. He thought that he could see a weapon in her hand, but again the tiny reflections disturbed his eyesight. Adding to the frame of the picture were tiny droplets of water which were being released from the leaves of willow trees all around the dreamscape and they served to fill the picture with morning mist. The body of mist contained a sweetened fragrance, and it caused Jonathan to momentarily lift his eyes to the branches above his position. That was when the focus of his eyes landed upon a single drop of water as it escaped the rounded contours of a leaf. He watched it as it fell from its perch, and just as it was about to strike him in the face, he woke up from the dream.

Unlike the sliver of silver on the edge of the passing cloud that would have smiled upon him, a perspiration-covered face appeared in his eyesight, and it was punctuated by a drop of the salty sweat as it struck him on the cheek. Jonathan could instantly smell the foul fumes of the man that stood over him, but before another drop of perspiration hit him, he rolled from beneath the portly gentleman and stood to his feet.

For a moment he wobbled upon his legs but was caught by the strong arm of a man who stood a good arm's length above him. Next to him, there was another man that looked like a mirror image of the first. Both were tall and lanky. Both wore dirty cloaks that hugged their forms and made them appear taller than they actually were. The phrase 'walking willows' came to Jonathan's mind as he spied the twin towers of their form. Their faces were gaunt and hollowed as if someone had completely drained them of fat and marrow and within their eyes there appeared to be waning lights like candles that had reached the end of their wicks.

Jonathan tried to observe all of this through the clouds of his own mind, and they were just beginning to naturally clear when they were suddenly blown away by the silvery quick tongue of the portly man who had been standing over and sweating upon him a few moments earlier.

"Wisekoff's da' name," the man snapped in a rough accent that seemed to emerge directly through his nose as he offered his hand in a shake, "Dese' here gents are, ah', you needn't to know der' names. Tis' not import anyway."

Jonathan refused to offer his hand in return but was quickly rebuked by the short man, "Come statue, release da' paw to me, it's not propr' in this parts not too."

He was a portly fellow indeed and it occurred to Jonathan that the man could have been mistaken for a child if it were not for his belly and balding head. His hair was a wiry gray and it fell off the back and sides of his dome like the ends of the straw sweep he had once used to clean the clay floor of the weapon shop with. His clothes were altogether different. The outer layer was a gray fur cloak that made Jonathan feel that much colder than he already was. Beneath that, he could see some sort of armless garb that half covered his frame and was made of some sort of golden cloth. And below that still, he could see a whitish shirt that seemed to be fashioned in the same style that he himself was wearing, that was, before they had been shredded by his recent ordeal.

"Here's da' chunks I promisd' ya'," Wisekoff said as he pulled some silver objects from his breeches and proceeded to hand them to one of the lurching men.

The figure that he handed the chunks to received them with his bony fingers, placed them in his pockets, and departed with his twin. Jonathan watched as Wisekoff was waving to the departing figures and could see an almost invisible string running from his hand to the pockets of the other. With a flip of his wrist, the silver chunks flew out of the hiding place of the tall man, and in the twinkling of an eye, Wisekoff reeled them in to the safety of his own pocket. Neither of the men noticed and continued to make their way out of the ravine they had just been in.

That was the moment that Jonathan began to distrust the short and rounded man and it was also the moment he finally got the chance to look about himself. He had been awoken from his slumber by the drops of Wisekoff's sweat which, incidentally, struck Jonathan as odd for the day was cold and windy with snow in various places. He was still a bit groggy and could feel a swimmy feeling as he turned in a semi-circle to get a lay of the land around him. The two were standing in the bottom of a ravine made of sand. They were about the depth of two horsebacks and were surrounded with barren rocks that were the same color of the sand itself. The stark landscape was something he had never seen in his entire life. The blandness of the place made him feel slightly sickened and if it were not for the patches of snow, he may have even thrown up for a peculiar smell was starting to turn his stomach.

There was no water present, and certainly no river running to that place. He knew that he had been carried by the current to a distant land, but after losing the strength to fight against it, he had altogether fallen asleep on the large branch that he had been clinging to. Now there was no sight of the river, the branch, or even his sense of direction and it caused him some concern.

"Where am I?" he questioned as he turned back in the direction of Wisekoff.

However, the portly man had already departed and was following the dry river bed in what Jonathan thought to be the southerly direction for the sun was still rising on his left hand side.

"Hey! Where am I?"

"Follow, statue, and you be seen' soon," trailed off Wisekoff's voice.

He was making his way around one of the s-turns that the riverbed had made and when Jonathan reached the corner, he could see Wisekoff continuing toward a wooden bridge in the far distance. Beneath his feet, he could see the strange man kicking up some kind of mud and it comforted Jonathan to think that water was close by. Perhaps even the remnants of the river that had swept him away.

His thoughts meandered in the direction of his homeland as he himself shuffled his feet a good distance behind, kicking the sand beneath himself more out of exhaustion than anything else. He would have many questions for the man out in front, but being at that distance he knew that he would have to catch up to him first if he were to ask any of them. More than once, he tried to pick up his pace, but the weakness of his body forbade him and merely left him gazing at the dust below, lost in thought. His eyes threatened to close on a number of occasions, but he struggled to fight off the feeling by keeping his mind busy.

His first thoughts began to betray him as tears for his mother tried to make their way to the surface. He wondered what must have been going through her heart the day following his disappearance. And what of the tiny heart of Samuel?

He reflected on the dream he had had and pondered whether the girl in it were the one he had been dreaming of for the better part of seven years. He pondered how far he must have been away from the realm and even questioned how long it had been since he had left. It wasn't as though he had meant to fall into the river, but it had been a great desire to leave the confines of his surroundings. He found it odd that he had just come to a place of acceptance when his destiny had swiftly and suddenly taken a different turn. Then his thoughts drifted toward Swift and whether she had survived the ordeal… Inevitably, the memory of his Da' and their disagreements coupled with their broken relationship sprang forth and it caused a hunger-knot in his stomach to make its presence known. Strangely, he suddenly found the energy to quicken his steps in his pursuit of the strange, portly man.

He, at long last, reached the place where Wisekoff had been kicking up the mud and was met with a stench so rancid that he had to hide his nose and mouth in the corner of his elbow to proceed. His clothes were still wet, and his arm was shivering. The shaking afforded an opportunity for the smell to reach his nasal septum and it stung to no end. In fact, his entire body was occasionally suffering periodic jolts of shivers as he fought to keep himself from falling apart all together. Wisekoff had finally stopped a good distance from the bridge and was watching Jonathan fight the elements of his new surroundings. Having spied his struggle, he turned to assist the young man.

"'Tis' a strange new land, hey wetted rat?" Wisekoff blurted out as he took one of Jonathan's arms and stretched it around his neck. Though the man was short, Jonathan could feel a previously hidden strength in him that was suddenly helping him in his ordeal, and he took note that there could be more to him than met the eye. However, with the proximity of his new friend being closer than he cared, the stench of filth flooded his head with ghastly thoughts of where the man must spend most of his time.

"What is that horrible smell?" questioned Jonathan.

"We be walkn' on da' sewage, statue."

"Why do you insist on calling me statue?" inquired Jonathan.

"From my perspects', everybody' be statues, statue." declared Wisekoff.

"I'd like to know where we are."

"You'd be no place like yer' house. Yes, you'd be far from dat' ind'ed."

Jonathan was just barely beginning to understand the rough accent of the man he had just met. Though repulsive, there was something about him that was endearing. He had appreciated the shoulder to lean on and took note that Wisekoff's height had fit under his own arm like a shelf that had been perfectly built to suit him. He was far from home, that much was for certain, but at the same time Jonathan could feel a certain satisfaction in being a part of an adventure to a distant land and even though his surroundings were stark, there was something endearing about them as well.

"So, where are we?" Jonathan questioned a second time.

"First of first, we likes to know more bout' ye'... I be havin' to know ye more ifn' I be showin' me secrits."

"Secrets. What secrets?"

"Me secrits. Cause I got plenty o' dem'. Dey' be secrits that only da' secrits demselves be knowin'. And what bout' ye? Tell me, statue."

"I wants to be sittn'," jested Jonathan to Wisekoff.

"Dat's jestin'. Good statue. I like some ribbn' meself."

Together, the two sat on the side of the dry riverbank. Jonathan was still shivering from the cold. The sun had gained some strength in the sky, but the wind continued to fight it back. At the same time, he was thankful that the stench was being carried away to some other unsuspecting noses. However, at times the sewage smell would be thrust upon them as the wind changed its direction. As he rested, he was able to concentrate on keeping his shivering under control and thought about what to tell the stranger. He was old enough to know how to choose his words carefully, and the short man seemed to be someone he thought he could trust. Still, Jonathan kept most of his information close to his chest.

"The name's Jonathan of Scharp, from one of the towns in the Realms of Irenay," he cautiously treaded.

"Ah, da' kingdom in da' highlands," surmised Wisekoff. "Can't say I'd been to dos' heights, my boy... What yer' papa' do?"

"He's a weapon master," thinking it harmless to tell.

"Ah, he make da' weapons for da' soldier. Intrestn'… And you make da' weapons too?" Wisekoff inquired.

"Some, but not like my Da'. He's the best there is." Jonathan was surprised by the way he spoke about his father and took note that he had still thought of him with an ounce of pride, albeit an ounce; but then again, those were merely the thoughts of a young lad.

"You be knowin' how to use da' sharpies?"

"Sharpies?" questioned Jonathan.

"Yah, da' weapons, boy. You be knowin' da' weapons?

"Yes. Some."

"Show it den'," stated Wisekoff, pulling from the folds of his fur cloak a sharpened dagger he gingerly held in his dirty hand.

The handle was a white substance that Jonathan had never seen before, but when he took it from Wisekoff's hand, he noted that its weight felt like it were hardly even present. It was lighter than anything he had ever felt. Out of the handle proceeded a blade that was irregularly colored for it was tinged with a reddish hue. Not stained mind you, but it was a crimson type of substance that felt as hard as metal, or stone, or something. Jonathan turned it over and over in his hand, measuring the breadth of the weapon as if he were a connoisseur of such items. And in a way, he was.

"What's it made of?" he inquired.

"Human bone…," Wisekoff said flatly. "Bone be the handle, and Redstone be da' blade."

"Right..." was Jonathan's reply as a repulsive look slid its way into his wrinkled brow.

As he stood, he looked about him for a target to show off his talent. In the distance, the wooden bridge stood about thirty paces from where they were located. Upon the side of the bridge, a cross beam ran diagonally and intersected with another. They were both made of large wooden beams and the engineering impressed Jonathan as he studied the framework for it spanned the entire distance of the sand bottom riverbed. The thought occurred whether a river, his river, had ever run beneath it.

"Art' ye' gonna' throw, or just stand in da' cold like a statue?" interrupted Wisekoff as he eyed the young man he had started to grow accustomed too.

Jonathan stood with his eyes studying the bridge, but when the portly man broke his thoughts, his eyes began to fix upon his target. The crossbeams were at least three times the distance as the tethers of Swift had been when he threw the fated hatchet days or possibly weeks earlier. After he had locked in on his target, he turned his head to look Wisekoff in the face and saw that his eyes had an unimpressed expression within them. All the same, he closed his own and shifted his weight so that he could maximize the strength of his throw.

When he let the dagger fly, he could feel the blade slip from his grip and suddenly heard a slicing sound followed by an instant of pain that shot up his arm. With his eyes still closed, he could feel a liquid substance leaking down his wrist and wondered what damage he had just inflicted upon himself. With a wince on his face, he opened his eyes and witnessed an awe inspired Wisekoff who was looking in the direction of the thrown projectile.

"Ouchhh," yelped Jonathan as he looked down upon a gushing gash that had been opened across all four of his fingers. Beneath it, he could see his own bones shining through.

"I failed to speak ye' bout' da' blade. Redstone be the sharpest' in all me realm," Wisekoff returned without even glancing in Jonathan's direction for he was still focused on the target the young man had thrown too. At the same time, he began to shred a small filthy scrap of cloth after blowing his nose into it.

"What realm?" he moaned. "What be your realm, and where are we?" he sarcastically griped.

"Come wit' me, now," replied Wisekoff as he wrapped Jonathan's hand with the filthy cloth. He then slung the young man's arm over his shoulder and began to pull him in the direction of the thrown dagger.

In the distance and upon the bridge, Jonathan was shocked when he finally lifted his eyes in the direction of his throw. He had known in his heart that he had hit the target, there was no question there. But what he had failed to know was that his thrown knife had found its way not only to the precise point upon the bridge where he had been aiming, but all the way through a woman's hand! She happened to be crossing the bridge at the moment and was using the railing to balance herself.

The elderly woman was in the process of pulling her hand against the resistance of the blade and was failing in her struggle to free her hand from the lodged weapon.

Jonathan broke free of Wisekoff's assistance and ran toward the bridge. The portly man continued to waddle behind him and when Jonathan turned to ask his help to free the woman, he just continued in the same cadence, yet was laughing jolly bellows. Jonathan slipped and slid his way in the muck of the sewage and more than one time, fell down in the sludge. The smell bit into his nostrils like tiny needles, but he continued to the rescue of his unfortunate victim. When he arrived at her location, he could see the woman still trying to free herself from the projectile and could only imagine the pain that must have been inflicted upon her. It made his own wound feel not as problematic. However, to his utter surprise, the woman displayed no pain whatsoever.

She was merely pulling against the resistance with a cold and emotionless gaze…

She was elderly and had long blackened hair that fell down her neck and back like long strips of rough cloth. Her dress was of shaggy grayed robes that were ripped and torn about the base, and looked as though hungry moths had feasted for days upon the material. Her feet were covered in muck and mud and beneath the grime, were clothed with leather satchels. In her left hand, she carried a bucket. As Jonathan grew close, she didn't even acknowledge his presence and continued to stare at her hand with a hollow and lifeless look. She reminded him of the taller twins he had encountered earlier but was in a deeper state of removal from reality. Wisekoff finally reached his position beneath the bridge and seemed to be unfazed by the sight.

"That be the most amazing tro' I ever spy," Wisekoff exclaimed.

"Why is she like that?"

"It don't matter. She can't be feelin' da' pain. She's got the Zomb."

"The what?" Jonathan questioned.

"Come wit' me..." Wisekoff said as he pulled the young man behind him and up the side of the ravine to where the bridge crossed it. Once they had reached the top, they made their way across the bridge.

The entire time that they were walking, Jonathan kept his eyes upon a sight that utterly mesmerized him, for once again he was looking upon a sight he had never witnessed before, and it caused him to walk in not so straight a line. When Wisekoff stopped to retrieve his dagger, Jonathan just continued to walk by, still in awe. The woman, once freed from her fastening, continued on her course across the bridge as if nothing had ever happened. When she neared Jonathan's position, she haphazardly bumped into him with the bucket and continued right along. As for Jonathan, he fell to the ground and to his side.

It was the perfect excuse that he had been waiting for because he had been feeling like he wanted to sit down once he had spied the sight that awed him so. Upon the bridge, he simply stared past the woman as she continued with her bucket to the edge of the ravine. Once there, she dumped the muck that was in it, the end product of the vast population of the massive city he had been looking upon… a city that stretched out as far as he could see...

Wisekoff laughed a hearty laugh, "Welcome to da' City of Gish, me friend!"

✝

The City of Gish

Jonathan stood to his feet, still dumbfounded and smelling of sewage. Wisekoff looked at his hand and could see the blood beginning to soak through the cloth he had applied, yet he was impressed by his own instinct for recruitment.

"'Tis' a shame to hurt hands wit' dat' talent. You be troain' those tros' in perpetuity, and I be takin' you to somes' that could use your giftins', statue." Wisekoff stated.

Unbeknownst to Jonathan, Wisekoff had been on one of his many journeys into the vast wilderness that was far removed from the sandy city of his own realm. The forest itself had always fascinated the portly man. In it, he had found some of his most precious treasures, and out of shear enjoyment, he would often comb the base of it to see what the great river had deposited upon its final shores.

When he discovered the unconscious young man lying face down across a branch, he thought that he had found just another wandering soul. Nevertheless, a wandering soul was just the thing that could fetch him a decent price in the city. He had long ago learned to bring along hired hands to help him retrieve any significant findings, and the two tall men were just dimmed enough not to question his authority, like elephants afraid of a mouse. When he ordered them to carry the boy back to the city's ravine, they blindly obeyed even though the distance was great. To preserve the young man in a state of stupor, Wisekoff had opened a small glass vial beneath the nostrils of the lad as he slept. So potent was the brew that the wandering soul stayed that way for three days which was good, for the journey took them two.

Together, the three bandits overshadowed the young man as he lay sleeping in the sands of the long-dead river that wound its way into the city from sandy heights in the distance. Those sandy heights were truly the southernmost edges of human existence and the few brave souls that had tried to explore beyond the dull range were never heard from again. Wisekoff had been trying to wake the boy for nearly twenty minutes when Jonathan had finally come around.

Wisekoff produced a small rope and began to measure the height and width of Jonathan's frame as he sat on the bridge still gazing at the immensity of Gish. Having witnessed the 'throw' he knew that he had discovered much more than a lost soul in search of something new.

"You be getting' up and follown' me, statue," Wisekoff urged Jonathan as he continued across the bridge.

Jonathan struggled to gain his footing once again and blindly followed, still awed by the sight of the city that surrounded him. He turned in circles and could see that it was everywhere. The City of Gish was vastly spread out.

The deep ravine that they had been in merely bisected the city, and the bridge was only the first in an immense number of them that crossed the ravine. It was built into the sandy hills that were more or less the foothills of the equally bland heights beyond. Other than those heights, Jonathan could see nothing else but the sheer enormity of the city's size. The buildings were so stacked upon one another like giant towers that the portion he was witnessing looked as though it were about to fall over. They were fortified by wooden trusses and connecting each were bridges that ran from one hovel to the next. The smoke that poured from the chimneys made it seem as though one great fire had perpetually burned for centuries. In most places the smoke was so thick that he could barely make out what lay beyond. It darkened the sky above, allowing him to look upon the giant orange fire ball of the sun which hung in the sky like a bobble that had been back-lit by a candle. He had never before been able to fully look into its shine and for a moment, it mesmerized him.

Looking toward the city once again and through the hazy atmosphere, Jonathan could also make out what seemed to be hundreds of figures meandering to and fro around the metropolis. He and Wisekoff were walking straight into the fray, and he again felt a pang of hunger make itself known. All the same, he didn't feel like he could eat even if a vast banquet were set before him.

As they made their way down into the dusty streets of the city, Jonathan was struck by the incredible uniqueness of each person he passed. Never before had he seen so many different types of people. There were women as well as men, but the different types of skin tones and facial shapes were striking. Equaling the vast array of bodies, were their diverse eye shapes as well. It would have been the greatest experience of his life, if it were not for an ominous commonality that began to present itself. In a sense, each soul seemed to be at different levels of dullness. Though they were functioning as normal people, it seemed as though each was mysteriously compartmentalized, or 'zombed' as Wisekoff had put it. Some were as deeply dimmed as the lady on the bridge, and others were at a different level just as the two tall men he had first met. There were even some who were at a level beyond the woman on the bridge, and those were the ones that produced the greatest amount of caution. At the moment, Wisekoff was stepping over a few of them which lay in the streets like deadened cattle. As they continued along the road, Jonathan himself stepped over one and looked into the person's face.

His, or he assumed it was a 'his' eyes were sunken into the gaunt figure of the face. The person was alive, but the eyelids were half closed. For a moment, Jonathan felt the urge to lift his lids and to look into them, but a sudden shudder of the figure kept him from performing the act. He tried to jump past the person to continue along his journey behind Wisekoff, but as he did he felt a tug on the sleeve of his leg. He then turned to see the figure trying to say something to him. Jonathan half bent down to hear what the person was saying. Instantly, a sweet and pungent aroma struck him in the face and nearly knocked him off his already teetering balance and he had to pull back some.

"Serpent's Breath... I need it," the raspy voice stated. "Serpents Breath..." it trailed off.

Jonathan could then feel a tug on his arm and turned to see a ghostly white skinned woman urging him to follow her. She was dressed in a multi-colored dress. She had more of the colorful cloth hanging from her form in various places like the one Wisekoff had blown his nose into. When she moved, she sounded like a goblet that was being struck with a utensil for she had about her body tiny golden colored bells. Binding her waist was a large leather belt that had notches all about it. Hanging on both hips were two of the bone handled daggers similar to the one he had thrown earlier. Jonathan instinctively pulled away from her feeling like he would have become just another one of the notches in her belt if he would have followed her lead. However, when he pulled away, he then fell into the waiting arms of an elderly man with teeth so filthy that they appeared to not be there whatsoever. The old man was leaning on a crooked cane with a knotted handle.

Jonathan could feel the hands of the man searching his clothing while he leaned against him. In a flash, Jonathan was reminded of a nightmare he had once had, and he had to fight to free himself from that as well. Though he knew that there was nothing the man would find within the folds, the groping forced Jonathan into a twisting motion that allowed him to break free, almost. Just prior to letting the young man go, the old man grabbed and held Jonathan's face in his hands, looked deeply into his eyes, and spoke in a raspy worn-out voice.

"Open their eyes," he stated. Then the old man let him go and backed away, fading into the crowd.

Jonathan's weight caused him to fall onto his back and upon the grimy ground. Instantly, he found looming over his body three of the lifeless and zombed people, descending upon him like vultures that had swooped down from the towering buildings above his position. For a moment, he felt like he was about to become a longed-for victual for the ghastly strangers. It made him feel sickened, but before he could think further upon the dreadful thought, a flying body flew over him and slammed into the figures. They looked like felling trees that were cut out by Wisekoff as he leaped like a human axe into their trunks.

Both Jonathan and Wisekoff then scrambled to their feet and fled the scene, Wisekoff grabbing Jonathan by the arm and whisking him away.

"You can't be givin' dem' a moment of yer' focus or they'd consume ya'." Wisekoff darkly stated.

Suddenly, the adventure of travel had begun to lose its luster for Jonathan. Thoughts of his homeland began to flood his soul. He thought of his family and the near-perfect newly cobbled streets of his hometown. The strange cityscape passed by his eyesight with a foggy blur as Wisekoff continued to lead him deeper and deeper into the heart of the city. All about, merchants were selling their wares. Brightly dressed women flitted about like lost hummingbirds, their eyes heavy with what looked like darkened paint. Old and hunched women were carrying buckets of muck that they had scooped from the disgusting streams that ran down the middle of the streets. In some places, the filth upon the dirt road they followed was so blackened that the mucky water just slid into the troughs that were hewn out in the middle of the street. Skipping back and forth over the central pools were filthy children who were being chased by old men trying to recover the items that had just been stolen. A sickening feeling continued to creep its way into the weapon-master son's stomach as Wisekoff suddenly halted their journey at the entrance of an ominous alleyway.

Towering above them stood a conglomeration of mud-packed hovels that had long ago lost its footing and had merely fallen into the structure that was adjacent to it. Rather than demolishing the building, the residents of that abode had simply propped it up with large wooden poles and adapted to living a leaning existence. To Jonathan, it seemed to optimize the city itself. That was, to simply accept what life had delivered, stabilize it up the best one could, and hope that the floor would not crumble beneath one's feet. Together, Wisekoff and Jonathan stared down the shadowy alley darkened by the felled structure.

"Wait." Wisekoff blurted out with his arm blocking Jonathan from moving down the alley (as if he would want to go there anyway).

"Wait for what?"

Suddenly, a rain of clear water fell from somewhere far above them and crashed onto the ground of the darkened alleyway.

"That's it," Wisekoff blurted out with the giddiness of a school child and grabbed Jonathan's arm once again.

Together they made their way beneath the leaning tower and turned into an alcove that was blocked by a stained oaken door. Wisekoff kicked the bottom of it with his foot. It opened for them.

They were instantly met with the same sweet and acrid smell that Jonathan had discovered on the near-lifeless forms in the streets, only it was attached to a misty haze that he would have thought to be smoke if it were not for its yellowish color. Standing next to the door was one of the two tall men that had been with them earlier in the day, and the stinging of the yellow mist in Jonathan's eyes caused him to look much taller than he had been before. In fact, as the young man inevitably breathed in the fumes, the tall man seemed to loom higher and more distant and all at once began to turn in a circular motion.

Jonathan began to stumble, but Wisekoff gathered himself under his arm once again and together they started to ascend a creaky wooden staircase which twisted and turned in a steep upward direction. As they arose, Jonathan could make out that the room at the base of the stairs had been some sort of tavern or pub at some time yet had long ago forfeited its patrons and had inevitably fallen into disrepair. Cobwebs could even be seen in the dusty corners where the floorboards met the walls.

He couldn't tell whether it was due to the leaning architecture of the crumbling building or the strange effect the misty atmosphere was having upon him, but as they continued to climb the staircase Jonathan had to keep his left shoulder leaning against the wall as they climbed, for there were no railings.

Higher and higher they ascended for what seemed to be an eternity. Occasionally, Jonathan would look down from the staircase and the dizzying effect of the height caused fear to spring up within his heart. More than a few times he had to halt their progress to catch his breath and the deeper he breathed in the air, the more intensely his fear gained strength.

Finally, they reached the top of the dilapidated staircase and found themselves in front of yet another door that was barely holding on to its wooden hinges. Jonathan took another glance down from his lofty perch and instead of feeling sickened by the ungodly height, he was surprised to suddenly feel elated. In actuality, it was the Serpents Breath that had broken through to a deeper level of consciousness and a switch had occurred where the fear was replaced by a euphoric feeling of strength, optimism, and bravery. For a moment, Jonathan felt like he could have jumped from that height and would have been able to land on his feet without injury. The thought was a crazy one and he immediately dismissed it from his mind and turned once again to the door behind Wisekoff. He was scarce to understand that the yellow mist of the air had made its way throughout his entire system and was finally having the effect that it was meant to have.

Beyond Wisekoff and the door, Jonathan could see a series of lighted candles or what seemed to be candles. Shadows were making their way around on the inside of the room and on one of the walls a shadow grew from tall to short and short to tall again as a figure within paced back and forth upon the floorboards. Wisekoff again kicked the bottom of the door and again the door was opened, only this time it was opened by the other of the twin towering figures.

"Wisekoff. Finally, you've returned… We have problems!" It wasn't the tall figure of the man that had been talking to them, but rather a figure arrayed in a black cloak that draped the entirety of the frame. As Wisekoff stepped through the doorway, he was careful to take a sidestep around a circular cut that was sawn into the wooden floor about three steps beyond the door. Wisekoff carefully led Jonathan around the trap and closer toward the figure in the black cloak who was just removing the hood that covered   her head.

"The devices have been discovered in Brigand Square." the female voice stated.

She instantly captivated Jonathan's eye. She had inky black hair that hung straight down but was curled inward upon the ends. Her eyes were just as black as her hair, and above he could see that she was wearing some purplish paint. Her lips were even painted in a black color and her cheeks were hollowed by a charcoal dusting of some sorts. "Who's this?" she questioned Wisekoff.

"A helpmate. I found em'," he retorted. "He's gotten' the best shot I been seein'." The woman motioned Wisekoff closer and out of earshot from Jonathan.

"Do you trust him, sir?" she whispered.

"He be too green to make a diff' if he ever got ill intents… We can use em'do'. He be provin' himself in time, be trustn' me."

The two broke up their huddle and the woman made her way over to where Jonathan was standing. When she walked, she seemed to be floating upon the air. Jonathan couldn't help but watch her feet as she did. Rather than walking heel to toe, she was swiftly gliding across the room with a toe to heel movement. It captivated him and even more so when she spoke to him giving him a name he could easily remember and commit to memory.

"If Wisekoff says he can trust you, then I can as well. He's the best judge of character I've ever known. His recruits have always paid off… I should know, I'm one of them." She stretched her hand out to him and Jonathan took note that even her fingernails were blackened with black streaks that ran up her hands ending somewhere up the distance of her forearms.

"I'm Katelyn."

Katelyn, it was dangerously close to his own mother's name, but her voice had seemed to wiggle its way into his heart.

"He hesitate to shake me hand too." Wisekoff chuckled.

"Jonathan of Scharp." Jonathan returned, looking deeply into her eyes, finally returning her handshake, and mentally took note that her hand was cold, and was dripping with fresh blood.

"Can I call you John?"

"Absolutely," he replied with a slight slur to his speech. All at once, his eyes grew heavy, and the room began to swim in his vision. Jonathan looked down at his hand and noticed that it was over-soaked with blood. In fact, the blood had also covered Katelyn's hand and was dripping onto the floor into a small puddle beneath him.

The loss of blood, coupled with the pangs of starvation, tripled with the effects of the Serpent's Breath, had finally taken over his faculties. All at once, his eyes rolled back in his head and he looked at the ceiling above him, a ceiling that he could have touched with an outstretched arm. However, it only served to make him feel that much more closed in. Then he began to fall backward, and Katelyn let go of his hand.

He fell fully backward without an attempt at breaking his fall, a fall that was directly through the trap door that was waiting behind him. It gave way with an eerily ripping sound as his body fell right through it.

✝

A Warm and Dry Place

Jonathan awoke with a splitting headache.

Upon grabbing his head, he discovered that the wound on his hand had been attended too. No longer was it dripping with blood. Curious to see, he removed the bandaging and saw that he had been stitched up like some kind of cloth sewn together, and yet the healing was working quite effectively. Looking about, he could see that he was lying in a bed made of the same cloth that had been used to bandage his hand. It was a pale white color and not the cleanest linen he had ever seen. It was filled with straw and the discovery made him think of his own bed at home. He thought how his mother would have never allowed the cloth to become so dirtied. Nevertheless, it served as a comfortable nesting spot for the moment. Oh, how he missed his family. He quickly tried to remove the thought and just lay in that spot for a few minutes trying to clear his head. He had no idea how long he had been in the room.

The space itself had no windows and only mud packing for walls. Pieces of timber stuck through at various places where one could see light from the outside. At the moment, a drafty cold breeze was blowing in tiny flakes of snow, and it caused the still misty air to swirl about like tiny dancing crystal formations. The chill in the air kept Jonathan longer in his comfortable bed as he tried to think things through.

No one else was present in the room, but beyond a door he could see that he was still in the building he had been in earlier. What he thought to be candles when he had first arrived were not candles at all, but rather small wick-like sticks that had been lit aflame. They burned slowly, and from the tiny yellow wisps that emanated from them, he surmised that they must have been the source of the misty atmosphere, an atmosphere that continued to cloud his head. For the moment, it was a peaceful and quiet place with only the snow-filled breeze making itself known as it sneaked its way through the cracks in the walls. However, that serene atmosphere was soon shattered when the door crashed open and the boisterous voice of Wisekoff broke the stillness:

"Da' plans got to be reworked, dat's all," Wisekoff nearly shouted to a group of fighters that were dressed just like the dark-clad girl had been earlier. When six or seven of them had come through, Jonathan could see that Katelyn was among them as well. With the intrusion, he closed his eyes and pretended to still be asleep.

"We don't have the time to," replied one of the men in the group.

"Keep your voices down," Katelyn interrupted as she made her way to the open door that separated Jonathan from them.

Jonathan could feel the eyes of Katelyn upon him as he continued to pretend to be asleep. He even let out a few snores to sell it. She then gently closed the door behind her. Jonathan opened his eyes, but then could not clearly hear the voices beyond the door. He quietly arose from the bed and made his way closer. That was when he discovered that he had been dressed in a similar outfit to the group of fighters that had filled the next room over.

His bottom half was arrayed in a set of black breeches that were loose enough to be comfortable and warm, but not loose enough to cause him to stumble. His top half was made of the same black fabric which more closely hugged his body with just enough tautness to be functional. Upon closer examination, he noticed that the cloth contained hundreds of tiny upside-down acorn looking attachments. Inside the objects, tiny filaments of fiber faced each other like miniscule spider webs. What they were for was simply a mystery to him. When Jonathan had made his way closer to the door, he felt the lightness of his feet which were clothed with a set of leather soled shoes that were fur lined in the interior. They allowed him to walk more quietly than he had ever been able to do before, and his stealthy approach to the door went undetected.

"We have to get the devices back today, Wisekoff," stated one voice. "They haven't done anything with them yet and that's simply because they don't know what they are. There's time, but not much," the voice continued.

"We think the gathering is still set for three days from now. The discovery won't change the rally, but the location will most likely change. I overheard them talking about Mocker's bridge," said another voice, this time female.

"We can't be havin' things always goin' our way. Dere' be times when we gots' to step back into the shadows. Besides, dem' leaders be knowin' sometins' happenin' and they probably gonna' suspend the talkings'."

Jonathan could make out that Wisekoff must have been a leader of some sort of fighting group, but it wasn't clear what they had been fighting for, who they had been fighting, and why. As he continued to listen at the door, one thing became clear and that was the fact that whatever they had been planning, they were calculating that Jonathan would be a part of it.

"We got's a fighter in da' other room dat' be the best shot I'd ever seen."

"But can we trust him?" A voice questioned.

"You be leavin' dat' up to me and Katelyn," Wisekoff told him.

"That's right, you know. We could use your help in some things," declared a voice behind Jonathan and it startled him so much so that he fell over.

It made him feel like the same kid that used to spy on his parents as they would discuss various topics after they had put him and Samuel down for the night. The voice belonged to Katelyn.

"I thought that you might have been faking," she continued… "It was the fake snorts."

"Where did you come from? You were just in the other room," Jonathan blushed.

"The first lesson that you should learn about our group is stealth… That's what the clothes are for."

Jonathan was again captivated by her beauty. She had come through an opening in the wall that seemed to be nothing more than a decayed part of it. "What group?" Jonathan asked brushing aside the fact that he had just been spying in on their conversation.

"We are a clandestine group that fights for the Nasgroth and Prince of Gish. We call ourselves, The Shade."

"Who are you fighting?"

"Unbelievers. There are people in this city that don't agree with the way things are run according to the rules of the

Gish. If we are to ever have our rightful place in this world, we must subdue any rebellion that threatens to rise up. There is coming a day when we will grow beyond the poverty of this city and extend our lands into other lands... even into other realms."

"Who is Wisekoff then?" asked Jonathan.

"He's the leader of The Shade. We've grown to over one hundred fighters and we've been given charge of quenching uprisings within the city, but we started with just two. Him and me. There are other groups as well, sects that move beyond the city to other lands. There are also scouts that are in charge of reconnaissance. Still, there are other tribes that are charged with other aspects of the kingdom's plans."

"The kingdom?" Jonathan questioned.

"Yes, but not the kingdom that you know. There's another one that's coming and will far surpass any that has come before. And our prince, our king, has promised riches beyond compare. He promises a life of abundance that we have never known not only in this life, but in another one to come. We want you to join our cause. Wisekoff sees a future for you in this grand vision."

"I can't join your cause. I don't know anything about it. I just... I just want to get home to the life I once knew." replied Jonathan.

"Are you sure? You hesitated. Did you really have the freedom that you desired? I know something of your former kingdom. It's a life of *nichism*." stated Katelyn.

"Nichism?" questioned Jonathan through a wrinkled nose.

"I call that what you were born into, nichism. It's the fact that the box of a life that you were born into, your niche, you can't ever escape from. It's a certain life, that you are destined to live in forever with no hope of ever changing. It's where you start and where you end. What kind of life is that?"

"How do you know these things?" asked Jonathan stunned by her knowledge as if she were reading his mind, or at least one corner of it.

"I was from your realm once. I know how stifling it can be. It was a life of laws and rules with little room for freedom. I was taken from there when I was much younger, and I'm grateful that I was," she triumphantly declared.

Jonathan could hardly believe what he was hearing, but nevertheless, he had been feeling the same way.

"What about your family?"

"You just met them."

The statement was followed by a long pause that Jonathan pondered upon.

"I remember you from the Blossom Festivals you know," continued Katelyn. "I also played the pig chasing games!" Katelyn shot at him with disgust in her voice.

Jonathan was dumbfounded and could not find the words to return with. For as many years as he could remember, he never thought that anyone had felt the same way that he did. He had for years tucked his frustration into the pocket of his heart and never allowed anyone to know. Yet, here was a girl from his own realm and God only knew how many miles away, with the same thoughts and feelings as his own.

"You should come with us tonight," Katelyn stated. "See what we're about. You will see what the rebellion is like, and you can make up your own mind whether we stand for what is right."

Jonathan felt a pang of guilt within his heart as if he were about to agree to sell his soul to something that he had always heard was a place of only darkness. His father had long ago made it clear that what lay beyond the realm was a place of not only darkness, but evil as well, a place he didn't have to think about. Sure, he had been faced with strange new things that had occurred. Sure, the city smelled like a constant barrage of sewage. Sure, there were ugly things in the streets, but in his darkest hour he had found help, he had been cared for, and he had been taken in as one of their own.

"Sure. I'll come with you... why not?"

He had been introduced to a group of ten fighters of The Shade which included Katelyn and himself and they departed from the tall, crooked building by the way that Katelyn had entered his room. As they squeezed through the crevice, Jonathan discovered that the walls were built together in such a way that everything was merely a leaning facade of what it stood before, thereby creating niches that were camouflaged by dirt and shadows. As they stealthily traveled, the thought that coursed through Jonathan's mind was that whoever had designed the city was truly a master architect. It was a different sort of 'nichism', and it was simply brilliant.

They were like leaping cats as they crossed from roof top to roof top, corner to corner although he himself felt like a bumbling idiot as they leaped lighter than air their leaps before him. More than once, he had made noises that caused the others to shoot him with looks of frustration as he tried to overcome the residual pain that was throughout his body and most notably in his hand. At the same time, he had impressed himself with the fact that he could keep up at all. Katelyn had more than one time tried to explain to him how to maneuver a certain set of obstacles, but he quickly discovered that it was easier to simply observe the others as they maneuvered before him. By witnessing their fluid movements, he surprised himself by the fact that he could mimic their efforts and more than one time, he felt like a human weapon rather than just wielding one.

They had been trained in some sort of acrobatic method and they moved silently upon the rooftops and through windows. The strange design of their clothing seemed to absorb the surrounding sounds allowing them to be that much more silent. The bridges served as springboards for great leaps from one place to another. The dugout windows served as mere step stools to higher buildings. Ropes used to dry clothes became death-defying swings from great heights to even greater ones and the thought more than once crossed Jonathan's mind that perhaps the city was created more for them than for the actual citizenry. Their clothes also afforded them the ability to hide in shadows undetected, or more appropriately, in the shade. At one point, Katelyn had stopped the group as they hid in the shadow of a roof top. Passing within a mere arm's length from their still bodies, residents walked by completely oblivious to their close proximity. It was altogether thrilling and ominous as Jonathan observed how easily the citizenry could have been taken out if the Shade had so desired.

He was just beginning to get a handle on the mode of transportation and was actually starting to enjoy it when the group had stopped at an overlook that was far above one of the squares that lay in the city. Far below, they could see that a group of men had gathered in the center of it to discuss some issues. They were too far up to make out the voices, but the men were holding some kind of objects in their hands. The devices themselves looked like tiny barrels made of wood not much larger that a child's hand. The men were turning them over in their hands as if they were trying to figure out what their purposes were for.

"They've found more of them. I'm sure they've discovered the whole lot," stated one of the fighters who had piercing eyes and possessed the same shadowy substance on his cheeks that Katelyn had. In fact, all of them were dressed so similarly that they looked as though they were one.

"We need to get them back sooner rather than later," stated Katelyn to the group. "Wisekoff should be making his way into the square within a few minutes, and we need to be in place when he does."

Katelyn motioned for the others to pull away from their perch and selected four of them to descend into the square. Three others were directed to take up defensive positions somewhat lower than they were, but still far enough above the square to attack if need be. Jonathan observed the girl as she directed the group with the confidence of a seasoned veteran, and he pondered in his heart how many of the 'attacks' she had orchestrated. She was a cunning warrior, and it left a lasting impression upon him. With the seven other Shade warriors ordered to their posts, three were left on the roof top… Katelyn, Jonathan, and one other.

"I'll need you to take out the men with the barrels when I tell you too, but we'll have to wait for Wisekoff's signal," she ordered the fighter. "I could use your help here as well," she stated to Jonathan.

The anticipation of the attack was palpable, and Jonathan thought about how much he had dreamed about such a moment. He would have never experienced anything like this in his hometown. He was more than ready to lend a helping hand simply for the fact that it would be the very first time that he had ever used his skills in real battle.

"I'm in," he replied.

Katelyn produced a bone-handled dagger from the folds of her clothing and handed it Jonathan. The other fighter had produced his own set of them.

"Wait for my signal, and don't cut your hand again." she said with a slight smile.

Far below, Jonathan could see Wisekoff finally making his way in the direction of the group of men still discussing the affair. The way in which he had moved made it seem as though he were just one more of the zombed people, for there were many other folks in the square as well.

'Quite the actor', thought Jonathan to himself.

From his height above, he could see that the people of the city were truly more aimless than he had previously realized. Most, it seemed, simply turned in circles without purpose and without direction. Then, a thought occurred to him. Perhaps the Shade's mission was to make a difference in the lost souls of the citizenry and in fact it was the rebels who were the ones that were making the situation worse… maybe even pushing the Serpents Breath upon them, thereby brainwashing and dulling their senses to the grand plan that Katelyn had talked about. Either way, it didn't matter to the young man. For the first time in his life he was given the chance to use the weapons he so longed to utilize and finally realized what he and his Da's weapons were good for. The whole experience was mind-numbing, yet thrilling.

The other fighter that had been waiting next to Jonathan produced a small vial and opened it to take a breath of the substance. Afterwards, he handed it to Jonathan.

"I created those devices you know, Jayden's the name," whispered the Shade member as he presented his hand to Jonathan.

"Yeah?" questioned Jonathan as he returned the handshake with his good hand.

"The contents are under a tremendous amount of pressure, see. Throw in some of my secret ingredients and…" Jayden pulled his hand back and made it into a fist and threw out his fingers to mimic the tiny barrel. "Here, try some. It'll sharpen your senses, but I didn't create this."

"Is it Serpent's Breath?" Jonathan questioned.

"Yeah, but a much lighter version," the soldier chuckled. "The heavy stuff, what's in the barrels, that will not only Zomb ya' instantly, but will kill you as well."

Jonathan hesitated as if something on the inside were warning him, but then decided to breathe in the fragrance which was sharp and bitter to the senses, but instantly a surge of energy shot through his mind, and he felt the same feeling he had when he had reached the top of the stairs a few days prior.

Katelyn and the two watched Wisekoff as he slowly meandered his way closer to the men holding the barrels. He pretended to stumble near them and as he did, a small explosion of smoke fill the air.

"Now," yelled Katelyn, "Take them out."

Jonathan watched as Jayden let his dagger fly. It was an extensive and high distance, but he had timed his throw so that the projectile lodged into the neck of one of the men holding a small barrel. He instantly dropped to the ground and the object rolled away freely. Jonathan was shocked to see the gruesome sight, but he could also see the first four fighters that Katelyn had sent into the square making their way in the direction of the scene. As they approached, they were hesitant for there were still two other men that continued to hold on to their objects.

That's when everything slowed down in his vision. Jonathan realized that he had been delaying the plan and his comrades below were waiting for the rebels to be taken out. The other fighter was beginning to throw another dagger when Jonathan spied his target, locked it in, and closed his eyes... the signature of his form... With all of his strength he let his projectile fly, being careful not to let the blade slice his hand again.

It tumbled end over end, and just as he was opening his eyes again, he could see the blade sink into the side of the tiny barrel that one of the other men had been holding. It exploded and released an inky black substance that filled the air with an acrid smoke.

The third man dropped as the second dagger of Jayden's sank deep into his back. He too slumped to the ground. As for the one that Jonathan had managed to wrench the barrel from, he was trying to flee the scene while gagging and running with all of his strength. Before he could escape the square though, the three other Shade fighters that were perched a little lower killed him with some arrow shots that knocked him from his feet.

The chaos that Jonathan was expecting in the streets far below never materialized as the three dead men became just three more bodies that the city had swallowed into its dark throat.

The remaining barrels were never recovered due to the deadly smoke that filled the square. Jonathan watched from far above as Wisekoff made a signal with his hand telling all fighters to return to the home base. Katelyn motioned to Jonathan to follow her, and together they commenced to scamper over roof tops and obstacles back in the direction that they had come from, only occasionally having to hide in the shadows.

When they had finally arrived back at the room, they were the first to get there. As the others trickled in, they eyed Jonathan with a wary look. Finally, Wisekoff entered and dug into him with the anger of a fierce jackal:

"Why you be hesistaten! We could have been killt'! And we lost our bangs! We brought you cause we taut' you could help. As it turned out, we lost all our barrels cause' you!" Katelyn was trying to calm Wisekoff's temper, but he would have nothing of it, "What be your answer, statue! Speak you!" Wisekoff continued.

"What's so special about those devices anyway?" Jonathan bit back.

"It takes us weeks to harvest those concentrations of Serpent's Breath," shouted the fighter that had been on the rooftop with Jonathan and Katelyn.

"You broke da' barrel instead of killin' da' man," added Wisekoff.

"I can't kill a man," Jonathan softened.

"You have to be killin' if you wants' to be a Shade!" Wisekoff screamed as he continued to dig into the young man.

Jonathan just turned his head away, "It's not my decision to make," he nearly whispered as adolescent tears threatened to leak out, for he was remembering the long ago words of Bart of the Forest.

"What you be sayin?" Wisekoff continued.

"It's not my decision to make!" Jonathan shouted.

"You right there… It be mine!" was Wisekoff's reply. "I'm da' Nasgroth of this group and my word stands firm!"

"I don't need this!" Jonathan shouted in return, "I don't even know what you're fighting for or who you're fighting. You yourselves may be the enemy for all I know. I may have a talent, but I'm not going to let you exploit it… Find someone else to do your thieven' work," Jonathan finished and made his way around the broken part of the floor he had fallen through.

For a moment, he stopped to look into it, and could see that it fell the full distance to the tavern far below…

"Dat's just…" Wisekoff interrupted his own thoughts. "Katelyn saved your butt as you be fallin' through, statue. Kept you from breakin' into a million pieces wit' her rope around your chicken leg."

"Is that true?" Jonathan asked her. She just nodded her head in acknowledgement. "Well, thank you then," he said and continued on his path out of the room.

When one of the Shade fighters attempted to block his path, to even his own surprise, he quickly made the man fall to his knees with a well-placed kick to them. Others quickly responded and followed after, trying to grab hold of the weapon master's son, but Wisekoff forbade them with a wave of his hand.

"You be getting' lost out in da' streets tonight!" Wisekoff yelled after him.

Jonathan turned upon the top of the stairs:

"I don't need you to survive. I don't need any of you. You're not my family."

"We be seein' how you do den'," Wisekoff returned. "You be not knowin' what's out dere jn da' darkness, boy."

Jonathan didn't even acknowledge him and simply continued down the creaky wooden staircase, ever descending closer and closer to the ground floor of the crooked building. At the bottom he hesitated, and for a moment looked back up in the direction of the room, but without another thought he departed from the building and into the darkened alley, thinking that he would never return to that place again.

The snow that had been falling had already begun to stick to the ground a few inches thick and as he walked into the streets once again, he was thankful for the new clothes he had been given.

That evening was spent in search of shelter. As the sun set, Jonathan noticed that there was a stirring in the streets of the city. Everywhere, the wandering souls that seemed to be aimless before were suddenly scrambling to find shelter. Alley after alleyway passed by him as he himself began to aimlessly wander the streets. Merchants were closing their shops and boarding up their stalls. It was as if someone had blown out the candle of the city. At all intersections, people sought places to get into the protection of the structures. More than one time, when Jonathan had tried to enter a pub or a tavern to get out of the elements of the night, he was denied a place to stay. As the sun cast its last shadow upon the streets, he felt as though he was the only soul not to have found a place of shelter, save for a few other stragglers who were deeply zombed.

He was not quite sure how long or how far he had traveled when he finally found a set of wooden boxes that were stacked up in the dead-end of an alleyway. With no other choice, he climbed into one of the crates and tried to settle in for the night.

The snowstorm had increased to the point where it was hard to even see the opening of the corridor at the street that ran by. Near the position where he was located, he could see that another person had failed to find shelter or had become too exhausted to make it to the set of crates that he himself was housed within. He thought about helping the poor wretch and was just about to leave the comfort of his box to assist the other person when he spied an ominous sight indeed.

It was a set of tracks, and they were making their way down the dead-end side street.

As the tracks came closer, he could see that it was actually two sets of tracks. To his shock and horror, there were no figures attached to the steps that were continuing in his direction. Side by side, invisible feet, supposing they were feet at all, were kicking up the snow that had been layered upon the ground.

The specters made their way to the person who had been lying in the alleyway. Then, invisible hands grabbed the unfortunate soul by one leg and commenced to drag him off into the fury of the storm. Jonathan could hear the protests of the person fade into the distance as the silence of the falling snow swallowed the cries.

He couldn't even begin to imagine what or who had taken the poor lost human, not to mention to what destination.

When all grew quiet again, Jonathan just sat in his box shuddering, not so much from the chill of the night's snowstorm, but more from what he had just witnessed. His ability to sleep failed him, and that left him longing for a warm and dry place; any place, if but to just rest, sleep…

Aye, perhaps even, to dream.

Chapter 5

Buying In

†

The Bridge Ordeal

Snow had fallen throughout the night, burying Jonathan's makeshift house beneath it. At some point during the storm the thickness created a blanket that contained his body's warmth; warmth that only came long after shivering for hours. If it had not been for the garments that Wisekoff had arrayed him in, he would have surely succumbed to hypothermia. As it was, the few moments he did spend trying to concentrate on keeping his eyes closed distracted him from the fact that his fingertips were beginning to suffer from frost nip. He would have tried to remedy the situation if he had not finally fallen asleep.

She approached his location like a cat clad in black. Perhaps she hadn't seen him, for she knelt down near the little creek to take a drink. Scooping the water into her cupped hand made her look as though she were a seasoned fighter for as she lapped it, she simultaneously scouted her surroundings. It was a precaution that he himself would have taken. The rippling light effect that the sun created as its rays glanced off the water, coupled with the morning mist, made the whole sight seem dreamlike. Jonathan continued to watch as she looked about herself. The contours of her shadowed face confirmed to his heart that she was beautiful indeed and he was captivated by her.

When she at last stood to her feet, Jonathan could see that a weapon was dangling at her side, having been slung over her shoulder with a leather strap. Its latter part was supported by one end of the said strap and it looked like some sort of cross, only there was a sinewy string strung across the beams. That's when he realized that the weapon was a crossbow.

He continued to be captivated as he watched her pull an arrow from a small quiver that was tied to her right thigh. She then loaded the shaft into its firing position and began to raise it in his direction. Her face was still hidden, and he was scarce to make out her features other than her silhouette. And then a thought struck his heart... Is she going to aim the arrow right at me?

He had been so captured by her image that his hands had started to fall asleep and the numbing effect screamed for his attention. When he tried to shake the feeling free, the motion woke him up.

When he finally came back around that morning, a burning and stinging sensation was making its way up his forearm and ever closer to his already slowly beating heart. Jonathan felt like a caged animal as he finally opened his eyes. His first sight was that of the wood-crate slats that held back the built-up snow above him. The first sound that he heard was the voice of an old woman mumbling and complaining to herself about the white stuff that had never fallen in such large amounts before as she passed down the alleyway next to his hovel. And his first thoughts were of how far he had wandered from everything he had ever known while growing up. Though he missed that life, it was quickly pushed to the back portions of his mind as he was then stirred by the fact that he would have to figure out how to survive in the strange new world that he had suddenly become a part of.

From the outside, it would have looked as though an animal were emerging from an eggshell. The ice and snow cracked in large chunks as Jonathan lifted the crate from off of his self. His hands were still stinging as blood rushed into the veins of his fingers, but at least they were still functioning. He winced as he threw the weight of his house across the alleyway and stood nearly dazed as it broke into several pieces.

The sun, reflecting off of the snow-covered landscape, threatened to blind him and made the people meandering past the alleyway appear as though they were merely shadowed figures. Hunger and thirst had also abandoned him, and he only had enough strength to shuffle his feet in the white substance that had blanketed the mucky streets of Gish. Jonathan tried to find traces of the mysterious tracks from the previous night, but the populous had already trampled them down. He swore at himself wishing he had asked the Shade fighters to give him something to eat. His head pounded as he tried to contemplate his next move.

If he had had the strength to survey his surroundings more closely, he would have seen that the alley had dumped him into the middle of a marketplace. And, if he had had the desire to listen to his surroundings, he would have heard the liveliness of the city that sounded as if life had been injected into it as some new rumor was being talked about. As it was, however, the cacophony of sound just echoed in the distance as he more or less tuned everything out and turned inward like a man that looks at himself from somewhere in the distance. Sometime between his contemplations of self-preservation and utter fatigue, he never realized that he was becoming like many of the other zombed folks of that place.

It took him all day to walk across the city and when he finally got to the outskirts, a barren desert stared him in the face, a flat lifeless landscape stretching out into the distance. If it were not for the icy wind that began to pierce the corners of his eyes, he most likely would have continued right out into the expanse and off into oblivion. However, the waning remnants of sensation served him well and caused him to turn away from the biting air and back in the direction of the city once again. With no other thought than to get out of the wind, he then began to walk back into the filthy streets that had begun to grow hard and frozen as speculative thought faded and foggy dimness set in.

Jonathan would not remember the days he spent completely wandering about the city like a lost sheep. However, even in his near zombed state, he had just enough wits to get out of the elements of the night that lurked in the streets of Gish when night had cascaded over the populous. Other than that, he was completely oblivious to his surroundings and meandered between slow and near-stopped cadences for three full days.

When night had begun to blanket the city on the third night, his demeanor had sunken so low that he most likely would not have even noticed the nightfall if it were not for the sudden thud of an escaped wooden cart that plowed right into him.

As for the cart, it hit him square in the backside and threw Jonathan clear across the street where he struck his face on the cold hardened ground. Consequently, it was exactly what he had needed at the time, and it served to bring him back to his senses.

Jonathan shook his head and wiped the blood free from his nose. It was warm on his ghostly white hand, and it reminded him that he was still alive. He found it difficult to stand upon his feet at first, but when he discovered the contents of the cart, life suddenly rushed into his being, for contained within the rotted wooden contraption was a plethora of moldy apples, some bits of crusty bread, some other bruised fruit, and leather-like pieces of dried meat which seemed to be smiling at him. To outsiders, it would have been a revolting meal, but to our homeless, wandering, would-be hero, it was a feast fit for a king.

Jonathan tore into it with the ferocity of a wolf and didn't even think about how it had come to him. In fact, he barely even noticed the form of an old man holding a crooked cane that lay just a few paces away. It was the same one he had encountered days prior. The old wretch had been pushing the cart when his strength had suddenly given away and his frame crumbled, causing him to shove the cart into Jonathan's back.

The food, as terrible as it was, brought strength to the young man who was thankful for the other old man's misfortune, for his life had suddenly become a game of survival rather than a mere zombed existence. He ate every bit of the disgusting morsels and it allowed him to think a bit more clearly than he had been for the past few days. The body of the old man still lay on the ground, and he thought it proper to make an attempt at finding a family member or friend. Surely, there is someone who knows the old creature, thought Jonathan to himself. Looking about however, he quickly discovered that he and the ancient man were the only ones in the immediate area.

Jonathan dragged the old man to a resting place near a side street. He was just starting to scurry away when the man whacked him with his crooked cane and reached out to him with gnarled old fingers, attempting to talk. However, only whispers came forth. Jonathan leaned in close to listen.

"Take the cart, I have no more need for it," Jonathan pulled back believing the man to be expiring, but he grabbed him once again, "Bring out the prisoners." He then closed his eyes and laid his head on the cold ground.

Jonathan, believing the old wretch to be truly dying, took the man's overcoat which was long and full of holes, nevertheless, it would be one more covering to drape over his still shivering body. He then took up the old cart. It was made of a ragged gnarly frame, similar to the man himself. The wheels swayed with creaking noises as it moved making it that much more difficult to pull. Regardless, Jonathan figured that the cart could be used for something; anything for it had suddenly become his only earthly possession.

He slipped on hardened mud that had begun to submit to the freeze of the waxing night once again. With much difficulty, Jonathan had managed to make his way down two side streets and around four corners. He then found himself in a square full of shivering people. The sun that was starting to sink deeper upon the horizon beyond the smoke of the city beckoned them to find shelter with its last rays. However, they continued to linger a little longer for the place was lit up with activity.

Parking the cart near a corner building, he stepped into the crowd of people that were talking amongst each other. There was an air of anticipation as nightfall approached and he spied a lady on the edges of a conversation who seemed to be listening intently to what a certain gentleman had been describing. The people of that area of the city seemed to have a little more life in them than any of the others that he had seen thus far.

"Yes, it will still take place tonight at Mocker's Bridge," answered a man wearing a long overcoat whose bottom was muddy and frayed. He possessed a long nose that looked as though it came to a perfect point on the end of his face, a face that was gaunt and sunken. In fact, if it were not for the skin covering, Jonathan thought that he could have passed for a living walking skeleton.

"Where is Mocker's Bridge?" asked Jonathan as he interrupted the man.

"You're not from here, hey?" questioned the man.

"No, just passing through."

"No one just passes through," chuckled the man. "But if you're interested, it's just down Straight Street there. Look for the lit torches. If nothing else, come for the warmth of the flames," he pointed over his shoulder.

The others in the small group of citizens looked at Jonathan with emotionless expressions. It never occurred to him that he was returning their gaze with the same emotionless look as they themselves had, but the prospect of warmth was intriguing.

"What of the trackers," asked the woman that Jonathan had been standing near. No one answered the question and left it hanging in the air like a swirl of smoke that refuses to dissipate.

"Does anyone know the owner of that old cart over there?" Jonathan interrupted again as he pointed to the dilapidated crooked contraption. He was met with more of the emotionless gazes as the people just shook their heads. "Well, at least I tried to help the man," he mused to himself, and quickly moved himself back to where the cart was located.

Even the meager amount of conversation had taken its toll on his still weakened frame, and he thought it better not to engage in any more of them. His thoughts drifted once again to his own survival, but what could he do with an old, abandoned cart? For the moment, he thought that he had better find a place to park it quickly as the rapidly approaching nightfall continued its curtain-like drop across the city. Apparently, the others in the square had thought the same thing for they themselves began to disburse as well. Jonathan managed to push the old cart across the street and down another one of the many dead-end alleys that seemed to be the end product of most of the streets in the City of Gish.

Nightfall then fell rapidly as if the sun had finally ducked for cover. Jonathan chose not to wander very far from the cart, and it was a good thing for every door that he had tried to enter was suddenly closed in his face yet again. A light snowfall began, and a chilling wind crept its way through the streets. The cold was bone-piercing and the thought of another appearance by the mysterious 'trackers' made the weather feel that much colder. Jonathan then found a purpose for the old apple cart. He flipped it over and made it his new home.

Approximately one hour into the darkness of the nightfall, he heard a commotion that sounded like a gathering of people cutting its way through the silence that the falling snow was trying to swallow. He remembered about the meeting at Mocker's Bridge, but the ever-looming image of the tracks appearing once again kept him hidden in his hovel.

Jonathan wrestled with the prospect for some time before finally giving in to the more curious, if not dangerous side of his nature. Lifting the cart with it still resting on his back, he peered out from beneath its protection and discovered that there was not a soul, nor a track to be seen. The decision to leave the relative comfort of his shelter was not an easy one, but nevertheless he made it simply for the prospect of the tantalizing warmth of the torchlight fires.

The black shoes on his feet kept them somewhat warm as he watched the snow scamper away with each new step. Looking about, he found himself to be at an elbow near the square that he had been at earlier. From there, he hugged the walls of the buildings and made his way in the direction that the man had pointed him toward. Finding Straight Street was easy, for although there was no street sign per say, it was the only road that stretched out in one continuous direction for more than an half a block and had no apparent dead-end. Peering down the expanse and through the silent falling snow, Jonathan could see a faint orange glow in the distance and surmised it to be the meeting at Mocker's Bridge.

He then felt like a mouse making his way beneath a sky full of eagles as he inched closer to the gathering of people. At long last, he arrived at a position where he could observe the gathering and still be hidden in the shadows that lay beyond the reach of the flickering flames upon the bridge. His instinct kept him from rushing to the fire's warmth, and he removed the old man's overcoat to take full advantage of the black clothing that had been given to him by the Shade.

The bridge itself was made of large blocks of stone. To Jonathan, it was the largest bridge he had ever seen. It spanned the ravine with a curvature thereby forcing it to have to be longer than any of the others. It had a bowing effect that was supported by large columns of rock at different intervals. Wooden cross beams made up the railings which were connected by rock pillars. In the middle, and at the apex of the bow, a tower was erected that was supported by two more arched rock formations that formed a tunnel beneath. The thought that struck Jonathan was that this was the only structure in the entire city, or at least what he had seen of the city, that was constructed of rock. Every other building, or structure, or square had been formed from the pale, shaded, mud-packed construction held together with endless amounts of timber.

Atop the tower of Mocker's Bridge, a small platform jutted out with railings that had shackles attached to it. Behind the platform, Jonathan could see that the walls were stained with the fruit and foods that were most likely used to mock whatever hungry prisoner happened to be present. Hence the name, Mocker's Bridge. What a person could do that would break the law in a place like the Gish puzzled him to no end.

At that moment, there were no prisoners, and no one was being mocked, but the bridge was certainly filled with people. Many of them were huddled near the burning torches and there was a small group of men standing upon a makeshift platform of large barrels. He was too far away to hear what they were saying but could see many in the crowd nodding their approvals. He thought better of trying to join the group on the bridge but was curious to hear what was being said. At long last, he decided to inch his way closer in the direction of the gathered crowd.

It was at that same moment that a series of small explosions occurred in quick succession one after the other.

They began on the far end and steadily grew closer to the group gathered to hear the speakers. Jonathan could see the puffs of yellow substance begin to flood the area. Then, upon the bridge closest to his location, more of the tiny explosions of deep yellow, almost orange substance made their way in the opposite direction. With each new explosion the crowd grew with panic as the floating acrid smoke began to drive the people toward the center of the bridge where the speakers were still upon the barreled stage. The speaking men fruitlessly began to calm the crowd. Suddenly, just as he was about to flee the area, Jonathan spied a shadowy image racing through the crowd of people and toward the platform. He then witnessed a sight so devastating that it would shatter his image of right and wrong for years to come.

It was one of the Shade members, and Jonathan seemed to be the only one to catch site of the shadowed figure. All at once, he recognized the one… It was Katelyn.

He watched, dumbstruck, as she made her way to the barreled stage where the crowd had been forced to gather. Through the feet of the people and at the base of the platform,

Jonathan could see her fidgeting with something. Even from his great distance, he could see that her hands were shaking terribly. Then, in an instant, the barrels exploded with such force that a wave of air lifted those closest to the platform completely from off their feet including Katelyn who was flipped into the air like a limp rag. Then the square became so thick with the orange turned black substance that he could no longer see any of the bridge, save for the mocker's platform far above.

Jonathan sunk deeper into the shadows, horrified by what he had just been a witness too. The smoke-like substance swirled in shapes that almost looked like twisted faces peering down at the victims underneath and it occurred to him that it was a terrible irony indeed for they had morphed into looks of mockery. Mesmerized by the sight, he stayed until the cloud began to dissipate, but it slowly segued into a much more menacing sight.

In what seemed to be all directions, people were being dragged away by the same invisible creatures that he had seen trudging through the snow, nights earlier. The yells pierced the air as bodies were being taken below the bridge, one by one. Among those still lying in a daze, the Shade warrior Katelyn was so stunned by the impact that she lay halfway over one of the railings on the bridge. He would have thought that she was stretched over it upon her stomach if it were not for the fact that her face was pointing upward toward the sky. She had been bent in two like a piece of rope that was slung over the railing. Something must have gone terribly wrong.

Without a thought for himself, he sprang into action before one of the specters could grab his comrade. Driving into the fray, he leaped through the chaos and destruction that was upon the bridge. The residue of the acrid smoke stung his eyes instantly. Immediately, he felt a dizzying effect followed by an instant of nausea. It smelled similar to the yellowish smoke he had already encountered, but it seemed to be rotted and foul. It took all of the little strength that he possessed just to reach Katelyn. Once there, he could see that the girl was still alive, but only barely.

"Katelyn?"

"John." Her voice was just as broken as her body. "How'd I do?"

"Great friend… you did great," having no clue to what she was referring too.

Jonathan tried to pull her from the bridge as gently as he could, but the pain must have been excruciating for a moment later, she had grown silent from it. He could hear a second wave of trackers taking people from somewhere behind him, but he continued to push back from off of the bridge.

His strength was failing, and his knees began to buckle not only from his own weight, but from that of the girl as well. He yelled and pulled himself further until he had finally arrived back at the overturned apple cart. It was half buried in the snow, but he was immensely relieved to see that it was still there. He raised it with great difficulty and had just enough time to push Katelyn underneath before passing out next to it.

He would have pulled himself underneath as well, but even in his dire condition, he thought it not the proper thing to do.

✝

Throne Under

His nest was rustled and the snow was swept aside, allowing sunlight to stream around the rotted wood of the old cart.

"How been your night, statue? You be froze like marble," came the cackling, nasally voice of Wisekoff.

Jonathan was repulsed and thankful all at the same time. The utter loneliness that had engulfed him for the past few nights, coupled with the bridge ordeal had allowed room for their previous encounter to instantly fade into forgiveness.

"Hey, you be in there?" Wisekoff asked as he more or less hammered on the side of the crate. "You be in a crate or a casket? Stay any longer and we be buryn' ya'."

"How'd I get in here?" Jonathan questioned from the interior of his tomb.

"Ah, Wisekoff and da' boys helped ya'… again." he chuckled. "We's startin' to form a habit o' this, statue."

"Where's Katelyn?" Jonathan's voice sounded raspy, tired, worn out.

"I think she be okay. How bout' you? You gonna' make it, dirt chewr?"

Jonathan crawled out from underneath his hovel like a worm emerging from an apple core. He was so ragged that it looked as though the apple cart had completely run him over, not once, but numerous times.

"Look what da' Gish coughed up. I don't tink' I seen a more pitiful sight in all me life," Wisekoff spewed out as spittle sprayed the young man.

"Is dat' yo' idea of a washin'?" mused Jonathan.

"Ah, der's da' wit again. Good. We friends'till. I tank' ya' for that… Follow, statue. I gots' to be showin' ya' something." Wisekoff waved him along like a giddy school child again and Jonathan knew what the implications could mean. Nevertheless, the endearing quality that Wisekoff possessed somehow captured his curiosity yet again, and off they went; the latter staggering like an old, achy wretch.

"You done a good ting', weapon master," stated Wisekoff as they both trudged through the streets of the city.

"Weapon master would be my father," replied Jonathan wryly.

"Don't be correctin' old Wisekoff. I knows' what I'm be sayin.'

They continued through square after square, past street after street, and down alleyway after alleyway. Many of them appeared to be dead ends, but mysteriously led to other streets. They had, however, appeared to be nothing more than roads leading to nowhere. It was not until one would reach the end that another would open. The optical illusion caused Jonathan's mind to become deluded again and he found it hard to concentrate as Wisekoff whisked him along as he done before.

Thoughts of the previous nights' ordeal surged through his brain like tiny electric lightning strikes. Feelings for Katelyn flooded his soul. Questions convoluted his emotions. People of all sorts, still zombed at various levels, continued to meander all around them, but unlike the time that he had first been escorted into the city by Wisekoff, not one of them bothered the young man. In fact, on more than one occasion, when a merchant or toothless old grinning woman came near with an ever-present outstretched beggar's hand, they would suddenly turn away as if to hide from him. All the while, the streets streamed by like passing arms that reached out to him. At times, he felt as though the city were attempting to beckon him, to gather him, to embrace him; and perhaps it was.

If Jonathan could have been hovering over Gish at some great height above the clouds, he would have seen that it was spread out like a great tablet. The streets of the northern sector, with their endless dead-end alleyways, all arched inward and toward the south. As has been mentioned, Straight Street was the only one of its kind, bisecting the metropolis from east to west. The infamous ravine ran the distance from north to south thereby bisecting the city. Together, they created upon the 'tablet' layout of Gish, a giant cross section that met at none other than Mocker's Bridge.

The myriad of people from that great height would have had no distinguishing features to separate one from the other like ants that all appear to be the brother (or sister) of one another. However, the common theme of all the citizenry, and what would be a stark contrast to that of ants, was the fact that they were not working together toward one goal, whether it be stockpiling food, building a better city, or fighting against some common enemy. No, rather, they looked like a lost litter of pups searching for their mother, or a scattered herd of deer searching for an oasis of water in some desert place.

As for Wisekoff and the Shade, and all of the other fighting sects of that realm, they had found their oasis at the southernmost tip of the city and the citizens had become mere shadows to them as if they were living just a few breadths above their surroundings. The south was where their master resided, and it also happened to be the very place where Wisekoff was leading Jonathan to at the moment.

They walked for hours before they finally arrived at a large piazza. At one time, it could have been considered beautiful, if it were not for the fact that the massive fountain had long been broken, the sub-fountains bone dry, the immense vessels that once housed elegant plants, deeply cracked and rotted, and the ornate buildings, half-crumbled to the ground in a twist of frayed and broken piles of sandstone rubble.

As they entered the square, Jonathan was at his strength's end. He fell to his knees to catch his breath and could see that they had entered the immense piazza by one of three streets that emptied into it. Not a soul was present, but an eerie feeling that they were not alone ran down his spine. He wondered whether the Shade members were watching them from shadowed positions, or one of the other tribes that Katelyn had talked about, or possibly the invisible trackers. An oddly placed warm breeze filled the square... odd because it was still the bitter cold months of winter. Be that as it may, it ran to and fro about the place in tiny circular effects that lifted the snow and litter of the square into the air causing them to dance to their own musical score.

"Wisekoff? Where are we?" Jonathan managed through an exhausted voice.

Wisekoff turned around having missed the fact that Jonathan had fallen to the ground. He turned to ease beneath the young man and lifted him to his feet once again where he was able to support his weight.

Jonathan pondered how much more of the trial his body could endure, or how little. It had been a very long journey thus far; much longer than he had ever dreamed of. He felt more or less like a leaf that had been liberated from a tree only to ride the winds of change and the end result, he surmised, was that he would be trampled upon by some passing war-horse or some rolling weighted-down wagon.

Wisekoff could see that his 'recruit' was at his wit's end. "It be almost over, statue. You be seen' that the ride's been worth it... Da' king of Gish has called for ye'. Forgets all you've been knowin', cause its bout' to change."

Wisekoff more or less carried Jonathan across the piazza and to a giant oaken door. It was fastened with brass fixtures and stood nearly four times their own height. Jonathan was quickened at its sight for he had always heard that only mysteries lay beyond the doors that led to thrones. He had often dreamt of what it would have been like to enter beyond the gates of Kalaw, if it were still standing. He also dreamed of what it would have been like to serve a real king. Alas, they were merely boyhood dreams. However, there must have been some sort of substance to them for as he and Wisekoff stood before the door, those very thoughts sprang to the surface of his being lending him the strength to continue without Wisekoff's help, and he pulled away from his newfound friend.

"Who is this king?" he asked with a reserved giddiness that matched Wisekoff's own.

"Official, he be called Prince Magreth, but we be calln' him our king."

Even before they reached their hands out to knock upon, the door opened for them of its own accord. Together, they entered, and never looked back.

It was a tremendous space that appeared to be a great dining hall and was not what Jonathan had anticipated. All of his boyhood dreams almost seemed dashed to pieces as they stepped into the hall that had long been forgotten. Ancient chandeliers had half-fallen from the ceiling and seemed to be hanging on only by the cobwebs that fastened them to the roof. The candles in them had long lost their waxy substance and were merely stubs of their former selves. So dusty was the floor that it appeared like some dimmed mockery of freshly fallen snow. The middle of the room contained a massive table that nearly spanned the length of the space but contained as much dust and cobwebs as the floor itself. On both ends two fireplaces stood large enough for both Jonathan and Wisekoff to walk into. However, they were merely the younger siblings to the one massive fireplace that stood on the far wall opposite from the door that they had just entered.

The musty air that filled the atmosphere made Jonathan constantly waver upon the edge of a massive sneezing attack, but in its midst, he could sense a trace of the sweet aroma of the yellow mist that had been at the Shade's base. Somehow it seemed sweeter, perhaps even cleaner, as if it were a more purified form of it. It was, however, quite the opposite of the spectrum from the rotted Serpent's Breath that had taken out the bridge. One thing was for certain, thought Jonathan; Gish is a multi-layered city, like an onion that's peeled away with each new step. Little did he know that he was about to cut right through to the core.

"This is his throne room?" he snidely questioned.

"Shhhh," Wisekoff rebuked with a hush. "It not be permitted to speak ere' or anywhere's' near his presence… til' asked." And in an even more hushed tone he continued… "Da' throne room… is under."

They approached the massive fireplace on the far wall after they had taken the journey around the elongated dining table. The food on it was ancient as well, but somehow it was still preserved, still intact, and un-rotted. A hunger pain leaped within Jonathan's stomach, and he grabbed it with his hand as it made a beckoning growl.

"I know. I be hungry too," Wisekoff gestured with his hands and lips without making a sound, and motioned Jonathan to keep following.

As they neared the fireplace, Jonathan could see that there was an opening beneath the metal grate that would have been used to hold logs. As it was, Wisekoff lifted it with his hand and a downward staircase opened below them. It had a narrow opening, and as they entered, the two of them had to practically get on their knees to pass.

It was made of a granite rock roughly hewn and it descended into a deep cavern. Far below, a sound like water rushing down a canyon wall met them. The sweet smell increased ever so slightly, and it strengthened the weapon master's son, nay, even elated him.

They climbed down without saying a word to each other. Deeper and deeper they plunged into the cavern. At some point, the stairs beneath their feet and the substance upon the stairs morphed from granite to marble. It was still roughly hewn but had taken on a cleaner sheen almost as if it were wet with rain. However, Jonathan hardly noticed the change for a sight altogether different had captured his attention. As they proceeded, the walls which were just as roughly hewn as the stairs had begun to give way to shelves filled with plant life that grew in a multitude of various varieties. Not only were they the usual green colored, but different colored ones were beginning to spring forth as well. And the more they descended, the more the variety and colors manifested. All the while, the sound of the river grew louder, and the aroma grew in greater thickness.

Jonathan continually tried to stop to admire and smell the different species, but each time, Wisekoff prodded and urged him to keep going. Finally, at a place where red roses grew in such abundance and were the most brightly colored flowers he had ever seen, he paused, for he simply could not take the curiosity any longer. Fortunately for him, Wisekoff had missed his stopping and continued on without him.

The moment lingered for what seemed to be an eternity as the sweet smell of the fragrance, which had been increasing throughout their descent, emanated from the pedals of the roses. Even the stems and leaves seemed to reek with it. Jonathan was completely captivated. It was the only beauty he had seen in so many days and he relished the change in atmosphere. If there were something redeemable about the Gish thus far, the roses certainly expressed it. They almost seemed to belong to an alternate world. He then reached forth his hand to pluck one of the tiny heavenly plants, but then quickly pulled back for when he had just barely touched one with the mere tip of his finger, it completely disintegrated into dust.

Instant death was the result of his reach. Thinking that it must have been only inherent in the one, he reached for another. Again, it crumbled at the touch. Then he realized that the sweet fragrance was not coming through the plants at all but was merely residual traces that had long ago settled upon them… a residue that preserved it in a façade of life leaving it teetering on the edge of death. Wisekoff interrupted him with a tap on the shoulder, which was followed by a yank on the arm.

Though the discovery was disheartening, the fascination still captivated Jonathan. Though the aroma rising from the depths of the cavern had preserved the plants in a curious state of suspension, their beauty had far surpassed anything else. They reminded him of the flora he had seen in his dreams about the girl, whoever she was. With each new step the cavern became more and more beautiful. Though dimmed, it drew him into a deeper appreciation for the strange city and its mysterious depths.

When they had finally reached the bottom of the staircase, they were met with a being so tall and lean that Jonathan himself felt like a mere sapling, not to mention the effect on Wisekoff. Whoever the being was, it would have caused even Wisekoff's tall twins to have appeared short. It came from behind them and the first sight of its flesh, if one could call it flesh, was of a set of long bony fingers. They could have easily bridged the distance of Wisekoff's forearm and possibly even Jonathan's. Its head was enshrouded, hiding the face somewhere deep within. It wore a long flowing robe made of some kind of shimmering gray substance and it appeared so light that one could almost see entirely through it. As it passed by them, it urged them to follow down a large cavern. The lengthened robe more or less floated behind the creature. As it walked, or floated, it was as silent and as diaphanous as a mid-summer night's breeze. Summer breeze, because it had grown oddly warmer, more humid, yet pleasantly fragrant.

As they followed the stranger, the sound of the cascading river grew fainter behind them and faded to a mere trickle somewhere out front. The mist continued to swirl about the cavern from floor to ceiling amongst the same assortment of plant life, or plant-like life as it were. After following the soundless stranger, they at long last arrived at the opening of another chamber from which emanated not only the sound of the trickling watery noise, but also thicker mists which bellowed forth from the room.

Without a word, the tall one bid them to enter, and then withdrew into the shadows.

"The Throne Room?" mouthed Jonathan to Wisekoff who returned it with merely a nod. Then they entered in hushed awe.

The marble floor of the room had been polished, so much so, that Jonathan could see the shadow of himself and Wisekoff in it. It was pure black with gold settings between each block. Pillars that were fashioned from the same polished stone surrounded the room but half the way up the height of them they blurred gray and segued to a pure white. The mist that filled the chamber wafted not from tiny burning sticks as earlier in his journey, but from the trickling of a creek which flowed from behind the far wall and beyond what appeared to be a great throne.

Captivated by the stream, Jonathan peered deeply into it and could not see the bottom for it was milky white with a tinge of gold. Its fragrance was sweet to the smell just like what he had been experiencing throughout his entire journey but absent from it was the innocuous dizzying effect. In fact, as the mist settled upon his skin, and as he breathed it into his lungs; he felt a strength that he hadn't felt in a very long time. Being in a state of devastating thirst, he could not help but scoop the liquid into his hands, pour it down his throat and into the total emptiness of his barren stomach. He could feel the liquid flow down the full length of his innards, and it was as if he had just woken up from the greatest sleep of his entire life.

Thoughts of cherry blossoms filling the hollow of Safehaven flooded his being. Feelings of family and friends sparked his emotions. And, in some strange way, he felt as if he had been there before as wave after wave of good memories flooded his soul. Then he remembered that the Serpent's Breath had only brought memories and feelings of darkness and fright. The two substances, though similar, were juxtaposed opposites.

Wisekoff interrupted and ushered the young man closer to the foot of the throne. It was raised above them upon a platform of stairs that mirrored the floor and pillars, half-black and half-white. The throne itself, however, was a pure white just as the upper half of the pillars were. In it, the carvings of birds of prey and wild cats of the forest were inlaid with green polished gems. They made him think of his own Emeralhearth stone, absent the flickering light within. He also remembered the blue stones inlaid upon his father's shunt and for a fleeting moment, a knot of remorse etched the contours of his expression. However, the memory of his father's face dammed the flow from fully forming.

Silenced, the young man stood in awe at the great sight which stood before him, for it was perfectly framed. Then, into that frame, entered a figure like an artist that steps into his very own creation. The form appeared from behind a crimson curtain and suddenly all else became paled in comparison.

Prince Margreth was a warrior of immense proportions. As he strode onto the platform, Jonathan's first impression was one of sheer power. His was the presence of a man who causes all to drop what they were doing and to freeze in their tracks. It was an unseen and magnetic force as if wherever he went, though alone, he was never alone. The muscles that rippled beneath his tightly fitted crimson leather garb reminded Jonathan of the strength of the war horse he had once ridden. The upper half of his body formed an upside-down triangle that was arrayed in hardened white with inlaid golden leather. Draping his powerful form was a shimmering whitened fur cloak with faint traces of crimson streaks. Jonathan couldn't tell whether the red streaks were blood-stained in battle or had just been part of its design. Seeing him seated upon his throne with his wavy black hair almost reminded him of his own, only it was much longer. His face, though milky white, had traces of black shadowing effects, similar to Katelyn's.

Wisekoff fell to his knees and prostrated himself. "Hail, my king."

Jonathan, however, dropped to only one knee.

After being seated, the prince gazed upon the young man for the longest time as if he were measuring the length and depth of the lad. Jonathan more than one time had to turn his eyes from the penetrating stare that looked upon him through yellow tinted irises. When the prince finally spoke, it was with a voice that almost sounded melodious. The end of each word was elongated to the point that they ran into each other like one continuous stream. It was alluring, yet intimidating, and all together commanding. At the same time, Jonathan felt that the language he was using, the one that he could understand, was not his original tongue.

"Do you know why it is that you are here?" questioned the prince.

"Sir, I…"

"You are here, because you have been lost… like an orphan left out in the cold, but…, you see, you are lost no longer because, we… have found you," continued the Prince of Gish with a pointing finger at Wisekoff, "Have you ever had the feeling…" and then he seemed to be speaking almost to himself… "That there is something, some kind of force out there that drives you to go places? I have. And... let's just continue to call it a force, drives you to destinations that you desire to be anyway? At the end of your journey, nay, life's journey, you find that it's the very place you always wanted to be anyway. Oh, you may have never voiced those desires to any other living soul, but you have certainly voiced them to yourself. It is not true?"

Jonathan was captivated by the speech. His voice was entrancing, drawing, overflowing. He observed as the great prince bowed his head and began to follow the contours of the carvings on his throne with fingers that were arrayed with precious jewels and colored stones and continued his discourse...

"This force that we are speaking of... It's like an invisible bird that follows you around. It waits upon your every thought. Though it cannot pluck the thoughts from your brain, it can wait... and it does. It can listen and, quite frankly, it does. Then, at the very moment that you release the thought, the very instant that you force the thought through your vocal cords, that... that is the moment that you give birth to your desire. Funny, one never knows when one is listening. Then, that bird of prey... that force, grabs your mouthed thoughts in its talons to carry it to a place that you know not of." Magreth then turned his eyes upon the boy again piercing his very soul.

"Young man, I heard your desire to leave your homeland. You wanted to leave it like... like a stone that is skipped across the water..."

A moment of deathly silence followed and hung uncertainly upon the air. A thousand thoughts raced through Jonathan's head. A multitude of questions were forming and fitting together like stones that assemble themselves to build a great bridge. In his mind, he was whisked back to the years he had spent skipping stones at the river.

He thought of the desires he had had in his mind back then. He thought about how he had longed to reach the opposite shore, to leave his surroundings, his father, his hometown. He wanted to ask the sage that sat before him many of those questions. Never before had he stood before one with such wisdom and in one short speech, his soul had been stirred. His mind was racing, and his lips quivered ever so slightly as he was tempted to pour out his heart. The only thing that kept him from breathing speech to his thoughts was a pang of fear that wrenched his stomach like a fist grabbing his insides. Teetering upon that knife's edge, the son of the weapon master would be spun around on the insides as he heard the very next sentence tumble toward him like a cascading waterfall falling from the lips of the great Prince of Gish:

"This has got to be the one… Come on, just once… just once, make it to the other side…"

These were Jonathan's very own words! They were his very own thoughts, his own desires… His own supposed hidden desires, spoken out loud when he used to skip stones across the river's expanse!

"You thought that the seventh stone had fallen short of the far bank, aye? No, the stone that you cast flew farther than you ever dreamed possible, and it was that stone that led you to this place, to this moment," finalized Magreth.

Jonathan was dumbfounded. He peered to his right where Wisekoff was still kneeling before his king. And then, ever so slowly, Jonathan himself dropped his other knee to the floor of the throne room and bowed his head.

"Katelyn has survived her wounds," stated the Prince of Gish. "And in saving one of my daughters, you have saved yourself," continued Magreth. "For that, I am grateful. She has more recovery, but she will make a full one. Meanwhile, you… my boy, will train. When you are finished training, that is, if you finish training, you will be promoted. Under the care of Wisekoff, and also under the mentorship of one of my greatest generals, we will break you down, and build you up again… Up higher than you thought possible, for I have heard of your talent with weapons, and I believe that you have the potential. So, if you so choose, we will make you a master of weapons and not merely a weapons master."

It cut to the heart of Jonathan's life. The prince was like a master butcher that cuts out the fat from within the choicest of meats and the phrase 'weapon master' had become that corpulent substance within his own existence. The son of the weapon master marveled at everything that he was hearing, and he knew that it was the offer of a lifetime. Wisekoff was right. In the few moments that they had spent in the throne under Gish, everything had suddenly changed. He had so many questions that still remained to be answered and he would have savored more time in front of the great leader, but Magreth had suddenly risen from his throne and was obviously awaiting an answer from the young man.

He stood with his hands outstretched in a 'join me' fashion and suddenly appeared larger and taller than when he had first entered the room.

Jonathan continued to kneel with the knot still in his stomach. Inside, his being wrestled with an unsure future. He had reaped a whirlwind through his deep desire to make a change, a change that had come simply by his own voiced craving spoken in a moment of passionate frustration. Why me? He pondered. His view of the world had suddenly and irreversibly been altered. He had, at long last, broken free from his life of 'nichism'. He had come to the apex of the mountain he had been climbing, or in this case, the base of the overturned summit. And it all teetered upon the cliff of his decision-making ability.

What if I were to refuse?

The thought was fleeting for the next moment would change everything.

"It would be an honor to serve you, my king." And he bowed his head deeply.

If he were looking, Jonathan would have seen Magreth depart with a satisfied and knowing smile, but just before he disappeared beyond the crimson curtain, he spoke one last time. This time, the words were aimed right at Wisekoff:

"I congratulate you, Dumbkoff. Your eye for talent is truly a gift. You will be greatly rewarded, as usual."

"Tank' you, sire." Wisekoff humbly continued.

Jonathan and Wisekoff stayed prostrate for a few more minutes. Jonathan could hear his comrade, his caretaker, arise and slip away. He didn't want to leave but knew that he must go on to the next chapter of his life.

As he rose, he could see the shade of his form in the polished marble floor once again, but failed to realize that it was only the shadow of his former self, the shadow of his adolescent former self. And then, John of Scharp walked away from his past, forever leaving it sealed away in that throne under and onward to his destiny…

To become a master of weapons, or so he hoped.

✝

The Road that Led Him

Not a word was spoken the entire trip back to the surface. Jonathan's mind was still numb. As for Wisekoff, he had received more than what he had been bargaining for. The two were now entwined like the beginnings of a newly forming tapestry. Once they had made it back to the streets of Gish, Wisekoff was lost in thought as Jonathan attempted to have some of his questions answered, but Wisekoff would have none of it for it irked him that he was now the 'caretaker' of the young man. He had plans of his own and at the moment, was having a hard time trying to factor Jonathan into them.

"Wisekoff," Jonathan tried to catch the attention of the man. "Hey, Wisekoff!" he shouted and stopped dead in his tracks.

"What'd you want, boy?" Wisekoff replied over his shoulder still meandering along.

"That's going to stop. No more 'boy'. No more 'statue,' and no more ignoring my questions. Got it?" demanded Jonathan.

Wisekoff just chuckled beneath his round frame and continued back into the hazy maze of the smoke-filled alleys and mucked-up streets. Jonathan again followed suite, but still attempted to catch his attention. Shout after shout, yell after yell, and plea after plea failed to produce results until finally he touched upon a subject that froze the small bounding man in his own tracks.

"Hey. Dumbkoff!" Jonathan threw out.

Wisekoff stood fast, not believing that he had heard what he had just heard, "Did he just verbally accost me?" he asked himself.

Slowly turning around, he then darted toward the young arrogant man and dove for his throat. Jonathan was astonished at the swiftness of the attack. He hadn't had the time to catch his balance or parlay his position and he found himself on the ground with the short man staring down at him with a verbal assault to match his physical strength:

"How dare you stab at me with your contempt! Just because I allowed Magreth to call me that doesn't give you the right to. Who do you think I am? I've now been placed over you as your 'caretaker', so that doesn't mean that you have the right to treat me like the other garbage you see in this city. Remember boy, you are only one step from the trash heap yourself. Twice, twice I've had to pull you from annihilation… from obscurity!" Wisekoff was tearing into him like a fierce tiger.

"Wisekoff…?" Jonathan tried to interrupt.

"By the way, you are a novice in this city. I could disappear around the next corner, and you'd be lost just as before…"

"Uh. Wisekoff?"

"… And not only that…"

"Wisekoff!" Jonathan finally screamed.

"What do you want?"

"Where did your accent go?"

The question was followed by an elongated pause as Wisekoff stared back at him, occasionally blinking. Then he arose, brushed himself off, and turned to continue along his waddling path speaking over his shoulder at Jonathan once again.

"Have you learned nothing about this city? Nothing, I say, nothing is at it seems," he continued, his hands flailing about. "You just trust ole' Wisekoff and he be leadin' ya' straight," he shot back with a chuckle.

"Quite a short temper you got there," quipped Jonathan.

"Der' ya' go again wit' the wit," Wisekoff jokingly replied.

By the time they had finished their bantering, they had arrived at a structure that was located on a corner street. The dirt road itself curved around it like a pulled back and broken horseshoe. It was at least seven stories high from what Jonathan could tell and on the second was a very active pub. A sign hung above one of the corner windows that read, The Turnback Inn. Underneath the title it read, 'Once ya' turn inn, there's no turnin' back.' Whoops and hollers were cascading from the windows and lively music was wafting from the place as well. It was the liveliest sound he had heard in the city save for the 'attacks; that he had been privy too, but quite the opposite atmosphere. Where the attacks had contained darkness and death, this was full of laughter and life, albeit riotous. Suddenly, a voice fell from the window beneath the sign. Jonathan recognized the man as Jaylan, the one he had fought alongside above Beggar's Square, the creator of the explosive devices.

"The first installment of your payment has arrived, sire," he swooned as though he were about to fall from the height. Wisekoff just waved him off, and Jaylan fell back into the structure with a thud… "Hey, John," came Jaylan's voice somewhere beyond the window.

The city had taken on a new air. It was still smoke, muck, and ruffian-filled, but something had changed. Or at least it had changed in that corner of the Gish. In actuality, it was someone, and even though no one had known it at the moment, that someone was following Wisekoff into his new home.

It appeared as though Wisekoff was going to walk into the front door of the building that jutted out into the street as if it were trying to force itself upon all who passed by like bait on the end of a fishhook, but he bypassed the front entrance and made his way around to the side street and down an alleyway. Needless to say, Jonathan was beginning to despise alley ways. He had been introduced, seduced, secluded, and disgusted by them all in a mere number of days. A slight edge of nausea crept into his mid-section at the thought of making his way down yet another. Wisekoff waddled along looking about like a cat ready for a nap. Twice he stopped mid stride to stretch and yawn. It was catching, and Jonathan yawned as well. Though he had felt a surge of energy through his being at the throne room, the fullness of his adventure had begun to catch up to him. If they were going to Wisekoff's home, he was hoping that he had some sort of straw bed to lie on for the next number of hours, or days, or possibly even weeks.

Wisekoff finally reached the end of the alley where various discarded items lay scattered about. There were buckets, crates, bottles, piled up chairs and tables with other odds and ends. Beyond them, Jonathan could see a small tunnel. Wisekoff made his way past the pile of junk and mumbled something about cleaning it all up but did nothing to lift a hand in that direction. Together, they made their way through the tunnel that led beneath the second story tavern. When they arrived at yet another door, Wisekoff produced a long iron key and unlocked it. It sounded like six or seven mechanisms releasing beyond. When they had finally finished their tumbling tones, the door opened to a room not much bigger than an alcove.

Jonathan surmised that if he and Wisekoff were to grab hands and reach for opposite sides of the place, they would have been able to touch the opposing walls. However, the thought of actually touching such filthy stained hands repulsed even the once homeless young man. Wisekoff could see the look on Jonathan's face and addressed his thoughts.

"So, have you learned anything from me yet?" he questioned with the polished speech of a wealthy merchant.

"Yes, nothing is as it seems, right?" Jonathan replied.

"That's it," Wisekoff finished and pushed against a brick that lay slightly sunken into the far wall.

Other than being slightly recessed, the brick appeared like any of the others in the cellar of a room, but what it produced was something different all together. The activation mechanism had caused that whole back corner of the room to slide away into some hidden shelf that was on the corner floorboard. Below, Jonathan could see a stairwell descend beneath them. At three lengths his own height, he could see that another polished marble floor opened up into yet another floor. A warm glow of torches emanated from beyond the curvature of the corner. Wisekoff extended his hand in an invitation gesture to the young master of weapons.

"What's with everything being below the surface?"

"That, my friend, is the heart of the matter... you learn quickly," retorted Wisekoff and slapped Jonathan on the back as they descended yet another mysterious staircase into yet another mysterious world. What they entered into was again, awe inspiring.

The space stretched out before them like an elongated bowl. Where stark angled corners should have been, rounded edges curved inward. Even the wall to floor connection was smoothed over. The floor, walls, and ceiling were one, and were hued in a peaceful light green color. The furniture was an ornately carved dark wood. Again, a table was stretched out before them with high back chairs, but rather than being old and full of cobwebs, it was immaculately arrayed with gold and silver plates and goblets. It appeared as though it had just been set, and it must have been, for a moment later a young servant woman entered with a large platter of victuals.

As she entered, she bowed toward Wisekoff who was enjoying watching the jaw-drop effect on Jonathan's face. Even the candles, which seemed to be in every nook and cranny of the place, were ornately carved and warmly burning in settings of silver. A chandelier above the table beckoned them into the space with thirty or so candles. Jonathan lost track of his count as the servant girl neared him, placed the succulent food on the table, and bowed to him as well.

"Uh, what is she doing?" asked the young man taken aback by the gesture.

"She's paying homage to her master," replied Wisekoff. At that, Jonathan burst into a fit of laughter so loud that it teetered on the edge of being embarrassing. So much so, that Wisekoff had to stop him. "Jonathan… Jonathan! Don't put her to shame. She is here to serve you." Wisekoff stopped him with a hand on his arm.

Jonathan was dumbstruck. Never before had he even heard of such a thing. Perhaps in the courts of a prince or a king could such a thing happen, but not in the presence of a mere peasant. As she continued to bow before him, he could not stand the gesture any longer and raised her to an upright stance.

"You don't have to do that… I'm just… I am not what you think… I'm… Can she understand me?" he inquired of Wisekoff.

"Not a word. She doesn't even speak. It's fruitless… She must treat you like this though." Wisekoff continued seeing that Jonathan was at a loss for words. "It was not long ago that she was roaming the streets as you were. She's thankful just to be out of the elements. I call her Lady Dael. She came here about a year ago, and she hasn't spoken a word. Just served me, like this… Now, she will serve you."

"Is all of this yours?"

"It was," he answered. "But it's now yours!" Again, Jonathan laughed uproariously. "Hungry?" Wisekoff continued.

"Starved."

Together, Wisekoff and Jonathan dug into the wealth of food that Lady Dael continued to bring to the table. Where it was coming from never even crossed the mind of the young man who had suddenly morphed from being a peasant boy from a tiny township to a near prince in a metropolis... all without paying a price for a thing. Little did he realize that the price, and it would surely be a great one, would come at a later date.

For the moment however, Jonathan was supping on the most succulent victuals he had ever tasted. There was a roasted pig, stuffed with wild game; grapes as fat as plums, chickens roasted with so much spice that one could barely see the cooked meat below. There was even venison, and it had been soaked in a creamy white type of sauce that tasted like honey… Then the drink…

It was a darkened substance so deeply red that it almost appeared as freshly flowing blood. Wisekoff had called it wine, but although the young man had heard of the liquid, he had never even seen it. It was the drink of kings, and even his Da', who had been in the company of princes himself, had never even seen it either.

It was bitter but sweet, and he sipped it from a golden jeweled goblet that took two hands to hold. The drink stung his nose ever so slightly, but the more he drank, the less it bit into him. Coupled with the meats, especially the venison, it made his mouth feel as though it were bathing in a pool of butter. So tender was the food, and so smooth became the wine, that his head slightly ached with the thought that at some point the meal would have to come to a close. He couldn't even remember the last time that he had a decent meal. And whenever it was (no offense to his mother), it would have been a mixture of bland potatoes and lifeless vegetables that had grown soggy in a river of watery soup.

Together, Wisekoff and Jonathan filled themselves to the brim with the wealth of victuals that seemed to have descended from the heavens. At one point, when Jonathan thought that the meal would come to an end, a whole new one began.

Wisekoff had called the substance chocolate and Lady Dael presented it warmly dripping from the contours of various fruits. Its fragrance filled the young man's nasal cavity from the outside with pure delight, but as he took it into his mouth and it slid down the back of his throat, it filled his nose from the inside as well. He described it as liquid gold when Wisekoff asked him what he had thought. Its sugary thick substance bathed his mouth with a warm delightful comfort. Lady Dael had coupled it with a series of small wooden cups filled with an even darker and thicker wine than the one they had experienced earlier. It was almost as thick and sweet as the chocolate itself.

Those were the two delights that Wisekoff and Jonathan savored unto the waning hours of the night. Somewhere during the waxing hours of the morning, a small, gilded bowl was filled with a yellowish cake-like substance that smelled just as sweet as the other delectable's but was set on fire where it smoldered ever so slowly. It released a curling smoke that slowly filled the place with a mind-numbing fog.

"What is this substance?" Jonathan slurred into a question.

"It's a form of Serpent's Breath."

"I don't understand."

"You will… in time," Wisekoff finalized.

As the hours passed in sheer bliss, Jonathan's head spun and swam as he tried to focus on a number of sporadically placed paintings and tapestries that were hung upon the wall in various places. In his state, they appeared to be mere windows into other worlds, and on more than one occasion, thought that the characters in them had mysteriously come alive. It seemed similar to his life and how it had become. The more he looked through the renderings, the more he became lost in those other worlds. It was not until Wisekoff would jar him awake, that he would be rescued from them.

While they ate, drank, and simply breathed in the atmosphere, they talked about many of the young man's questions regarding the mysteries of Gish. Many of his questions were answered, only they were answered in a way that Jonathan would never remember, for the new lifestyle had begun to take its full effect and had managed to steal his capacity to remember any of it.

Thus, Jonathan of Scharp fell into a state that would make this only the first of many days, or more appropriately nights, where he would not be able to remember a thing. As dinner party after dinner party, week after week, pub after pub, and month after month blurred into one giant and elongated period of debauchery, the young man became more and more entwined within the underground of Gish, and like roots growing out of a cellar, the city packaged him deep within its bosom… (The details of which would be better left to the imagination of the reader than to the description of the writer)

Suffice it to say, Jonathan experienced no daylight hours during that phase of his life, for they were spent in a sort of mind-numbing suspension where one dare not cease the frivolity of the night lest the dream come to an end, or so he thought.

A word should be said about those hazy nights, for a dark dependency had managed to hook its lethal claws deeply into the heart of the weapon master's son, claws that would not loose their grasp easily. Such were the nails that emerged from the fingers of such a lifestyle, nay, of all such lifestyles. Jonathan existed in that dark, dark place until he was suddenly and violently shaken free from that riotous living.

†

To The Train

"Get up, you corpse!"

Jonathan could feel the entirety of the canopy bed that he had been sleeping upon shake with a jolt.

"Get out of that nest, soft hands!" bellowed a gruff voice.

Jonathan tried to rollover to face whatever giant had come knocking, but his sore back refused to twist as it became hung up on a point between two joints of his spine.

"Get up I said."

The next kick to the bed jolted him past the edgy point of the joint and produced a pop so loud that his eyes shot open: The face that jeered down at him was foggy through his post-catatonic eyes and it pulsated back and forth in his view as the blood within his head beat against the inner sides of it.

He tried to focus but was more or less hoisted out of his so-called nest by the strong arms of what he surmised to be the general that Prince Magreth had talked about nearly six months earlier, yes, six months earlier… The bill for the price of his surroundings and of his lifestyle had at last come knocking on the chamber door.

Jonathan had no clue how long he had been out but watched as the bed he had been sleeping within (an oversized and deeply grained box that had a carved canopy over it), disappear beyond his view, for he had been swiftly draped over the shoulder of the giant. The view of his whole world bounced away as he was carried past the banquet table, which had been immaculately set yet again, up the hidden staircase, down the old familiar tunnel, out the alley past the trash heap which had never been cleaned up, and finally into the streets of the Gish where he was bound hand and foot with ropes and slung over the rump of a war horse that seemed vaguely familiar.

His head continued to pound, his nauseated stomach threatened to reverse course, and his voice refused to operate. His eyes stubbornly stayed at half-mast and his ears heard only echoes. He had no choice but to surrender to the ride as the horse carried them through the streets of the city and out into the barren wilderness of the sand landscape that surrounded the giant metropolis.

A deadened log would have even been a welcomed sight as they crossed that barren expanse.

Convulsive wretches poured from his being like numerous fleshly volcanoes of vomit. The rider, or general, or whoever it had been that abducted Jonathan still had not said a word as he succumbed to the sickness that threatened to envelope him entirely. The young man remained draped over the back of the horse, his bones aching as he tried to adjust himself in his slung over position. He began to feel his muscles going numb as the sun began to set somewhere behind him, and a few creepy shivers made their way up his back. He finally lost track of the direction that they were heading as he watched the sun sink beyond the horizon and into the thickness of nightfall. He wretched, bringing up only the acid that was left in his stomach and shivered himself to sleep, but still the rider continued into the night.

The sun had run its complete circuit twenty-one times before Jonathan had finally awakened from the bondage of his addiction, so deep were the claws embedded. It was dawn, and he had been wrapped in a fur blanket and placed in a tent upon a rocky overlook. Beyond his view, a bird that appeared to be an eagle soared majestically high over a deep canyon in search of prey. His eyes followed the flight path of the fowl until it dipped down into the canyon like a flash of released lightening. In what seemed to be mere seconds, it again rose upon the windy currents. It had within its grasp an unfortunate and much smaller bird. The victory cry of the eagle echoed throughout the canyon and brought a smile to enlighten the young man's face. Then another face appeared in the entrance to the small tent.

"The eagle has caught himself a snipe," came the gruff voice from the face.

The sight was that of a face that had been, at sometime in the past, cut from one side to the other across the forehead and completely through the right ear severing it in two. The former slice lay just beneath the flowing red hair that cascaded from the head of a man, "Do you know what a snipe is?" he asked.

"I have no idea," Jonathan shakily replied through a pounding headache.

"You are, or will be, one day… You're feeling the effects of your endless parties and elongated nights, hey? Tell me, was it worth it?" The man scowled down at him. "I have a remedy for that nonsense." At that, he grabbed both of Jonathan's hands and began to bind them together with rope. "The name's Thomas Dodd, but you can just call me, Thomas Dodd."

"You seem familiar to me, like we've met before."

"Steal any war-horses lately?" Then Thomas more or less dragged Jonathan out of the tent, jerked him to his feet, and pulled him to the very same horse that he had stolen nearly a year earlier.

"Where are we?" searched Jonathan as he pondered whether the giant of a man was from his kingdom or from his former kingdom. Before coming to any conclusion, Jonathan found himself atop a ledge overlooking a deep canyon. The rocks and crags of the landscape were jagged and the deep fissure in the earth fell away with reddened clay.

Thomas had set up a camp, three tents held up with wooden poles surrounding a fire pit among some gangly tree trunks that were perched upon the edge of the cliffs. Jonathan tried the best that he could to survey his surroundings but was forced to concentrate rather in trying to stay upon his feet as Dodd began to lash the other end of the rope to the horn of the saddle that was set upon the back of the steed. Dodd had saddled the horse and started to ride down the backside of the mountain that they were upon. A moment later, Jonathan was jerked free from his standing position and had to run just to keep up with the courser. More than once, he fell and was dragged and he had to struggle to gain his footing once again. Dodd never even stopped for him.

They rode, ran, fell, and ran some more for what seemed like hours. In the process, the young man had sweated so much that his clothing was soaked through and through. He was no longer wearing the mysterious black garb that he had been given, but sometime during his 'hazy days' had been given a set of leather brown breeches and sturdy leather boots. His shirt was still a blackened material, but it flowed freely and fit him rather loosely. A belt was girded about his waist and his forearms were arrayed in black leather bands that were hooked around his thumbs. He was thankful for them, for the rope would have easily dug into his arms as the steed continued to pull him along.

"Where are we going?" shouted Jonathan to Thomas Dodd.

"To the training grounds," Dodd yelled back.

"Yeah... Right." Jonathan's voice shook as he continued to scamper behind.

Finally, Dodd stopped the horse near a small creek. The corners of Jonathan's mouth were white with the foam of thirst. The water seemed like a heavenly drink in the sight of the young man who had sweated nearly every ounce of fluid out of his system, and consequently, poison. Dodd dismounted and made his way over to Jonathan who was looking at him like a man who was desperate for relief. After untying the binding, he motioned for him to partake of the water from the stream.

Jonathan ran for it with desperation, like a hind that searches the wilderness for relief. Once upon the edge of the trickling stream, he fell to his knees, the rope dragging behind. He then prostrated himself and slammed his face into the water to drink. Suddenly, with a thud, something bounced off the exterior of his head.

"Ouch! What was that for?"

Dodd had produced a long bow from his surplus of weapons and commenced to whack the young man on the top of his head. "You failed."

"Failed what?" cried Jonathan.

"You know better than to lose track of your surroundings."

"But I knew you were watching."

Dodd was silent for a moment, but having the need to maintain his superior position, he chided Jonathan again with another hit to the head. Whack! "You'll be fighting alone when you're finally released from my care."

"It shouldn't be that way," Jonathan argued.

"Well, it is… Now get some water and let's get going"

That was only the beginning of a relationship that would last close to a year, for Jonathan, at long last, had found that the deeply ingrained and passionate seeds of soldiery had found the light of day and flourished within the garden of his desire… and he made it seem effortless.

The training ground was located in a forested mountain region that was on the edge of the barren desert through by which lay the metropolis of Gish, even though it could not be seen from that distance. Little did Jonathan know that he was actually closer to Safehaven than to Gish, but the thought had never crossed his mind during that time, for he was caught up in becoming another man altogether.

For months, Dodd taught Jonathan all there was to know about the way of the snipe warriors. Jonathan's strength grew, along with his agility, and even morphed into a near religion of sorts. The mornings always began with some quiet moments overlooking the canyon and Dodd never even knew that he was doing it. Most mornings, the same eagle that Jonathan had first seen when he arrived at the training camp would make an appearance for his morning hunt. There was something endearing about the bird and Jonathan could sense that the eagle knew that he was being watched.

Secretly he studied the way of the bird of prey. For instance, he observed as it waited aloft the canyon's updraft winds where it hovered, watched, and waited ever so patiently. It was more than just waiting for an opportunity to strike though. It almost seemed as if the bird were waiting for the prey to surrender itself. It was an art form of sorts. The bird even seemed to be enjoying itself, for a peaceful air always surrounded it at all times. It was not hurried, nor was it anxious.

As morning after morning passed, Jonathan came to call the eagle Talonshard, and their time together became special for it strengthened him, helped him to focus, and sharpened his very own fighting style. It was at this time that a newly formed concept found its way into the young master of weapon's heart, and he made a decision that his particular art of war would be of a different way from any other. He, like Talonshard, would patiently wait and at the same time, be at peace, un-anxious, unnerved.

The remainder of the mornings would continue with strengthening exercises including agility drills and finger-strengthening routines. These were followed by the usual runs to the training grounds away from the camp. Not only had he learned combat techniques, but more importantly, he learned the way of stealth that would be the hallmark of his position.

For example, he learned how to conceal his scent behind a veil of mud, or even dung, whatever it took as he hunted the animals that would consequently become his meal during his months in training. Jonathan also learned how to blend into his surroundings by shading his face with charcoal left by their nightly campfires, or wetted clay from the surrounding earth. Dodd taught him how not only to utilize the natural flora, but also the direction and movement of the wind through the trees. He also became a master of the shadows, learning how to 'feel' his way through the shades not only of the daylight, but the night as well.

In that time, Dodd had explained the driving force of their movement, and that the great Prince of Gish had long ago set his sight on a kingdom that would rule over all other realms just as Gish itself had been ruled. It would be a kingdom where the prince would be the overarching commander-in-chief, but the soldiers themselves would become the leaders of the lands, townships, and even the cities.

Jonathan was mature enough to understand that Magreth was all about self-fulfilling power and control, but he and his comrades would be given the ability to live lives of extravagance and excess. In essence, they would become the ruling upper class. That would have been enough of a motivation in and of itself, for he had experienced a taste of that type of lifestyle during his time in Gish and knew that he was merely in the process of truly earning it.

However, there was an even deeper motivation for Jonathan because he often thought about how much his former realm could benefit from such a kingdom and king. (Had it not been ruler-less for ages?) He dreamed about how he could elevate his family to a great position in his very own realm. The thought was a tantalizing one, but nothing was more so than the day that he would be able to return to face his father as the soldier he had always longed to become… The soldier that his Da' had always kept him from becoming.

It was a sweet essence of a thought, and it pushed him to train harder than any other student that Dodd had ever trained.

In the course of his preparation, Thomas Dodd had given Jonathan the task of learning the art of the bow, the signature weapon of the Snipes. He had supplied the young man with one from his own cache of weaponry and Jonathan spent hours trying to perfect the form. Not only would he have to shoot more accurately than any other soldier, he would have to do it from the shadow of his concealment. The Snipes, as they were called, would be not only reconnaissance warriors, but assassins as well. They were the elite servants in the service of Magreth. Their means of fighting would put them in lonely positions for hours on end. Most often, their exploits would go unnoticed by any other, but Jonathan came to realize through the tutelage of Dodd, that their service would exact great feats and would serve the overall vision of the kingdom. And, that it would exact even greater rewards for they were honored above all others.

Many times, Dodd would force Jonathan to spend days hunting for his own game, having to conceal himself and wait for his prey to come to him. On more than one occasion, Jonathan had missed his shot and was required to go hungry for days, watching Dodd feast on his own captured game. The young trainee came to appreciate the talent of his mentor, for their many sparring sessions almost always ended with Jonathan on his backside, completely exhausted. Nevertheless, that whole time, their relationship deepened as they shared their thoughts on a myriad of subjects.

The training had done exactly what Magreth had described. The young master of weapons was not only broken down but was also rebuilt again. Built up in body, in mind, in strength, and in thought.

As the year had begun to come to a close, and as Jonathan neared the time when his training would come to an end, Dodd had continually challenged him with different tasks to accomplish, but the one that had stood head and shoulders above all the rest would be the crowning achievement of his training and would mark the very hour when he would have fulfilled his schooling.

Much to Jonathan's disliking and chagrin, he was assigned to hunt down and kill the very eagle he had grown fond of, the one he had named, Talonshard. To Dodd, it would test the soul of the young apprentice and his commitment to the art of assassination, for it would be a sacrifice near and dear to his heart. As for Jonathan, it was a conundrum, and it delayed the completion of his training for weeks and weeks. However, after many days and hours of contemplation, the young apprentice had at last come to a solution to solve his personal dilemma.

Jonathan had risen long before the sunrise, arrayed himself with the long bow and projectiles, and snuck his way out of camp to position him upon a ledge that was about a third of the way into the depths of the reddened canyon wall. He had concealed his form by stripping down to only his loin cloth and completely covering himself in the red clay of the surrounding landscape. Having carefully descended to a precipice, he situated himself near a tree that had been growing out from the side of the cliff. Once there, he virtually became invisible as he patiently waited for the eagle, his eagle, to make an appearance.

However, Talonshard's usual one-day-furlough extended further than Jonathan had anticipated.

It was as if the bird had known that there was a hunter awaiting its arrival. For three days Jonathan stayed in one place waiting for Talonshard. He hadn't slept the entire time simply for the fact that if he would have fallen asleep upon that great height, he would have fallen much deeper than anticipated; fallen to the rocks far below. Just as he was about to abandon his quest however, Talonshard soared into the canyon with a piecing howl. The young trainee had grown fond of his friend and was always amazed not only by the sheer size of the predator, but by the beauty of it as well.

Its head was pure white with blackened streaks down the sides that blended into its inky black body. Its wings were immense and when opened, spanned nearly twice the height of Jonathan himself. The bird's talons were what caused the young man to lend its namesake, for they seemed to be as long as his own fingers. At times, they would reflect the sun's rays if they were struck at just the right angle, creating shards of light. But what fascinated Jonathan even more than the talons was when the bird of prey would dive toward its hunted victim. The wings would form a V as if for victory, and the speed at which the eagle dove was mind boggling.

As Jonathan spied his friend from his concealment, the bird did just that.

Talonshard dove with ferocity, at what, Jonathan could not see. He watched the eagle as it slowed itself near a felled tree that had long begun to decay into the surroundings of a dry riverbed. When the eagle arose once again on the spiraling updraft winds, it had in its powerful talons a long black snake. The eagle released a long echoing victory cry that brought a smile to Jonathan's face. However, he knew what he needed to do to complete his training and loaded his weapon for firing. He then commenced to pull back the firing cord.

The muscles in his arms, now more powerful, flexed as he held the missile in position. With piercing eyes, he watched the bird of prey circle on the wind near his position, the snake dangling from its claws. His arms began to strain against the pull of the bow as he contemplated his shot. Thoughts of unforgettable mornings flashed through his mind as he remembered the days when the silhouette of Talonshard floated past him, a beautiful sunrise in the backdrop.

He remembered that all of the bird's victims were still alive when he flew away with them and pondered whether the eagle would actually let them go somewhere due to the shear sense of artistic sport. It was a fleeting thought, but it would prove to be an endearing one. A voice from long ago echoed in his mind as he remembered Bart of the Forest telling him that it was not his decision to take another's life. Though Talonshard was only a bird, the test would define the master of weapons motivation for the rest of his life and Jonathan knew that to be true. He closed his eyes, and he let the shot go.

It flew straight and true. The eyes of Talonshard spotted Jonathan just as the arrow was released, and the war eagle let out a great cry. Jonathan opened his own eyes just as the missile neared its target. He felt confident that what he had been aiming at would be hit for sure, but he questioned his own ability to lead the target. If the eagle could have voiced its thoughts, they most likely would have been thoughts of betrayal, however, 'betrayal' in a different sense of the word. It would not be a betrayal because the bird himself had been shot, but betrayal because the thick black snake that Talonshard had just successfully hunted had been plucked right out from beneath its great talons!

The master of weapons had not shot his friend, but the snake right through the top of its head!

Thus, Talonshard would have to return on another day and would have to hunt with a different partner, for the young apprentice had completed his own training with that one impossible and immeasurable shot.

Thomas Dodd stood silent behind a tree atop the cliff edge. It had become the norm for Jonathan to think one step beyond Dodd's own understanding. The shot simply amazed him, and he knew that the young man had not only completed his mentorship, but had infinitely surpassed it. A smile slid its way across his mouth as he pondered the young man's future. If he could have been seeing it through a magical looking glass, it would have been a cloudy one indeed. He knew that he would see him again, but on which side of the coming war, he could not know.

Dodd made his way back to the camp where they had spent nearly a year together. He looked about it with a fondness he had never felt for a student before, and he had prepared a scroll for the young man. Producing it from the folds of his cloak, he laid it upon a rock next to the fire pit. He then saddled his white war horse and contemplated whether Jonathan would be able to complete the one final test that was written upon it.

It would have to be death defying, and he had never assigned it to any other student he had ever trained. Thomas Dodd wanted to know for sure; he wanted to discover whether the young man could complete a task that, according to legend, only one other individual was ever able to accomplish.

That individual was Prince Magreth himself, the Nasgroth and undisputed king of Gish.

Chapter 6

Meanwhile

†

A Safe Haven No More

The road home was a difficult one. Remorseful tears had ear-marked most of the trail as the fractured search party returned to the township of Safehaven, their thoughts of the gentle butcher and the missing Jonathan weighing heavily upon their hearts. Their arrival back at the home of John and Katherine of Scharp was a rueful one, for the place reminded them of the fact that they were now a broken family in search of answers. The grounds around the old shop and cottage were a stabbing reminder as well, for it was still deeply fissured from the storm.

The heaviness was palpable as Katherine led her husband and son around the pitted landscape. Jacqueline was asked to stay that first night due not only to the fact that they all had a terrible day, and her strength was sapped, but also due to the fact that Katherine had begun to grow fond of her and wanted to get to know her more. They had left the door open when they began the search and as they entered into the small cottage, they discovered that it had been ransacked. It was the first time that any such occurrence had ever happened in the township of Safehaven.

After cleaning the small house the best that they could, they settled in for an evening of victuals and well-deserved sleep. During the meal, Katherine excused herself for a moment, remembering a certain valuable item and made her way into her son's room. After a moment, she came back with a dark cloak draped over her arm.

"I want you to have this… It was Jonathan's."

"No, I couldn't," Jacqueline replied.

"Please. I feel like you should have it."

"I don't know what to say, but… Thank you."

Katherine smiled silently and hugged Jacqueline. Then she retained her seat, and they all finished the meal together.

Afterwards, both John and Katherine wept themselves into slumber. Samuel and Jacqueline stayed in the only other room of the two-room cottage. Samuel asked the 'princess' what seemed to be a million meaningless questions, more out of misplaced emotions than curiosity. Jacqueline obliged him, understanding his little boy sorrows. Besides, she herself needed some relief for her feelings, for the elder of the weapon master's sons had grown exponentially in the short time that she had spent with his family.

When Samuel had more or less mumbled himself to sleep, the princess was left alone with her own thoughts. After a few moments of staring out the small window through which moonbeams slid, she rose to walk about the space. She had never been a part of a real family and the thought made her feel warm on the inside. The glow of the fire from the common living space flickered off the walls of the room like little joyfully dancing shadows and she found herself lost in thought…

Hers was a life of a daughter to mother relationship. Having never known her own father, and having had a mother who was constantly serving the town's Nasgroth, she more or less lived a life on her own except for the times that she would assist her mother in her duties. At such times, the Nasgroth of Marshai had taken an interest in the young girl seeing in her a semblance of herself and that led to an apprenticeship as a Council warrior. Jacqueline was more than happy to accept the invitation to train, for she too had an insatiable appetite for adventure similar to Jonathan's.

From the moment that she saw the young weapon master's son in Bart's pig stall long ago at the Blossom Festival, she had taken a liking to him. Unbeknownst to Jonathan, his attack on James the Younger had made an indelible impression and over time, had become Jacqueline's first lesson in how to deal with a bully figure. Consequently, the lesson carried her through many confrontations as she trained to become a soldier of the council. Although there had been many women in the army of the king over the centuries, including her very own mentor Brenda of Hilt, it remained a challenge for a young woman to claim her rightful place in the world. Many a broken nose or slashed arm had been afflicted upon those would-be bullies that would confront her, leaving a thin if not veiled bitter root of anger which had a tendency to reach toward the surface at odd times.

The core lesson that young Jonathan had taught her was that the only answer for a bully was to strike with the swiftness and fierceness of a mongoose. In fact, that was the name that she ended up inheriting from her peers.

Jacqueline, as a woman soldier, had an inherent determination not only to accomplish any task that was set before her, but to rise above the others in study and training. She had chosen the crossbow more out of happenstance than personal choice. The weapon itself had been delivered on a trial basis only. Most thought that the weapon master, John of Scharp had come up with the crazy design out of his own imagination, but in actuality, it had been revealed to him as he continued to study the Willowfeld Shunt that had been mysteriously given to him. Jacqueline was the only student brave enough to set her determination upon mastering it. Many a misfire and broken finger earmarked her trials with the weapon. Her breakthrough finally came, however, when a contest was announced by the Captain of the Guard, Nathan.

The prize would be an opportune chance to ride with the said captain's elite force of scouts that he himself would personally lead. The person chosen would inevitably fare well, for anyone chosen to ride with the captain would end up being a leader in the king and council's army. Nathan would only allow the most talented of cadets to ride with him. It was not a matter of pride for the great guard, but a matter of fact that he intuitively knew, for his own life would prove to be one of the greatest prizes the enemy could claim. It was a reality that he had to carry with him at all times and could ill afford to have anyone less than the very best riding at his side.

When the contest arrived, the chosen younglings were gathered together that morning in front of a series of targets, each growing smaller in succession and standing upon thin poles that stood about thirty paces in the distance. As they assembled their weapons, they were clumped together in a group. Some of the competitors chose long-bows, some short-bows, and some even throwing daggers. When Jacqueline chose hers, a yet untested crossbow, she was teased by the others, out of earshot from the leaders, of course.

"What's the mongoose got," mocked one slightly under his breath. He was shorter than her by about two hand lengths and as round as a pastry.

"Don't you mean featherless goose?" shot another, this one a little taller and considerably larger than Jacqueline.

As it turned out, the latter; the taller bully, would never even get the chance to compete, for he had been taken to the infirmary after having had three of his fingers on his firing side mysteriously broken into so many angles that it appeared as though he had been deformed from birth; the end result, I suppose, of one of Jacqueline's aforementioned bitter roots... And, of course, the larger boy would have never confessed to have been beaten back by a mere girl. Alas, the occasion was merely a microcosm of the life of a woman called to soldiery.

Even after the unfortunate 'accident', which none of the other trainees believed to be a true accident, others still persisted in calling her names; names like wild mongoose or just simply goose. The names, however, usually didn't faze her though, for she had become used to being set apart. Unbeknownst to any others, she had long been acquainted with a life more or less lived alone. What they also didn't know about her, was that she had turned her unfortunate existence into a passion for training. Consequently, it was the loneliness that had carried her through many a dark night as she trained and trained, even at times by moonlight.

When the contest finally commenced, each candidate took their turn at the first target, and they were all successful in splitting it, for it was a large watermelon that had been piked' upon a pole. The next target was a grapefruit, and all contestants easily subdued them as well. The great Captain of the Guard was pleased to see that the year's recruits had all possessed the talent to be competitive.

However, when an apple was placed upon the poles that had held the targets, nearly a third of the students failed to complete the task and were dropped from the competition.

Among the successful were James the Younger and Jacqueline of Marshai. Alas, it was a grape that was placed upon the tip of a stick that cut the field down to a mere three competitors, James, Jacqueline, and Timmons, another would-be warrior from Trelane.

Timmons was the first to fire at the tiny piece of fruit at a distance of thirty paces. His weapon of choice was the long-bow and when he fired, it missed the target by a mere wisp. When James lined up, he split it with a well-placed dagger that passed right through it and stuck into the hay bale beyond. Then it was Jacqueline's turn... She could feel the mocking faces of her peers, angry more out of spite than out of teasing, for she had narrowed the field to just two competitors when she took aim with her new weapon of war. The grape didn't even stand a chance as it was split asunder as well, the power of the weapon forcing the projectile completely through the roll of hay. Nathan and the other leaders had never seen the contest go beyond the grape stage and were at a loss as how to proceed until Brenda, who would become Jacqueline's mentor, suggested that they use a pomegranate seed held up with a tiny, sharpened stick.

She called it, 'the blood fruit'.

It was hard enough just to stabilize the tiny target let alone hit it with a weapon. Jacqueline was the first to line up before it. The mockery had dissipated and the name calling ceased and would be gone forever if she were to actually hit the piece of fruit; a truth that weighed heavily upon her heart. Her hand slightly trembled as she raised the weapon toward her would-be enemy. Peering down the site, she breathed one last nervous breath before tucking the said nerves into the back of her heart. Releasing all air from her lungs, she poised her shot on the edge of silence. She knew that a slight bit of inspired air would ruin her aim. Waiting to the last second, she fired the projectile.

It whisked past the target and completely through the entirety of hay. At first, it appeared to have missed the mark, but as Nathan approached the seed and picked it up, the blood fruit released its juices and ran down the great Captain's hand. The arrow had split just the top portion of the seed so cleanly that it didn't even fall from its perch nor release its contents. It was declared a hit and the others, at long last, cheered the young mongoose.

James the Younger was the next to line up in front of the target. Another tiny seed was precariously perched, and silence once again prevailed. James chose his usual throwing dagger and with one arm outstretched toward the target and the other grasping the knife, he steadied himself. He relished the fact that all eyes were upon him. He had inherited his father's desire to be the center of attention, and he let the moment hang in the air like low-lying fog. As his pause approached near to causing embarrassment, not for James, but rather for all those that were watching, he suddenly changed weapons in the flash of a moment. The would-be warrior, in one fluid movement, replaced the dagger into its hilt and unsheathed one of his narrow swords, spun three hundred and sixty degrees for velocity, and fired it at the blood fruit.

The sword tumbled end over and completely destroyed not only the tiny seed, but the perch that was holding it as well. Nathan approached the destroyed target and had a hard time trying to find the seed amongst the broken wood pieces. He finally found the felled target, but only found the seed itself. The 'blood' and the sheath that surrounded it had soaked into the dirt, leaving the seed sitting all alone. It was a debated call, but Nathan had declared it a strike.

Thus, both Jacqueline and James had earned a spot in Nathan's scouting party, as we have already seen. It had only been a year of training before the search for the weapon master's son had become Jacqueline's first real mission that she had ever been personally given. Needless to say, the thought of failing in her very first duty focused her determination to accomplish the task, a task that was put on hold due to circumstances beyond her control.

She spent that first night in Jonathan's bed which sat across the room from Samuel's and the next day, returned to her home township of Marshai. That year, she split her time between two homes, Marshai and Safehaven, for Katherine more or less demanded that she visit them often. Each town had become just like the others in the realm and was busily building the walls that would help to protect them, an order that had been given by Council of the Castle and announced by James the Good at the previous year's Blossom Festival, festivals that were put on hold indefinitely.

There were not many scouting trips during that time, for the first step in the Council's plan was to protect the homeland. In the process, Safehaven had grown economically due to the rock quarry as had been forecasted. However, the disappearances continued, the black serpents remained an ominous mystery, the walls slowly grew around the towns, and the Snipes continued in their reconnaissance. All the while, John of Scharp created as many weapons as he could for the growing army of the Council, Samuel having become his new apprentice.

"Good morn," Jacqueline said as she entered the smoky weapon master's shop.

She was always like a breath of fresh air and both John and Samuel were ecstatic to see her, or in John's case, to hear her voice. He and his son had been working on the latest order of long-bows and were in the process of stringing them with their firing cords. Nearly a week had been spent twisting them into a braid of three-fold cords. For years, only two twisted strands had been used, but John had learned that the strength of three had never failed in battle.

It had been born from the fact that he and his family had been left as such and he knew that together, the three of them would survive whatever seemed to have been coming against the realm like a gathering storm. The pains of missing a son plagued his heart, and he was often found in silence, trying to imagine what had become of his first-born. The three-fold concept had been one of the comforts of his heart and the weapon master found that he, his second son, and his wife had grown tremendously close. Whenever Jacqueline would show up, it was a bonus and a delight.

"What new news?" inquired John.

"Six of the seven townships have completed their walls; all except for this one. Unfortunately, it has lagged behind considerably because of the quarry," Jacqueline cautiously related. "I've come to see what I can do to help."

"You have a good heart, dear." John seemed to be in a melancholy mood and Jacqueline perceived that he had been low in spirit.

"Samuel, can you show me how your playing has progressed?" she inquired.

"Can I, Da'?"

"For a short time, sure," replied the weapon master.

Jacqueline had been speaking of the boy's newfound talent to play the lyre. Samuel had a dream whereby he had seen himself playing an instrument of strings. In it, he had been standing in the corner of a great room, which he told his Da' and Ma', had an oversized chair that had been set high above a number of steps. From underneath the steps, he continued, flowed a stream of liquid gold that created a mist that filled the entire hall. At first, the instrument had been playing of its own accord, but as he picked it up, he was able to mimic its melodies. Shortly after the dream, John, able to understand such mysterious things, fashioned the lyre according to Samuel's description.

The weapon master continued his work and Jacqueline took up where Samuel had left off. Samuel obtained the instrument and from the moment that he plucked the strings, the atmosphere in the hovel changed dramatically. To both Jacqueline and John, it felt like someone had suddenly poured that same liquid gold that Samuel had described from his dream down upon their heads. The chords had found the crevices of their hearts like streams that seek low ground.

Katherine had been in the garden area and was trying to dig through the hardened soil to prepare for the coming planting season. She had hung the previous season's clippings in the back of the weapon shop to keep them warm, and when she heard the music, she decided that it was time to check in on them.

She entered quietly and walked over to Jacqueline with outstretched arms. They hugged for some time for it had been a while since the last visit. After the greeting, the three sat quietly and just listened to the soothing flow of melodies as they bathed them in warmth. Samuel had truly been given a gift, a gift that always brought comfort and healing to their hearts.

They bathed in the invisible 'liquid gold' for some time until Samuel had come to a place of hushed tones. Jacqueline boldly seized the moment to inquire of the weapon master about his past, questions no one else dared to ask.

"How did you lose your sight, John?" she asked.

He had evaded the question for years, and even his wife was vague as to how it had happened, but many things had changed as of late. Katherine quietly shook her head at Jacqueline, trying to dissuade her from the line of questioning, but was amazed as John broke his silence:

"Well, let me tell you. Without going into too much detail…" Silence prevailed as Samuel continued on a subdued rift… "I had been commissioned as a soldier of the king and council shortly before the Campaign of Eight."

Samuel almost dropped his lyre and the music suddenly ceased at his Da's revelation. He sat opened mouthed.

"Please continue, Samuel," said John and continued his tale, "Like you, Jacqueline, I had earned a spot alongside the great Captain of the Guard. Nathan himself became my mentor, but he was much more than that. He became a close friend. People only know a fraction of the greatness of that man. Without him, I would not be here. He saved my life many times."

Katherine released tears as she recalled the time that she had nearly lost her first love. She silently wept as her husband continued.

"Beyond the great southern forest and past the reaches of the river lies a vast and barren desert. Through that wasteland there lay an enormous city shaped like… Well, it's shaped like a gravestone. It's called Gish." John's voice cracked at the recollection, but he managed to continue, "Gish is named for its mysteriously darkened depths. I was taken there, against my will…"

Samuel was finding it hard to continue his playing but perceived that the music was somehow helping his Da' work through his painful memories. He changed his tune, and when he did, his Da' nodded at him.

"Thank you, son." John straightened his back in his chair and continued again after clearing his throat. "The Campaign of Eight brought us to a valley that lies just east of the tail end of the river. You know it as the Vale of Decision. It's the very one that our king was killed within… One hundred and twenty of us had gathered on horseback just north of the deathly expanse." Again, the weapon master found it difficult to continue.

"You don't have to tell us." Jacqueline declared.

"No, I have too… It's all right my dear. You should know. You should all know. Our mission was to reach the dark mouth of the cave on the far end of the battlefield, a cave so ominous and foreboding that it strikes fear just to look into it. But it's what we had been working for, training for, preparing for. The enemy had lined the edges of the bowl-shaped valley from one end to the other… There were hundreds of them… It was the most fear I had ever felt. The very wind of that place seemed to jeer at us. As they awaited our charge, they beat their drums of war so loud that the dirt and rocks beneath our horses actually shook in response.

We were vastly outnumbered, but we knew that what lay beyond that gate was a treasure so valuable that even the king gave his life trying to attain it."

"What's the prize, Da?" Samuel burst in.

"I don't know, boy. I never made it through the gate. None of us did. We were slain like sheep before the slaughter. I didn't even make it halfway across the expanse before I was struck from my horse. I had so many arrows in me that I lost count before I passed out. What happened after that, I don't even know…"

The silence hung thick in the air. Samuel's tune became shaky.

"I woke up high above a bridge that overlooked the largest, dirtiest, and darkest city I had ever seen. They called the place, Mocker's Bridge. Below me, thousands had gathered. They were everywhere. They threw anything and everything that they could find at me. I was struck so many times. Between moments of utter blackness, which I will never recall, they shouted and threw and threw. The pain was unbearable. Finally, as night fell over the land, the crowd suddenly dispersed and I was left alone… and locked there… Left to suffer the terrors of the darkness… Left to the claws of…" John finally broke down at the recollection and couldn't continue. His weeping segued to a flood of tears so great that Samuel flushed with embarrassment and had to leave the shop, crying himself.

As he left, Katherine spoke to him, "Samuel?" He stopped without turning. "Can you please get your Da' a towel and some water?"

"Yes, Ma'"

They waited for his return for far too long. When they finally decided to see where he had disappeared to, all they found was a dropped cloth and a felled wooden cup lying in the mud of the courtyard. Tracks with drag marks made their way beyond the stone gate and toward the direction of the river and the great southern forest, which some had named, The Dead Forest.

Katherine yelled so loudly that she passed out and never fully came back around. John, the weapon master, fell on his face wailing and covered his head with the dirt of the courtyard. It would be days before he would rise again.

As for Jacqueline, she quickly mounted her mocha-colored horse and pursued the enemy with all of her heart, determined to fulfill her mission.

That was, to find both sons of the weapon master.

Together, the horse and rider raced in the direction of the great woods armed with not only a string of daggers down her left arm marked by red stones, but with a crossbow slung over her shoulder and resting upon her back. She also wore the dark cloak that was Jonathan's at one time, and it flowed in the wind behind her.

✝

The Princess and the Prophet

Jacqueline plunged headlong into the thickness of the woods. Her determination to catch up with the young lad Samuel and who or whatever had taken him caused her to barely notice the great whirlpool as she whisked past the spot where it had once threatened to swallow the entirety of the search party. She and her horse danced back and forth ducked and darted as they flew under trees over brush brambles and around stumps.

Only occasionally would she look for any sort of tracks, putting more of her focus on time rather than methodology. When not only her adrenaline had slowed, but her cadence as well, she realized that a more seasoned warrior would have methodically and patiently tracked her friend and his captor.

Be that as it may, she suddenly found herself in a thickened wood with no sense of direction and not knowing which way to turn.

Dismounting her horse, she fell to her knees and let out a cry that echoed throughout the trees. She had been trained to corral her emotions, but the occurrences of late had gotten the better of her and for a moment, one of the thin roots of anger wept its way toward remorse. Alas, it felt good to let her feelings roar. That was when a mysterious figure emerged from the woods in her direction leaning upon a crooked cane.

"What's all the noise about?" emerged a grumbling voice.

By instinct, Jacqueline produced one of her daggers and poised herself ready to strike, "Who are you?"

"Ah, the real question is… Who are you?"

The old man was hunched over and had a face that was kind but lined with the wrinkles of years-worth of pain. In typical fashion, whatever hand that was not holding the crooked cane, was holding the small of his back for he often switched from one to the other and was constantly shifting from one hip to the other hip. His clothes were made of some sort of fur, but they were furs that had been pulled apart and more or less appeared as motley scraps of cloth hanging from his frail frame. Jacqueline figured him to be a beggar of sorts that had long ago been banished from… somewhere.

"I ask you again, young lady… WHAT'S ALL THE YELLING ABOUT!?" he hollered with his cane lifted into the air!

"… I'm seeking a friend. He was taken from the township of Safehaven… Have you seen a small boy with anyone… or anything?" she asked as she unconsciously slid her dagger back into one of her arm hilts.

"What do you mean by anything?" inquired the old fellow.

"Have you not heard about the plague of serpents in the realm?"

The old man began to chuckle at her question. "There has always been a plague of serpents in this realm; nay, in all realms. It just depends on how you interpret the term, serpents. If you are speaking of the one's that have been trained to steal your people away, then yes, I have been aware of them."

The man spoke with mysterious underlying themes that Jacqueline had picked up on right away. He seemed to be wise, and she could only guess at what age the man had reached. He was kind, almost jovial, and she felt comfortable in his presence. There seemed to be hardly a crooked bone in his body even though his back, arms, and fingers were attached at various angles.

"Come with me," he motioned with his wrinkled hand.

"But I have to find the boy. I'm in a hurry."

"There's your first problem. You're in too much of a hurry. You have always been in too much of a hurry. Everyone has been in too much of a hurry. Where is everyone running too? They go here, they go there; they just go, go, and go. Here, there…"

The man began talking to himself and trailed off into mumbles as he limped back into the woods that he had emerged from. At the edge he stopped, half turned around, and spied Jacqueline beyond the bridge of his long elbow of a nose.

"Now, now all of a sudden you want to stop? I thought you were in a hurry? Well, hurry up and follow me then. I'm only an old man you know, and I'm beating you already…"

Again, the man turned, and his voice trailed off as he disappeared into the thickness of the forest. Jacqueline grabbed the reins of her horse and hesitated to follow. Against her common judgment, she decided to follow the old fellow, for there was something endearing about the old wretch that hustled her feet to catch up, her courser trailing behind.

After a few minutes, she caught the man who was still hobbling along. He had grown silent and was intent on placing one foot in front of the other. Another summer had dried out the vegetation and the heartier of the trees had completed their battle against the aggressive undergrowth, some having won the fight and some having lost it. The losers were bone dry, and the young soldier remembered that the forest had been named the dead forest for such reasons, although when she was a little girl, she had always thought that it was called such a name for the dangers of the place.

As she closed in closer to the stranger, she found that she suddenly felt safe near the old man who had finally reached an opening in the trees and approached a giant rock that sat in the middle of a glade.

As they neared the enormous stone, Jacqueline could see that it had been more or less hollowed out to form a cave into which home-like features appeared. There was a small, thatched bed, a chair or two, a small table made from willow branches, and a fire pit over which two rabbits were roasting on a spit. She found it strange, as if the old man had been waiting for someone to join him for the meal though she did not voice her opinion.

"I have been waiting for you," he stated as he took the reins of her horse and motioned for her to take a seat at the willow table.

He then commenced to tie the mare to a nearby post, "Have you named her?" he inquired.

"Have I named who?" asked the young lady.

"Now, that's a question I could really use to make your head spin. But, for now, I'll keep it simple since you're new to the ways of the realm. You must be what, sixteen or seventeen now?"

"Aye, seventeen, sir. I'm just about to have a birthday."

"Ah, yet another opportunity to make your head spin. You really make this fun, you know that?" The fellow hesitated, looking deeply in Jacqueline's eyes.

His, in return, seemed to glaze over as if he were looking beyond her outer appearance. His mouth released a slight smile almost as if he were hearing someone talking to him. Then he continued again, "You have a good heart. You speak the way of the shadows, so I know that it's good. I would call it… a purity."

Another pause hung in the air.

"The horse, have you named her?"

"No, I have not." Jacqueline said somewhat embarrassed.

"You have to name her. She's what carries you, moves you, bear's your burdens. Believe me, in the fray of battle, she can become your very best friend… your only friend." He was looking away to some distant place and perhaps to some distant time as well… "So, name her now," the old man snapped back into focus, "But whatever you name her, know that she may just become her namesake."

Jacqueline had never thought to name her faithful horse. It had been given to her from the Nasgroth of Marshai, she and her mother's benefactor. It was a gift for being accepted to the royal academy. From the moment of her appointment to the military institute, the young soldier's life had moved at such a fast pace that there was hardly time to think, only time to react. Though the mocha-colored horse had been a faithful friend, and at times a confidant, she had never recognized the fact.

Jacqueline took the time to think about what she had been to her in the past and what she expected of her in the future. The old fellow had made his way to the roasting rabbits and was testing them for their readiness. The young soldier could smell the aroma of the meal, and her mouth watered ever so slightly as her furrowed brow revealed her mind's inner search for a namesake.

"Everheart", she finally said, "For she has, and will always, carry me steadfastly through whatever I have to face in the future."

The old man turned from the spit with the meats in hand and smiled at the young lady. "That name will ring true even through the greatest trial of your life… which is coming your way. But take heart, for you will prevail. Yes, you will prevail, my dear."

Jacqueline felt a chill trickle down her spine, but it was not out of fear. It was rather out of a knowing that what the man had just said would one day return to her. For the time being, however, she placed the words on a shelf hidden within her heart and joined the man in a delicious meal.

Not a lot more was said as they supped together on victuals that tasted heavenly. They had been flavored with aromatic spices that Jacqueline had never tasted nor smelled before.

"They come from the forest… and other places." stated that man through a full mouth responding to her thoughts.

"What comes from the forest?"

Again, the man chuckled, but waved off his thought. "The spices… You were just thinking about the spices."

"How do you do that?" asked Jacqueline.

"It's simple… I listen. So easy a child could do it. Actually, come to think of it, a child is much better at it than an adult. You're in between the two, but not for long." Again, the man peered into her eyes as his appearance glazed over again and another smile slid its way across his face.

"The child that you seek has gone underground… The young man, his brother, has gone high above it. You will see the latter right where I have told you, but you won't perceive it. You will see the young one many days from now like the shadows of another scroll being unfurled. The mission that you have set your heart upon will only be completed within the protection of numbers, and the stone will glow white hot. And that's a good thing, for it will light your path, nay, it will light all of your paths."

Jacqueline watched as the man dug into his food once again. A tear slipped from the corner of her eye, but it was a tear of happiness. After some time passed, the man spoke again.

"May I ask a quest' of you?" inquired the old prophet.

"Yes, of course."

"Take the pathway east of here."

"What path?"

"That one," he said as he pointed over his shoulder.

In the distance, Jacqueline could see that a small trail meandered up a hill. She hadn't seen it before even though she thought that she had completely surveyed her surroundings as her training had taught her.

"I want you to see something… Take that pathway and follow it to the end, only walk lightly and keep your head held high. It will lead you to a revelation that has been a great concern of mine. With the knowledge that you will receive, you will know how to combat one of the greatest evils in the realm… It's been nice to speak with you, dear. I don't get many visitors you know. Not anymore… I bid you farewell."

Jacqueline knew that her time with the stranger had come to a close, but she didn't want it to. Her insides were buzzing with excitement. She had never sat at the feet of such a wise person. The man seemed so familiar that she felt like he could have been her grandfather, or even her father. She had never known a father-figure save for her trainers, but they were too busy teaching the art of war to take the time to speak with her. The emotions that rippled within her were like waves of joy cascading over her heart and filling the pools of her soul.

"It's time to go, my child," stated the old fellow. "… At least for now."

"Aye, sir… Thank you."

Jacqueline made her way to Everheart and mounted the horse of war. Settling herself upon the mare's back, she patted the neck of her friend and cantered across the glade. She wanted to look back but was not sure whether the old man and his rock would have even been there. She chose not to and ascended the trail that he had directed her to with great thoughts of hope filling her soul. Little did she know that a horror of colossal proportions was about to meet her head on.

It was not long before the forest grew dark again and the sky above disappeared beyond the canopy of the trees. An ominous sound began to grow in her ears. She had wished that she were not alone. If only the old man could have been a much younger man, or a valiant prince, or even a strong farmer that could have ridden with her, she mused. However, she took strength in the man's words that there was a reason for her to take the journey and that his prophetic words seemed to speak of a vast future beyond her current situation. At the same time, he had told her that success lies in numbers. Things were quickly becoming cloudy and confusing, and she was fearful… doubtful. Then she realized why.

Holding her head high, as the mysterious man had said, most likely proved to save her life for as she continued along the trail, she not only heard the sound of hissing but saw the vine-like breeding grounds of a million tiny serpents.

If she had not become aware of their presence far above her and hanging from the limbs of great trees, she would most likely have made noises that would have stirred the army of little beasts. As she caught sight of them, she became aware of a strange yellow haze that floated just above her head but descended almost to ground level further up the trail like smoke that fills a confined space. Halting Everheart, and with as little noise as possible, she dismounted and walked the horse to a safe distance where she loosely tethered her friend to a tree.

Then she continued up the trail on foot and alone.

From what Jacqueline could tell, the baby serpents were sleeping, or hibernating, or germinating, or something. Either way, they were oblivious to the presence of the young woman far below them. The mist that emanated from their breathing was heavy. When Jacqueline had reached the point in the path where it hovered close to the ground, she crouched down and continued on hands and knees. She continued that way up a hill and to a rise. Rolling onto her back, she peered up to see if the numbers of serpents had lessened. To her shock and horror, they had become so think that she could no longer see the branches of the trees that they hung from. It sickened her in the stomach and bile crept its way into her throat. Fortunately, and unfortunately, she had reached the end of the trail and could continue no further through the macabre tunnel of terror.

The snake-like passageway paled in comparison to what she saw over the cliffs that she was perched upon. Far below, a massive pit opened right out of the forest. Ten or twenty Brittle Marshes could have easily been dumped into the cavity. As far as she could see, there was an expanse so wide that it seemed a whole ocean could be housed within its depths. It was filled with workers that looked like dead people walking and there were hundreds of them. They appeared to be soldiers as well for they wore the armor of warfare and supported weapons, some of which Jacqueline had never even fathomed before. Their faces were shrouded by coverings that hid everything save for their eyes. It was a massive army of soldier/workers, but what they were doing horrified the young lady even more.

Everywhere that she looked, pits full of the tiny vipers were being crushed into great vats like grapes that are smashed for their juices. The blood of slaughter was so deep that some of the workers waded knee high in the crimson flow through pools that the vats were constantly filling. The workers that tended them carried elongated and woven scoopers that they were using to filter a steaming yellow liquid substance that they collected into barrels. Other soldier/workers would then seal the massive wooden barrels and roll them great distances to where they would dump them into long rectangular shallow pools. Jacqueline was in awe of the sheer amount of yellow substance filling the shallows. If it were in a more pleasant place, it would have appeared as almost beautiful, but a pleasant surrounding would have been impossible. There was yet another workforce that was setting the shallows ablaze with fire. Once aflame, the orange glow emanated an acrid smoke that made the air around it waver with gaseous fumes. The final step in the process appeared to be a yellow cake-like substance that yet more assemblymen were shoveling into baskets. Where the baskets were being taken, she could only guess.

Jacqueline observed the ominous 'factory' of workers and was in awe at its efficiency and sheer grandeur. How it would be a revelation that could combat a great evil, she was not certain. What was for certain, however, was the fact that it had been the most wretched site she had ever seen, and quite possibly, would ever set her eyes upon again. She observed for as long as she could stand the site, but what caused her to abandon her position was not expired time, but rather her stomach that reversed course so she could not hold the earlier meal of roasted rabbit any longer…

Her throwing up awoke the multitudes of serpents above her position!

A hissing commenced so loud that she thought that her eardrums would explode. Along with the fury of the little creatures as they discovered that their nest had been disturbed, came a thick and sickening acrid and somewhat sweet aroma. At first smell, Jacqueline was tempted to just lie still in the fumes to breathe it in, but her consciousness saved her, and she raced back down the trail in the direction of her horse. Only a few steps into the cloud, however, she began to stagger upon her legs. Her path became crooked as the trail ahead became twisted. Her mind began to grow tired, and her breathing became labored. She wanted to lie down and go to sleep, and one step further, she would have done so if it were not for the fact that Everheart had galloped right into the cloud to assist her master.

The horse bucked and then nudged Jacqueline. The soldier's eyes felt heavy, but she had just enough sense to fumble for the reins. Once she found them, she swung herself to the saddle with the little remaining strength that she had and spurred her horse to flee. As they ran, Jacqueline could hear the thud of falling snakes behind her but had not the strength to turn and see.

Somewhere in the midst of the chaos, Everheart had carried the two of them off the path that they had been following and raced deeply into the forest. If Jacqueline had not finally passed out on the back of the horse, she could have halted the mare. As it was, they both ran so far into the depths of the great southern forest that they became utterly and completely lost in its vast wilderness.

Once there, they were doomed to wander in hopes that someday they would find civilization again, but that would be quite a while, if ever…

✝

The Peaceless

The sudden and hot wind that struck the war party on the rim of the bowl-shaped vale had merely been the beginning of their troubles. Not only were they struck from the backs of their horses, but they had also lost their footing and tumbled down the steep bank of the mountain. At the bottom of the fall, Edgemont, James the Younger, Brenda, and the six other Council warriors struggled to regain their wits… six, because one of them was dead having been thrown against rocks and deadened Willowfeld trees. James had sustained a broken left wrist that was twisted to his medial side at nearly a forty-five-degree angle and was swelling immensely. The others fared better, for they mostly suffered from more bruises than breaks. They were given no time to mourn or feel remorse, for the enemy was quickly converging on their positions. James and the war party scrambled.

The enemy sentries were caught off guard when the mighty rush of wind bellowed from the mouth of darkness. They had been stationed in the Vale as part of the normal rotation. (We have already been made aware of one of the enemy soldier's other rotations, the snake pits.) The Vale rotation was a quiet post for the most part, but the great wind had suddenly announced the intruders and it shook the sentries into action. Their numbers were thirty-nine strong, Magreth's protocol for the protection of the cave that sat below the Sturmstone tower. There would have been a multitude more if word had reached the enemy of an impending attack, but then again, it was originally meant to be a scouting party.

When James and his comrades were more or less spilled into the bowl of the valley, they swiftly became a war party and the inevitable fight for their very lives hung in the balance.

The advancing Magreth soldiers dared not tread upon the floor of the Vale of Blood. No one ever did unless absolutely necessary, a fate that will be revealed in time.

The leader of the thirty-nine, a man named Chion, ordered them to be split into two squads. After climbing down from the Sturmstone 'nests', twenty of them followed him around the blood-soaked valley to the right on the bottom edge of the bowl. The other nineteen made their way around to the left. Paths had long been carved around the edges that served to make their march that much easier.

Edgemont spotted them across the vast expanse of the valley and recognized their tactics immediately. He knew that the enemy leader had meant to pinch them between the two, thereby creating a two-front skirmish. Edgemont quickly devised a plan of counterattack. He ordered the party to take up defensive positions as high up the side of the bowl as possible. He wanted to take advantage of the high ground. Unfortunately, due not only to their injuries, but the sheer steepness of the valley's sides, they were forced to conceal themselves in wind swept and gangly tree trunks. James scrambled to the one that his already dead comrade had been ensnared by.

The thought of using not only the tree trunk, but the body of his comrade for shielding made him slightly wretch and he quickly spat out the vomit, for the enemy was advancing rapidly.

"Hold your positions as long as possible," shouted Edgemont du Val. "Fire as many projectiles as possible and make every shot count. Once we're out of ammunition, we're going to make a sprint for the cave."

"Pardon my words, but have you lost your mind, Edge?" questioned Brenda. "We can't make it across the expanse with these kinds of numbers."

"Bren', we're heavily outnumbered. It's our only chance out of this," he responded as he motioned for Brenda to look at the others. They were greatly concerned, and she relented.

"Your right, sir. I'm sorry."

Chion and his soldiers were approaching the halfway point when he stopped to signal to the others on the opposite side of the valley. He had seen that the Council warriors had been given the order to take to higher ground so he himself wanted to get his soldiers as high as possible as well and thereby attempt to descend upon his enemy. With open arm motions he spoke to the second half of his squadron in code, who responded to him in like manner.

Edgemont recognized the move and knew that his options were quickly diminishing, and his 'last stand' tactic loomed larger and larger. With the revelation, he knew it was time to address his crew of a mere six soldiers.

"Gentleman… My lady. Across that hideous blood-stained floor lays our only means of escape. My first command still stands, but when it comes time to make our break, we will… And we will make it together. What waits for us out there is difficult to explain. I can only say that we face more of the enemy than just the ones that you can see with your own eyes… Look long and hard at the floor of that valley. It was stained with the blood of our king himself. What lies beyond that cave is a treasure so great that he himself died in an attempt to get there… all by himself. We, we are six strong."

His soldiers were watching him intently. They knew what his words meant to them, and they all were thinking the same thing when Edgemont continued.

"Make no mistake comrades. Some of us will not make it out of this, but now is the time to read the writing on the walls of your heart and ponder their meanings… It is the time to ponder the common oath that we all took as soldiers of the kingdom. Whether you believe those words or not, the core of our oath is to gain the treasure within that cave… Now is the time to make your decision a firm foundation upon which to lay down your lives… For that treasure… is our people… They are our brothers, our sisters, our mothers, and our fathers. They are in vast prisons beneath our feet and only one of us needs to get the message to them. Remember the words of your oath. These advancing soldiers will do anything to keep us from reaching the prisoners, for that is their oath… Are we going to let them? Well, are we?"

"No sir," the remaining five yelled in unison.

"This day, we will make our lives memorable!"

"Aye!" they responded as an arrow whisked past them and stuck fast into the tree that James was concealed behind. It was duel pronged, and it served as a beacon which declared that the fight had commenced.

The party of six hid in their redoubts as a volley of arrows rained down upon them, striking two of them and killing one. It was Brenda, and she had been struck right through the neck and jugular vein. The remaining five rose from their hiding and returned fire. Three attacked to their right flank and two to their left. Five of the enemy soldiers quickly fell dead in their tracks.

Chion continued the advance as his soldiers obeyed his command to continue. Each flank would advance one step at a time as they lined up three soldiers side by side. It would have been a wider wall if the path had not been so narrow. After one group of three would fire from kneeling positions, three more would fire from standing positions. Then another three would advance around the kneeling ones and it would all start over again. The result was a near constant barrage of arrows that looked like a great caterpillar of death advancing toward the Council warriors who were using up their own ammunition quickly.

The right flank diminished more rapidly than the left, for they were being counterattacked by three, whereas the left were by two. The Council soldiers didn't lose another person for some time as they fired as fast as they could. Edgemont counted the enemies' losses at approximately ten on his right and five on his left. That would put their diminished number at twenty-four.

As for James, he was once again proving himself in battle. His training had solidified his soldiery. Having a severely broken extremity made his fight difficult, but the adrenaline of the fight-or-flight system within him more than overcame the pain. He was right-handed and had long spent the number of daggers that he had on his person. He had even thrown one of his slender swords and it had felled two enemy warriors in one throw, for it had passed through the one and into the thigh of the other thereby lodging into the latter's femoral artery which quickly drained the man of life-sustaining blood.

Chion, seeing his numbers quickly diminishing, gave the order to charge and both flanks broke rank to run wholeheartedly at the five defenders. That's when Edgemont gave the order to make a break for the valley and the deep cave in the distance. The enemy perceived the order and pursued them into it.

As James hit the floor of the Vale of Blood, he felt the strange sensation that he was running across a snow like landscape. The dust of the valley floor was so dry and cold that it dispersed from around his feet like escaping flurries. At the same time, he felt heated wind slam into his face head on.

Nevertheless, he ran with all of his might towards the heart of darkness.

James was the type of lad that had never accepted the message of the Shadow Scrolls, neither had his parents nor family members. To him, the scrolls were too incomplete of a story to put much merit in. The first spoke of how the king had been killed in the vale... To what end, he didn't know. The second spoke of how the same king had been lowered into a bottomless pit... Again, to what end, he didn't know. As for the third Scroll, there was no third.

He had been taught that there was perhaps another, but it had never been found, let alone read by anyone of his generation or any recent generation. The Scrolls had never even given the king a name and the whole concept of 'kingdom' had fallen into near obscurity. When the Council of the Castle had assumed control of the realm, the succession of seven Nasgroths had watered down the stories over time until they had fallen into mere fable. He had read the Scrolls during his education about the history of his realm and how there were moments in time when belief in the Scrolls would re-surface on a larger scale.

The Campaign of Eight provided one such moment, but for the most part, it had failed to accomplish its task of completely delivering the realm from all enemies foreign and domestic even though the hearts of the entire kingdom were sewn together toward one common victory under the banner of the Scrolls. James also found it strange that the Oath of Soldiery, which he took upon completing his training, contained the words, 'to fight for the King's prize.' He not only misunderstood it, but had never really em-braced it either. However, having just re-read what was written on the walls of his heart by the taking of that oath, the son of James the Good, Nasgroth of Trelane, was running for his life in the hope that somehow, and in some way, it would prove to be the truth.

The sword hit him in the upper right thoracic region of his back, piercing his body completely.   He spun around one hundred eighty degrees. The pain caused by the cold blade felt sharp and stinging. Though it struck on the lateral side, he felt the pain in his midline and his heart skipped a beat. With the spinning motion, came the view of his scrambling comrades rather than the ominous cave that he had been sprinting toward. All of them had already fallen in battle and he was the last one to fall.

He landed in the shadow of one of the Sturmstone pillars that poked skyward through the floor of the bloody vale. In fact, he had been running so fast that when he fell, he slid into the foot of the immovable object slamming into it with such great force that he was nearly knocked unconscious. He ended up on his side, facing the direction of his fallen friends. Chion, the leader of the enemy horde, was walking in his direction his weapon having hit its mark. Beyond the figure of the man, James was stunned and horrified to see the ominous sight of his friends and comrades being dragged hand and foot by invisible creatures into pits that had opened up to swallow them whole just beneath the jutting pillars of crumbling marble.

James tried to rise from his position, but the exhaustion and blood loss had sucked the strength right out of him.

As Chion came closer, he produced a dagger and was going to finish his work which he had begun on the young man. Out of a sense of shear survival, James tried to block the stab with his remaining good arm. The knife struck him in the forearm and fastened to the bony substance of his ulna. Though pain filled, it gave James the chance to strike the enemy leader across the face with his other still broken arm. More pain than he had ever felt in his life shot through the dendrites of his entire nervous system. Then, both of them found themselves lying on the valley floor, skirmishing with hits and head butts…

Until the two opposing soldiers felt a strange sensation; a sensation that was a wrapping itself around their ankles like a life constricting serpent.

Chion kicked and screamed just as loudly as James did as they both, now equals and equally afraid, tried to escape the clutches of creatures that they could not see. They both, however, could certainly feel the invisible claws that were starting to firmly lodge into the meaty portions of their calf muscles. And no amount of fighting the specters could accomplish anything. Then, both men were simultaneously dragged against their wills below the surface of the Vale of Decision.

The war party's fight occurred nearly one year prior, and the battlefield had never coughed up any soldier back upon its bloody dust-filled barren expanse, not even one soul, including James the Younger.

Chapter 7

A Rise to Power

†

The Vale of Decision

Jonathan knew instinctively that he was the only one left at the camp for he did not hear, smell, or sense any other. The first thing that he saw was the scroll that Dodd had left for him lying on a rock. Unfurling it, he read:

Farewell my friend, until a more opportune time. If you are reading this script, then know that you have completed your training. It has been an honor and a privilege to have had you as my student. Never before have I seen such natural talent and cunning intuition. Your eye and your shot are truly one, with one motion aimed for one kill. Though I know that you have not the heart to take another's life, you may just have to when there is no other choice. I say, kill or be killed.

For one final test, which you have the freedom to attempt the task or not (for only one other has ever completed the trial, and it could cost you your life) is to retrieve your own Willowfeld branch from The Vale of Blood. If successful, fashion your own long bow from it, and you will be most revered, even as Magreth has been, for he is that 'only other one'. The Vale is due west of the camp. Fare thee well.

~Thomas Dodd

It took Jonathan a day and a half to reach the Vale of Decision. Thomas must have stopped there on his way to wherever he was headed to, for when the young master of weapons had arrived, he was an expected arrival. The sentry soldiers greeted him with growls.

"Aye Flynn, we've got our chummy here," hollered one of the sentries to his captain who answered with an equal growl.

"Send em' over."

Flynn was a stout warrior who looked battle hardened by many a skirmish. Upon his head was a leather helm that curved around the contours of his face and had protrusions that met at his nose, thereby protecting it. Jonathan wondered whether he had the helmet made before or after he had sustained a cut to the face, for a large chunk was missing from his nose. "You think that's bad, look at this," Flynn continued, spying that Jonathan had caught sight of his past wound. Flynn turned his leg to show Jonathan that most of the meat on the back of his leg was missing. The wound had healed, but made it appear as though he had a wooden leg.

"How'd you get that?" asked Jonathan.

"I received it about ten years ago… out there," Flynn replied with a nod of the head. They were located high atop the Sturmstone pillar that arose above the mouth of the cave of darkness. The bowl-shaped valley was spread out far below them, its rim far above. "Funny thing is, I didn't get it from an enemy soldier. It came from the Nephim, and the thing stripped the muscle right off my bone." Flynn's voice trailed off as he looked out across the expanse of the battlefield… "Do you know how disconcerting it is for your leg to go missing by a creature you can't even see? Well, it's very disconcerting."

"The Nephim?" asked the young warrior.

"Yes, the fallen ones…" Flynn then re-focused his eyes on Jonathan once again. "Why are you here, anyway?"

"I've been sent on a quest."

"A quest… For what?" asked the leader of the sentries.

"For a Willowfeld branch," retorted Jonathan at which Flynn roared with laughter.

"What? What is it," asked the young treasure hunter.

"Thomas has sent you on a snipe hunt. You know what a snipe hunt is? It's like trying to catch the air. No one ensnares the snipe bird," stated Flynn and continued to chuckle.

"I've seen it done."

"Oh yeah? Where?"

"I witnessed an eagle catch one the first day at training camp."

"Hah!" By that time, others had made their way over to where Flynn spoke with the newling. "The lad wants to go into the Vale for a Willowfeld branch!" Flynn announced in a sing-song voice and all those gathering cackled into laughter.

Jonathan turned and started to head down the outcropping and into the vale without a word.

"You really goin' in there? Hey, hey!" Flynn bolted in front of Jonathan and placed a powerful hand on his chest to stop him. "We've all had a good laugh now, but you can't go in there. The Nephim don't play games… They'll shred you to pieces. No one makes it out there. Not us. Nor our enemies. Not even animals survive out there."

"Someone has, right?"

"So they say, but it's only a legend."

Jonathan smiled at the leader and grabbed him by the shoulders. He was taller than Flynn and when he spoke it was from above. "Let's create a new legend, eh?"

"All right, but if you hear wind... you're already dead."

Jonathan had made his way down to the valley below and stood on the edge of the wicked expanse with his toes just over the demarcation line between the natural soil of the surrounding landscape and the dusty, blood-stained soil of the battlefield. With determination furrowing his brow, he surveyed his surroundings. It was his first sight of the infamous valley that he had only heard about in the scroll stories and the re-enactment plays and for a moment, caused him to question his own doubts about the scrolls for it was truly a hideous sight to behold. Above him, the edges of the rim rocks loomed large and cast shadows throughout the vale; shadows that looked like some sort of dragon. He saw the Sturmstone pillars poking through the floor of the field just as he had been told by his childhood teachings. Also present were the Willowfeld tree trunks that had been wind swept and deadened.

Standing out above all of the rest, was the macabre cave that spit out sulfuric yellow mists of vapor. It sat to his right and almost seemed to be beckoning the young soldier to come and take a look into its gaping mouth. There was no sign of the Nephim, but then again, they were invisible.

Jonathan could hear the sentries placing bets as to whether he would survive from the Sturmstone pillar above the grotto, but his mind was made up. He would complete his task or die trying. However, putting a name to the invisible specters did make the whole thing a bit more... ominous.

"Fallen ones," he murmured to himself.

Jonathan spotted a particular root system that appeared promising though, but unfortunately, it was close to the mouth of the cave. Like a man that contemplates a high leap, he stood on the edge of his sprint knowing that if he waited too long, like the said jumper, it would never get done. He left his place before his mind could convince him otherwise and headed out into the battlefield.

The dust around his feet reminded him of the days when he had trudged through the streets of Gish. The valley was exceptionally quiet like those long-ago snowstorms and their eerie peacefulness. He zigzagged his way through the battlefield like a cat that stalks its prey. Intuitively, he utilized his stealth ability by staying in the shadows that the pillars cast and crept from one to the other. When he had finally reached the last one closest to the felled tree trunk, he saw that it was a good choice. The tree itself had long ago been blown over by some gale force wind and its roots presented previously bent sticks. The forceful wind must have emerged from the cave, surmised Jonathan. As if something were reading his thoughts, his first step toward the root system was met with an ominous sound from the deep.

As he crept, the noise froze him where he stood. Somewhere behind the rotted mossy veil of the cave, a bellowing sound was emitted. At first, it reminded him of the forger's bellow that he and his Da' had used to forge weapons with, but as it grew closer, it sounded more like a fire storm. Jonathan ran to the tree trunk and produced a dagger from his hip hilt. Knowing that his time was short, he hacked away at the root. Its materiel was as hard as an iron sword and try as he might it would not bend; it would not give in to his blows.

"Get out of there!" he heard Flynn's voice from far above as it echoed down from the cliff side, but it was too late.

Jonathan continued his struggle with the root system, a sudden shiver running up his spine and his hair on the back of his head stood on end. He froze once again and dared not to turn around. An instant later, a hot wind struck him with such force that he fell to his knees having been knocked off balance by it. That's when he heard the wheezing sound of an invisible being approaching his position from the depths of the grotto. Turning around in the residue of the dirty floor, he could see that more of the dust was being lifted into the air by the heated wind which created a steadily growing dust devil. Trailing it, tracks came closer, pausing now and again as if made by a leopard that prepares to pounce. Jonathan could hear the being breathing and could even smell its breath. It was putrid like sulfur and dank like mold. Its very presence was overwhelming. Although he was not able to see the being, he knew that the Nephim was much taller than he had ever imagined and, at the moment, was standing tall and fierce.

Then he saw the tracks leave the dust as it must have leaped toward him.

Instinctively, Jonathan threw up his hands to parry the attack. By happenstance, the young soldier had placed his hands so that the sun streamed through them at just the right angle and its rays struck his eyes as if he were peering through green leaves at eventide.

Then it happened, and it would become the stuff of legends.

From his vantage point, Jonathan suddenly witnessed a flash of light so bright that it glowed blue. It was a massive sword, and it appeared out of thin air. In that same moment, he could also see the face of the Nephim and its hideously sunken face… but it wore a look of fear. Wherever the sword had come from, in another blink of an eye, it connected with the figure mid-pounce causing it to vaporize into dust that fell like ash flakes around the young man.

The once invisible enemy had been vanquished instantly!

A moment later, another blue flash of the sword of light whirred just above Jonathan's head and right through the Willowfeld branch he had been struggling with. It fell to the ground with a thud in front of the master of weapons. And then all fell silent again.

Jonathan, stunned by what had just occurred, stared at the branch for what felt like forever. Then another burp of wind came from deep within the grotto causing him to scramble to his feet, grab the felled branch, and sprint out of the Vale of Decision.

As he emerged from the blood-stained field, he heard a cheer rise atop the rocky pillar and could see two sentry soldiers scampering down the backside of the valley's rim. Flynn descended the rocky tower and came down to meet him with arms in the air.

"Whatever that was my friend, you are highly favored." Flynn grabbed him by the back of the shoulders and walked him to where the others were waiting. Jonathan used the Willowfeld branch as a walking stick, for he was sweating profusely due to the leftover adrenaline that had been surging through his system. "By the way, you owe me five gold pieces. I regret to say… I bet against you… Cheer him boys! Cheer this soldier!" And they did.

Flynn ordered two of his men to escort Jonathan back to Gish upon horseback and provided one for him as well. They took him as far as the city and pointed him in the direction of the Turnback Inn. When he arrived, Wisekoff was leaning against the door to the building and was cleaning his teeth with a toothpick. It was a gesture that Jonathan saw as purely symbolic for he knew that Wisekoff and clean teeth were on two different planes all together.

"Ah, the good eagle has arrived at my doorstep," said Wisekoff with his highly refined tongue.

"The what?" asked Jonathan.

"We've all been told about your exploits. They say, 'an eagle has arisen among us...' Would dat' be you, me laddie?" barked Wisekoff in his rough accent once again.

"Aye, it would," Jonathan replied as he dismounted his horse and held the Willowfeld branch high into the air, "On to bigger and better things."

Wisekoff wrapped his arm around his long lost friend, "With the Willowfeld branch as our symbol, we'll just ride the winds of the city, my friend. Me, you, and the Shade... We'll ride the winds to wherever they take us... And I'll be your rudder... (I guess that would only work for a boat wouldn't it?) Ah, no matter... Come wit' me to da' Turnback, John. We got friends that want to say hey." Wisekoff escorted Jonathan up the stairs and his voice echoed off the halls... "Ah, da' Turnback... Remember it?"

They both spoke simultaneously, "Once ya' turn in, there's no turnin' back!"

They opened the door to the second-floor tavern and were met with a cheer that was heard for blocks and blocks around the building.

The cheers wrapped around corners, down streets, and into squares like bubbling ale flowing through blocks that were already abuzz with the news that a great warrior had risen among them. What excited the zombed street people of the city the most was that their new hero had once been homeless like themselves, and for the first time in many, many years, a new hope seemed to bubble up within them like sparkling red wine in their blood…

And they were warmed by it as many of them slept in makeshift hovels made of old crates and overturned apple carts.

✝

Rising in Rank and Order

They partied like they had done a thousand times before, but with one big difference. Jonathan held himself in reserve. He still saluted and gabbed with the others, but rather than allowing the atmosphere to swallow him whole as he used to, he rode above the cacophony of swills armed with the fact that he had been called to a higher purpose and refused to be swayed by distraction, save for one, and she walked through the doors arrayed in the black clothing that he himself had once worn:

"The would-be soldier and his Willowfeld branch," decried Katelyn.

All others in the Turnback Inn paled in comparison, and as Jonathan watched her enter, he could see that she still supported her weight with a slight limp in her left leg. Other than the limp injury, she more or less glided across the room still in her heel to toe manner.

"I believe that we have a seat set aside for you, my dear," Wisekoff's voice rang through the cackle. He felt safe enough to remove his 'rough' mask in his own pub and amongst his closest friends. He met Katelyn with open arms and assisted her to a seat on Jonathan's left... "Ever thought that you'd be a princess?" he whispered to her out of ear shot of even Jonathan.

"My lady," Jonathan greeted her with a nod and laughed. "It's a relief to see you in good health."

"Thanks to you, my hero." she quipped and returned his laughter.

Jonathan had been given a place of prominence in Wisekoff's pub. They had set him in the middle of three high back chairs that almost appeared to be thrones and in a sense they were. The chairs had been acquired from a manor house on the far reaches of the city, chairs that had been once owned and sat in by one of the many lords of Gish before Magreth had overcome them in his quest for power. Jonathan sat and watched the revelers as they played games and carried on, Wisekoff on his right and Katelyn on his left. It was the life he had always dreamed of, and he was quickly becoming comfortable being the center of attention. Still, he could not help the thoughts that drifted in and out of his swelling mind. Wisekoff, recognizing his prize recruit's rising star, arose from his chair, a giant gold goblet in his hand.

"Ladies and gentlemen... Excuse me, ladies and gentlemen!" The partiers quieted as he held his cup high. "A toast to our new friend and hero...

"He has survived the trials of training. He has saved one of our own. And, as of this morning, has even survived a foray into the Vale of Decision. I say we drink a draft to him my friends. May he turn this city upside down, or rather, right side up," and Wisekoff overturned the goblet allowing the contents to drain down his throat.

The cheers that arose spilled over into the streets as the Turnback Inn nearly shook upon its foundations. Wisekoff, ecstatic over the festivities, flew over to the nearest window and flung them open yelling down to whoever happened to be in the streets and invited them inside for warmth and drink. Moments later, the place was so filled with people that both Jonathan and Katelyn had to escape out a window to prevent being crushed by the throngs. Once down, they made their way through the crowd and down the alleyway to where Jonathan's 'apartment' was located.

They stopped in the shadow of the tunnel.

"It was really good to see you doing well," Jonathan said shyly. "I thought that we might have lost you." He still had his Willowfeld branch in his hand and used it to lightly hit the wall trying to chase away the awkward moment.

"The great prince has a way with the art of healing…" A silent moment lingered in the air before Katelyn continued again, "John, I was trying to give my life for the cause."

The dart hit Jonathan like an icicle. "What? What are you talking about?"

"We consider it a great honor to lay down our lives. Martyrdom is a powerful statement… the most powerful one we can make… especially from a leader like myself." She was sincere and Jonathan found the whole conversation suddenly turning ridiculous.

"You've got to be jesting. Thomas never explained these things to me. Is that really the way Magreth has run this city… by the blood of his own people? He wishes you to die, and then helps you recover when you don't? Why, so you can die again? It's madness… stupidity!"

"It's the way he's always run this city."

"Yeah, and look at it. It's rotten. The people have no hope, no purpose, and they're zombed into lethargy by his devilish Serpent's Breath." Jonathan's blood was beginning to boil.

"There's no other way to control the population, John. Our cause is just," she argued.

"Our cause… is to serve the thirst of Magreth's passion for power and control… to serve his unrestrained ambition. It has nothing to do with the city or her people."

"There's no other way, John."

"Yes… Yes there is, and it's about to be revealed if I have anything to do with it."

"You don't mean to stand up to the prince, do you?" Katelyn looked around as if she were scared to be a part of the conversation, and suddenly made subliminal movements revealing her desire to be somewhere else, anywhere else.

"Not right away, but to answer your question, of course I do… and I don't care if he knows. You heard the rumor… 'A great eagle has risen.' Well, here I am," he stated with pomposity swelling within him.

"It's senseless to try to stand up to him. Many have tried before, and all have failed miserably. Besides-"

"Not this time," Jonathan quickly interrupted her, his neck veins swelling with anger. "Mark my words, this city will never be the same again." Jonathan could see the look of shock in Katelyn's face, and softened his tone… "Join me, Katelyn. Wisekoff and I have discussed plans for the future of the Shade. With the power of an eagle, the three of us can become great… greater than Magreth himself."

Katelyn turned away, crossed her arms and spoke to him with her back to him. "I can't… I can't join you," she shook her head while looking at the ground.

Jonathan approached her, placed his hands on her shoulders and spun her around. "You can try… That's all I'm asking of you. Just try."

"I've heard that you defeated one of the Nephim in the Vale… Is that true?"

The moment hung suspended in mid-air…

"Dere' you be. I thought I lost ya's," Wisekoff's voice broke the silence. He handed Jonathan a small scroll and reverted to his normal accent. "It came by herald." It was sealed with the Prince of Gish's private seal. "You have also been summoned to the throne room immediately. Prince Magreth desires to speak with you." Unrolling it, Jonathan read it in silence… "What's it say?" piped in Wisekoff.

"It's my first mission," replied Jonathan with a somber look on his face.

"Come, I'll escort you to his throne," Wisekoff stated.

Jonathan stared Katelyn in the eyes as Wisekoff motioned for him to follow. "I'm not going to his throne… I'll do his missions, but I won't give him the satisfaction of seeing me bow before him. None of us will! Right, Katelyn?"

Another silence prevailed as Wisekoff stood slack jawed awaiting her answer. If it were a 'yes', then their plan would be launched immediately.

"Sure… Fine, yes," she finally stated.

"Wisekoff, can you have some tools sent down? I need to get started on the bow as soon as possible. In the meantime, I suppose I should expect a shipment of armament."

"It's already been arranged," stated Wisekoff.

"I'm sorry Katelyn. I have to go."

"Sure," she replied.

"Trust me, it will be well worth it," Jonathan continued again. "Wisekoff, thank you for the toast; I bid the two of you, goodnight," and he humorously bowed before them.

The young master of weapons then headed through the remainder of the tunnel and to his old front door. He had held on to his key throughout his training period and remembered the long nights that he would spend tracing its contours with his finger contemplating its meaning while training. Contemplating and planning. It had become more than a key to unlock his door though, it had become a symbol of the city. Even more than that, it had become a symbol of a deeply tucked away and secret ambition which had just suddenly and irreversibly been let out of the bag.

As he placed the key into the lock of his home, he chuckled to himself because of the fact that his plans had begun to unfold faster than he ever imagined like a pre-determined story that unscrolls before one's steps. His thoughts drifted to the mysterious sword of light and found that it had given him the strength and confidence to proceed. His ambition…? To one day become the Nasgroth of Gish himself. He dreamed of rebuilding the city in all its grandeur. He had already been one of its peasants. He now desired to be one of its rulers. He even found within his heart a desire to rule it from his very own personally designed 'throne room'. Knowing that it was a thought that could seemingly travel in the air all the way to Magreth's throne was a risk he was willing to take. The firing cord had been released though, and there was no taking the arrow back.

When Jonathan opened the door to his place and activated the sliding floor of a door, he was met with the sweet aromatic fragrance of finely refined Serpent's Breath. His home was filled with the yellow mist still. Jonathan breathed in the scent remembering how sick he had been the last time that he had to be detoxified from the substance. It was tantalizing and through the swirls of cloudy substance, he could see that the space had been transformed from one of being a party den, to one of being weaponry. The walls were lined with a myriad of them. Bows, daggers, arrows, and an assortment of Snipe clothing decorated the place to its fullness. Beyond the main hall, he could see that his bedroom remained the same and the bathing pool had been recently filled with steaming hot water.

Suddenly, Lady Dael appeared from beyond and welcomed him to her master's home with her usual silent bowing coupled with hand motions. It had been a long time.

She was urging her master to relax and enjoy a bathing. Jonathan stopped in mid-stride and contemplated. He thought about the plans that he had enacted… plans that had seemed as if they had been made for him. He thought of the sword that had saved his life. Perhaps it was his destiny to reform the city, he thought. Perhaps it was his calling. He visualized his months and months of training. Talonshard came to his mind, and he recalled how the bird had unknowingly taught him his own art of war.

A moment later, as Lady Dael had still been bowing and urging him to soak himself in the air around the place; he grabbed her by the shoulders and lifted her up. Looking into her eyes, he spoke to her:

"Lady Dael. Can you understand what I'm saying?" The tiny Asian looking woman nodded in response. "Good… It's nice to be home. Thank you for all that you have done for me. No more parties here though, no more Serpent's Breath, no more long nights. Understand?" Jonathan could see that she understood his words and was actually surprised to see that she had a relieved look on her face. "I'm sorry for the way I've treated you and I'm sorry for the times the place was left a mess for you to clean up alone… but no more. No more." Lady Dael nodded, bowed again, and when she rose up to look into his face, she had a tear in her eye. "Is there anything I can do for you? Is there anything you need?"

Lady Dael just nodded side to side and humbly bowed her head once again. Jonathan could tell that she had more to say, but he passed by the opportunity to listen and selfishly took a deep breath of the atmosphere. Breathing the mists into his lungs brought elation to his heart and he instantly felt the dizzying effects of the refined drug. Apprehensive, he looked to his servant and asked her if she could fan the fumes out of the room. If he were to be successful in his ambitions, he would have to remain clear-headed. At the same time, the feeling of elation tempted him to just get lost in the swirl as he had so many times before.

"Dael?" he called. She turned to face him. "No more mist," and he reinforced the statement with hand motions.

Lady Dael directed him over to a cabinet and opened it up for him. Inside, there were three buckets full of the yellow cake-like substance. Jonathan bent down to examine it and a thought occurred to him. Where does this come from? Upon closer examination, he caught sight of blood that had been dried to the sides where someone had carried the bucket from a place that Jonathan could only imagine.

"Take the buckets and sell them," he said to his servant. "I don't need this anymore. The street value is tremendous… But keep the money for yourself, Dael. Consider it my homecoming gift." Lady Dael bowed in thankfulness and commenced to fan the substance out of the home after snuffing out the burning wicks.

Jonathan made a lap around the room examining the contents of weaponry and clothing, re-examined the mission scroll he had been given, and retired to his room on the far end. That night, he fell asleep in the bathing waters, having soaked in the fullness of a season's passing.

He awoke early, long before the sunrise, and arrayed himself in the armament of the Snipe. Having chosen a sandy colored full-bodied garment, he armed himself with a long bow, a quiver of arrows, some wrist daggers, and a small coil of blackened rope. The room was silent, and he made his way across it with equally silent steps. Passing by the cabinet that housed the buckets of Serpent's Breath, he stopped and opened it. Lady Dael had done what she was told to do, and no buckets remained. He then headed out into the darkness of the early morning and made his way silently through the streets of the city.

The mission scroll he had been given directed him through the streets and to the northern sector of the metropolis. He hadn't been to the north since his first arrival in Gish. The scroll had called it the Asian sector and pointed to a large structure. The only other directions it gave were, 'floor six' and 'kill priest'. The meaning had sunk like a knot in his stomach when he first read it the night before and it remained throughout the morning.

The pre-dawn darkness still reigned when he arrived at the structure. It was tall and constructed of a greenish painted brick and stood in stark contrast to anything he had ever seen in the city save for Mocker's Bridge. Surrounding it were two and three-story structures that appeared to be shops and homes that formed a distinctly common area. Jonathan surmised that the tall, greenish structure was some sort of temple. Paper lanterns littered the block everywhere having been strung across the streets in loom-like patterns. Not one of them was lit and not a soul stirred in the section of the city. Jonathan blended into his surroundings and stayed in the shadows. Earlier that morning, he had covered his face in an ashy substance that made him appear like the lanky fellow he had seen in Magreth's throne room with his sunken cheeks and shaded eyes. The thought made him stop momentarily to ponder... Then, he shook his head free of the cobwebs and continued on.

As he continued into the kill-box of his mission and out of the darkened streets, he searched his surroundings for a means of egress. For his facial camouflage, he had created elongated eye sockets sharpened to a point on the exterior ends similar to Lady Dael's Asian look. He accomplished this by burning small sticks and used the leftover charcoal residue.

The Snipe made his way around to a corner of the structure and found a drainage pipe that ran up the side. After scaling it, he entered the structure at the first floor. Once inside, a hallway ran upward in a spiral direction to his right and contained hundreds of tiny doors that stood only as high as Jonathan's waist. They were on both sides of the hallway. With only a hand breath between each door, the would-be assassin surmised that there must be much more than mere hundreds; there were probably thousands of them. Most were closed and locked, but sporadically one or two of them would be open. He sneaked his way past them, but finally out of sheer curiosity, went into one.

The floor was a crimson color and padded. It sunk beneath his knees as he crawled in. On the far end of the miniscule room was a small wooden desk whereby a would-be kneeler could rest their elbows. Other than the desk, the space was stark and barren. No windows, no lamps, no sources of light. As he stayed there in silence, he could hear the sound of voices. It puzzled Jonathan as to what the room had been used for. They must have been centuries old, for grooves were worn into the ancient wood of the desk. Before leaving the confines of the cubicle, he was finally struck as to the purpose of the rooms. They were places of prayer. Suddenly feeling uncomfortable, he exited and continued his way up the spiral hallway.

The only way that he could tell that he was moving from floor to floor was that a landing would open up into a large room on each passing level. On the outward facing side of the landing, windows looked out over the city. They were tall and arched at the top and had glass that was stained in different colors of the rainbow. He could see that the sun was just beginning to break the darkness beyond them and knew that he would have to rush to complete his mission before the city awakened. He started to continue in the direction of the upward sloping hallway but saw that the room had a balcony which overlooked the interior of the structure as well. Peering over the railing, he could see that far below him, a pool of water was resting on the bottom. The water was still and putrid, and a stench arose from it that filled the entire structure with smell. A thought crossed Jonathan's mind that, perhaps, if need be, he could jump into in an emergent case. The thought, however, was a disgusting one and he tried to file it away. He hoped that he wouldn't have to use that means of exit.

With the thought still lingering in his mind, he continued to the six-floor platform. Once there, he discovered that the top floor was where the multi-door hallway had ceased, and one huge floor opened up. It still contained the stained-glass windows, but they seemed to be one continuous window that segued into an inverted dome above his head as well. It was awe inspiring and Jonathan was again struck by the fact that the city of Gish was truly a multi-leveled mystery.

In the center of the room, one smaller room was situated but was completely suspended from the ceiling by four huge woven ropes. Below, the entirety of six stories fell away to the putrid pool of water far below. The smaller room was connected to the larger outer ring by a small wooden foot bridge. Other than that, it was suspended by ropes from the glass ceiling. Jonathan could smell the putrid fumes funneling upward from below and hoped that the ropes had not been rotted by the continuously acrid stench.

The Snipe made his way over to the bridge and peered inside the small room.

He discovered that an elderly woman was seated in the center of the room upon a large red cushion. Her head was cocked upward, and her arms were outstretched and she looked oddly familiar. She was whispering and Jonathan thought that she must have been praying in that position. She was dressed in the garbs of some sort of priesthood. Jonathan un-slung his bow and loaded an arrow. He fixed his eyes on the woman's throat and thought how easy it would have been to take the breath life right from her, but that was not his style. He side-stepped his way across the creaky bridge and closer to his prey, remaining in the shadows that were cast by torches that flickered off the walls of the circular room. As Jonathan hesitated, and not having the stomach to snuff the woman's life out of her, the priestess suddenly dropped her head and looked straight at the assassin.

She had a strange smile on her face; it seemed almost to be glowing.

Jonathan felt as if he were looking directly into the eyes of Lady Dael. The woman almost looked like her twin, only older… much older. A thought that she must be related to her clung to his mind. Could this have been his servant's very own mother?

The thought reverberated inside his consciousness as he remembered that Lady Dael had been orphaned years prior. Even the way the woman's mouth was slightly crooked looked just like Dael's not to mention the fact that Dael had hesitated when asked if she ever needed anything almost as if to suggest an unstated desire. Poised and ready to strike, Jonathan momentarily con-templated his future and the future of his and the Shade's plans. Sparing the priestess would work not only into his planning, but it would also directly oppose Magreth's will. Besides, at this point, he had to know for sure whether she was Lady Dael's maternal parent. Suddenly, the shuffling footsteps of approaching feet from somewhere down the hallway made up his mind for him.

The peaceful woman just watched the goings on as Jonathan retreated to the underside of the foot bridge. The swaying and precarious perch would test his stealth abilities, but he had no time to find an alternative. Like a bat in the dark, he clung six stories above the putrid pool of water. If need be, he knew that he could drop into it, but was still not aware of the depths of the pool.

Slowing his breathing and even his heart rate, he clung to the edge to await the approaching sound. It turned out to be another assassin. Magreth must have sent two of them to be sure that the job would be accomplished, thought the young master of weapons.

The stealthy character walked right past Jonathan's dangling form without realizing he was there. Jonathan had to stop his supposed comrade if he were to know for sure who the priestess was, and if she had ever had a daughter. He could hear the back-up Snipe loading its bow and could only imagine what the formerly praying woman must have been thinking.

In one swift movement, Jonathan swung himself aloft the swaying bridge that he had been dangling from and quickly brought out the rope he had taken along. Tying one end of it to a slat, he dropped it and carried the other end with him as he made his way over to the figure, who was poised to fire.

Coming from behind, he quickly wrapped his arm around the figure's face, burying the pocket of his elbow into his foe's mouth thereby subduing him in silence. Jonathan looked past the figure and could see that the priestess still had an oddly peaceful look on her face. Jonathan pulled back on the figure's form and utilized his position to leverage the assassin to his knees and held tightly until the figure passed out. That's when he discovered that the figure was not a man at all, but rather, a woman. Katelyn, thought Jonathan for a moment, but it was not her. He quickly wrapped the rope around the girl's legs tying it securely, and threw her over the edge of the platform where she swung back and forth by one securely fastened leg, still unconscious.

Jonathan knew that his time was limited and rushed to the priestess. "You'll have to trust me," he said and reached his hand toward the woman. "Do you understand?" he asked at which the priestess nodded but still hesitated to follow. "Did you ever have a daughter? She would be grown now."

"Yes, yes. Many years ago! What does this mean?"

"I don't have time to explain. Come with me."

The priestess's legs were shaking when she stood to her feet. She must have been in that position for a very long time. They could hear that the woman Snipe was beginning to come around. Jonathan couldn't wait for the old woman to gain her wits, so he scooped her up, slung her over his shoulder, and raced back across the foot bridge and down the circular door-filled hallway. Some of them were just beginning to be unlocked for the morning, but Jonathan didn't stay long enough to see any of the pilgrims or be seen by any of them. Upon reaching the bottom floor, he asked the slung over priestess which way to an exit, at which the hunched over old woman spoke.

"Put me down now!" she demanded through a thick accent.

"As soon as we are in the streets," he flatly replied.

"That way then," and she pointed to a door that had morning sunlight streaming in, and around its frame.

The door dumped them onto the awakening streets of the Asian sector of Gish. In a moment's time, Jonathan produced an old, tattered cloak that he had stowed away and wrapped it around himself putting the hood over his head. He then took the priestess by the arm, told her to conceal herself as well, and began leading her through the streets, only his charcoaled eyes peering from beneath.

Merchants were just beginning to set up their carts and shops. Others were beginning to fire up their spits. Still others were beginning to dump their overnight sewage filled buckets into the central troughs. The sight brought back memories to Jonathan, and he thought that, though the city had become a dark and deadened place, there was warm feeling in his heart for it… or rather, for its people. Many of them greeted the priestess as they passed, having recognized her, with nods of the head and slight bows. Magreth had long ago forbidden any prayer activity and they were obviously being careful not to reveal their affiliation with what would surely be a controversial community figure.

'So, he had not conquered and controlled the city entirely', thought Jonathan, the would-be rebel to himself.

Jonathan stayed in the hunched over position throughout the journey from the northern sector. Without a word, he led the priestess back to the Turnback Inn. It was well into the morning when they finally arrived. Leading the old woman up the steps, he opened the door to the tavern and directed her to sit in his own seat at the far end of the room. He could barely move his back into its proper position and had to take a moment to stretch out his sore muscles. He then left to retrieve Lady Dael from the apartment that Wisekoff had provided for her. When he returned to the Inn, Wisekoff had already come down from his abode on the top floor and was talking with the priestess, not knowing where she had come from or when she had arrived… and he certainly didn't know who she was.

Lady Dael entered the Turnback Inn in humble silence. Jonathan had only told her that she needed to come with him. Walking across the room to the far end produced a revelation that shocked not only Dael, but Wisekoff and Jonathan as well.

"Mother..? Mother!" Lady Dael audibly spoke for the first time in a very long time and sprinted across the room to the arms of her long-lost mother.

They hugged and clung to each other, speaking a language that neither of the two men could understand. Dael's ability to speak had caught them both by surprise, but to interrupt the reunion to take the time to question the servant would have been unheard of. Both Jonathan and Wisekoff silently slid their way out of the room and down into the lobby on the first floor. They could hear the noise of the reunited mother and daughter above them and it warmed their hearts.

"I don't know what guides you or how you are guided, my friend, but this city will never be the same when we're through with it," Wisekoff stated and proceeded to tell Jonathan about more of the plans and political strategies that he had conjured up.

Wisekoff had plans of his own before he'd recruited Jonathan. Jonathan's mysterious talent to rebel against the status quo of the city had sold Wisekoff whole heartedly and he was satisfied by the fact that they were both on the road to permanent change. Wisekoff himself was a product of the city, having been born there, so his fondness for her and her citizens matched that of Jonathan's, melding their partnership together. His hatred for Magreth had climaxed and the fruits of revenge loomed sweet.

The Snipe warrior and unwilling-to-kill assassin simply smiled back at Wisekoff, listening to his friend spout, and knowing in his heart that the road would be a rough and bumpy one. Nevertheless, Jonathan was confident in his own abilities to overcome whatever obstacles would be in their way as they ran the gauntlet of the road that led to a city-wide takeover.

✝

The Drums of War

Jonathan would remain in his stealthy rebellion against Magreth's status quo for nearly two years, although it was shaded by his passive resistance. He had finally answered the call to Prince Magreth's throne room after months and months of multiple requests. Jonathan had thwarted a number of assassination attempts on his and Wisekoff's life, the source of which the royal house had always been careful to conceal. Needless to say, when he had finally complied with the prince's request for the sake of propelling his plans forward, it had not fared well for the young Snipe, and he barely walked away with his life.

Magreth had only spared him because, by the time they had met face to face, the people of Gish were resoundingly behind Jonathan having clung to the hope of a better future that he and the Shade had offered to them. Having taken out his aggressions on the young master of weapons by beating him to within an inch of his life, Magreth finally relented and allowed Jonathan's transgressions to fall to the wayside. Unbeknownst to Magreth however, Jonathan had thought through his plan completely and was ready for the inevitable beating before it even began and only offered meager, almost mocking attempts at fighting back.

Shortly after regaining the monarch's respect, and being given his own authority, Wisekoff had leveraged the Shade into a position of power whereby virtually all missions would come through their office, which they housed in the Turnback Inn.

Jonathan had long removed himself from being personally directed by Magreth's decrees and Katelyn had finally joined them in their control of the city. The executive orders still emanated from the throne of Magreth, which she always personally delivered, but he had released such power to them that all sects began to answer to the Shade, save for the Snipes themselves, which Magreth maintained control of. The Shade were always careful to fulfill the overall vision of the Prince of Gish and were extremely successful in quenching any city wide rebellion to that vision, yet still maintained their own shadowed master plan.

The Shade rose in prominence above all others and their numbers increased dramatically. The recruits were captivated by Jonathan's ability to teach them how to subdue their enemies without taking a life, an art form that he had personally perfected, having spent most of his studies on vulnerable subjugation tactics rather than one-shot-kill procedures. Even the elusive Thomas Dodd, one of Magreth's greatest generals, had joined Jonathan in the training of new recruits having embraced the 'art of war' that the master of weapons had inspired. He never forgot the famous snake and eagle shot and held it up as the prime example of the art of taking authority without killing an opponent at the beginning of every training season.

The symbol of Jonathan's power had become the Willowfeld bow that he had fashioned into a powerful weapon. In stark contrast to Magreth's own, he had used it to mete out mercy rather than death. Over the course of the years, his merciful methods had gained the respect of the entire population of the city, and those that had received his graces were more than willing to join his cause... so much so that the number of fighters had approached the number of citizens that Gish contained, and all were more or less citizen soldiers.

Rifts between the houses of Magreth and the house of the Shade always lingered just below the surface though. One of the most prominent fissures was the Magreth inspired suicide attacks. The martyrdom influence had been his brainchild, and his personal Snipes were forced to continue in them faithfully. Jonathan had imagined it to be an atrocity which he forbade his own followers to carry out. His art had taught them tactics that made the archaic practice of self-destruction obsolete. At long last, and after much political conniving on Wisekoff's part, Thomas Dodd had convinced many of Magreth's own troops to abandon the practice. Needless to say, it left Magreth seething with anger.

The production of Serpent's Breath had slowed to a near crawl as well. Jonathan had been assigned to the rotation of soldiery that oversaw the serpent fields which produced the deadly drug, a penance he was willing to pay for his transgressions against the throne. (It was, he surmised, just another rung on the scheming ladder to the top of the heap) After spending nearly three months in the bloody pits of the serpent fields, he personally vowed to put a quench on its manufacturing if he ever got the chance. He knew that he couldn't stop the substance being produced all together, for it had fueled Gish's economy for centuries and was used to 'Zomb' the citizenry into submission. To combat the long-ingrained tradition however, he devised a plan to win the hearts of the population by giving them a vision to pursue instead. Together, he and the Shade swayed the population to take an interest not only in cleaning up the city, but also in rebuilding its ruins. They were careful to make everything appear as though it was Prince Magreth's vision, but the way by which Jonathan and the Shade achieved persuading Magreth to ascribe to the vision was a stroke of genius.

The plan was to remove Serpent's Breath from public spaces, and with the lack of the narcotic circulating throughout the streets, the city even seemed brighter and was certainly a more hopeful place. With that mere fact alone, the population began to slowly arise as one great purposeful entity, and that pleased Magreth immensely for it began to magnify his own persona… and therein lay the heartbeat and success of the Shades plan. It was solidified when the citizenry even began to repair the broken-down structures of their homes and businesses.

Jonathan, Wisekoff, Katelyn, and the newly affirmed Dodd knew that the secret to their overall success lay in the way in which they would interpret the royal decrees that were handed down to them. They knew that Magreth's ability to carry out his passion for power and greater influence overarched his need to exact cruelty. His passion lay in sheer numbers and had grown into more of a lust for control, not only of the population, but of the landscape as well. In essence, it had become the new currency that fed his insatiable appetite.

He wanted to influence behaviors beyond the city itself and called for a massive army of citizen soldiery to be prepared if they were to expand territory. In other words, the more the fighters, the larger the Prince's army would grow, the easier it would be to confiscate properties and even other realms. One such order was so broad in its interpretation that it sparked an idea within the Shade's four leaders; an idea that would prove to propel them beyond the forefront of all the other would-be sects. It was only a one-word decree and it read, 'Exploration' and that was all.

The Shade immediately drafted a plan to send a patrol, led by Jonathan himself, across the expanse of the barren desert to the south in search of civilization. It had always been believed to be a death sentence, but the Shade's leader had learned by experience that most things never appeared to be as they actually were. They had sent Katelyn with the proposal before Magreth's throne, and one day later, their request was replied to. It was a resounding yes and Dodd was ordered to join Jonathan in the search.

It was not so much that Magreth was interested in the exploration itself per say, but rather that he had ascribed to the thought that the expedition would be a sure death sentence for the two of them, and Jonathan knew it. He also knew that the population of Gish understood it as well, something Magreth had been blinded to due to his utter seething for the traitors. Having seen treachery in Thomas Dodd's move to join the Shade, the prince's hatred for him equaled that of his hatred for Jonathan.

After much revelry and reunion, the once pupil and mentor, Jonathan of Scharp and Thomas Dodd, led a group of twenty-one soldiers south of the city of Gish. They traveled for three weeks into barren nothingness and had lost six of their numbers to sheer exhaustion and other such obstacles. The weary party finally ascended some snow-covered tundra atop the mountains, which they apply named, The Reaches. Once there, they happened along a city frozen in time.

By some great catastrophe, the city had fallen into silence many ages past. The population had been suddenly struck by some great and freezing wind and the citizens remained virtually frozen in their tracks for the wind had carried with it a crystallizing substance similar to volcanic ash. Though juxtaposed, the atoms in the elements of heat and cold had somehow been split and sewn together in a sort of alternate element. Alternate and ominous, that is. Some of the people even had smiles on their faces as if they had no idea what was coming. Victuals were even solidified on the tables, mid-meal.

However, what were also encapsulated by the furious storms were vast treasuries.

The scouting trip had proved to be an overwhelming success, but they had barely escaped. Moments after leaving the heights that the city was perched upon, they discovered that the violently intense windstorms would occur without warning, suddenly immobilizing all in an instant blast of alternate substance. The party had only escaped by timing, nothing more and nothing less.

Once Jonathan and Thomas had returned with their diminished numbers, they became even greater heroes in the eyes of the population, for it would prove to bring great wealth to the citizenry of Gish. Although they refused to personally appear before his throne, (another denied request) Jonathan and Dodd sent huge amounts of treasure to Magreth which he reveled in, yet was also furious about, for he knew that they had saved the very best items for themselves, which he naturally surmised, but let stew.

Over the course of six months and seemingly endless wagon trains later, so much gold and precious jewels had poured into the city that a month straight of revelry swept through, filling all with complete euphoria. The city began to be centered not on the throne room of Magreth, but on the Turnback Inn, which did not sleep, being consumed by more and more added numbers.

The Shade leaders knew that the expedition had sparked a great desire and an even greater vision to advance their culture beyond the city. Its coming was inevitable. Wisekoff wanted them to consolidate their own control by solidifying their power base within the city's borders, but Jonathan, Dodd, and even Katelyn could not see a way of taking a step back from their fierce expansionism without bringing the wrath of Magreth and his inner circle of Snipe troopers upon them. Therefore, the majority vote was for further expansion, but it would prove to be their downfall.

It had been three years, two months, two weeks, and three days since Jonathan was the toast of the town after successfully returning from the Vale of Decision with his Willowfeld bow. He was turning nineteen years old and had truly turned the city upside down as Wisekoff had (unknowingly) prophesied. He once again found himself seated in the Turnback Inn and upon his 'throne' with Wisekoff to his right, and on that night, Thomas Dodd to his left. Katelyn had not shown up for the celebration due to an argument between herself and Jonathan for he had refused yet again to receive her 'advances' a practice he was not only a total novice to, but also felt that it would only cloud his thoughts.

Together, the leaders of the Shade had become the rulers of the most powerful sect in the newly formed Realms of Gish, for the city had expanded beyond its borders and actually took up habitation beyond the Reaches Mountain Range at the frozen outpost of a city that had yielded so much treasure.

The building that had housed the Turnback Inn had also seen a transformation. No longer was it run down and dilapidated. As a gift from the people of the city and by the authority of the Shade, they had banded together and had completely rehabilitated the headquarters. It was still seven stories tall, but four of them had been opened up so that when one entered the great hall, one would look up to see a domed ceiling upon which a mural of the 'future' city was painted. A spiral staircase ascended to the top and passed each floor just as Jonathan had seen at the Asian temple in the northern sector. Upon each floor, revelers had the luxury of enjoying a vast amount of room, and it was always full. Lady Dael had become the curator and ran it with distinction for she had been given a staff of twelve. Jonathan had long ago vacated his apartment in the basement and had moved to the top floor where his abode was the entire seventh floor. Wisekoff remained on the sixth, and Katelyn had acquired the fifth. Thomas Dodd went to… wherever Thomas Dodd went, for he often disappeared for weeks on end. The structure had become the headquarters and the Great Guild of the Shade, an accomplishment his Da' would most certainly have been proud of, for Jonathan had effectively become its Nasgroth.

Wisekoff stood to his feet raising a great goblet of gold and quieted the crowd of more than four hundred people. All eyes turned to the Master of Politics as he prepared to speak. Not a sound interrupted him.

"Ladies and Gentlemen," his voice sounded forth echoing off the innards of the vast chamber. He had long forsaken his fake accent, having abandoned the façade of being just another street creature, "I would like to raise a toast to our great leader, but before I do, Jonathan of Scharp, one of your friends has a gift for you that she commissioned and purchased on behalf of us all." Wisekoff cleared his voice, thereby giving the signal for a servant to bring forth the gift.

Lady Dael emerged from the crowd with the present that she had purchased with part of the Serpent's Breath money that she had acquired years earlier. When Jonathan saw the gift, he was speechless. It was a decorative shield of finely crafted gold and precious jewels. Its back was covered in fine velvet crimson fabric. On its face, it bore a symbol. When it was presented, Jonathan had to fight back tears of joy, for impressed upon it was an engraving of a Willowfeld long bow with arrows on one side and a set of keys on the other. Across the top and bottom were emblazoned the words, 'Nasgroth Scharp, Master of Weapons.'

A great cheer was raised throughout the guild hall and Wisekoff had trouble calming the crowd again. When he was finally successful, he raised the golden goblet once again.

"To our great leader," and a 'hear, hear' resounded. "May the keys of the…"

Suddenly, the door of the guild hall was swung open with such force that the door splintered after crashing into the wall and barely clung onto its hinges.

It was Prince Magreth himself, and he entered with an entourage of ten Snipe soldiers and one woman, Katelyn. His majestic and powerful form struck an audible awe throughout the crowd. He was dressed in his royal attire and was wearing upon his head a Willowfeld crown that had been coated inside and out with pure gold and silver. He entered with all of the pomp and circumstance that was due his name. When he spoke, the authority that rang in his thunderous if not melodious voice struck fear into every heart.

"I would like to be a part of this toast as well," he bellowed.

Lady Dael fearfully scrambled her troops to produce goblets for the great leader, his guards, and Katelyn to drink from. The air grew thickly cold and silent as they waited. Embarrassment arose from the crowd like a vapor while they lingered for the drinks to be given to the previously uninvited guests, save the one. Once they received their cups, Magreth raised his in salutation.

"Please Dumbkoff. Please continue."

Wisekoff remained silent, seething in the mockery that the great captain had flung at him.

"Then I will", Magreth continued, "To the great master of weapons, may he fare well in whatever endeavor I command of him. May his cohorts..." the word sounded like it had been dipped in poison... "May they fare well." Magreth then turned to Jonathan and walked closer, never taking his yellow tinged eyes off the young Snipe. "To the great Shade warrior Katelyn, who has faithfully kept me in the loop... on everything."

It was an arrow that pierced deeper than Jonathan ever imagined, for though he had restrained himself from her advances, he had just begun to trust and love her... He took his eyes off Magreth momentarily and shot a glance at Katelyn. She merely returned his with a devilish stare. The Shade had been betrayed even from the beginning of their rise to power. A cold chill ran down Jonathan's spine; it was the same cold feeling he felt when he first shook Katelyn's hand many years prior. He silently cursed himself for ever trusting her, for it was she that had allowed the group to rise in power, but it was a power controlled by the puppet master Magreth... his sidekick, Katelyn, manipulating the strings, and which together, had been rolled into one large ball of betrayal.

"Jonathan," continued the Prince, "I have another mission for you. I want to show you how grateful I am for your achievements which you have wrought for this great kingdom... my great kingdom. And it comes in the form of a two-stage campaign.... The army has grown greatly, and they will follow you into any fight, correct?" He didn't wait for an answer. "I have received word from my Snipes that the Council of the Castle of the Realms of Irenay has decreed a new campaign. They have amassed an army of three hundred to attack in the Vale of Decision two days from today. They're calling it, The Campaign of the Missing." Magreth shared a look with Jonathan that very few in the immense room could possibly have understood.

Silence prevailed over the guild hall.

Jonathan could feel the subtle venom of Magreth's words leaking into his heart like soupy black ink. He knew that Wisekoff was quickly coming to his boiling point and up and to that moment, Jonathan had remained calm. He knew in his heart that a confrontation with the leader of the Realms of Gish would one day occur, but he had never calculated that it would be suddenly sprung upon him during his birthday celebration, not to mention that it came through one of their own. Katelyn had a look of satisfaction on her face as she knew that it would prove to be the beginning of the end of the Shade's rise to power. Jonathan understood that Magreth had ill intent but knew not how it would be meted. He and Wisekoff had been totally taken off guard as Magreth, the conniving politician that he was, continued staring down the former Snipe.

The eyes around the room penetrated Jonathan's soul like a thousand needle-sized daggers. He knew that his identity was on the edge of being betrayed and felt that his three years' worth of tireless work was beginning to crumble like the old Sturmstone pillars of the Vale. In that instant, he remembered the words that he had stabbed his father with so many years prior… that, "one day the people would turn on you Da'…" Then Magreth continued…

"After you lead my army to the Vale of Decision and become victorious… and become victorious," he repeated, waiting for the inevitable cheer from the crowd which they did like dogs conditioned for such a response. Magreth was truly the master of the speech that Jonathan had remembered him to be, and the prince played the tune to its fullness… "Your victory in the Vale will carry us beyond the great northern forest and into the Realms of Irenay itself. My command for you, my dear friend, is to begin the attack at the township of Safehaven… leaving no survivors… not even one… But that miserable little hamlet is not our prize. No, our prize will be beyond that and to the great Castle of Lock Kalaw itself, the greatest of all the seats of power!"

The roar was deafening.

Jonathan's heart sunk at the thought. First of all, he knew that three hundred Council warriors were no match for Magreth's thousands, that is, his own thousands. Secondly, he had just been ordered to slay his own flesh and blood. He was still in shock of the announcement. In a mere moment, Prince Magreth had torn his authority asunder, leaving it teetering on the edge of destruction, offered a way to rebuild it, and recaptured the hearts of the people firmly into his own grasp. In that same moment, Jonathan saw his own grand schemes crumbling into dust like the plants that he had seen leading to the leader's throne room and finally knew the reason for their existence.

The crowd within the Turnback reveled in the great plan to expand Gish to the greatest of all Realms, and to the greatest of all castles. Magreth continued to hold his cup high, waiting for Jonathan to return the toast, which he did but did not swallow.

After the toast, the Great Guild Hall of the Shade emptied like an overturned wine bottle as the army began to prepare for war. Jonathan himself was the last to leave. He wandered the streets of Gish that night shrouded beneath his cloak where no one could recognize him. He had been played like a musical instrument, manipulated like a forged piece of metal, and was about to be used to lead an army against his own people… And there seemed to him that there was nothing that could be done about it.

That night, he slept under the protection of an old wooden crate in the end of a darkened alley. The next day, he made his way to Mocker's Bridge and spent the day loitering below the raised platform. He had never spent any time actually upon the bridge save for the time he had rescued Katelyn from it. He silently shrugged his shoulders, knowing that she didn't even want to be saved, but instead wanted to give her own life in the archaic form of war that Magreth had invented, a form that he was sure would return with force. As he meandered around the bridge, he found a clandestine memorial dedicated to those who had suffered there. It was etched into the stone of the bridge in tiny lettering that would have been overlooked if it were not for his sharpened and trained Snipe eyes. There, he read the names of the fallen.

Jonathan haphazardly read until he came to one name in particular… and it was his own!

It read, "John of Scharp hung here until blind. May his path always be illuminated by light." Jonathan was awestruck. His own Da' had been to Gish! His own Da' had hung from Mocker's Bridge, ridiculed as an enemy of the people… And his name was memorialized by those that had rebelled. His own Da' had been a true patriot of the Gish as he himself had wanted to become.

Jonathan silently wept convulsively all the way back to the wooden crates. When he arrived, a familiar face was seated upon them. It was the old man with the crooked cane. He was hunched over and was humming a tune and very much alive. He never once lifted his head or opened his eyes. The song was very slow and methodical. Though the man's voice was raspy, it was soothing, beautiful, inspiring. As he listened, Jonathan felt like someone was pouring liquid gold upon down his head. It ran down the full length of his frame and a wave of peace followed in its wake. When Jonathan attempted to approach the gentleman, he stood without saying a word and walked out of the alleyway, his soothing tune fading into the distance.

That night, under the cover of the crate once again, Jonathan made a decision. He would have to fight in the Vale against the Council's Army, for he knew that he could not sway his, or rather Magreth's, thousand soldiers otherwise. But when it came time to attack Safehaven, he would steer them against Magreth and his Snipes. He knew that he could play on their merciful heart strings, for he had shown them his own mercy. Then, strangely, he slept the most peaceful sleep he had ever experienced.

The next day, Jonathan was at the head of one of the mightiest armies ever assembled in the history of the realms and was poised in defensive positions around the base of the infamous Vale of Decision.

He, Katelyn, and Magreth along with Magreth's personal bodyguard of Snipes stood atop the Sturmstone tower after giving the command to assemble and prepare for counterattack. Jonathan felt like a prisoner shackled with invisible chains beneath Magreth and Katelyn's penetrating eyes. The son of the weapon master of Safehaven had truly won the hearts of the army, but what they were being utilized for was clearly out of his control. It had been so long since he had thought about his homeland. He was like a man absent from his body as he recalled his time with his family by the river on breezy summer days. He wondered what Samuel had grown to become. Thoughts of his mother flooded his being and threatened to paralyze him completely. Regrets about his treatment of his own Da' bit into him. Those thoughts and more bounced off the innards of his mind when the Council's tiny army of three hundred appeared at the opening of the Vale. A tear escaped from Jonathan' right eye.

They were immediately met with Magreth's drums of war as every single soldier that Jonathan was leading began to beat on the sides of their shields with such great force that the ground beneath him began to literally shake.

The king's army began slowly. At first step, they cantered into the Vale, but soon picked up their pace as they flooded into it on a gallop. Jonathan could hear the familiar bellow of wind deep within the cave that he stood above. Then the massacre occurred. The hot wind of the cave met the council army head on removing the entire front line of soldiers from their horses.

As they fell to the floor of the battlefield, they were dragged beneath it by the tens and by the twenties.

By instinct, the blood lust and adrenaline of war pulled Jonathan's own men into the fray. Swords clashed, arrows flew, limbs were severed, and bodies were dragged. In an instant, the entire battlefield was filled with a mass of twisted bodies and screaming, painful cries. Fiery arrows rained down from every-where. The Vale had been apply named as the soldiers of the king struggled to reach the mouth of darkness. What gave them the passion to reach it, Jonathan could only imagine. It was worse than the young man had ever imagined as soldier after soldier including his own were struck down. There was no more rank and order, no more form or fashion as the melee continued uninhibited and lost in the dense fog of war. If it were possible, Jonathan would have thrown up his arms to stop the entire thing, but he had been stripped of all power and authority.

Nearly every soldier had emptied onto the blood-stained field as far as Jonathan could tell. There was so much smoke and dust that it was impossible to see who was who. Suddenly, out of the ashes of fire and smoke rode one single Council warrior that was making a sprint for the cave. The helmed rider rode past felled bodies and through falling arrows, untouched by any defenses leaving no one to parry the attack save Jonathan himself. He knew that his time had come to perform just like the puppet that Magreth had created him to be. His heart screamed at his own mind from within.

Jonathan remembered the words written on the scroll that Thomas had given to him when he completed his training. 'There will come a time when you may have to take another's life. Kill or be killed.' The young man knew that his job was to stop the advancing soldier. His plan must stand firm if he were to turn his forces back at Magreth once they were beyond the Vale and out of Magreth's controlling eye.

His emotions rumbled within him like an ocean that had been released as a flood. The actual shot was an unquestionable one. He knew right where to place the death blow… to the center of the chest, just off to the right. Jonathan raised his great Willowfeld bow and aimed it straight for the heart of the approaching council soldier. Steady was his gaze, true was his aim. He followed the bouncing of the soldier's form as the mocha-colored horse carried the rider closer and closer to the cave, and just as he was about to fire, the soldier spotted him atop the Sturmstone tower and raised her head in Jonathan's direction...

And she was wielding a crossbow…. Jonathan could see that the soldier had thick darkened hair that was blonde at one time… And her hair fell over her face in ringlets.

And then he realized who it was…

It was Jacqueline, his princess, and she fired up at him with his very own Da's designed crossbow!

Jonathan was dumbstruck. A sudden rush of emotions flooded into his being like a cascade of a thousand rivers. He didn't fire but was rather fired upon. As he remained frozen in time, Jacqueline's arrow struck the son of the weapon master in the right shoulder, spinning him completely around, full circle. Pain shot through the entirety of his being. He staggered toward the cliff edge where he watched the rider pass below his feet and into the mouth of darkness. He didn't know what it meant for the rider to enter the cave, but he didn't really care either.

Standing on the edge of the tower, he fell to his knees, overlooking the hideous valley floor.

That's when the Prince of Gish slowly walked up behind the young master of weapons and placed his strong foot between Jonathan's shoulder blades.

He could feel the heavy weight of his former king resting upon his back when he leaned in to speak to the former assassin.

"You have missed the mark, Snipe," whispered the Prince of Gish.

Then Magreth, his muscles flexing, shoved Jonathan over the edge where he fell head over heels to the floor of the Vale of Decision. He landed on his back, and it took his breath completely away from him. The last thing he saw was dust being kicked up as tracks emerged from the dark mouth of the hideous grotto.

After that, he was dragged away to a place of utter darkness for his fullness of time, and the price of his ambitious lifestyle had, at last, finally come.

Chapter 8

The Darkest of Cells

†

The Three-Fold Prison

He had survived his fall, but only barely. He awoke to utter blackness, his face resting against a cold and hardened ground. Not a sound could be heard save for the slight trickle of flowing liquid from somewhere near his location... other than that, an occasional echoing of a faraway wind which bounced off distant walls.

Jonathan could feel that his wrists and ankles had been shackled, but he had not the strength to lift any of his limbs. Through his swollen eyes, he thought that he could see prison bars, but the seething pain that ran throughout his body from head to toe shoved him back to into unconsciousness once again.

A scream of pain snapped his eyes open. It sounded like that of a woman in sheer agony. Then it was followed by others. After some time, they died down and all he could hear was the slight trickle of the liquid once again. Jonathan could smell dank mold mixed with the sewage-like smell of sulfuric fumes. Again, he tried to lift his arms and legs, but they were still too heavy. His eyes still swollen half shut. He had no idea how long he had been out since the last time he had awoken. Then he fell asleep once again.

Sometime during his slumber, he had shifted his head to face the opposite direction. He must have tried to roll over as well, for he could feel the piercing pain of the arrow that was still lodged into his shoulder and the weight of his upper body resting upon it. His eyes didn't feel quite as heavy as they had been, and he was beginning to adjust to the blackness of his surroundings. He caught sight of the shackles that were around his wrists and the chains that were attached to them. The links were massive. He could have put his whole arm through one of them, but that would have been impossible for the shackles were tight around his wrists and the chains were attached to shackles.

Jonathan knew that he would have to attempt to dislodge the arrow if he were to prevent any onset of infection. He had seen who it was that had shot him, and that it was from her crossbow. He couldn't help but chuckle by the irony of the fact that the arrow was most likely one of his father's as well, or that he may have even fashioned it himself years prior. Regardless, it being a crossbow shaft, would have had four barbed blades on its tip and he knew that it would not come back the way that it had entered. He had no choice but to try and push it through entirely. With gritted teeth, he raised his shoulder and slammed it down again.

The pain knocked him out and he slept yet again.

When he came back around, his eyes rested on the wall where the chains before had disappeared into the darkness. He could see that the four of them were attached to a wall around one large iron loop. The loop itself was secured to an iron plate that was in turn driven into the wall with massive spikes. It seemed that a hundred men could not pull it free. Flowing down the walls were beads of a liquid, milky-gold substance that had been the source of the trickling sound that he had been hearing during his awakened moments. Sliding his forehead through the dirt and peering in the opposite direction, he could finally see the prison bars more clearly. They ran from the ceiling to the floor and were just far enough apart that he would be able to push his head through.

His shoulder was still in pain, and he could feel the pulsating flow of blood around the wound with each heartbeat. Jonathan surmised that it must have been his self-healing mechanism kicking in to fight off the onset of the infection that he had been trying to prevent. The arrowhead itself had been pushed through to the backside of his shoulder, so he had been successful in his first stage of dislodgment. However, he knew that there was one more step to go. Jonathan maneuvered himself into a position so that he could use the arrowhead as a fulcrum between one of the chain links. After wedging it in, he once again gritted his teeth. Taking a couple of breaths, he yanked his shoulder free from the projectile and fell onto his back wincing in pain. He then found himself looking up to a roof that had been carved from shear rock. Tiny roots that had been poking through had begun to sprout with greenery. That time, he did not pass out from the pain and took it as a sign that he was beginning to regain his strength, but the moment of hope was fleeting.

It started as a faraway bellow from some unknown depth below his cell. He listened as the sound reverberated off what sounded like tunnels, but as it grew louder and louder, Jonathan could hear the voices of hundreds if not thousands of people crying in fear. Someone nearby began to yell loudly:

"No, no, not again!" the voice pleaded. And then it hit.

It. A blast of hot wind that filled the cavern. Jonathan knew that it was a cavern for the wind had made its way from somewhere far below his location and had funneled upward in a spiraling direction. He had seen twisting winds and their dev-astation on his expedition to the Reaches Mountain Range, and thought that this must have been similar, yet with one big difference, this was hot. At least it began as hot, for in a matter of moments, the wind became super-heated and furious.

It flowed through the bars with ease and circled around his body. He was already lying on his back and tried to stay that way, but it became so strong that it began to lift him off the ground. The heat only intensified, and he could feel it burning his skin. The pain began slowly, but quickly became excruciating. At one point, only his fingertips and heels were still touching the floor as the fury of the storm threatened to suck him right out of the cell. In the midst of his trial, he could hear voices beginning to come closer to him.

At first, the voices were subtle, almost kind.

"Safehaven…haven..," it echoed. "Blossom Festival… festival…" Whatever was the source of the voice, it was coming closer to Jonathan as he was gritting his teeth trying to maintain his sanity. Then he heard a whisper in his ear, as if the being had suddenly snuck up next to him… "Your Ma' and Da'… Your brother…. They are all dead!" and the voice cackled with laughter.

"No, no!" cried Jonathan in return.

Then he could feel claws slowly being dragged just above his legs from his upper thigh to his ankles where the hand stopped at the shackles. Even though they didn't touch him, it felt like knives had penetrated his flesh. He tried to lift his head to see what it was, but the fight against the super-heated wind was too intense and sank into sobs…

"Oh, God!" he cried.

More of the sinister laughter came in return and the young man could feel something breathing on his face as another claw followed the contours of his cheek bone, millimeters from the surface. It felt like a long centipede creeping across his skin near his nose and mouth. Then all at once, the storm subsided.

Jonathan fell back to the floor of his cell and was left staring at the ceiling completely in shock. He could hear the crying of thousands as he himself sobbed and shook. Through his welled-up tears, he could see the tiny roots that had been trying to grow through the hardened rock. They and their miniscule sprouts were on fire. He rolled to his side and saw that the threads of the tattered remains of his clothing were on fire as well. Rolling back and forth served to snuff them out. He then lay on his side in silence, shaking uncontrollably. In time, the crying throughout the cavern subsided and there was nothing but utter and complete silence.

It stayed that way until, at long last, tiny trickles of liquid bubbled from the ceiling and beaded down the walls once again. Jonathan, hearing the soothing sound, slipped off into a deepened sleep where he dreamed of a far-off time and a far-off place…

The brook was truly babbling, and it was speaking of things that were beautiful. The surrounding forest was in full spring bloom as mountain wildflowers blanketed the landscape. A mixture of Aspen and Willow trees stood like thin majestic pillars that held up a canopy of shimmering leaves which were quaking in the morning breeze. Jonathan found himself still watching the black clad and hooded figure rising from her position of drink and he knew that his recurring dream was once again visiting him. It all seemed to be slowed down. She removed her hood, freeing her long hair that fell into her eyes in ringlets. At long last, he saw who the figure was that had visited him often in the dreams. It was Jacqueline, and she smiled at him.

He was thinking to himself about how beautiful she was when her smile turned to a look of concern. He could even see her pupils dilate as the adrenaline within her system suddenly rushed through her body. She then knelt in an attacking pose and swiftly pulled her crossbow from her back. Raising it toward Jonathan, she pulled the firing mechanism, and the arrow was let loose. Jonathan watched the four finned arrow tip zipping toward his right shoulder, and could not help but cry out loud…

"No!" he screamed and opened his eyes with a start.

Jonathan's dream had ended, but his nightmare was still with him. He was looking out of the cell through the bars and beyond, where he could see only utter darkness. It was the kind of darkness that is so deep it seemed to have shadows that played games with his eyes. The fury had sapped him of the little strength that he had been regaining but had just enough to begin to pull himself toward the bars, the weight of the massive chains dragging behind him. The closer he got to them, the more clearly he could see that a door had been built into the cell, but it was closed.

The four chains by which he was fastened to the far wall allowed him to reach just beyond the door of the cage so that he could slip his head thorough. Looking out, he could see that there was nothing but a cliff edge outside and it dropped off into shear blackness like a bottomless well of darkness. Again, it was not a normal darkness, but a tar-like one which was thick and inky… and wavy. He directed his eyes to the walls below him and could see that there were not just a few other cells, but hundreds of other cells. The reality struck him that the prison that he, and thousands like him, were housed within the sides of a cavern and all were locked behind closed doors. He assumed that each was chained hand and foot to the back walls just as was. In essence, all of them were all in three-way prisons.

"Jonathan…" a whisper came from outside of his cell.

Jonathan withdrew and scampered into a corner. The voice sounded just like the one that had tortuously taunted him amidst the storm when he wanted to get as far away as he could from the edge of the abyss. He suddenly felt thirsty. In fact, he was parched. Feeling the moisture of the tiny trickles on his back, he turned his face to the wall and away from the exit where he slurped the liquid right off the side of the enclosure. The taste of soil was metallic, but at the same time, the fluid itself tasted sweet almost like honey.

"Jonathan of Scharp," emerged another raspy whisper from outside of the cell.

Jonathan turned his head and slurped more of the liquid. It was more to keep himself busy than anything else.

"Jonathan," entered the voice once again.

It wouldn't relent, so he decided to slowly make his way toward the door once again. Peering through, he waited.

"Who is it? Who's there?" Then he heard a sinister chuckle once again followed by a whisper.

"You're as good as dead!" boomed the voice. "No one knows you're here and no one cares…" The raspy voice laughed and fell away into the blackness of the cavern like a bat falling from its perch.

Jonathan scampered back to the corner of his cell like a scared little animal. His nails had been growing, and he suddenly saw a use for them. Digging into the hardened floor of the cell caused his fingers to bleed where the nails were attached, but the more he dug, the more the dirt gave way. He tried to keep himself busy. His body shook in fear and the digging helped him from going mad altogether. When he had dug a few inches deep, he found the wiggly figure of a worm. The morsel tasted bitter, but it was all he had to eat, and it brought with it a sense of normality.

If he could have seen himself from above, he would have seen that his skin was beet red and peeling. His hair was singed and long. His fingernails were hook shaped. What had felt like a mere few days of torturous existence was, in actuality, a few months. The deathly cavern and its utter darkness had a way of making time stand still. The prisoners were on one last stop before the bottomless pit of inky blackness before the cavernous throat would swallow them whole. There was no distinction between man, or woman, or child. Race, creed, and color were of no consequence or question. Foe and friend alike had been housed there for centuries, carved out of the soil and rock that made up the crust of the earth.

The liquid that slipped its way into the cell was the prisoners' only means of survival. Little did they know that they were sustained by its healing properties for it was the residue left over after the healing waters of Paraketh had been blocked and stopped up ages ago. But, although the fount of the spring had been quenched, the sheer force of pressure that created it in the first place had forced it through any crack or crevice it could find. It was like the human heart's innate ability to bypass a blockage by collateral circulation and the liquid of life had found its way into each and every cell in that awful place, thereby healing and preserving the people ever so slowly.

"Jonathan?" emerged another voice into the cell as he slurped more of the liquid. "Jonathan of Scharp, is that you?"

"Go away, get out of here. Leave me alone." He wanted to cry but began to realize that it was probably just what the specter had wanted. The hideous Nephim, if that's what they were.

"Jonathan of Sharp, I'm from the Realm of Irenay. We have known each other for years. My name is Younger... James the Younger."

"I don't believe you," Jonathan replied.

"My father is a Nasgroth in the Realm of Irenay... Jonathan, it's me! Just come to the door. Listen, hear my chains?"

Jonathan could hear the chains and they sounded just like his own. He reluctantly yielded his fear and decided to take the chance. Making his way across the floor of the cell on hands and knees, he poked his head through. Turning to his left, he could see a man looking back at him.

"James?"

"It's me." James was weeping.

He had been in the prison and in that particular cell for years, although he had completely lost track of time. His hair was long, nappy, and matted with filth. His face was as equally coated. Through the darkness, Jonathan could see that his teeth had long fallen out. His eyes were somewhat bugged, and he had a look of insanity beyond his tear welled eyeballs.

"How did you get placed here?" Jonathan asked.

"I fell on the field of battle, John. I had been commissioned to scout the Vale for enemy movement and we were attacked. I failed... I failed miserably." James began to laugh and cry at the same time. He suddenly pulled his head back into his own cell.

"James? James..?" It was clear to Jonathan that the voices and the wind had started to get the better of the man, and he felt for him. He himself had already been affected by the sinister voices in his short time, or what he believed to be a short time in the grotto. Finally, James appeared again.

"We can't talk long. It's forbidden."

"Were the voices from the Nephim?" asked Jonathan.

"Yes, only a lower-level form of them. There are different sects… or levels of them. Those were merely the gate keepers. They can't touch us, but they can taunt us. And believe me, they will."

"Why?"

"John, they have one goal… To get us to throw ourselves down there! They'll nag, gnash, hiss… anything they can to get us to surrender our wills, but you can't give in. Do you hear me? You can't give in!" Jonathan was silent. "How'd you end up here?" he inquired with a shaky voice still.

"It's a long story. I can only tell you that I failed in battle as well…" Jonathan fell silent again, trying to hold back his own tears. He had come so far in the past four years… So far and, so low. At the same time, he was puzzled that both of them had felt equally and guiltily condemned even though they each represented an opposing force. It was as if the prisons had a way of magnifying each man's shortcomings. Unbeknownst to both of them, they most certainly did magnify their shortcomings for they had allowed the words of the Nephim to seep into their hearts like sinister poison.

"Meaning what, John?"

"Meaning, I was a terrible… snipe."

"Snipe!"

"Yes, I was a Snipe warrior."

"Wait a minute," James maniacally chuckled. "Are you telling me that you turned your back on our homeland? You actually fought for our enemies…? You're my enemy?" James' anger sounded through in this stinging accusation and Jonathan could feel it in the pit of his stomach. He pulled his head back and placed his forehead on the cold hardened floor of the cell as James continued tearing into him… "I may have failed my comrades, but at least I didn't betray them… You have really helped me, you know that?" he chuckled. "I haven't felt this good in… in forever. Thanks, my traitor!"

Jonathan was just lifting his head to argue with his childhood competitor when he saw a figure outside of their cell floating in the air and peering in at the both of them, and it had a wicked smile on its hideous face.

He could only see the facial features for the body disappeared into the darkness. Its eyes were black and blood shot. It's teeth, long and slender and appearing as though they had come to razor sharp points at some time in the past, had been ground down to mere stubbles from its continual grinding. It sounded like two granite stones being rubbed together and it began to chuckle through the repugnant sound causing a wrinkled anxious response on both men's faces. Emerging from the darkness on its right side was a slender pale-gray arm holding in its yellow talons what appeared to be a ram's horn. It moved the instrument to its mouth and breathed in deeply with the smile continuing…

"No, please don't. I can't take anymore. No!" pleaded James, but it was too late.

The gate keeper of a Nephim blew its trump and a great bellow was heard in the deep followed by the sound of rushing wind… Jonathan once again scampered into his cell in search for a hiding place, but there was none to be found.

✝

A Deep Revelation

The fury of the storm lasted twice as long as the previous one. The pain was deep and penetrating and the voices of the fallen ones had stabbed at his heart.

He had no clue what James had been going through or what had been spoken to him, but in the midst of the torture, his screams had sounded blood curdling. He had protested the fact that his family was already in the prisons somewhere else, but his words faded after he had supposedly been told that they had already been swallowed by the deep. The final words he heard out of James' mouth were a confession…

"You're right, okay, you're right! The prisons exist because of me… because I failed as a soldier. There. Are you happy now? I FAILED. That was right before Jonathan had passed out from utter pain.

He must have slept through the cacophony of hundreds of voices weeping. He was finally awakened by the sound of shuffling feet and dragging chains. Pulling himself to the edge of his cell, he slipped his head through the bars once again. Below and beside him, Jonathan could see that a number of the prison doors had been opened including the door for James the Younger. It was an eerily ominous sight.

Careening to the left, Jonathan caught site of James approaching the edge of the opened door and heard the sound of his chains being unlatched. One by one, the chains fell to the hardened floor of the cell. Jonathan could see three Nephim hovering around his one-time nemesis as they taunted and tempt-ed him, rings of keys hanging from their skinny arms and their teeth sounding like grain being turned beneath a great millstone. He couldn't hear what they were saying to him for they were in hushed tones, but he could see that James had a flood of tears streaming down his cheeks. The tracks looked like crevices forming as they washed away thick years of built-up dirt. After being freed, he shuffled to the edge of the abyss and peered downward.

"James… James…" Jonathan tried to get his attention, but the specters had captured it completely with their lying phrases.

James grabbed hold of the prison bars and leaned outward over the thick tarry blackness. Jonathan looked below him and saw that others were being led to the pit as well. One woman, much older than the two of them, suddenly let go and jumped into the darkness screaming as she went. It eventually fell into a long fade. Jonathan was horrified.

"James the Younger of Irenay!" Jonathan pleaded. "I am Jonathan of Scharp. We've known each other for years. We were children together. Hear my chains… I am a prisoner like you…" Jonathan continued to try to snatch James from the trance-like look he was caught in. Two of the Nephim spun around and darted over where they jumped around in front of him yelling in his face and trying to shut the master of weapons up.

"James, it was not your fault…"

sounding like grain being turned beneath a great millstone. He couldn't hear what they were saying to him for they were in hushed tones, but he could see that James had a flood of tears streaming down his cheeks. The tracks looked like crevices forming as they washed away thick years of built-up dirt. After being freed, he shuffled to the edge of the abyss and peered downward.

"James… James…" Jonathan tried to get his attention, but the specters had captured it completely with their lying phrases.

James grabbed hold of the prison bars and leaned outward over the thick tarry blackness. Jonathan looked below him and saw that others were being led to the pit as well. One woman, much older than the two of them, suddenly let go and jumped into the darkness screaming as she went. It eventually fell into a long fade. Jonathan was horrified.

"James the Younger of Irenay!" Jonathan pleaded. "I am Jonathan of Scharp. We've known each other for years. We were children together. Hear my chains… I am a prisoner like you…" Jonathan continued to try to snatch James from the trance-like look he was caught in. Two of the Nephim spun around and darted over where they jumped around in front of him yelling in his face and trying to shut the master of weapons up.

"James, it was not your fault…"

"Shut up you fool… Stop now, Scharp!" screeched the voices.

"James… Whatever they said to you, it's a lie. That's all they ever say… Lies." The specters again began to hover around James more or less screaming at him. He was staring wide-eyed into the deep chasm… And then he blinked…

"That's right James. Don't believe them. Step back from the edge."

"You don't understand, John. My comrades have gone under. I was the last one on the field of battle and now I'm the last one here."

"It doesn't matter. That was their choice. They chose that fate. You don't have too."

The Nephim caught James' audible thoughts and harped on them like they were playing a tune. They began to taunt, tease, tempt, and torture with their wicked words.

"James… It's not your fault. James, listen… I am your friend! Yes, your friend. As a friend, I'm asking you… Just back away. There's got to be a way out of this, but even if there is not, don't let them have the satisfaction…" Jonathan finished.

To his surprise, James backed away from the door. He could hear him shuffling back to the far side of the cell and heard the shackles being placed on his arms and legs once again, the key rings clanging in the dark.

Jonathan backed away himself. He was still in intense pain from the previous fire storm but felt relieved that James had heard his voice. He strengthened himself with his own words that he himself had used. He utilized them to arm himself if there were any future furies. Little did he know that it would come sooner, rather than later.

He had made his way to the back of the cell to sip on the fluid that had finally found its way back into the cell when a cold feeling crept its way down his spine. As he drank, two raspy voices breathed sulfuric mist into his face as they gnashed at him.

"You'll regret that weapon master. We've been told of your heroics, but they'll die here forever… Wait and see." said the cackling voices as they flew over the edge of the abyss and faded into blackness.

Jonathan expected the worse, but the worse turned out to be much worse than he ever imagined.

The furious storm started as usual, from the depths of the well of darkness. However, unlike the others, an even deeper darkness swept over the prisons as the tarry substance of utter blackness crept around the cavern like a great shadow of death. It was almost palpable as Jonathan watched it slink into his cell. He had heard the familiar bellow and he had braced himself for the super-heated air. Lying on his back, he observed the cell that seemed to be stained with the shade. When the wind finally reached his cell, and the inevitable torture began again, Jonathan tried to cry but the tears merely turned to small spurts of steam under his eyes as his skin beneath began to peel away. It was hotter than before, and the liquid that was flowing down the back wall also transformed to vapor, adding to the burning sensation. It lasted for what seemed to be an eternity, and Jonathan questioned whether he would survive at all. The Nephim had filled his cell in such numbers that he felt as though he were a captive in the midst of the most furious of bee hives. They flitted back and forth, yelling accusations at him that hit him like a million poison tipped daggers. They had used every stinging lie that they could think of, about every person that was ever near and dear to his heart. Their words pulled up seemingly every mistake he had ever made. When it finally reached a crescendo, the young man was at his wits end and began to contemplate tossing himself into the pit. Anything would have been better than to endure the mockery any longer. He was just starting to rise to his feet when the fury suddenly quit as quickly as it had begun.

Like the passing of the eye of a storm, all fell quiet with only the sounds of wailing souls filling the cavern.

In that macabre stillness, Jonathan was faced with his worst fear yet and could hardly believe what he was seeing. He watched as the three hideous Nephim that had warned him about his transgression, opened the door of his cell snickering as they did. Out of the blackness and into his prison appeared two thickly massive creatures that looked like Snipe warriors, only they were almost transparent to the eyes as they 'flashed' in and out of Jonathan's eyesight.

At their sides were slung four swords apiece. They were girded with doubly thick belts that contained nearly numberless knives. Each had long bows that were made of some sort of marble looking substance. Each had arms that mirrored the immense muscles of their legs. Their skin was a deep gray that was almost black and was scale-like hardened. In fact, the skin was their armor. Jonathan knew that they could tear him from limb to limb just as easily as they breathed in the inky black substance. However, they were merely the soldiers at arms commissioned not only to guard, but to usher in the coming of their master.

He arrived on a cloud of swirling black smoke. It was like the smoke that emanates from a completely fire-engulfed structure. It was thick and ash filled. However, the blanket of smoke merely served as the carpet upon which the prince had arrived. It was Magreth, and he appeared to Jonathan in his spiritual form.

His face had been transformed to a milky white watery color and was thin and bony. His thick muscles had been replaced by thin and long ashen colored arms which emerged from a flowing white cloak. He had a thin crimson cape draped over the cloak and it floated like a flag in the wind. On the end of his elongated sinewy fingers, claw like structures for finger nails sharpened to a razor thin tip. He moved upon the air and as he floated toward the young weapon master's son, he seemed to be at ease in this state as if it were his more natural for him. He even appeared to be at peace.

The larger Snipe-like Nephim that served as Magreth's bodyguards (what they had to protect him from Jonathan could only imagine) grabbed the young man by his arms and lifted him up to face the great prince. He snickered as he neared.

"It strikes me as funny to think that you actually believed you could rule my kingdom better than I. Do you see the futility of your ways?" His voice had taken on a more melodic tone as if he were on the edge of song. Jonathan refused to answer him, still in utter shock and pain. "Do you see?" the prince raged. "Do you, boy?" His temper was like a volcano, and it was about to explode.

Jonathan tried to lower his head and avert his eyes to the ground once again, but the prince's ghoul squad prevented him from doing so. Magreth had calmed somewhat, but his demeanor had taken on a more sinister, more deprecated look.

"No," he laughed. "No, I think you still don't see. Here, let me help you!" In one swift movement the Prince of Gish darted over to Jonathan holding out his immensely sharpened claw-like fingernails and quickly slid them into the young man's eyes like sharpened daggers into blocks of lard burying them up to his fingertips.

Jonathan's screams produced no sound. The pain was beyond audible, and his voice failed him completely. It felt like Magreth had pierced his skull with red hot swords that had just been taken out of the fiery billows of a forger's hearth. As the prince held his hand in place, the shearing sting grew greater and greater. Finally, Magreth pulled his hand back and it sounded like he had just removed them from the side of a piece of hung meat. Jonathan crumpled to the ground in a heap, the chains weighing more heavily than ever.

As Magreth had arrived, so he left, upon a carpet of swirling black smoke.

Soon thereafter, the fury began again but Jonathan hardly noticed for he was reeling in agony. His skin burned black, his hair was half singed off, his eyes wept with blood. He curled up as tight as he could and just shuddered in the darkness having been utterly defeated in body, soul, and nearly in spirit.

When the storm had subsided and silence once again ruled, he could hear beyond his cocoon of misery that James had finally given in to the voices of the gatekeepers. He tried to cry as James' voice disappeared into the abyss, but his vocal cords were inoperable.

He turned into himself and laid that way for weeks praying that he would die. Any hope within him had long faded and a mere flicker of light barely blinked within his soul like an eternally fading star that had died ages ago, the end of its light having not reached the beholders yet.

Weeks turned into months as Jonathan lay motionless… and emotionless. Fortunately, no more storms from the deep had struck the cells and only an occasional faded voice fell into darkness. Other than that, the constant flow of healing streams turned to mere drips as even they began to fail in the prisons beneath the Vale of Decision.

†

A Piercing Light

At last, a night finally arrived that was different from any of the others that had occurred while the son of the weapon master was housed in the cells, and it changed his life forever.

Jonathan had still not moved from his position when he heard a distant thunderous sound from somewhere far above the prisons. It sounded like a stampede of horses as clumps of dirt fell from the roof of the cavern. Then the sound died once again. Whatever it was, it had brought a stir to some of the prisoners as a voice sounded out:

"They're fighting on the Vale again!", it echoed off the walls.

Shortly thereafter, the sound of a great door being raised was heard. Then it was opened, and a shaft of light pierced the darkness of the prisons. Jonathan turned his head, and even in his state, he could just make out the glimmer of light for its sharp contrast was self-evident. He pulled himself to the end of his chains, made his way to the edge of the door and to the ledge upon which he was perched far above the black pit. He looked up in the direction of the ray of daylight and heard the voice of one calling down to the hundreds if not thousands of prisoners including his self; and it contained a message:

"I have come in the name of the one true king!" it echoed down the cavern.

Jonathan strained to listen to the mysterious voice from above.

"The king gave up his life in these prisons. Do you know why? So that you might be free! He was lowered into this abyss by ropes that still hang from the ceiling! They are blood stained and blackened, but they are still there! You have been lied to these many days, months, and years. Your prison doors are not locked, they are merely closed! Your shackles are not binding, only latched! You have only been deceived to believe so."

Suddenly, a great bellow from the deep exploded in the depths and began to shake the prisons, but the voice from above continued…

"The keys of your keepers are false keys. There are no more keys! They have been forever dashed to pieces! You are free, if you choose to be!" The last phrase was yelled as loud as the voice could manage.

The raging wind began to fill the cavern with a mighty rush. Its fury seemingly aimed at the messenger high above, but still the voice continued…

"Only the truth can set you free! God speed you poor souls!" and the door was closed again with a thud just as the storm thrust its way upward past the cells rather than into them.

It was so strong that the cavern continued to shake for days. It was as if whatever beast, entity, or being that had been housed deep in the well of darkness had been shot through with an arrow, a simple arrow of mere words.

The storm raged for three days as the anger in the abyss was redirected upon the prisoners. Jonathan merely tucked himself into a ball once again as his hope was again dashed to a million tiny pieces beneath the utter pain of the fiery trial. Torturous and taunting Nephim poured into the cell once again as if from a nest of vipers. Those that were permitted to touch him poked and prodded him with stinging daggers. His body merely responded like a cadaver that shuttered underneath their prongs for his spirit had retreated once again into the depths of his soul where it smoldered there like a hearth fire that dimly glows on cold winter mornings.

When the three days had been completed, the cells had been shaken with such force that fissures had formed in the ceilings and walls. The heat had been so intensely hot that the healing waters of Paraketh had dried up deeply into the rock and refused to flow anymore. Unlike any previous storm, weeping and wailing did not follow the passing of the raging condemnation whose fire singed their souls.

Only darkness and utter silence ruled as each and every prisoner suffered a wrath that left them numb and catatonic. And Jonathan of Scharp was lying among them.

†

The Shadow of Light

On the third day, he rose from his stupor. Jonathan was a battered being barely able to lift himself up. He struggled just to get himself to a seated position. His mind had been bent and broken and he suddenly found it fascinating to try to polish the shackles that were around his wrist. A meaningless motion… one would think. He could just see the glimmering reflection of himself in them if he held them within inches to his wounded eyes. His sound was the only one that scuffled in the darkness until it gradually gave way to another sound altogether.

It started somewhere beyond the fissures that had been formed in the cell's solid rock. In Jonathan's prison, the substance of the sound began with one single drop of milky golden liquid. The drip welled above his head, and he didn't even know it until it had swelled enough to be fattened. At last, when it was finally set free, it fell and struck the very shackle that he had been furiously polishing.

The fluid suddenly splashed into his eyes, and he became motionless.

Slowly, he began to recall the words that had come down to him from above the cavern, he knew not how many days prior. It seemed to have been years ago. Recalling them lit a spark within his heart like flint stones being struck together to light a flickering campfire deep within his being. Could they have been the truth, he thought to himself.

Was there really one true king and was he really real? Did he actually go through the agony of my captivity?

These thoughts and more captured Jonathan's heart as the noise that filled the cavern was finally caught by the source of its sound. Like a spring set free, milk-like golden liquid began to pour upon him and upon all of the prisoners. They were refreshed like never before. It was like a gentle rainstorm in springtime, the cool liquid pouring upon them from above. In actuality, the fount of Paraketh had been momentarily shaken free from its pent-up captivity and the drops of healing liquid once again healed the hurting and preyed upon inhabitants of the cavern.

The prisoner's skin was restored, and their bones were strengthened.

Jonathan himself stood and turned his eyes upward to allow the salve to fill his eye sockets. He opened his mouth and drank deep drafts from the refreshing springs. His filth was being washed away moment after moment in the shower of life. He stole a moment to run his hands around the contours of the shackles around his wrists.

As he did, he made a decision to allow belief to rise within him. He permitted the words of the messenger to seep deeply into his soul. Feeling for the latch that lay beyond the lock of the shackle around his right hand, he gently moved it with his fingers… And it fell to the ground!

Then he tried the one on his left hand, and it fell as well.

He then set himself free from the leg irons.

The absent burden of weight that the chains had created were not the only heaviness that he left behind, and it made him feel lighter than air. The son of the weapon master, and the master of weapons then felt as though he were floating as he crossed the floor of the cell to where the door was located. He stood momentarily before it. And then, rather than pushing it open, he took one step back and kicked at it with all of his newfound strength. It dislodged completely and fell end over end into the black pit below.

Jonathan stood on the edge of his cell, free for the first time since his horrific arrival. He looked above, below, and to each side, and witnessed a thousand doors falling like great felled trees while the cool rain continued pouring forth. The euphoria he experienced was entirely sweeping away his utter desperation.

He tried to look across the cavern to see if there were truly ropes that hung somewhere in the darkness, but he could not see any. He decided to back up to the back of his former cell. When he did, the rain of milk-like golden liquid ceased its flow. Somewhere, it had been dammed up once again.

Jonathan knew his time was short. In that moment, an instant of hope caused him to make a run for the door and he threw himself as far as he could out into the darkness of the pit with arms outstretched!

He fell for what felt like an eternity. Somewhere in the midst of the fall, however, he was slapped in the face with a thick rope soaked in blood and he clung to it with all of his heart. The crimson flow covered his body in its red stain, and he slid down the cord for three times his own height… The truth was real! More real than anything the son of the weapon master had ever known or would ever now!

Once he had stabilized himself, he then slowly began to lower himself down the rope and a spontaneous laughter welled up from within. It was a joyful, hilarious roar, and the young man couldn't control its uncorking.

The rope shook as others jumped to their freedom as well. Far below, Jonathan could see a wooden foot bridge that had been spanning the cavern. He saw prisoners such as himself leaping to it as it swayed just as precariously as the rope had, but it remained steadfast. Only inches beneath the bridge, the tarry substance of darkness hovered like a thick black lake of ink. Men, women, and even children had begun to fill the bridge. Once upon it, he could see them escaping into tunnels hewn out of the sides of the cavern. Their numbers amazed him, and as he slowly descended, he could see that most of the prisons had been emptied, but not all them.

Finally, Jonathan took his turn to leap from the rope and landed on the bridge. The jump was just a bit short, and he was forced to hang on to the sides. His legs dangled over the edge and into the soup-like substance of darkness. It felt strangely cold considering that superheated air always flowed from somewhere below it. It wasn't liquid, but an overburdened cloud of heavy air. The bridge swayed under his weight, and he nearly lost his balance, but it had been fashioned in an almost web-like weave similar to a fish net. As such, the jumpers could catch it at various angles and could still gather themselves onto the bridge. Once he had scrambled to the top, Jonathan had the choice to go one of two ways and he contemplated which to turn to until a familiar bellow sounded lower than he was.

It immediately started a panic as the conditioned prisoners scrambled for an escape, being keenly aware of what was coming next. Jonathan could see the blast of hot air rising from the inky lake-like cloud and it began to push the bridge back into its standing position where it had been latched to the wall. Unfortunately, he was still on it. He rode it all the way up, but just before it slammed into the wall once again, he jumped free and into a cave that led in multiple directions.

For the first time, he was thankful that he had been conditioned to exist in the darkness for he was able to feel his way in it as he followed the tunnel. The wall felt like a cubed crystalline substance as he ran his hand along it. Behind, he could hear the sound of the rushing wind as it filled the cavern. However, it, and the familiar screams of terror faded into the distance the faster he ran. He had emerged from the bridge with many others but had suddenly found himself alone in a myriad of maze-like tunnels that led in multiple directions. When he had gone a considerable distance and was hearing the sounds of the prison no more, he finally sat on a stone and rested.

It would have been impossible for him to know how long he had been in the cell, and his body was apathetic. He was weak and wanted to sleep but knew that he had to keep going for he was sure the Nephim would soon follow. Rising, he staggered onward.

Jonathan surmised that the tunnels must have been narrowing for he could hear his own breathing more clearly. The floor became softer and slightly upward in motion. The crystalline substance had given way to rock and dirt. Still feeling his way along, he suddenly struck his head on the ceiling of the cave and for a moment, it stunned him. Sitting in the dark of the tunnel system gave him the chance to feel the dirt below and it was soft. Continuing in an upward angle, he made his way on his hands and knees crawling through the dust. The cave system continued to narrow until Jonathan found himself shuffling upon his stomach.

His distance was soon measured in inches as increment after increment made the ceiling seem closer and closer to the top of his head. At the same time, his pathway made a more vertical turn up toward what he hoped to be some kind of surface. More than one time, Jonathan had to halt his progress to grab hold of his emotions. His fear of small places loomed over him like a long-forgotten specter. Halting his advance once again, he recalled the time that he was caught in a similar circumstance as a child…

It had occurred during one of the family's journeys to the river's edge. His Da' had been felling trees and cutting them up for the winter's stockpile. His Ma' was busy helping John because of his condition. Therefore, Jonathan was left to play by himself amongst some of the trees. He had built himself a hovel with some of the larger branches by placing them between two boulders. He was only five years old but was proud of his own ability to construct the wooden structure. He had even fashioned windows in the side of it with some of the smaller sticks. Once he had accomplished the task, he began a game of make believe.

He pretended that his hovel was a great fortress that he had to defend from a vicious and hungry pack of wolves. He envisioned them advancing against his fort from all sides. His first thrown rock hit the leader right between the eyes and served to only stun the animal. The next throw was behind him, and as he tossed it over his shoulder at them, the rock bounced off the one killing it, then the other where it felled that foe as well. That left three more including the already wounded leader. Two more quick throws felled two more, leaving only the leader to defeat.

Jonathan imagined that the large male dog leaped at him through his make-shift window where they began to wrestle on the ground, arms flying, teeth gnashing, fur shedding, and legs flinging. Sometime during the main battle, the young boy kicked the roof of his hovel and it fell on him pinning him beneath the pile.

With his imagined battle suddenly interrupted, he waited there for what seemed to be hours. In truth, it had only been a few minutes, but he remembered thinking that he may have to stay in that one position forever. It was dark and he couldn't move any of his limbs. At one point, just before his rescue, his mind snapped, and he began to struggle with all of his strength to no avail and just had to quietly weep. Finally, his mother pulled the logs from him and removed him from the pile.

That's what Jonathan was working through in his mind as he lay in the dusty tunnel that had him wedged in between the floor and ceiling. He reached behind his head and felt the roof of the cave. He could feel that roots had been growing through.

It was a good thing for he must have been getting closer to the surface. He struggled to twist and turn his body around so that he was resting upon his back. From that vantage point, he began to dig in an upward motion with his long fingernails. Unfortunately, his action produced a crisis. What to do with the dirt? If he were to dig and push it down towards his feet, he could actually seal himself in his own grave if no surface was ever found. The other option was a worse one because it would mean that he would have to return in the direction of the prisons. He envisioned Nephim stalking the prisoners in the tunnels and either dragging them back to the cells or killing them on the spot.

He chose to dig.

Jonathan dug for hours through the soil which, fortunately for him, was soft with only occasional rocks appearing. The roots were more of a problem because he had to bite his way through most of them. The larger ones he just tried to dig around. By pushing the dirt behind him, he might have truly sealed himself into a tomb. However, his digging proved to be one of the best decisions of his life.

Jonathan could hear the breathing of creatures searching in the tunnels just beyond his sealed-in self. He froze as they searched just beyond his position. One of them even began to dig around in the dirt for he could hear the scraping of claws against the rocks and roots he had surpassed.

Closer and closer, the claws dug. He began to feel the dirt near his foot begin to loosen. And then, all of a sudden, the scraping ceased. Shortly thereafter, the breathing became muffled as it faded back into the direction that it had come from.

When Jonathan finally began to breathe again, he breathed in thick dust that made him choke. It was hard to catch his breath because he had wedged himself upright into the wormhole he had created. Continuing to dig, he found the roots to become thicker. His fingertips were a bleeding and filthy mess. His head and hair was matted with mud. His face black with dirt.

Then his hands felt moist grass and fresh air. He had, at long last, reached the surface.

His emergence started with just a fingernail, then a finger. The air felt cool and light. He had no idea whether it was day, night, spring, or summer. There was no snow, so he imagined it not to be winter. Finally, he pushed his hand though to the outside world and dirt fell into his face. He then wedged his second hand next to his first and felt the warmth of sunshine on them.

The weeping began immediately, and Jonathan could feel his own warm tears tracking down his cheeks. His ordeal had finally come to an end, and he was finally emerging from his darkness. With the touch of fresh air, he began to worm his way upward through the soil.

From the outside, it would have looked as if one were emerging from a grave, for he had come up right through an ancient burial ground. After his hands had come through, his elbows and arms then emerged. He was then able to rest his arms above ground and use them to lift his head and torso through. He was like a man returning from the dead, a man being reborn as he pulled the rest of his body out of the graveyard soil.

The sunlight was blinding, or it would have been if he were not already blind. Jonathan tried to adjust his eyes, thinking that his time in the caverns was the problem, but it wasn't. Magreth had left his mark on the man and his eyes were beet red and weeping. The only thing Jonathan's eyes finally adjusted to was a watery misty-like world. No matter, the smell of freedom was enough to elevate the heart of the former Snipe. He sucked in the fresh air with gusto and just lay on his back allowing the sunlight to warm his stricken body. His face tingled at the sudden influx of rays radiating down upon him. His skin soaked in its vitamins. He was weak, pale, still apathetic, and he was deeply winded. But he was free!

Though he lay in the midst of a graveyard with unmarked mounds of dirt all around him, he had not a care in the world. It was only by happenstance that he did not emerge from within another's grave. All the same, even if he had, it would have been a liberation unmatched by any other.

"Master of weapons, you have been set free. What will you do with your freedom?" emerged a voice majestic and true.

The voice sounded commanding and kind. Jonathan sat up to see who it may have been, still in the habit of naturally using his eyesight. He remembered his condition, but to his utter amazement, he was able to see the one from which the voice had come to him.

Standing before him was a creature that appeared to be a man, but twice the height of any he had ever seen... even Magreth would have seemed small in the presence of the being. Jonathan figured that it was a creature of some sort, because furled upon his back were silky white and nearly transparent wings. His tunic was a light blue shimmering substance. His hair was blonde with long waves. Thin bands of transparent gold were wrapped tightly around his forearms. He wore sandals on his feet and a massive sword hilted upon his back. His arms were crossed, and he was looking down at Jonathan, awaiting an answer.

"I was thinking of returning to my homeland," he replied.

"And so you shall," came the thunderous voice. Light seemed to be emanating from out of the massive soldier's pores. His eyes were penetratingly clear. Jonathan felt small and insignificant. "Follow the sun's setting for two days journey from here. On the third morning, turn north for one more. You shall be tested thrice, but fear not, for they are not battles that you cannot overcome. From the Vale you have emerged, and to the Vale you shall return. You will have sight that few others see. When your time has come, it will serve you well… you and the other sent ones." His voice finished and his form began to fade in Jonathan's line of sight like a mirage.

"Wait… who are you?"

Still fading he answered. "I am a Guardier sent to you from the presence of the King. This was my second journey to you…" and in a moment, the powerful soldier disappeared.

Jonathan was left dazed. He had traveled from the lowest of lows to the highest of highs. His journey from the village of Safehaven so many years prior had changed him forever. He had grown up during those travels. He thought of what his life would have been like if he had never fallen into the river, nay, never desired to fall into the river. He had been stripped of his peasantry; pried from his family, had wandered deadened streets, had been trained as an assassin, been exalted almost to be the ruler of an entire city, been sapped of his humanity, robbed of his eyesight, and raised from the dead.

Facing the sunshine once again and feeling its warmth, he surmised that it was late into the spring and the warm summer would soon arrive.

He felt like a new man, tattered and torn but, nevertheless, brand new. Leaning back on his arms, he figured that it was time to go home. It seemed like the best place to begin life afresh for there was no other place like it in all the earth.

Rising to his feet, he kept his face toward the sun, being guided by its warmth, and followed it Westward, even unto its setting.

Chapter 9

A Reunion of Sorts

†

The Lever and the Door

The king's army had been devastated. Some had been killed, some had been captured, and a mere few had escaped. Jacqueline had escaped. Following her triumphant ride beyond the mouth of darkness, and her dead on shot at the soldier poised and ready to strike back atop the Sturmstone tower, she had made it as far as the lever and the door.

The door was not a normal one though. It was more like a drawbridge really. At about thirty paces beyond the sulfuric grotto's entrance, she had found it lying on the ground but only barely. It had been concealed with dirt. While she searched the area at the back of the boxed in cave, she tripped over the chains that were attached to each side. They were buried as well. Following them, she found that they led to wooden wheel contraptions which were fixed within the walls. At first, she tried to pry up the door from off the floor, but it was much too heavy. With the chains leading to wheels within the walls, she surmised that there must be some sort of lever to activate it with. Try as she might, it was a puzzle that at first she just could not figure out. While she sat and contemplated, however, she had an encounter with the gatekeepers.

The gatekeepers were the same ones that Jonathan himself had encountered. They were the lower level Nephim that specialized in the lying arts. It was Jacqueline's first encounter with the spiritual world. Two of them had been assigned as sentries within the cave's entrance and watched from beams that were attached to the far walls like night owls that are on sentry. When they saw her, they seized upon her weaknesses... And her main weakness was her relationship to her father. How they had obtained the information so readily was simply a mystery. They started by accusing her of being the reason that he decided to leave the family in the first place. Then they harped on the lie that he had been killed because of her. Jacqueline, who couldn't see the beings, was vulnerable, and scared.

"It's your fault," she heard as one swooped near her.

Although the young warrior could not see the specters, she tried to swat at them, but the Nephim had an uncanny way of throwing their voices.

"He has tried to contact you, but you were too weak… too selfish…" another flew past.

One would think that the Nephim would call for others to assist them in their preventing the soldier from opening the door, but their inherent and seething pride prevented the thought from ever crossing their minds. It was hard enough for just the two to be in the cave together, let alone mount any coordinated defense. It was a hierarchy where the concept of unity was more or less null and void.

Jacqueline, though fearful, had been well trained by Brenda of Hilt and quickly remembered that the lower level Nephim could not touch her, but their stinging words were difficult to deal with all the same. She had been trained for the ride into the cave, and had been told of the creatures, but it was much different when actually dealing with the venomous beings and their accusative tongues. More than one time, she nearly crumpled into emotional exhaustion as they continued to swoop down from their beams and flit about circling just out of eyesight. Her only combat was to focus on the task at hand and she began to search for the all-important lever that would activate the door; which consequently, was the very best strategy that she could have chosen in such constraining and difficult circumstances. Finally, she found what she was looking for, but it would prove to be a whole new puzzle.

On the far wall of the grotto, Jacqueline spied the wooden beams close to the ceiling. They had been previously hidden until her eyes had adjusted to the darkness. There was no reason for them to be there, so she figured that one of them must have been the activation mechanism. Running to the back of the cave, she jumped as high as she could, placed a foot against the wall and used it as a springboard to the higher beam. The first time, she was unsuccessful and of course, the Nephim mocked her for it. However, the second attempt proved otherwise and as she grabbed and hung from the beam, it lowered, and she heard an unlatching sound, but the door failed to open. The other beam was a full leap away, so she pulled herself up to a standing position on the first and jumped to the next, which lowered and unlatched another mechanism. Unfortunately, when she left the first, it was raised once again, and the latch was reactivated. Somehow, they both had to be pulled down simultaneously leaving her with another puzzle to solve. Still continuing their incantations, the Nephim floated just above her head for she could feel the breeze of their flapping wings and that gave her an idea.

Jacqueline, standing atop the second beam, slowly made her way to her hands and knees and slipped underneath the beam holding on by her arms and legs. When she did, she heard the voices of her enemies go silent for they had suddenly become puzzled themselves. Then, the young kingdom soldier allowed her legs to fall away ever so slowly using her core muscles to do so. Once in the dangling position, she simply closed her eyes and allowed a peaceful presence to surround her. Still, the voices of the flapping Nephim were silent. Jacqueline knew that she didn't have a lot of time but continued to hang quietly and at peace. Inside, however, she was still afraid.

Her muscles began to shake, but still she maintained her position. And then, beyond her eyesight, the two Nephim began to do just what she was hoping that they would do. Together, they gently landed upon the other beam that protruded from the wall and neither said a word, not even a whisper. They were completely enamored and mystified as if they themselves had, at one time, experienced the same type of peace. All the while, the other beam slowly lowered, and Jacqueline heard it activate something in the far distance.

The door gently rose horizontally, and from the space below, a sulfuric and acrid air met Jacqueline in the face. She continued to hold on with all of her strength as the door moved in her direction. Once it had been opened, she found herself staring into a bottomless pit around which hundreds of cells lined the cave walls.

A hot wind began swirling far below and she could see that a draw bridge had just been lowered into place as well. The activation of the door also had activated the bridge. Jacqueline could see that the wind was increasing its intensity as the bridge began to swing back and forth. She shouted down the message that she had long before tucked into her heart, and it bounced off the walls all the way down the to the bridge which she figured to be approximately forty fathoms.

The hot wind had just started to strike her, when it forced her to let her arms go free. She did so by swinging from the beam that she had been hanging onto and swooped to the far side just as the great door was slammed shut once again. Rolling out of her fall, she turned to see the door shuttering beneath the blast of wind.

The voices of the Nephim suddenly sprang to life; they were furious. They began shouting at her in screaming shrieks that threatened to burst her eardrums. She quickly made her way to Everheart, mounted, and galloped out of the grotto as quickly as she could and into the swirling smoke and fire that was still on the battlefield. The residual effects of battle helped to conceal her escape, almost.

It was Katelyn that first spotted her trying to flee. Magreth immediately assigned her to assemble a hunting party and commanded her to pursue the young soldier relentlessly and to not return until she was dead. Jacqueline escaped out of the vale on the far side of the battlefield and had a ten-minute head start before Katelyn with ten others chased behind and into the thick forest. For Jacqueline, it was the great southern forest. For Katelyn, it was the great northern one. However, unbeknownst to Katelyn and Magreth's hunting party, Jacqueline had been lost in it, but then had found her way in it as well. In the process, she had learned most of its secrets.

Time passed, and the hunt had entered its fourth week when the first encounter between the two women occurred. Katelyn and her party were relentless in their search and Jacqueline was tireless in her elusiveness. She had learned how to live off the land. For example, she learned which leaves, roots, and berries were edible and which were not… and the ones which were deadly. One in particular, she had named the Breathless Bush.

During her time surviving in the forest, she was in the habit of trying miniscule amounts of any edible item before eating it. When she had come upon this one in particular, it was deviously tempting. The leaves were full, with a reddish tinge to them. Between each, sinewy strands of silky threads connected one to the other. Its blossoms were scented with a rich fragrance as well. However, its deadliness lay not in its flowers, but in its tiny berries. Just smelling them produced a gagging attack for the poison was most potent.

By the fourth week, Jacqueline unfortunately had found herself within striking distance of her would-be hunters. Somehow, they had figured out her track and re-tracking puzzle that she had left for them in hopes that they would get lost themselves, and she was caught unawares. Fortunately, she had been hiding near a dale that was full of the Breathless Bush. Having to invent a last-minute plan, she allowed herself to be seen trotting upon Everheart opposite the dale from Katelyn and her soldiers. They made a charge into the small valley in pursuit of their foe and the galloping of the charging horses through the brush created a poisonous cloud that instantly subdued just over half of them. Six were lost completely to the breathtaking fragrance as they choked and gasped to death. As Katelyn and the four remaining soldiers contemplated how to attempt to rescue their comrades, Jacqueline was able to escape. Another three weeks would pass before another showdown would occur and it wouldn't fair as well for the young Council warrior.

Against her better judgment, Jacqueline had started a campfire due to an extraordinarily cold spring night. She hadn't had much to eat save for the small edibles that she had discovered. However, the miniscule amount of protein that they had contained was hardly enough to keep her strength up, let alone her natural heating mechanism. Though blanketed under her cloak and bed roll, she could not keep from shivering. Although the camp's fire was merely twigs, it produced enough glow in the dark to attract the four remaining hunters.

After tethering their horses, they sneaked through the forest and converged on the glow of the makeshift fire from four different directions. Jacqueline was oblivious to their approach since they had been sharpened and polished in the ways of stealth. With the quiet-clothes, as they called them, they adapted their ways to the forest floor and were able to move within a few paces before being discovered. It was Everheart that finally gave away their presence with a strange whinny.

Jacqueline recognized the noise from her horse and rolling in a backward somersault she barely avoided three arrows and one dagger that would have struck her right in the head. Following the near miss, a foot race then commenced beneath the canopy of trees in the thick of night.

Jacqueline ran as fast as she could, ducking beneath low lying branches and through dense underbrush. She could hear the trackers moving behind her just as quickly she was. The foot race continued for a considerable length of time until it was suddenly and dreadfully interrupted. Jacqueline saw the pit one moment before it was too late, and she fell headlong into it. Fortunately, she had been running fast enough to fall to the other side of the cavernous hole where she slammed into the far wall with a thud. It left her breathless, but not fight-less. Two of the four soldiers fell directly into the cavern and fell the complete depth, with a couple of bounces off the walls. Jacqueline counted five loud cracks apiece before they struck the bottom. The third warrior had been so close to her that she had landed right next to Jacqueline and immediately clung to one of her legs. Needless to say, one good kick left that woman falling into the pit as well. That left only Katelyn. Unfortunately, she had seen the others disappear over the edge and stopped short herself.

With Jacqueline struggling to cling to the root of a tree that had been growing out of the side of the dirt wall, Katelyn merely raised her crossbow in her prey's direction and fired. Jacqueline saw her release the shot and swung to the left at the last moment. She knew that the next one would not miss.

Within the short time that it took Katelyn to reload the weapon, Jacqueline was able to use the first fired arrow as a step to help get up and out of the cavern. She stepped on it, sprung to the top edge, and began to run again through the thickened forest. Within minutes, Jacqueline had gained so much ground away from Katelyn that she was able to disappear into the thickness of the forest. Not long after, Jacqueline's faithful horse had found her and together they continued to elude the Gish warrior.

That would be the last confrontation between the two before the final showdown would occur… a showdown that only one would walk away from alive.

†

Adjoining Journeys

Jonathan, still blind, had been using the sunlight to guide his steps during the first day out of the deadly prisons. At sunset, the sun's rays fell behind the trees, and he knew that it was time to sleep for the night. His blind condition had been a difficult adjustment. He was forced to feel his way along. As one could imagine, he had sustained a number of injuries due to his constant stumbling. His was a misty and watery world that he had to try to adjust to. With each new obstacle, he gained a deeper empathy and admiration for his Da', who had learned to live with the condition for many years.

Not only was the journey a difficult one full of obstacles, but it was also a slow and tedious progression. The warrior of light had stated that the first two days would consist of following the sun westward, but how he could have calculated his speed or lack thereof was a puzzle that truly perplexed Jonathan during his journey. By the end of the first day, he had already begun to feel utterly exhausted in body and mind. That first night, he hardly slept between the myriad of eerie sounds that the great southern forest had harbored.

The sunrise gently awakened him the next morning. Knowing that he had to travel westward, he kept the warmth of the sun behind his head and faced the cool shadows of the opposite direction. It was his only sense of any sort of direction. As he journeyed, he could smell the forest and its trees, its shrubbery, and its foliage. The morning dew had magnified them, and he found himself captivated by his new sense of the surrounding world. The harmony of the different birds as they seemed to communicate to each other was an experience altogether new and exciting. However, amidst his elation at the discoveries, another sound and feeling began making its presence known louder than any other, and that was his body's language.

The hunger pains and accompanied noises began to yell louder and were beginning to be more pronounced than the surrounding forest.

The burning of his skin screamed for relief as well. His muscles ached and his eyes pulsated back and forth in his skull even though Jonathan had learned to put the pain out of his mind the best that he could. However, with his lessening strength and stamina, his ability to thrust the pain to the back of his mind was overridden.

As the sun began to approach its highest point in the sky, he was forced to stop and rest until he could feel it on his face once again. Jonathan felt around his location for any suggestion of food, but found none. To venture very far from his course could be devastating, but the need for sustenance begged him to do just that. Unfortunately, when he gave in, the stray nearly did cost him his life.

He had traveled only a few breadths from his position when he could smell the fragrant scent of some sort of flowered plant. The closer he got, the stronger it was. As he approached, he reached his hand out and felt for them. They had some sort of silky threads connecting them, but they also had berries nestled among their leaves as well. He grabbed the berries and brought them closer. When he did, they stole his breath away and the acrid fumes choked him from the inside out. Dropping them instantly, he backed away and began to rub his fingers in the dirt to get rid of the residue of the poison.

Struggling for life, he tried to maintain his breathing, but it felt as if he was being suffocated one gasp at a time. To make matters worse, his heart was racing, making the oxygen demand on it difficult. After some desperate moments, he was finally able to quiet his breathing and heart rate. Afterwards, he listened intently and felt for the sun, for he had strayed from his path and was desperate for direction once again. Within earshot, he could hear a distant stream, and it would prove to be a life saver.

The sun had not yet reached his face, but he could feel the rays on the top of his head. The previous experience still lingered in his system and his constant coughing threatened to gag the life out of him once again. Throwing caution to the wind, he shuffled forward toward the sound of the brook. It was much further than he thought and by the time he had gotten near, the sun had long passed being his compassing directional guide. Exhausted, he struggled to find the source of the creek. With each effort, more strength was leaked from his body. At last, at about seven paces from the edge of the stream, he was completely and utterly sapped of all energy. It would be impossible for him to continue any longer and equally impossible for him to find his direction again.

The young man from Safehaven had been through too much for his humanity to withstand any more demands. Besides, just being freed from the tortuous prisons had been as complete an experience as a whole life lived. Jonathan, satisfied with having fully lived, laid down his head, listened to the sound of the water with the forest accompanying the orchestration, and fell asleep. A sleep that he was positive would be his last upon the earth's surface.

He slept an uncommon coma-like sleep that hovered near a deep cliff…

Upon that precipice of death, he was finally awakened by the smell of sizzling fish and the warmth of a fire within arm's reach of his position. His stomach growled with ferocity. He could hear the sound of someone nearby scooping water from the stream and into some sort of basin.

"Who's there?" Jonathan's voice box barely worked, "Hello?" But no answer came.

He could hear the person, whoever it was, making their way closer to him. Suddenly, he felt a hand upon his feet. Then he felt cool water being poured over them. After that, the hand was joined by another, and the two hands began cleansing them, washing away the filth of the prisons and his seemingly endless journey. Still, there was no voice attached to the servant. He then heard the sound of a cloth being dipped into the basin and felt a hand upon his face. At first, he wanted to protest, but the cleansing was the most soothing thing he had felt in a very long time. Besides, he had not the strength to even resist.

It was refreshing… It was healing. Whoever it was that was helping him began to wipe his face with the cloth, wringing it out, and letting the water run down his cheeks. The task must have been a tedious one for the person, for it took some time.

At last, Jonathan felt the hands of the person upon both of his cheeks. They felt strong and powerful yet gentle enough to be soothing. He surmised them to be the hands of a man, probably a soldier of some sort. Jonathan lifted his hands to the stranger in response and felt… gouges and scars… and old arrow piercings. Suddenly, he felt the person's thumbs pressing on his eyes that began to wipe them from an inward motion to an outer one. Again and again, the hands wiped the filth free. In his head, Jonathan could feel warmth like the warmth he had felt when the old man had sung his song back in the streets of the Gish. It was calming like liquid gold being poured upon him. Then, to his astonishment, the man began to hum the very same tune that the old man had sung long ago in the streets of the city.

The old prophet, thought Jonathan to himself. Then the man arose to his feet and began to walk away.

"Wait…," he tried to say through wounded cords, but there was still no answer.

Jonathan tried to look in the direction of the fleeing figure through his watery eyesight. To his shock and amazement, his vision began to clear. Sunlight and colors began to stream into his view causing him to squint. Allowing the tears to escape his eyes, he began to clearly see the figure of a man walking toward a massive white war horse in the distance. The man was neither old nor bent over, nor was the man the soldier of light that Jonathan had seen earlier. The man was, however, wearing a flowing white fur cloak and had hair that was wavy and rather long. Through continual streams of tears, he watched the stranger grab the golden horn of the saddle and effortlessly swung himself aloft the giant war horse.

And then he knew… The man was the king himself!

Jonathan sat dumbstruck as the rider then rode into the forest and Jonathan saw him no more, but lying near the still sizzling fish was an old, crooked cane.

That evening, the son of the weapon master enjoyed the most fulfilling meal of his entire lifetime and just before he fell asleep upon a thick, soft bedroll in the recently built camp, he gazed at the stars and tried to count the number of them, but they were too innumerable.

The next morning he arose to a glorious new day. Everything around him was alight with the newness of life. He walked seven paces from the camp that the stranger had set up and down to the edge of the stream. He took note of the sun's reflection from the water and how it flickered in the morning light. A light breeze was slipping through the trees, and they danced in unison like an orchestrated ballet. His eyes felt cool and refreshed. The colors in the surrounding forest were vibrant and alive. Never before had he seen such an absolute contrast between them. Where before, any forest had only been a collage of backdrop, each leaf suddenly had a life of its own. He thought that he could hear their language as well for they seemed to be singing… singing just to be alive. Kneeling at the water's edge, he turned to look upstream. When he did, he caught the glimpse of a woman's figure arrayed in a black cloak with a hood over her head.

The woman was leaping from one side of the stream to the other and concealing her scent by the water's passing beneath her form. And she was coming toward Jonathan.

He knew that it was the exact fulfillment of the recurring dream that he had been having for years. The thought alone kept him from moving as he observed his prophetic premonition now unfolding before his very eyes. As in his dream, the woman was captivating in real life, but even more so. At about forty paces upstream, the woman kneeled down to take a drink. She had a smile on her face for she knew that Jonathan was watching her.

When she removed her hood, he could see that it was Jacqueline as her ringlets fell into her eyes. He was enthralled. When she turned her head to look in his direction, he could see her long eyelashes blink and they reminded him of angel's wings. A moment later, she began to stand to her feet and un-slung the crossbow upon her back. He was still frozen in time when she pointed the weapon in his direction and fired. Jonathan could imagine the four barbs of the arrow zipping toward his right shoulder again…

Then, the arrow flew right past and into someone behind him. The former master of weapons could hear breath being released with a whimper and knew that the person had been struck down. Turning, he saw that it was the Shade warrior, Katelyn, and she had been holding a long, jagged dagger. She was about to plunge it into the back of Jonathan's neck when Jacqueline had killed her. Jonathan was dumb-struck again.

He went to her side to see if she were still alive, but alas, she had perished. Jacqueline silently made her way to where Jonathan knelt near the body. He had his head bowed in silence.

"Would you mind if I joined you in your journey?" she asked, but he did not answer.

✝

The Reunion

Jonathan had not said a word, so Jacqueline spoke once again, "Did you know her?"

After a long pause, he replied. "No. I never knew her… I would love for you to join me in my journey, but let's bury   her first."

Together, they dug a deep hole for the Shade warrior, wrapped her in the bed roll and covered her over. Then, at the direction of Jacqueline, they headed in a northerly direction towards the Realms of Irenay and home.

However, just after breaking camp, Jonathan grabbed the crooked cane to use as a walking stick. North was the way that Jonathan would have traveled anyway, for the still rising sun was on his right side so he was moving just as the warrior of light had told him to, three days earlier.

They began their travels, taking turns holding the reins of Everheart the famous mocha colored horse, and exchanged stories of their adventures.

Jonathan was still the novice when it came to girls and was pleasantly surprised to discover that the young woman from Marshai was a novice as well. For the first time, Jonathan learned about where she had come from, how she had trained, and how she had joined his family in the search for him when he had disappeared so long ago.

Jacqueline, in return, learned how the young man had such a desire to leave his homeland, how he had been to great cities, and how he himself had been trained to become a warrior. If there was ever any connection between two people, then the bond of that journey through the great southern forest was one of them. And yet, there were certain facts that each could not bring themselves to share with the other. The sub-textual facts, coupled with their mutual shyness, kept the conversation just above the surface of a deep pool of commonality and both of their minds bounced around the facts that neither of them felt comfortable sharing.

For instance, Jonathan found that even the memories of his time in the prison were difficult to stomach. His ragged clothing and worn demeanor spoke volumes about the trial he had endured, and Jacqueline didn't have the heart to press him on the issue. He, therefore, left that out of the story of his time away. She, in return, had a number of things that were difficult to share as well. For instance, she wanted to blurt out the fact that he had been such a tremendous influence on her life even from the time of their first meeting as children at the Blossom Festival. In time, she was able to break the sad news about how and why Bart of the Forest had been lost, after which followed a long and lingering silence. He could not bring himself to share the fate of James the Younger, a subject that would have been lost in translation due to their past issues anyway. She, in turn, could not find the words or the moment to tell him of his missing brother, a fact that she surmised he would find out soon enough. Alas, Jonathan had not the desire, nor the moment, nor the bitterness to tell her that it was she who had shot him in the shoulder. The confrontation had long lost its meaning. Besides, if he could have found the strength to tell her, he might even have thanked her for it. During the trip, she never even discovered that he had been a Snipe warrior for the enemy. Thus, there was much that they could have said, but in fact, most of the connective tissue of their lives stayed buried just be- the surface.

One full day of travel brought them to the river across from the canyon that would take them back to the Township of Safehaven and to the homestead of Scharp. They stopped directly across the river from the place where Jonathan had, in his past life, skipped rocks in hopes of reaching the far side. It was eventide. The river had subsided, but the carved canyons remained. The water continued to flow with a strong current, but it was shallow and easily passable. Jonathan, overwhelmed with emotions, had to sit beside the water and attempt to gain control of his self. Jacqueline quietly sat next to him and watched the currents flow. Neither said a word to each other for the longest time, until the barrier ice covering their conversation was finally broken.

"Jacqueline?" Jonathan started. "I'm not the man that you think I am. I've done terrible things and have had terrible things done to me."

"We've all done things we've regretted."

Jonathan found himself collecting stones as he lowered his head, "I turned my back on my family and my realm," his voice began to crack. "I turned my back on my king… I wanted to leave this place so badly that my eyes were blinded by my desires for soldiery. I… I would have done anything to attain it… I did do anything, and everything."

"You don't have to tell me," Jacqueline interrupted. She could see that he was struggling quite a bit.

"I served our enemies…" he began breaking. "I was our enemy," he finally sobbed and buried his face in his hands. Jacqueline quietly placed an arm around his shoulder to comfort him. Jonathan raised his tear-stained face toward her. "I just watched as our own people were killed by my soldiers. I watched them as they were dragged beneath the Vale of Blood by the Nephim," he wept.

Jacqueline hugged him and then Jonathan just sank into her arms and cried, where he remained until the sun began to glance off the water and set upon the horizon, its pink and purple hue reflected in the swirling rapids. Jonathan finally arose from his slumped over position and walked to the water's edge where he began to skip rocks across it. He didn't even realize that he had gathered seven of them, and only seven.

Try as he might, he just could not span the distance of the river with the stones and the opposing shore was still out of his reach. Where the river had once stood as a border that, in his own mind, had kept him imprisoned in his homeland then stood as a border to keep him out. After spending his cache of rocks, he was left just staring at the unbridgeable span until Jacqueline crept up next to him.

"Here, try one more," she said and handed him what would be the most perfect skipping stone he had ever seen. It was his Emeralhearth stone, a stone that was able to float upon the water and it was full of the abundance of life.

"Where… Where did you get that?"

"I think your mother knew it was in your old cloak when she gave it to me. The cloak's underneath my horses' saddle."

Jonathan turned the treasure over in his hand and it was glowing with light deep within. Turning to his right, he gave Jacqueline a smile over his shoulder and threw it. The throw was a picture of perfection, and it skipped the entire distance of the river, finally spanning it, and landing on the far shore where it continued to glow. Just thirty paces beyond its resting place was the canyon path that led to his home, and the stone was pointing them toward it.

†

The Reconciling

They made their way across the river upon the back of Everheart, for its depths only reached to her underbelly. When they had crossed, they started up the canyon, but only after Jonathan had grabbed the Emeralhearth stone once again. It was a treasure he could not forsake and was much more valuable than fine gold… much, much more.

The defensive wall around the town had never been completed, and the house of Scharp, the weapon master of Safehaven, had fallen into great disrepair. Though a light spring breeze was blowing the night that Jonathan returned home, a cold air wafted from the courtyard. It seemed lifeless and empty.

Jacqueline joined Jonathan as they made their way through the gate that the two of them had left by. Not a sound could be heard save for the creaking of a chair coming from the inside. The door had been left open and leaves swirled in tiny circles near the entrance.

Jonathan stood in the doorway and pushed the old door the rest of the way into the room and there sat his father, swaying back and forth in the chair. He was older, disheveled, and was holding the hatchet that Jonathan had thrown years prior. The weapon master was running a sharpening stone up and down the blade.

His son stood dumbfounded, for the house was filthy, empty, and hollow.

"I know you're there just staring at me. Who is it, and what do you want...? Well, speak you ghost." John's voice was broken, as if hope had long leaked from it, but the axe had been sharpened to a razor's edge.

"Da?"

John froze... And then dropped the hatchet where it stuck into the floor, the blade sinking deeply into it.

"Jonathan? Is that you, my son?" Though dimmed, John's eyes seemed to light up with life.

"It's me, Da!" Jonathan ran to his father, swung his arms around him, and wept in his lap. "I'm so sorry, papa. Oh, I'm   so sorry.

"My son has returned... My son..." and they both cried like little children.

"Da', Jacqueline's here as well."

"Jacqueline, my dear. We thought we had lost the lot of you children. Oh God, thank you... thank you..." and Jacqueline joined Jonathan on the floor of the cottage hugging the weapon master and crying.

"Where's Ma' and Samuel?" Jonathan asked still buried in his father's lap.

John raised his son and Jacqueline to an upright position. "Jacqueline?"

"I didn't have the heart to tell you, Jonathan… I'm so sorry," she cried and crumpled to the floor.

"What? What is it, Da'?"

"He… he was taken, son."

"No… No… NO!" Jonathan shouted. "Don't tell me this. Don't…" and he ran out of the cottage and started pulling on his hair and tuning in circles looking up at the sky. He then suddenly stopped and returned to the house where he asked a question he dared not to, "And Ma'? Where's Ma'?"

The bedroom was silent and Katherine lay wide eyed and staring at the ceiling. She was covered in blankets up to her neck. Her face was a pale white, almost gray in color. Jonathan was speechless as he stood in the doorway looking at her. He silently prayed for a breath to come to her being. He held still, not wanting to believe what his eyes were seeing… Then, her lungs slowly expanded as they filled with air. Jonathan's eyes leaked more tears as they silently rolled down his face, followed the contours of his quivering lips, and dripped from the bottom of his chin.

"How long has she been like this?" he asked his Da' without turning around to face him.

"From the day of Samuel's disappearance… She never recovered from the grief."

"What's happened, Da'?"

And John went on to explain to both Jonathan and Jacqueline what had transpired over the course of their absence.

He described a flood of enemy soldiers that emerged from the canyon through and around his very own gate. Hundreds he described them to be. Like a flood of locust that swarmed into the Realm right through the weapon master's back door. They had even silently moved through his own house as he lay in his bed next to his wife. One of them had found the Willowfeld shunt, for he had heard them talking about the unique weapon, but strangely left it in its place next to the fire pit when John went searching for it. Though they were enemy soldiers, they had been mysteriously found to be civilized.

John went on to explain that the very next day the citizens had been summoned by escort to meet in the town's square. When they had gathered in front of the three-tiered stage, their leader stood and spoke to them. "Do you remember a man with red hair?" John asked his son… "I was told by someone near me that he had a scar across his forehead that ran all the way through his right ear." Jonathan nearly fell over when his Da' relayed the story!

It was Thomas Dodd, and he had been Jonathan's replacement after the Vale fiasco. The great general had led the army through the dead forest and through the gate of the weapon master's home and shop. Along the way, he had confronted the army of soldiers and persuaded some of them to remember where they had come from. He asked them to search their hearts about attacking the innocent. "Remember the goodness of the Shade," he had said. "Remember how you yourselves had been shown mercy when the Shade had come to your home." His effective speech had persuaded three hundred of Magreth's army to defect. He nearly had a revolt on his hands right then and there in the dead forest as those that didn't have a change of heart wanted to fight it out. However, Thomas's further persuasions had prevented the blood bath and put the inevitable battle off for the time being…

"He went on to explain that the great leader Magreth would come back for his vengeance," John explained.

"… And his fury will surely cause him to seek his desire. His heated ambition will one day lead to the castle, our realm's symbol of power. He desires to expand his own kingdom and to rule not only this one, but all others… And he's not of this world, Da'."

After getting cleaned up and experiencing further reconciliation, Jonathan and Jacqueline assisted the weapon master with the repairs to the Scharp household. Jacqueline gave Jonathan back his cloak and told him the story of the night that it was given to her. Together, they cared for Katherine dutifully, hoping that their presence would bring her around. However, she remained in her catatonic state despite their tender loving care and words. A few days later, Jonathan was in the weapon shop holding the crooked cane he had brought with him from the forest, and they spoke of things past.

"I remember the first day that we worked together in this shop." John stated. He hadn't touched the place nor had even stepped foot into it since Samuel had disappeared. In fact, the lute instrument still lay on the ground where he had left it.

"Were there any clues to Samuel's abduction," Jonathan inquired.

"He…," John choked back tears. "He had gone for some water, and we found the cup and cloth lying in the courtyard. Only tracks and drag marks led away."

"Which way did they go?"

"Out the gate and toward the river," John quietly finalized.

Jonathan found himself somber and choking back tears. So much had occurred since he had left. He remembered his name etched at the foot of the bridge, and looked at his Da' with fondness, almost awe.

"Why didn't you ever tell me about the bridge, Da'?"

"Bridge?"

"Mocker's Bridge… I found your name etched into the stone at the base of it. You're a hero to people you don't even know."

"I was no hero, son… I was caught in my own web of deception. I joined the soldiery… I truly believed that what we were fighting for in the Vale was a worthy cause. I took the oath; I believed in the door; I believed in the king… Now, I…" John was at the end of his treasured faith, and on the edge of apostasy. Jonathan knew that, and he interrupted his confession…

"It's true. The stories, the king, the door, the prisons… it's all true. What the king did in the Vale of Decision paid the price for my freedom… I was one of those prisoners, Da'." His voice shook at the recollection. "If that door had never opened… If that soldier had never fought his way into the cave, I would still be there… I would still be… burning to death."

The weapon master could hardly believe his ears. Tears began to well up in his eyes as Jonathan looked at his Da'.

"The king is alive. I saw him in the forest, Da. I…," he paused, measuring his next words carefully, "I came out of the prisons blind. I spent two days seeing as you see. You once told me that your world is a watery one full of mist and shadows, remember? That's how I was… But on the third day out, I was in the forest half-dead when a stranger touched my eyes. I had seen him before the prisons, only in a different form, I think. Moments later, I could see, and what I saw was a white-fur-caped man straddling a white horse with a golden saddled horn. Has there ever been a Shadow Scroll stating such a thing; stating that the king still lives?"

"It has been rumored to exist, but it's never been found."

"Da', he left this behind… I think that he wanted you to have it."

Jonathan placed the crooked cane in his father's hand. John ran his own hand up and down the length of it. The head fit into his palm perfectly. Its length was the exact height for him. Its base was thick and strong. He leaned on it, and it held him upright, giving his walk strength, for he still suffered from the limp he had sustained the night his first son had left his life.

"Jonathan, a long time ago I lost my sight on that bridge. I never told you how it happened because I wanted to keep you from the darkness and the shadows. I'm sorry, son. I only did it because I loved you so very much. I tried to keep you here in Safehaven for the very same reasons. Now, I realize that our king rules much more than a realm that we can see with our eyes. He also rules our hearts, if we let him… I believe that this is his way of letting us know that he is with us, no matter where we travel to. I love you, son."

They were hugging and weeping together when they heard the sound of an approaching horse and rider. Jonathan made his way to the door of the hovel and saw an arriving herald with a white and gray war horse trailing behind. He was bearing the flag of the Council of the Castle and had an official looking scroll in his hand.

"Would you be Jonathan of Scharp, son of the weapon master of Safehaven?" he spoke down to him.

"I would," Jonathan replied, wiping his eyes. John had emerged from the shop and stood next to his son, leaning on the crooked cane.

"You are hereby summoned to appear before the Council immediately," the herald stated and handed him the scroll. Jonathan broke the seal and read it to himself.

"What does it say, son?" asked John.

"It's true. I am to comply immediately and go with this gentleman."

"Then you must, son. Whatever you must face, remember what we have talked about," John stated as he wrapped his arms around Jonathan.

"Yes sir," he said to his Da'. "May I say goodbye to someone?" Jonathan asked the herald.

"I'm sorry. My orders are to bring you immediately. No exceptions."

"Aye then." He straddled the extra courser and followed the herald past the entrance to the cottage, hoping to catch a glimpse of Jacqueline as they passed by, but she was not there. Surely she had heard the arriving rider, thought Jonathan to himself. Just as they were out of eyesight of the homestead, Jonathan heard a voice calling his name…

"Jonathan? Son?"

Jonathan turned to see. It was Katherine, and she was standing with the assistance of Jacqueline just outside of the entrance to the cottage. "God speed you, son. I love you," and they both waved.

"May we stop?" he asked the herald.

"I'm sorry, sir. My orders are firm."

Jonathan watched them as he rode over the rise that separated them from the township of Safehaven with tears in his eyes.

The herald led Jonathan and the white and gray war courser through the Township of Safehaven. It had changed little, with the exception of the wall which had begun to surround it. Citizens were re-building the walls and the place was abuzz with noise. When they passed by, the workers stopped and pointed at him and the herald talking as they did. He could see that the butcher's shop was still empty, and he thought of Bart of the Forest and how thankful he was for his sacrifice.

Once out of town, they commenced at a gallop's pace in the direction of Trelane. Beyond, Jonathan could see the castle Lock Kalaw perched high atop its pocket below the Range of the Unknown. Smoke was emanating from around its keep in various places. It seemed to have been occupied. It was nice to see it after such a long time. He could see why Magreth had coveted it so much, for it was truly majestic even though half-felled. He could just make out the waterfalls of the castle as they poured forth from beneath its foundation. They reminded him of the healing waters in the prison. Though it was a harrowing experience, he was glad to have gone through it. Though he had been excruciatingly blinded, he was happy to be seeing with new eyes.

The Realm of Irenay, his home, was more beautiful than he ever remembered. He thought of the people of Gish, and how they would have loved to be seeing what he was seeing. He had often thought about them for he was, at one time, one of them. He thought about Dodd, and his heroic effort to preserve the kingdom. He wondered where he was. He wondered whether he would ever see him again. Continuing behind the herald, his thoughts drifted toward Samuel. His heart ached at the thought of his missing and innocent brother. He prayed a silent prayer for the monkish looking boy. The remembrance brought a smile to his face... a smile that dissipated quickly. What's to become of me, he thought to himself. What will they do?

After traveling over hill and through dale, they came within eyesight of the city of Trelane. It had been surrounded with great walls that stood ten horse heights high. The road that they were following ran uphill all the way to a great gate. He had only been to the city once in his lifetime, but it was then merely a township like Safehaven. Jonathan was impressed by the city's grandeur and thought of the Nasgroth, James the Good. Inevitably, his thoughts and prayers went out to the family for they must have surely missed James the Younger. One day, I will have to tell them how he died, he thought to himself. As the herald led him through the massive gate and into the city, he was surprised when they had traveled completely through and beyond.

"Where are we going?" Jonathan inquired of the herald.

"To the castle… The Council has taken up residence once again."

Jonathan had never been to Kalaw and his heart leapt at the thought. Though he was heading to an unknown future, he had often dreamed of visiting it. He had heard so much about it as a child, but now it suddenly seemed more awe inspiring as they began to ascend the steeps which led to it. The meaning of the king's ride from ages past had found a new meaning and given purpose to his heart. He was humbled to think that he had descended the very same road that they were now traveling up. He believed in the ride, was fascinated by the ride, for it was the ride that had saved his life.

It took them over an hour to finally reach the basin in which the castle sat. The three distinct waterfalls were much grander than he ever imagined. The castle itself loomed even more immensely as well. From his life in the realms below, it had appeared as a fraction of the size that it truly was. The Range of the Unknown towered above it into what looked like infinity, the heights still shrouded in clouds and mist beyond. When they drew near, Jonathan could see that a great canyon separated the foundation of the castle from the surrounding terrain. A long and sturdy bridge spanned three quarters of the great distance, its architecture supremely surpassing even the construction of Mocker's Bridge in Gish. As they began to cross upon the sturdy wood expanse, a trumpet was heard beyond the keep and an immense draw bridge began to lower for them thereby completing the expanse. Jonathan couldn't help but steal a look behind him at the realms below. It almost made him fall off the war horse that he was riding upon for not only the view, but the sheer height was breathtaking.

As they strode beyond the gate, the keep was filled with people working feverishly. Tanners, fletchers, blacksmiths, stablemen, weapon forgers, and builders alike were busily about the labor of the Council. Something had been planned and they had been called to enact it with great fervor. Jonathan surmised that they had heard of the coming war and were in preparation. The immense courtyard was much larger than Jonathan could think was possible. A whole city could have been housed within its confines. He could see soldiers training on the far-right side of it. Even the training grounds had come alive with activity. As they continued closer to the actual castle walls, they passed under an arched walkway that was as wide as it was deep. Beyond, another expanse opened, within which a town was erected. Wooden and stone lean-to structures lined the inner walls of the castle where Jonathan could see stonemasons moving about upon constructed scaffoldings. The inner yard was as fervent as the outer.

Rather than proceeding directly to the main structure however, the herald led Jonathan around to the left side where there appeared a series of cells with iron bars carved into the wall. A series of stocks were also present in the yard for law breakers. All of them were filled with captives. He recognized them as his own men and women that he had trained and sent into the Vale of Decision. Some of them recognized him in return, and merely nodded at him remaining silent in their captivity. Jonathan's heart sank at the thought of being thrown into yet another prison. His forehead instantly beaded with sweat as his heart began to race out of normal cadence at the prospect. His hands grew clammy, for he was sure that his fate had been sealed when the herald stopped in front of one of the cells, but it was already occupied.

For the most part, the herald had been silent, but finally the messenger turned and spoke directly to the former Snipe. While he did, he produced yet another sealed scroll from his saddle bag. "You have a very important decision to make, and your choice will weigh heavily. Therefore, choose wisely," and he handed Jonathan the scroll.

Jonathan broke the seal and read…

Your name and your actions have been spoken of and weighed

Before the Council of the Castle, in the name of our great King.

You have now been placed in the scales of a precarious balance.

It has been determined that the time has now come to weigh your actions.

Before you is housed a prisoner who has committed a grievous crime against

Not only you, but your family as well. His future is inextricably tied

To not only yours, but the others who are currently being held before

Your very eyes. Let it be said that a leader is inseparable from those

Whom he leads. Approach, listen, and choose your reaction, for that

Choice will define all your future actions.

Fastened to the bottom of the scroll was a single key.

Jonathan had never heard of such a judgment. Nevertheless, he was relieved that he wasn't being thrown immediately into the prisons himself. As he dismounted the horse, a thought invaded his mind. He remembered that the soldier of light had said that he would be tested three times. He knew that this would be at least one of them.

Approaching the cell, he didn't recognize the prisoner for he was badly tattered and torn. His head was bowed, and he was chained to the interior of the cell by hand and foot. It reminded him of his own captivity beneath the Vale of Decision.

"Prisoner, raise your head!" shouted the herald. Unbeknownst to Jonathan, it was a signal. Beyond and high above the herald, a crimson colored curtain was drawn back within a window of the castle.

The prisoner complied, and Jonathan looked into the prisoner's face. It was the face of a filthy, badly burnt, and battered Wisekoff!

"What happened to him?" Jonathan asked as he turned to the herald.

"He was thrown into the prisons beneath the Vale."

"My God, he's barely alive!" stated Jonathan. "What has he done to me?"

"You must ask him. His confession is one of his terms of imprisonment."

Jonathan made his way to the bars beyond which Wisekoff was imprisoned and broken. Placing his hands on the bars, he tried to look into the eyes of his friend, but they were swollen shut and weeping. "Wisekoff… Wisekoff…" he called, but no answer was returned. "Wisekoff, it's Jonathan."

Finally, a reply. "John?" his voice was utterly severed. "John, I have hurt you tremendously," he whispered.

"What do you mean? How?"

"I… I… Oh, John. I took your brother and sold him to Magreth."

Jonathan stood silent, unable to comprehend the fathomless repercussions that little Samuel must have been enduring. Then the pain hit him. He had endured physical sting beyond belief. His body and mind had been put through some of the most devastating hurts imaginable, but not one of them could compare to the piercing of his heart that he had just been struck with. It was inner and infinitely deep. Its depths had matched the heights of the Range of the Unknown… It was a fissure that was beyond any that a human could comprehend.

Wisekoff had no more words to say. He knew that he had devastated his former friend and partner. All he could do was to wait for the judgment.

Jonathan collapsed, his hands sliding down the bars ever so slowly. He was shaking on the inside and out. Never before had tears literally sprung from his eyes. They began to drip at a frantic rate. He had the key to Wisekoff's fate in his very own hand. The test and judgment were almost too much to bear. He, clutching the piece of metal so hard, brought blood to his palm as the edges dug into his flesh. He wanted to throw it at the short round man. He knew that he could sink it deeply into his brain if he wanted too. Right through the eye socket, he thought. He had never personally taken another human being's life, but he wanted to for the first time ever. He opened his hand to contemplate, and saw the blood beginning to pool there…

Then, another tear fell from his eye and struck the metal object. And he remembered…

There was another moment when a drop of water struck a metal object… Had the waters of Paraketh merely been the tears of a devastated king? Could they have been the residue of an infinitely wounded savior… his savior? The very thought was like the rolling of a tide…

In that moment, that tide pulled his anger out into a great sea. Then, replacing the reseeding waters, were waves of forgive-ness cascading into his heart. They found the cracks and crevices of his pierced soul. The waves were beyond human ability. Though they failed to wash away the pain, they soothed every bitter question that ever bit into him as to why he had to endure what he had to endure. His questions had been as many as the sands upon the sea-shore, but the moment brought them all together, creating a beach of oneness.

Jonathan slowly and silently rose to his feet, staring at the pathetic figure of a broken man and then waited for the longest of times...

He then methodically placed the key into the lock, for it was certainly locked, turned it over, and entered the prison. With the key still in hand, he moved across the floor of the cell and unlocked the shackles from around his friend's hands and feet. The heavy chains fell to the ground like a succession of numberless links. The son of the weapon master then scooped Wisekoff into his arms and carried him out of the prison.

"Where can I take him to have his wounds cared for?" he asked the herald, tears streaming down his face.

"We have an infirmary. You can take him there."

"Lead me to it then, herald."

"Yes, sir."

The crimson-colored curtain in the window high upon the castle's wall, was then re-drawn.

Chapter 10

The End of the Beginning

†

The Judgement

Jonathan was exiting from the door of the hospice when the herald met him face to face.

"You are to appear before the Council at once… sir." added the herald with a newfound admiration for the man. Jonathan just nodded and followed the messenger across the grounds of the inner courtyard of the castle.

They came to an immense gate composed of two massive oak and iron doors. It was the famed Eastern Gate. Just beyond was a stone tunnel covered with grape vines that were full and their fruit was being cared for by a gardener perched atop a wooden ladder. He had his back to them, but as they passed through, Jonathan watched the elderly man pluck a ripened grape and hold it up to the light. He measured it like a master artist, and bit into it.

"Yes, it is fully ripened."

After passing, the herald continued to lead the master of weapons through the outer courtyard of the castle itself. It was full of plant life. They approached a massive arched doorway that stood about ten times the height of Jonathan. They stopped and awaited its opening.

As they were, Jonathan reached out to one of the flowers that grew near him. Hesitating, he touched it with his hand… and it did not crumble. Suddenly, he heard the sound of the humming of a familiar song. It was coming from behind him near the grapevines. Jonathan swung around to see, but only caught a glimpse of the gardener as he was exiting the great Eastern Gate. The massive door that he and the herald were standing before opened for them, and they entered Lock Kalaw itself.

Though the exterior and the interior of the giant castle were broken down in places, its tremendous beauty was awe inspiring. 'How many times I dreamed of entering this place', he thought to himself. It was the fulfillment of a lifelong dream. Jonathan continued to follow the herald, but hardly took notice of where they were going for he was transfixed by his surroundings. Ironically, there were many similarities to Magreth's own throne under the City of Gish. Massive marble columns rose from the floor to the ceiling. They were at least twice, if not triple the size of the ones he had seen in the throne under. The floor was a pure white marble without spot or blemish. Though some of it had been upended by some great shaking from ages past, its beauty was beyond description. Jonathan lost count of the columns lining each side of the massive hallway that they were following. He imagined it filled with hundreds of people at some point in time. At the moment, however, only their footsteps echoed off the walls and reverberated to the ceiling, the height of which was almost beyond sight.

When at last they reached the end, an inner sanctuary opened through simple wooden doors which must have suffered from the same ancient quake for they were hardly hanging on to their hinges. That was the place where the herald stopped and silently waved Jonathan beyond the doors to face the Council alone.

Though the unhinged doors were simple, the inner sanctum beyond was certainly not. The floor was a pure gold. So pure in fact, that it was nearly transparent.

Jonathan could see right through it and just below the hardened surface, water gently flowed, for the entire room was slightly tilted upward. It wasn't just a stream here or there but was flowing throughout the entirety of the space beneath his feet. It was as if he were walking right on top of the water. Peering across the room to locate the source of the spectacle, Jonathan could see that it was also flowing down the entire side of the far wall. So gentle and peaceful was the flow that he had to strain to hear its hushed tones. The sight brought chills to his spine for it reminded him so much of the gentle flow of the waters within the prisons. It even produced a mist which blanketed the room in a peaceful and perfectly temperate atmosphere.

However, beyond the mist was an even greater sight to behold. A grand throne sat upon a platform of seven stairs. It was made of a whitened substance that was all-together familiar to Jonathan for it had been finely carved and deeply polished from a single massive chunk of a Willowfeld Tree. By comparison, it made Magreth's white marble throne look like a mere piece of overturned river rock. The lines of it flowed with masterful strokes. A light, which was flowing into the space through perfectly placed windows, caused the shadows within to be cast in such a way that they created around the throne a poignant frame for it to sit within.

Jonathan was speechless, almost breathless. He began to make his way across the golden floor where each step closer to the throne brought with it the soft sound of the familiar tune. The humming was ever so gentle, but unlike any other time that he had heard the song, it was harmonized with accompanying string and wind instruments. The resonant orchestration seemed to be flowing right through the very walls themselves. He felt like falling to his knees and could only imagine who and where the music had been originating from. He actually had to make a conscious effort to keep himself from falling face down all together, the atmosphere was that heavy and thick with the substance of peace.

Below the throne's platform, a round table had been placed on the floor of the court. It had seven ornately carved high back chairs plus one. Jonathan had almost reached it, when seven figures entered the room from the right side beyond one of the many crimson curtains that adorned the lower portions of the room. At the head of them was the great Captain of the Guard, leader of the Council, and keeper of the castle, Nathan.

He was arrayed in his royal attire crafted of finely spun silk. His darkened skin magnified the grandeur of his clothing. As soon as the young man saw him, he dropped to one knee and bowed his head. Following him, six others entered the space as well. All of them were dressed in similar royal apparel and they silently took their places around the table with Nathan directly in front and below the throne. It was also directly across from the one empty chair.

"There is no need to kneel before this council," the council leader started. "Let your heart know that your prostrating should only be before the throne of the great king. And we assume it to be so. When your reverence is complete, then rise and take your seat at the table," decried Nathan. His voice was commanding, but not condemning. It had an air of justice, but it was also sprinkled with mercy.

Jonathan remained bowed as he allowed the statement to sink deeply into his heart. When it had fully soaked in, he slipped his other knee to the ground as well. He stayed that way until his nervousness began to subside ever so slightly. At last, he arose and made his way to the seat. Regardless of his movement, he could not chase the inner quaking away as he faced the seven Council of the Castle members.

"Your decision was most wise," continued Nathan. "Do you know why we allowed you to make such a decision?"

"No sir, I don't," replied Jonathan.

"We were informed of your conduct beyond the great forest. Your friend, and ours, Thomas of Dodd, explained your actions to this council. We knew of your great love for your brother. Therefore, measuring your reactions would speak volumes to us about what your heart was full of. We are sorry for your brother's unfortunate fate. Our thoughts and prayers are with you and your family."

"Thank you, sir."

"Are the rest of them well?" inquired Nathan.

"Yes, I think so sir."

"We have sent for them. They will be joining you up here soon. We have provided housing for your family and have requested the assistance of your father in our needs," stated one of the women Council members.

"That is most generous, madam… May I freely speak?"

"Within reason," stated another of the Councilors. He had hardened facial lines and Jonathan took note that he should not make too much eye contact with the leader.

"Thank you, sir." Jonathan continued. "Where is Thomas?"

"He has been sent on another mission beyond the great forest," stated Nathan once again.

The next series of questions came in rapid succession from nearly all the Council members, and Jonathan knew that the conversation had touched upon the one subject that they all were heavily vested in.

"Is it true that you appeared before the throne of Prince Magreth himself?"

"Yes, madam."

"Is it also true that you began to lead a revolt against his leadership?"

"Aye, sir."

"How many hearts were won under your and Dodd's leadership?"

"I would calculate them to be approximately half of the population of the city."

"Among those, how many warriors? How many trained soldiers? How many Snipes?" three of the councilors questioned.

"Well, sir… madam… I would say not one of the Snipes. They remained firm in their support of the prince. As for the others, Thomas and I calculated our numbers to be nine hundred eighty-four highly trained subjugation soldiers.

Unfortunately, I've heard that only three hundred had a change of heart... Of which, I have seen but a few," Jonathan explained. His next question, he knew, would place him on a precarious perch. "Where are the other men and women? I'd like to know what has become of them?"

"Your tongue has a sharpened edge to it. You may fare better with a softer approach," said the hardened one, "They've been held under house arrest at the barracks in Trelane where they've been extensively questioned as you are being now. We are gathering as much individual information as possible to corroborate all the stories that we have heard. The fates of you all hang in the balance. I suggest that you walk carefully," finalized the member.

"In time, you may see them again," added another.

"Your honors, what is to become of us?" Jonathan flatly stated.

"Tell us of your subjugation tactics, first." Nathan had thrown out the statement as a segue to his previous question. Jonathan recognized it as a political tactic that favored himself. With a knowing eye, he followed the captain's lead.

"During my training with Thomas, I had the good fortune to observe the ways of one of the great, if not the greatest, hunters in all realms. It was an eagle that I named Talonshard." His story seemed to pique the interest of the Council for some of their postures adjusted to a more attentive position. Jonathan's training had taught him to observe such signs. "I watched the bird of prey as it patiently waited aloft the winds until the opportune time to strike. When it did, it was with swiftness and accuracy. It was its art of war..." Jonathan let the words sink in before continuing. "Day after day, I observed the great hunter capture its prey. I was fascinated, mesmerized. I began to notice that Talonshard was always careful to carry its prey away without ever killing it. Then I realized that the bird was not hunting for itself at all, but for others. It was carrying the prey to its eaglets. It was Talonshard's tactics that gave me the inspiration about how to turn the hearts of the people away from Magreth. We, the Shade that is, showed the people mercy rather than murder. Favor, rather than fear. At every turn, we spared their lives. It backfired on more than one occasion, but for the most part, it was extremely successful." Jonathan could see that he had captured not only their attention, but possibly even their hearts as well. "Fortunately, it was a risk that worked. We…"

"Did you really strike the snake from the talons of the eagle?" One of the members enthusiastically interrupted.

"Yes, sir… It was what I call, subjugation tactics." Jonathan could see that Nathan's inquiry had led the council down a certain path and he stealthily acknowledged his help with a sublime nod of the head.

"Interesting… We must further discuss what will become of you," Nathan began. "But while we decide what your fate will be, it is this council's desire for you await our decision here within the castle grounds. You will be placed under house arrest as your troops have been. Only one escorted hour outside of doors will be permitted per day. I suggest that you comply fully until our decision has been handed down to you at the proper time. You are dismissed for now."

"May I ask that my leaders, the ones in the stocks and cells, be moved to house arrest as well?"

"They have been the most difficult ones. Our will for them must remain for the time being, but fear not, they are being looked after and well cared for."

"Very well… Thank you, your honors." Jonathan left the chamber in silence not sure what his future would hold. He dreaded the thought of more time in prison if that were to be his lot. His head was full of questions, but it was not the proper time to ask any of them.

The herald met him back at the entrance of the throne room. He was accompanied by two armed guards, and they escorted Jonathan out of the castle and to a small cottage that was near the fore gate. Once inside, they locked the doors behind him.

Three long days past without word. In that time, Jonathan had been allowed to leave the cottage by escort only once a day. He had been re-united with his family once again and they were allowed to stay with him in the cottage. His meeting with his mother was a tearful one and the family spent an entire day together. Most of the discussions were over Samuel and the piercing pain that lingered just beneath the surface of each and every conversation, coupled with the fact that Jonathan had changed so tremendously, kept their time together a bit on the icy side. Jacqueline had departed to be re-united with her mother in Marshai, but they had already begun to miss her company for she would have been the warmth to blanket each of them.

Jonathan stayed true to his morning quiet times that he had grown accustomed to since the time of his training beyond the great southern forest. At the break of each new day, and with an escort of two guards, he had found a certain overlook beyond the walls of the outer courts and training grounds which saw the entirety of the realm and beyond. His fondness for Jacqueline grew exponentially during her absence and he had not heard word about her well-being. He often wondered whether they were admiring the same sunrise.

He had tried to look in on Wisekoff, but every time he inquired, he was turned down. It pained him to think that he couldn't see his old friend. Perhaps it was for the better, for their relationship had been seared deeply. Jonathan's own heart had been completely washed clean of the transgression and he marveled about how forgiveness, true forgiveness, had a way of setting one free from the fetters of the soul.

Jonathan also sought Samuel, if only in his dreams. Seated atop his overlook, he often thought of the good times they'd had together as children. He could see the peak where he had spent a freezing night after attempting to escape upon Dodd's horse so many years ago. He remembered when he had finally returned to the supper table that night and how Samuel had reacted to his return. It seemed so long ago, and it was.

"Quite the view, eh Snipe?" It was Thomas Dodd, and he had found Jonathan at his overlook.

"Thomas!" Jonathan returned and the two locked arms in a hello gesture. "It's been quite a while."

"Yes it has, my friend. How are you?"

"It's been… a long three days."

"I was with the council last night," Thomas explained. "I presented my findings for over four hours. And we debated for an additional three. The old council 'cackle' as I call it." Thomas had made the statement below his breath for the watchful guards remained near

"Aye." It was good to laugh once again, thought Jonathan. It was even better to see his old friend after so long. In fact, he couldn't even remember the last time that he did. "Thank you, Thomas."

"For what?"

"Right," Jonathan jested. "I recall a little soirée in the dead forest that just, oh… more or less saved the kingdom as we know it."

"Let's just call it a moment of inspiration… It wasn't even my idea. It was yours, statue. I just delivered the message."

"Yes, speaking of Wisekoff, I'm surprised you could deliver it with such eloquence as I'm sure you did. I know that I couldn't have."

"It stayed the tide of war for the moment," Thomas explained with a more serious tone in his voice and continued… "My report was not a pleasant one I'm afraid…"

He went on to explain the extent of Magreth's movements. Thomas had been behind enemy lines and spied even to the depths of Magreth's throne room itself. He described the rage of the enemy leader as a whirlwind with volcanic ash mixed in. The army had been growing exponentially since Jonathan's time in the prisons. Its growth was even greater than they had thought, and it was all in a very short time. It had swelled to over three thousand strong, all willing to give their lives in the most archaic of forms. He went on to explain that the production of Serpent's Breath had been increased exponentially as well, with additives that produced a delirious rage in its users and abusers. Magreth's engineers had even begun to produce huge barrels of the deathly potent form of the drug that could be hurled by massive trebuchets. The wheels of the prince's war factory had begun to turn in much greater circles and the time was short. Thomas had also discovered that Magreth, in his fury, was determined to annihilate the Realms of Irenay totally and completely and planned to simply rebuild from the ash heap that he would leave behind.

"Jonathan, I saw your brother," Thomas continued cautiously.

"What did you say?" questioned Jonathan.

"Samuel is alive."

"What? How… Where is he?"

"He's in Magreth's throne room. He's been made a slave as the prince's personal musician. John, he plays day and night for the monster; and that without rest."

"You couldn't get him out of there? What's wrong with you?" Jonathan was agitated to no end and practically shook with frustration.

"I couldn't risk the mission. There's no way I could have sneaked him out of there without alerting hundreds. The piazza leading to his throne room is now guarded by two hundred Snipe warriors. I was fortunate to escape with my own life. My findings would have never made it to the council, John."

"I suppose you're right… I'll just have to go myself. Thank you, Thomas." Jonathan began to tear off in the other direction but was quickly stopped by Dodd who grabbed his friend by   the arm.

"Jonathan. What are you doing?"

"What do you think I'm doing? I'm going to get my brother."

"You can't."

"Why not?" Jonathan was incredulous with his friend.

"John, if you leave now, before the judgment, you'd be sealing the scroll on the Council's decision. Not only yours, but the entirety of the Shade. You'd spend the rest of your life behind prison bars. I know what you went through under the Vale… John, you can't leave."

"What of Samuel? The boy is only ten years old by now. Ten…" He turned away as tears of frustration threatened to well up.

"Be patient my friend… I'll do everything that I can to get him back, I promise."

They were interrupted by the approaching of the herald to their location along with Jonathan's mother and father.

"It's time master Scharp. The council has come to a decision. Please come with me and the guards."

Jonathan looked into the eyes of his Ma' and Da' and hugged them fiercely.

"Believe in the goodness of the king, son," the weapon master stated with tears in his eyes.

"I did my best to convince the castle of your good acts," said Thomas. "That's what I spent most of last night trying to do."

"I'll be praying, Jonathan," cried his mother.

"Thank you all… I'm ready," Jonathan finalized. He slowly followed his escort back to the castle and Thomas trailed behind, but before he left the company of the weapon master and his wife, Katherine spoke to him.

"Thomas, you once promised me that you would bring my son back from wherever he had run to, and you did. Thank you."

"Katherine, I know there's another out there and I'll do everything that I can so you can see him again. I give you my word."

Jonathan entered the throne room of the castle once again. The mist and music were a soothing reminder of what his Da' had told him. Nevertheless, his nerves threatened to get the better of him. For a moment, he found himself alone before the Council's table and he bowed his head and said a silent prayer. It was a prayer not for himself, but for his brother.

The seven council members entered as they had before, from beyond the crimson curtain. Upon the round table, a leather book had been placed along with a long quill pen and a container of ink. They filed in silently and found their seats in equal silence until Nathan finally broke it.

"It has been said that there is no greater threat to our enemy than the one who has been to his depths and back." Nathan looked around at his comrades. By the wear on their faces, the deliberations had been heated and Jonathan had wondered if they had even slept for the past three days. Their shoulders were slumped, and their eyes were heavy. "We have come to a decision." Nathan looked at his comrades one more time, and then continued. "Jonathan of Scharp, we have found your actions beyond the great southern forest to be most commendable and the majority of us are in favor of you joining our cause, but it will come at a great price. Therefore, you will have a choice to make between two sentences. But before you hear them, however, you must know that your soldiers will be handed down the same sentence as their leader. Do you understand?"

"Yes, sir. I do."

"Choice one, will be to surrender to a lifetime of service to this council. With this option, you and the Shade will do as we say, when we say. In this, the whole of you will also be forbidden to marry, for you will be inextricably tied to the will of the kingdom. The burden of your missions will not afford you such luxuries. Son, from this day forward you would be living a life tethered to a very short chain... The other choice would begin with an indeterminate amount of imprisonment for you and your soldiers. After such time, you would be sentenced to a lifetime of servitude as castle attendants, and you would be bound to the castle grounds. We have recently passed a decree to rebuild Kalaw and the help would be much needed. In this option, the whole of you would be permitted to marry and raise families, within the confines of the castle, of course..." Nathan paused to let the sentence sink fully in, and then continued. "What say you, son of the weapon master?"

Jonathan took the time to think through the penance.

Over three hundred futures rested on the edges of his lips. Personally, his childhood had been spent dreaming about becoming a soldier. It would be an easy burden to carry. As for the Shade, they had carried much heavier loads under the leadership of the dark prince, so he was positive that they would be in agreement. Marriage, on the other hand, had only just begun to cross his mind as of late. Until very recently, he had dismissed it from his heart for the residue of a forced union had been like a poison to his soul, but Jacqueline had sweetened that bitterness. Though they hadn't discussed marriage, he had sensed a strong connection between them... a strong and unspoken connection. With his sentence, he supposed, it would have to remain unspoken.

It could prove to be a bitter pill for him and his soldiers to swallow, but a life of imprisonment and arrested servitude would be much bitterer than that.

Jonathan did, however, have one major issue with the sentence that had been handed down to him and he responded with carefully weighted words. "If my sentence is to serve in the soldiery, then I and the Shade wholeheartedly accept. However, if we are to fight for this council, and for this council alone, then I decline. But, if our skills are to be used in the service of the one true king, mediated by this great council, then I humbly accept the penance, as long as the king's will reigns supreme in all that we do."

Nathan smiled a broad smile. The others did as well, save for one. They took from their sides daggers and held them high.

"Then so shall it be done," Nathan proclaimed, and in unison the members of the Council of the Castle plunged them into the table where they stuck fast. Only one of them abstained, but it was not the one with the hardened facial lines.

Nathan then slid a key across the table where Jonathan caught it in his grip… Another council member slid the leather bound book to him as well. "Sign the ledger beneath the oath of soldiery and then go and set your soldiers free. Prepare them for orders… You shall receive them by nightfall."

"Aye, sir. Thank you." And he took the pen and signed the oath of office not having the need to read it for he had already lived it.

Jonathan, the master of weapons, then left the chamber, his heart a prisoner of the one true king.

†

The Turning of the Point

Jonathan, the soldier of the king, walked through the great hall and into the outer court where Thomas was waiting without escort and without guard.

"Am I witnessing a free man?" asked Thomas.

"More free than you can imagine, my friend."

Together, they headed for the Shade troops that had been held at the cells and stocks where Wisekoff had been imprisoned, and they set them free one by one. They were the Shade's leaders of tens and twenties. The reunions were sweet as the cells were opened and the chains fell to the ground. Both Jonathan and Thomas reveled in the comradeship that was inherent in the shared stories of past battles. Many ribbings took place throughout the morning as both were teased to no end. Afterwards, they saddled horses and visited the others at the barracks in Trelane. They stayed with them throughout the day and were given a great feast. In the evening, Jonathan made his way to the cottage where his family was housed while Thomas lingered behind. When he had arrived, a white and gray horse was tethered to a post.

Jonathan made his way over to the horse and realized that it was the same war horse that he had been summoned to the castle upon. It was a magnificent animal. The coat was almost silver, and the gray palomino-like spots blended perfectly into its coat. Stretching his hand toward the courser produced a nudge in response, and it was vaguely familiar. The horse eyed Jonathan deeply, and there seemed to be a common spark. After spending some time with the animal, Jonathan made his way to the door of the cottage, opened it, and stepped in.

"Jonathan!" He heard the voice of his tearful mother but saw his father walking toward him with his crooked cane in hand. In his other hand, he held a Willowfeld bow. Also standing in the middle of the room was the great captain of the guard, Nathan.

"I believe that this belongs to you, son… I re-worked it a little, but not much. Your firing cord was off just a bit," jested the weapon master.

"Where did you get that?"

"Your friend, Thomas, left it standing near the Willowfeld Shunt after he had come through our home."

"I… I don't know what to say."

"We've heard the good news," cried his mother and she moved across the room to hug her eldest son. "Your father and I have been given favor as well. Da' has just been made the royal weapon master and I, one of the royal gardeners. We are to live here at the castle during its reconstruction."

"And beyond," continued Nathan. "I've come to deliver your mission to you as well," he declared. He had another official looking scroll in his hand. "It's all written here, but I wanted to deliver it by word of mouth first."

"Sir. Thank you." He was almost at a loss for words.

"Jonathan, I know that what you had to endure within the prisons beneath the Vale was horrendous. When you heard the message that set you free, many others were freed as well. Sadly though, most that are ever liberated from those chains find themselves as captives once again for many various reasons…

You and Wisekoff were among a small number of the fortunate ones. Son, the cells have been filled again. We need you and your Shade warriors to ride to the Vale with the message to them."

Katherine began to weep beneath rolling emotional waves. Jonathan made his way over to her, held her shoulders, and looked into her misty eyes. "Ma', I've been there... I've been to that darkness... Whatever realm someone belongs to is of no consequence there. There is neither friend nor foe in those prisons. They're equals, and they're utterly perishing. They need to hear the truth... It will be all right, Ma'. I'll be fine," he comforted her. "Nathan, what of Samuel?" Jonathan asked without turning to the captain of the guard.

After a long pause, he answered. "The council's will must be done... But this, letter of the law," Nathan continued while holding up the scroll. "It doesn't specify how long you have to get to the Vale, you know... Our hearts are with you, and the heart of the king is with you as well." Nathan's voice had simmered from one of authority, to one of a more personal tone. "I, uh, noticed that you don't have a horse to take you to where you need to go. There's one tethered outside that I think that you could have."

Jonathan retuned to the door and looked out at the white and gray horse.

"Did you not see a familiarity in his eyes?" asked Nathan.

"Sir?"

"I recovered him from the far end of the river many years ago when he was just a colt... He was Swift's colt."

Jonathan's heart was alit with fondness as an instant connection bound the two together. Katherine and John were equally heart struck.

"I bid you farewell and God speed," Nathan finalized by handing him the scroll.

After Nathan had left, the goodbyes were heartfelt and emotionally trying for the family. And, as so many years prior, John and Katherine of Scharp's eldest son departed into the night. That time, upon a horse rather than running after one. Unlike before, the couple was hopeful knowing that he had been trained as a soldier; that he was serving a purpose much higher than they ever imagined possible, and that he would be surrounded by his comrades in arms. They had no idea of how many were with him.

Jonathan was making his way out of the courtyards of the great castle of Kalaw and toward Trelane where Thomas and the others were waiting. When he neared the great drawbridge that spanned the distance between the castle and the rest of the realm, a shadowy figure stepped out in front of him to block his path.

"Who goes there?" inquired Jonathan.

"Long live da' Shades," came a voice in return. It was Wisekoff, and he had broken out of the infirmary to see his friend off. "I been hearn' of your journey, me friend."

Jonathan stopped his horse, dismounted, and embraced the forearms of his friend. "You're feeling better?"

"Aye… I'm so sorry, John."

"Wisekoff, we'll find him. We'll get him back." Jonathan re-mounted his war horse. "Now get back to the hospice and make a full recovery. The Shade needs their spokesman back."

"Aye sir," Wisekoff replied and bowed dramatically deep.

When Jonathan had arrived at the barracks, Thomas had one hundred and twenty of the Shade warriors ready to ride, for they had been given the numbers to ride with by herald. Not a word was passed between them as the battle-hardened soldiers knew what they would have to face in the Vale of Blood.

They rode for six days straight and had taken a route previously cut through the forest by a long-ago war party. Covering ground as fast as the clouds moved above their heads, they stopped as little as possible, only for watering and feeding the horses for they were the ones that were doing most of the work. Along the way, the two leaders Jonathan and Thomas discussed an impossible plan that would be even more of a miracle than the one that they had been given by the Council if they could pull it off.

By the evening of the sixth day, the Shade warriors thus far had not encountered any of the enemy Snipes nor any of the serpent breeding grounds on their trip to the Vale. They had expected to confront at least one of Magreth's warriors but had not. Even more than their expectation of a confrontation in the forest, they surely expected one on the outskirts of the City of Gish for the leader's plan had carried them all the way to the desert bound city. For the moment, however, the Vale and the prisoners would have to wait.

They encamped on the northern outskirts and sent spies into the streets of the filthy city. After half a day, the spies returned with the news that the enemy soldiery had grown so thick throughout the population, that they could be found on nearly every street corner of the city. They also reported that their former home had decayed into a militaristic society that was sinisterly darkened by the mind-numbing, soul-sucking and Zomb-producing Serpent's Breath that filled the atmosphere with an acrid smoke. The Shade leader, Jonathan, hung his hopes on the spies' report that nearly every street corner was covered. Thomas remained in charge of the army and was asked to stay encamped no longer than one more day before departing to complete the mission to the Vale of Blood.

"Thomas, I need only one day, making our journey seven in total. Only seven to the Vale," Jonathan had said.

He left his horse and most of his weaponry including his armor guarded by the army. Dressed in the loose black clothing of the Shade, with its sound swallowing attachments, and armed with only his Willowfeld bow, he set a course for the Snipe infested throne room of Magreth to the rescue of his baby brother. It would take all his stealthy ability if he were to make it there, and even more to make it back.

†

Shades in the Shadows

Making his way across the cold desert sand, Jonathan could see the city in all its immenseness. It was lit with millions of torches, and if he had not known the truth about the metropolis, it would have appeared as a sparkling diamond in the rough wilderness that lay before his vision. The truth was that it was a gem, but it contained deeply ingrained flaws that had only grown darker under the violence of Prince Magreth's wicked will. Jonathan's heart went out to the people he had once tried to help. He knew of only one place where hope may still be in existence. Thus, it was to a six-story green temple in the northern sector that he set his inner compass to... a stop that would bring him to the Asian sector.

Stepping into the shadows that were cast upon the first street was like walking into the past for the Shade warrior. Muck still slid into central troughs off the wax-like filthy dirt which brought back memories long forgotten, or almost forgotten. It was nighttime, and Jonathan knew what the implications could mean. Not only would he have to elude any Magreth soldiers he came across, but he would have to be mindful of the invisible Nephim as well.

Leaning against the first structure that he came to was a series of wooden beams lined up side by side. They had been left over from the city's push to re-build when he and the Shade had been in power, or rather, in an appearance of power. Jonathan could see that they had not been touched in years, for spider webs with hundreds of cocoons as large as his fist coated the entire underside. With his back to the wall, he slid along trying not to make a sound, but at the same time, not to brush up against them lest they break open and spill their contents onto him, or even worse, into his hair. Once he reached the end of the makeshift tunnel, he found himself to be on the edge of a city square. He knew that beyond the square's central fountain lay another darkened street that would lead him another four blocks to the temple. The only problem was the fact that the whole city had been lit by the multitude of torches, and the spy's reports proved more true than he cared to think about.

Jonathan counted twenty soldiers in that square alone and they were patrolling by two's down each and every street that emptied into it, thus leaving ten near the fountain who were vigilant to not shirk their duties. They had become more disciplined than ever before, and Jonathan wondered what Magreth had threatened them with. Their vigilance left him with three choices. He could enter the square in plain sight with his bow strung with an arrow and with others in his hand ready to blaze, which would have been suicidal not to mention that it would have been bad form and not his own. Another choice was to climb high overhead and skip across the roof tops, but a quick look above revealed that more of the enemy soldiers were standing sentry there. The puzzle left him with only one more choice, and that was to go under them.

Jonathan backed himself through the web infested leaning beams and to the darker area where he had first entered the city. At the mucky trough, he knelt down and scooped the sewage into his hand while keeping an ever-watchful eye on his surroundings… and he covered himself in the filth from head to toe.

He then lowered himself into the dugout trough that ran down the center of the street and inched himself along like a slug through the muck.

It took him over an hour to make his way past the sentries. At times, he had to completely halt his progress and lower his face into the liquid while holding his breath. At least it's not accompanied by a superheated wind, he thought to himself beneath the small puddle. Though disgusted, the thoughts of little Samuel kept him focused on his side-quest, and he was more than willing to pay whatever price he had to pay to reach his goal. When he made his way beyond the square and felt as though he was at a safe enough distance to raise himself out of the rut, he slid his way to another crumbled wall and continued along.

He was forced to zigzag his way down the street from one side of the roadway to the other as the flickering shadows created by the lit torches afforded very little shade in between. At last, he finally reached the familiar Asian sector and was saddened to see that the life of the lit lanterns had been long snuffed out. The temple was still green, but in the darkness of the night, it appeared more like some slime-colored tint rather than the emerald hue it had previously been. Finding the corner where he had once entered, he grabbed the loosened bricks of the building and paused. Examining them, he found that they were loosened not by some shaking of sorts, but rather by thousands of sword and arrow strikes. With little time to contemplate the fate of the temple, Jonathan sprung up the side of the structure, and it was just in time for around the corner appeared two sentries making their rounds.

Like an alerted cat, the former Snipe perched himself upon a ledge of a window and waited their passing. They had not heard his climb and were talking to each other of things that concerned the temple. From his vantage point, Jonathan could see that the two were not Magreth warriors, for they were dressed in the commonality of the Asian peasantry.

"When will they attack again?" asked one to the other.

"No one knows. There has been no rhyme, nor reason from the enemy."

Jonathan didn't know how he was able to understand their language, but he was, for although they had spoken in a tongue foreign to his own, he could make out what they were saying and surmised that they must have been placed as temple guards. His thinking had been confirmed. Hope and resistance were still alive, at least in that area of the city. After their passing, the stealthy assassin-trained soldier made his way into the structure itself.

Following the hallway proved to be revelatory for Jonathan, and he was flabbergasted by what he encountered in the spiral hallway where thousands of tiny prayer doors were closed and locked from the inside. The song that he had been hearing throughout the entirety of his journey was being hummed yet again, and the tune echoed up and down the full six stories of the structure. While he had been absent from the city, the song had become an anthem for the resistance, and he was then hearing it by the hundreds and hundreds of voices, all in unison. As he con-tinued up the hallway, the sound emanated from each and every doorway, like a common prayer being raised toward heaven. He could still catch the stench of the water that lay unmoving from the ground level as he passed between floors, but the sounds that filled the cavern more than made up for the temple's shortcomings. Jonathan hoped beyond hope that Lady Dael's mother would be seated upon the red cushion in an attitude of prayer, for no other person in the city knew the secrets that lay within. When he at last reached the narrow bridge that led to the central and inner prayer chamber on the sixth floor, he did find a woman's figure seated there, but it wasn't the former priestess.

"Lady Dael?" asked Jonathan in hushed tones.

Dael looked elegant in her mother's robes. She brought her tilted head back down and looked at Jonathan with a smile on her face.

"Master Scharp, I'm not surprised… pleasantly not surprised." Dael rose from her prayer cushion and ran to her former master embracing him with streams of tears bursting from her eyes. "I knew that you were not dead… I just knew it."

"How are you my dear friend?"

"My mother, sadly, is no longer with us, but we are carrying on her wishes. She urged us on her death bed, to carry on with the resistance. 'To the last soul,' she commanded… How wonderful to see you."

"And you as well. I have little time, and I need your help… The city is so infested with Magreth's army that I fear I cannot make it to his throne room through the streets. Can you help?"

"I think so… Come with me." Lady Dael led Jonathan out of the inner room and across the bridge to where the stained-glass windows which overlooked the city were located. "I'm sure that you remember these."

"I certainly do… beautiful for sure."

"Do you know what they are pictures of?"

"I never took the time to examine them."

"They are of the city before the decay of Magreth. He built upon the old ruins. Below, the city still exists as it did in ancient times… At least the streets do. Don't you see? It is a map of the underground."

Jonathan was dumbstruck once again by the shear layers of mystery that were inherent in and under the City of Gish. He followed the contours of glass which were melded together with smelted gold. Each color met another at golden intersections. And the gold itself was the streets of the city, or former city. It was awe inspiring and only served to deepen his affinity for the metropolis.

"Do you see?" asked Dael.

"Yes, I see it."

"Do you know what the colors of glass are for?"

"No, but I've never seen so many different colors in all of my life."

"They are people groups… they're every tribe, every tongue, and every color under heaven… See?" Lady Dael pointed to a portion of the "map." "This is where we are located; it is represented in a beautiful yellow hue…"

"But the temple is green," replied Jonathan, still in awe.

"Master Scharp, buildings are of no consequence. It is the people that make up this city… That is why we, and you, have never been quelled by the outer appearance…" Dael began to chuckle a laugh of joy… "You should see this window at sunrise in springtime. It only happens on one day of the year when the angle is just so, and when the light strikes it, the gold streets shine so brightly that all the colors blend together to create a unified one with no distinction between any other. Light consists of color you know."

Jonathan had no words to respond with, so Dael simply continued.

"Here we are," she pointed then followed a certain pathway to a broken piece of glass toward the southern sector. "This is your destination… The only broken piece in the entire window is the location of Magreth's throne."

"Even the broken piece has a meaning," Jonathan said in a hushed tone.

"I could not have said it better."

"… And the other windows around the room?"

"They are the other realms… Each one is different and unique."

"Where is my home realm?" inquired Jonathan.

"Upon the floor of the central room. The one where I pray from… The floor is made of glass so thick that it is unbreakable, but it has been covered over by dust for years awaiting the light from the glass ceiling to strike it. When at last, the smoke of the city has lifted, the sun will stream through and enlighten both… Would you like to know where the door to the underground is located?" asked Dael knowing Jonathan was running short on time.

"Yes… please," he stated with a newfound respect for his former servant.

"Come with me once again." Dael led Jonathan to the narrow bridge that led to the inner room and stopped upon it… "It's down there," and she pointed to the stench-filled pool of water six stories below. "It's not the cleanest water, but then again, you're not the cleanest Snipe in the world either."

Jonathan laughed and slung himself over the edge of the bridge. "Thank you Dael, thank you for everything."

I will see you again, master Scharp. Your story has only just begun. All of us here will be praying for you as well as the realms."

With that, Jonathan let himself fall into the water far below.

Strangely, it was approximately the same height of the prison cavern beneath the Vale. Plunging into the water, he sunk deeply into it leaving the filth of the former streets behind and searched for a sub-liquid and sub-terrain entrance to the under-ground, and the ancient streets of Gish, if that was its name.

✝

The Sub-Setting

He held his breath for as long as he could, and at the last moment an underwater current pulled him into a deepened river of fresh flowing water. Far below the surface, the current entered the cylinder of the cavern beneath the temple in one direction and dumped it on the other side without ever disturbing the surface. It was that river that caught Jonathan by the legs and took him into the tunnels beneath the city. Just beyond the location where the river exited the cavern, he found surface air and suddenly discovered that he was being whisked along through one glorious cave after another. It was like a whirlwind tour of the underworld. He merely had to tread water and the river did the rest.

The city beneath the city was amazingly beautiful, or at least what he could see of it. The temperature was perfect. Plant life was abundant and flourished with the constant flow of water feeding it. Majestic pillar-lined hallways rose beside him as he whisked by. So did sporadic piazzas. Even ornate homes which had long been deserted sat as if waiting to be occupied. They were littered with potted plant life and ornately carved urns. Actual walkways carved from marble lined the sides of the river. Jonathan could have swum to an edge of it, and he would have been able to free himself from the river, as he desired to do, if it were not for his determination to complete his mission. Continuing to allow the current to do the work for him, he traveled swiftly underneath the enemy-army-filled streets of Gish above him.

In time, the river flowed gently along, having left the siphon effect of the cavern far behind. Then a thought struck the former Snipe. To what destination is the water being pulled? It was not long before he discovered exactly what it was.

Jonathan could hear the sound of a great waterfall somewhere ahead of him. The current had picked up its pace considerably, and he remembered the sound of a mighty rushing of water near the location of Magreth's throne and surmised correctly that he was nearing it. Making his way to the edge of the river, he caught himself at a set of smoothly hewn stairs that led right to the water's edge. It proved to be the perfect landing spot, almost. Trying to pull himself from the current, he miscalculated the slippery moss that had been growing on the stairs and he fell. The landing dumped him right back into the rushing current. He struggled against it for a few moments, and with much effort, was able to make his way back to the stairwell where he clung to it with all his strength. He could only guess where the falls would have taken him.

Standing on the edge of the river, he could see that the plant life was more abundant than anywhere else that he had seen thus far on his express trip to the space under the throne. At first, it appeared as though he had landed at the end of the line, but he had long learned that the Gish had held secrets close to its chest, and he assumed that the city under the Gish contained the same qualities. Searching the back side of the cavern proved just that as he discovered a moss-covered cave-like hallway that led into utter darkness. He followed it blindly for what seemed like ages, something he had grown accustomed to doing. At long last, a flicker of light shone on his pathway. The closer he got to the source, the more the plant life surrounding him began to appear pale.

Suddenly, a familiar smell entered his nasal cavity, stopping him in his tracks. To his left, he spotted a small marble shelf full of roses. Jonathan reached out to them ever so gently… and they crumbled like dust at the touch. Magreth's throne room, he thought to himself.

He remembered the last time that he had been to the place. It seemed so long ago. Still present, however, was the feeling that he was being watched and he now knew where the feeling was coming from. He was sure that the underground fortress would be full of the Nephim. Silently slipping through the shadows, he moved further down the cavern until it began to open into a hallway. It was the very one that led to the heart of the dark kingdom.

Jonathan had come to the junction where he had once descended to the bottom of the stairs and where he had made a right-handed turn and headed in the direction of the throne room itself. It was the same junction where he had seen the tall and ghostly figure of an usher, but the specter never materialized. Contemplating his approach, he waited for his eyes to adjust once again to the light that was now filling the great hall that led to Magreth's throne, and it was a good thing that he did.

He had been thinking that the so-called great hall was a cheap mockery of an imitation of the true great hall he had seen within the walls of Kalaw, when it appeared as though the pillars that lined it began to melt. Jonathan thought that the Serpent's Breath had been getting to him, but then he remembered that his last visit had been strangely absent of the effects of the drug. Upon closer inspection however, he discovered the source of the melting sensation that he was witnessing as the hall had begun to fill with the fallen ones, the Nephim.

They were hideous and came in all shapes and sizes. What Jonathan had discovered was that when Magreth had deeply wounded his eyes in the prison, he had unknowingly 'opened'   them to what lay beyond the veil of his natural eyesight. Jonathan watched as the Nephim flooded the space like an overturned ink bottle. They must have sensed that a threat had drawn near and were conglomerating around their leader to protect him. Jonathan instinctively slowed his breathing and even his heart rate. They hadn't caught sight of him yet, and he remained hidden near the bottom of the stairwell.

His first thought was to quickly make an ascent on the stairs to get to safety, but he had not come all that way to fall just short of his goal. Samuel must have been somewhere beyond the next threshold, for Magreth's throne room lay through the doorway that stood across the great hall and beyond the macabre gauntlet of the fallen Nephim. Bowing his head, he said a silent prayer. Then, like a light in the darkness, the words of the Guardier, the warrior of light, came tumbling back from time and into his mind.

He had said that a stone would light his way in the darkness!

Jonathan felt for the Emeralhearth stone within the folds of his clothing, and it felt warm. Producing it, he found it to be still glowing deeply within, but it was an intensified glow. There must be a reason for the light to come alive like it is, he thought. Throwing caution to the wind, he then quickly un-slung his bow and tied the stone to one end of it where his Da' had re-strung the firing cord and left some residual line. The green hued light immediately streamed into the darkness.

The former Snipe watched the Nephim as they appeared to be oblivious to the light. They hadn't even reacted to anything out of the ordinary. Jonathan stood to his feet and cautiously stepped out of the shadows and into the great hall holding the long bow horizontally out in front of him. Still, there was no response as the stone continued to glow from within. He silently made his way down the hallway, but the Nephim, breathing sulfur, just continued in conversations which they had begun with each other upon entering the great hall. If there was ever a room filled with backbiting, backstabbing, and condemning conversations, that was it. Their hatred for their leader and anyone else that was un-fortunate to come up in their discussions was so poisonous that it almost made the air feel sticky. The residue of their rants hung like graveyard fog in the atmosphere.   Still, Jonathan moved undetected past the multitudes of sulfur breathing Nephim and all the way to the far room.

With the mass of Nephim behind, he stepped beyond the doorway closing it behind him and into the throne room itself. However, just beyond the entrance to the polished marble mockery of the king's own throne room, he encountered a single foot soldier left behind to guard the treasures.

It took all of two blinks of an eye for Jonathan to subdue the soldier under his foot, where he held him to the floor by the neck. The former assassin had his bow strung and poised to strike the young man below him. The soldier was shaking and had already wet himself in his abject fear.

"Where's the boy?" he spoke through gritted teeth.

"What boy?" the scared soldier asked.

"The musician, where is he?"

"I tried to stop him… I promise, I protested the whole idea, but his anger could not be assuaged. I took care of Samuel, I watched over him for three years, but it didn't matter in the end." The soldier was shaking like a leaf.

"Where… is… he?" Jonathan lowered the tip of his arrow and rested it against the forehead of the guard, slightly piercing it.

"He…"

"He what."

"He threw the boy into the prisons beneath the Vale… I tried to stop him… I promise I did."

Jonathan's face flushed with rage. He let out a grunt that sprung up from the depths of his being. The soldier beneath his foot considered himself a dead man, but Jonathan retracted his arrow and let it fly toward Magreth's throne. Jonathan followed the projectile with his eye and just before it sunk deeply into the chair, Magreth himself appeared seemingly out of thin air.

The arrow passed right through him and penetrated the eye-socket of one of the great cats carved into the marble. Jonathan turned to face his foe and allowed the soldier beneath his foot to escape.

Magreth began to chuckle and produced his great Willowfeld bow and raised it in the direction of the son of the weapon master. Jonathan froze with fear as the great prince loaded the firing cord with an arrow that contained no flight feathers and he did so with lightning quick reflexes. The arrow itself was more of a beveled spear than a mere fletcher's arrow. Pointing it, he aimed directly for Jonathan's heart. The former Snipe warrior had no time to react when the Prince of Gish let it fly…

Jonathan began to fall back knowing that the shot would kill him instantly…

But as quickly as the shot had been fired, Thomas of Dodd flew through the doorway and stepped in front of it. It entered his armor through the mid-sternal region and stayed fast not passing entirely through.

Thomas had in his hand another Emralhearth-type stone, only it was blue. Turning the best that he could with an elongated arrow through his body, he placed the stone in Jonathan's hand and lifted his head to speak. Magreth had already begun to load another immense arrow into position from across the room.

"Go Jonathan… Get out of here. This stone will keep you hidden from Magreth's eyes as well as from the Nephim… Go.!"

"Thomas, I can't without you."

"You must. Go, complete your quest, master of weapons."

Thomas died on the floor of Magreth's throne room, but Jonathan didn't have the time to mourn, for Magreth had fired another missile. Only the stone's shining light saved him from the death blow of the second shot, having temporarily blinded the   dark prince.

Jonathan narrowly escaped the underworld full of Nephim, not hidden in the shadows, but wrapped in a cloak of light. The rock had shrouded the Shade leader beneath its shadow of spectral blue-hued color. The stealth training that he had received from his friend, Dodd, carried him past Magreth's physical army once he emerged onto the streets of Gish once again.

Jonathan's mentor had poured himself out to the uttermost, thereby completing his own quest and fulfilling his own sentence that had been handed down to him by the Council of the Castle, that was, to watch over and protect the son of John, the weapon master of Irenay.

✝

The Sent Ones

On the morning of the eighth day, the Shade appeared at the mouth of the infamous Vale upon horseback and ready for war.

Jonathan sat upon the white and gray Sire by Swift, for so he had named the war horse. The Shades numbers were one hundred and twenty-two strong. A heated wind blew at them from the mouth of the cave on the far end of the valley. The drums of war began to beat, and it shook the dirt beneath them. Jonathan strummed the firing cord of his Willowfeld bow almost like a lyre to test its ability to fire and still hold the blue stone that he had been given which was tied to one end of it. Jacqueline had joined them, having found the gathered army at the outskirts of the City of Gish.

"Can you see them?" Jacqueline inquired of the Shade's leader.

"Yes," Jonathan replied.

"How many are there?"

"Hundreds of the Nephim are with the enemy troops," he replied as he surveyed the surrounding landscape. The hot blast of wind began to swirl on the floor of the valley below them as dust was kicked up.

Jonathan then looked up toward the sky above the rims that created the bowl for the Vale of Blood to be housed within and continued… "But, there are thousands more who are with us… Do you remember the plan, Jacqueline?"

"I do."

"Repeat it one more time…"

"I go to the door first, open it up for you…" Jacqueline looked to Jonathan.

"And I go in. That's it… Listen to me, people of the Shade." He addressed his army of troops. "You know what needs to be done. I may be gone for a very long time, and where I'm going you cannot follow. Under that valley floor are our families, our brothers, and our sisters. And somewhere under there is my own flesh and blood… I'm not coming back until I find him… In the name of the one true king, it is time to move forward, my friends."

The king's troops began with a mere trot, but it soon gave way to a gallop as they fixed their eyes on the cave at the far end of the field…

And great winds did swirl about them…

The End

of the Beginning!

Soon to come…

The Shadow Scrolls

Book II

The Well of Darkness

By PD Lorenz

Will be available at

choicepublications.org

breathofalmighty.org

Amazon

Barnes & Noble

And Booksellers everywhere!